W9-CAA-855

PROLOGUE

Siddharth Arora has no way of knowing it, but today is the last day he will ever see his mother. He is on the armchair in the family room, straining his ears so he can hear the television. His father and Barry Uncle have been making a racket all morning, and Siddharth has been trying to watch a game show. His mother thinks he is too young to watch game shows. Thinks he should spend time on better things. Going to friends' houses, or having them over. He enjoys these things. But would trade them all in for the television. He could sit in front of the television every waking hour of the day. He wouldn't mind sleeping in front of it.

His father hates the television. Thinks it is evil. A cancer that will ruin the greatest civilization on earth. His father thinks he should spend more time reading. Arjun reads a lot. Arjun studies and gets good grades. In two years, Arjun will be away at college. The thought of his impending departure sometimes keeps Siddharth awake at night.

Siddharth clicks his tongue. Says, You wanna keep it down?

Barry Uncle is perched on a ladder behind one of the sofas. White leather sofas that Siddharth's mother has recently purchased against his father's wishes. Barry Uncle says, in his raspy voice, Hah, boy? Speak up.

Siddharth scowls. Says, Keep it down!

Barry Uncle chuckles, then coughs. Says, Boy, you don't need to hear that show. You don't need to listen to those blondes. Just sit back and admire the beauty. Barry Uncle rests a knife on the leather sofa. Wipes his shiny brow. Says, Have a look at that redhead. I'd buy a washing machine from her any day. I'd buy ten. Reminds me of my ex. Before she blimped out, that is.

Gross, Siddharth says. But he is pleased that Barry Uncle has spoken to him about women. He turned ten five months ago, and thinks they should speak to him like a grown-up. They should speak to him the same way they speak to Arjun.

His father, Mohan Lal, is wearing shorts and a green collared shirt that is stained with paint. He says, Siddharth, didn't you hear your mother? Get off your butt and go!

Two minutes, he says. The show's gonna be over in two minutes.

Mohan Lal says, With you it's always two minutes. He hands Barry Uncle some sort of tool. Says, Try this, it's wider. It will give you more leverage.

Barry Uncle says, Gimme a dull rock for all I care. Says, Mind over matter. You hear that, boy? When it comes to the hard stuff, it's always mind over matter.

Whatever, says Siddharth.

Mohan Lal and Barry Uncle are removing the old wallpaper from the family room. The wallpaper is a mural of trees and a river from some national park that Siddharth has never visited. He wants the family room to look sleek. Modern. Like a mansion in Beverly Hills or Fairfield County. He wants the family room to have a modern black lamp from Europe, a modern black lamp right beside the new leather sofas. When his mother bought the sofas, she told Mohan Lal to relax. That she knew how to care for their household. Mohan Lal exploded. Said, Yes, I'm an idiot! I know nothing about caring for my household.

Siddharth hates it when they fight. Each time they fight, he worries about divorce. He has learned at school that half of all marriages end in divorce. But his parents usually make up quickly. The night they fought about the sofas, Siddharth stayed up late with his ear pressed to their door. At first, his parents exchanged angry whispers. But then he heard rising laughter. His father's laughter. His mother has a harder time laughing after fights.

The sound of footsteps. It distracts him from an advertisement for a toy he wishes he could own. His mother's footsteps. Shit, he thinks. Shit is no longer a new word, but he still feels a small thrill upon uttering it. The Connor boys from next door started using it first. Eric and Timmy Connor have taught him many new words. Cunt. Dyke. Motherfucker. He feels older when he uses these words. Stronger.

He turns his head and glimpses his mother. Swallows. Knows he must accept that his time in front of the television is over.

His mother says, Siddharth?

Yeah?

What did I say? Go get ready.

But I am ready.

He watches his mother check herself in the hallway mirror. The mirror hangs beside the ugly Indian sculpture that her sister gave them on her first and only visit to America. His mother is parting her closely cropped hair down the middle, patting it down with her pudgy fingers. He misses her long black hair, which used to fall in a braid down her back. But Mohan Lal prefers this new manly style. He was the one who encouraged her to chop it all off. Mohan Lal said short hair is the mark of a modern woman. The mark of independence. Arjun said, Dad, this is a free country. Let her do what she wants.

Siddharth notices his mother is showered and ready, wearing pants and a tucked-in shirt. A silk shirt with a floral print. She is ready, in case the hospital calls her in. The VA hospital that she hates. The VA hospital where she has worked for the past twelve years. Today she is on call, and Siddharth hates it when she's on call. For then he might have to be alone with his father. But today Barry Uncle is here, which means there will be laughter if she goes. There will be chatter, even if it is about Gandhi, Warren Hastings, or the Mughal Empire. Siddharth hates it when they talk about India.

His mother says, Don't be smart. Go get the brushes, fill a cup with water. Use a paper cup. And put some newspaper down on the table.

It is Saturday, and his mother gives him art lessons on Saturdays. Together they make cubes, bowls, and cups. They shade them in with special pencils. Lately, his mother has been placing various objects on the table. A pear, a candle, a spoon. And he has had to draw these objects. After he sketches them in pencil, he and his mother mix watercolors on the back of plastic yogurt lids and paint them. She keeps all of their art supplies in a brown plastic tackle box. He wishes they would use the box for something important, like fishing. Mr. Connor is an expert fisherman.

He sighs. Says, Okay, in five minutes. I'll do it in five minutes. He wonders if it won't be so bad if his mother gets called into the hospital. Just for a few hours. Then he'd miss his art lesson. Then he'd get to stay on the armchair.

Barry Uncle whistles suddenly. Says, Looking sharp as usual. But I miss that long black hair of yours. That hair was something gorgeous. It was sexy.

Siddharth grimaces. Says, Gross.

Mohan Lal says, Chief, your problem is that you are always looking backward.

Barry Uncle says, Boss, I don't know why you've always been so ashamed of tradition.

His mother clears her throat. Says, Barry, I'll let you know when I need your opinion.

I love you too, sweetheart, says Barry Uncle.

Siddharth sits up, stretches his arms toward the ceiling. Heads toward the closet outside of the bathroom to get the brown tackle box with the art supplies. But on the way there the phone rings, and he turns to grab the yellow receiver. In case it's the Connor boys. In case it's his brother, checking in from Hartford. Something might be wrong in Hartford, where Arjun has been for the past two days at a youth-in-government conference. Something might have happened to Arjun.

His mother beats him to the phone. She says hello, then laughs. But it's not a happy laugh. She shakes her head and rolls her eyes. Says into the receiver, What can I tell you? We could have avoided this. Says, I told him not to do it, but he's always in a rush. He never listens. She puts the phone down, grabs her purse from the white leather sofa. Grabs her keys from the drawer under the phone that holds the yellow pages, the takeout menus, and the postage stamps. Kisses him on the head and walks out the door.

Many years from now, he will blame himself for wishing that call to come. He will wonder, as a rational, atheistic adult, if the universe was trying to teach him some sort of lesson. But in that moment, all he feels is relief. Contentment. In that moment, he feels powerful. Lucky. Wonders if he should wish for other things. For money. For his parents to buy a Japanese luxury sedan, or perhaps an Audi. For Barry Uncle and Mohan Lal to shut the hell up. For them to be called away too.

The rest of the day slips by in a blissful haze of game shows, cartoons, and reruns. His mother calls once to say that she will have dinner at the hospital. She'll probably sleep there because they might have to operate on somebody in the middle of the night. He is disappointed, especially since Barry Uncle has gone, and his father has become grumpy. Mohan Lal has made him change the channel to public television, which is airing a program about the fall of the Berlin Wall and a new era of peace and prosperity. As Mohan Lal watches his program, Siddharth lies on the leather sofa with his feet on his father's lap. He daydreams. About Chris Pizzolorusso's birthday party next weekend. It will be at Skate World, and it will be his first boy-girl party since the first grade. He daydreams about their upcoming family vacation to Florida. Maybe Arjun and he will pick up girls. They have plans to go snorkeling, and he wonders if they might find a sunken treasure in the middle of the ocean. Then they'd be rich. Then his mother wouldn't have to be on call anymore, and he wouldn't have to be alone with his father on Saturday evenings.

Mohan Lal interrupts his reverie. Says, Son, time for a shower, I think.

I just showered yesterday, says Siddharth.

Mohan Lal laughs. Says, Son, I can smell you from here. Go shower.

It's your farts, Dad. You're stinking up the whole room.

They both laugh.

Arjun gets home at seven, and the three Arora men eat dinner together. Mohan Lal has prepared his famous tacos, made with hard El Paso shells. Red kidney beans, raw onions, and grated orange cheese. Arjun tells them about his youth-in-government conference. Explains that he and Adam Aaronson designed a bill that would discourage people from staying on welfare.

Siddharth is growing bored. Doesn't like the fact that his father listens so attentively when Arjun speaks.

Mohan Lal says, Son, a strong state must protect its vulnerable citizens.

Siddharth isn't totally sure what vulnerable means. But he knows his father has said this word incorrectly, pronouncing the *v* like a *w*.

Mohan Lal says, Arjun, I'm proud of you. One day you'll make a great politician. One day you'll be a man who will make a difference.

Arjun says, Thanks, but politicians make diddly. I'm gonna be a radiologist.

Siddharth and Arjun go to bed around eleven. Within minutes, Arjun is snoring. Siddharth is happy to have his brother nearby on a Saturday night. Usually, Arjun is out on the weekends. Out with Adam Aaronson. With his friends from the cross-country team, the school newspaper. Sometimes they go drinking. The drinking makes Siddharth nervous, but he has agreed not to tell his parents. His father doesn't need another excuse to get angry with Arjun. Mohan Lal blows up when Arjun isn't working hard enough. For his mother, it's the opposite. She gets annoyed when Arjun doesn't take time out to relax. Siddharth agrees with her. He thinks Arjun needs to learn how to chill. Thinks Arjun should watch more television.

Siddharth falls asleep peacefully, contented by the knowledge that his mother will have the next few days off. He thinks, Maybe we'll have our shitty art lesson tomorrow. Thinks, Maybe art lessons aren't so shitty. At six in the morning, a thunderous pounding wakes him up. He struggles to open his eyes, the light feeble outside his window. At six in the morning, he stares from his bed as his father barges into their bedroom. Mohan Lal shakes Arjun. Mohan Lal's wispy gray hairs are tousled, and he is wearing nothing but his tight white underwear.

Arjun groans. Says, Dad, what the hell?

Siddharth cringes because Arjun has said hell in front of their father. Now Mohan Lal might erupt. But Mohan Lal doesn't react. He just says, Get up, son! Get up. I need to talk with you.

If it were later in the day and he weren't so sleepy, Siddharth would protest. He would say that he is old enough to hear whatever is about to be said. But once Arjun follows Mohan Lal out of the room, Siddharth closes his eyes. He closes his eyes and falls back asleep.

He arrives at the Connors' just before six thirty. Eric and Timmy are still sleeping, so he sits in their family room and watches cartoons on their big-screen television. Mrs. Connor is beside him, smoking cigarettes and ironing the family's church clothes. Siddharth is jealous of this large television. He is jealous that everybody from his school gets to meet up at church.

Eric and Timmy wake up at a quarter to eight, and he is relieved. The three of them head out to the garage and examine Eric's new bike jump, which he constructed with spare plywood, nails, and two-by-twos. Eric is three years older than Siddharth, and now in junior high school. Timmy is two years older than Siddharth, but he is only in the fifth grade because he stayed back when he was eight years old. The Connors are his best friends, but he thinks Eric is cooler than Timmy. Eric is like a superhero, the way he can build jumps and do back handsprings. The way he can do a flip in the air without taking a running start.

Mr. and Mrs. Connor adopted Eric and Timmy from Laos, a place Siddharth can't locate on a map. But his father has told him that America has ruined that part of the world. Mohan Lal says that the only reason the Connors adopted Eric and Timmy is because they screwed up their first kids. Their real kids. His mother gets upset whenever Mohan Lal says this. She tells him to be more compassionate. To mind his own business.

After admiring the bike jump, the boys grab Timmy's brand-new Daisy air rifle and head to the backyard. They stray into the Aroras' back lawn, and Siddharth is glad to be closer to home.

Realizes now that he has been uneasy at the Connors. He has been uneasy even though he usually loves it there. He tells himself Arjun will pick him up soon. That his mother was just having a little car trouble and they shouldn't be much longer.

Timmy Connor says, Your dad needs to cut the grass. He always lets it grow so freaking long.

Siddharth feels ashamed of his father. Annoyed by Timmy. Says, He'll mow it. He's a busy guy.

Timmy says, Your dad's tractor sucks. You know what my dad says when your dad cuts the grass? He says, Hey, guys, grab the popcorn, old Hajji's at it again.

Siddharth isn't sure what this means but knows it isn't nice. Says, Whatever, I bet my dad makes more money than yours.

Eric Connor says, You both got no fucking clue what you're talking about.

Eric takes aim at Siddharth's mother's squirrel-proof bird feeder, which dangles from the maple tree behind their screened-in porch. A cardinal is nibbling at some seed there. Siddharth wants to tell him to stop. Wants to tell him that this is his mother's feeder, and he shouldn't shoot. But he also wonders if Eric will actually go through with it. Wonders what it will look like to see a dead bird.

Eric turns from the feeder toward Siddharth's old jungle gym, which is being claimed by the woods. Is engulfed by vines and the branches of a black cherry tree. He fires. Hits the metal slide, which clangs loudly. The Capasso kids, who are enemies with the Connors, can probably hear it. They can probably hear it all the way down the street. Siddharth isn't sure if he likes the gun. The noise. Eric fires again, and the clang echoes more loudly. It's a frightening sound, but one that fills him with adrenaline. He can picture his mother. Imagines her lecturing him about shooting BBs in the backyard.

Eric tells Timmy to raise his leg in the air. Says he wants to shoot Timmy on the sole of his sneaker.

Siddharth can already picture the blood dripping onto the grass. Says, You sure that's a good idea?

Eric says, Don't be a pussy. You'll see—I'm gonna shoot you next. It hurts less than a bee sting.

Timmy raises his foot in the air. Siddharth swallows.

And then the bell rings.

It's Mrs. Connor's bell, calling them in for lunch.

Eric says, Dangit!

Timmy laughs.

The three boys run toward the Connors' white two-story home. Naomi, the Connors' black mutt, trots alongside them. Mr. and Mrs. Connor are on the back deck, which is adjacent to their inground swimming pool. Siddharth has swum in this pool many times, but he will never swim in it again. The wooden picnic table is set for lunch. Mrs. Connor has made Hamburger Helper and boiled vegetables. He hates his parents' Indian food, but it tastes better than this putrid stuff. It even smells better than Mrs. Connor's cooking.

Everyone sits down. It's late May, but already very hot. Siddharth wipes the sweat from his brow with his T-shirt. Asks, Did my dad call? He's starting to get a little worried. Wonders why they are taking so long. Thinks, They must have gone out to lunch after dropping the car at the garage. He feels a surge of irritation. Of envy. Why do they always do things like that without him?

Mr. Connor adjusts his big steel glasses. Wipes his hands on his fraying jean shorts and takes a bite out of his sandwich. Says, Sit tight—your brother will be here soon. And don't worry. If he's late, we'll take you to church today.

Mrs. Connor bounces a hand off her red curly hair. Shoots her husband a look.

Siddharth definitely doesn't want to go with them to church today. Wonders what that look was all about. Wonders if they're acting weird. Yes, they've been strange all day. Quiet. And nice. They haven't yelled at Eric and Timmy even once. Usually they're always hollering at them. About their chores. About making their beds and not drinking too much Coke. Siddharth gets to drink as much Coke as he wants at his own home. He wishes he could be on one of his new leather sofas right now, drinking a cold glass of Coke.

Mr. Connor shrugs his shoulders. Says, with his mouth full, What? It might do some good, Rita. Relax.

Mrs. Connor says, Siddharth, honey, how about some ice cream for dessert?

Ice cream? says Siddharth. He puts down his sandwich. Something is definitely awry. The Connor boys are only allowed ice cream on very special occasions. He wonders what has happened. Has something happened to his mother? No, that isn't possible. It isn't possible, because he has just considered the possibility of it happening. When he imagines something bad occurring, he knows he is negating the possibility of it ever actually taking place. He tells himself that the Connor boys must be in trouble. Maybe they've found out that Eric has a girlfriend and has gotten really far with her. The Connors go to church a lot, and they probably wouldn't like that. Siddharth's mother doesn't go to church, but she wouldn't like that either. When Arjun said he wanted to start dating, she was the one who got angry. The one who said he was way too young.

His train of thought is disrupted by the sound of the doorbell. It rings three times, in the way that Arjun rings doorbells. He is relieved. Wishes he hadn't eaten so much Hamburger Helper. He could have waited and had lunch with his own family.

He and Arjun walk silently down the Connors' driveway, which they get repaved every year, so it's always smooth and shiny. Unlike the Aroras' cracked driveway, which, as Timmy Connor frequently points out, hasn't been repaved in ages. Since before the Aroras moved into the house.

He says, Arjun, we're taking the long way home.

So? says Arjun.

So, why? Why are we taking the long way home?

Arjun doesn't respond, just places a hand on his shoulder and squeezes. At first this squeeze feels nice. A love squeeze. But Arjun presses down harder. Much harder.

Ow, he says. Quit it.

Mr. Iverson is in front of his mud-colored raised ranch home, washing down the fanged wheels of his yellow bulldozer with a garden hose. Mr. Iverson drives a Harley-Davidson on weekends. He used to have a ponytail and a beard, but he chopped off his hair and now just has a mustache. He waves. Says, Kiddo, tell your dad I got his part for him. I'll bring it over in the morning. Arjun waves back. Says, Sure, no problem. Siddharth tells himself that everything is okay. Mr. Iverson will bring over a part tomorrow morning, so everything must be fine.

They pass the ever-present puddle in front of his bus stop, which he and the Connors use as a skating rink in winter. Pass Mr. Hines's Mercedes, which is parked on the street for some reason, with a green cloth draped over it. Siddharth loves that car, the only nice car in the neighborhood. Wishes his father would spend less money on books—and that his mother wouldn't make them go to India—so that the family could be seen in such a car. The sight of the cream-colored vehicle peeking from under a corner of the cover makes him forget about Arjun's heavy hand.

There are way too many cars parked in front of his own drive-way. There's a car he doesn't recognize, a long Lincoln, and there's Barry Uncle's Accord, even though he's supposed to be in New Jersey on business. But his mother's LeBaron isn't there. Maybe's she's sick, he thinks. Maybe her shitty boss made her work again, even though she's supposed to have the day off after being on call.

When they get to their mailbox, Arjun pauses. Siddharth doesn't look at him. Doesn't want to hear whatever Arjun is about to explain. He stares at the daffodils and crocuses sprouting at the base of the mailbox. His mother planted these bulbs several weeks ago, and he'd grudgingly agreed to help her. The flowers look pretty now, and he might like to paint them. He wants to charge toward the house, break into a run, like he always does upon reaching the mailbox. But Arjun's hand squeezes him again. Hard.

What the hell! says Siddharth.

I need to talk to you, says Arjun.

He stares at their single-story home. Thinks, Eric Connor is right. The wooden exterior looks shitty, and they should get aluminum siding. Arjun kneels down, so that he is eye level with him. Siddharth notices that his brother's glasses are smudged and stained. That his brother's eyes are red. That his brother's breath reeks like he hasn't brushed his teeth in several days. Siddharth wants to cover his ears. To place his hand over Arjun's mouth. To run back to the Connors'. But he stands frozen. And Arjun tells him.

Upon hearing the news, he feels like spitting at his brother for playing such a cruel joke. But knows that Arjun will hit him hard, so hard that he'd cry. And he doesn't want to cry. The last thing he wants to do right now is cry. He says, Fuck you, Arjun. He has never said fuck in front of his brother before, let alone to him. It makes him feel better.

Arjun's face scrunches up. He begins to sob. Pulls him into his chest. Siddharth stays there for a minute, breathing in his brother's sweat and tears. Then can't take it anymore. He pushes Arjun away and charges toward the house. So that he can tell on Arjun. So that he can find out what's really going on. So that he can tell his brother that he's an asshole. A baby.

He sees Barry Uncle on the sofa, and as soon as he walks in, Barry Uncle looks away. There's an Indian woman there, and he knows her, and there's a white man with a big belly, and he knows him too. But he can't locate their names anywhere inside his brain. He sees his father in the kitchen, pouring hot water from a kettle into mugs. Mohan Lal, who wears sweatpants and the same collared polo all summer, has on a thick gray suit. He's wearing a thick, gray suit even though he doesn't have to go back to work until September.

Mohan Lal puts down the kettle and smiles a faint smile.

Siddharth steps toward him. Thinks, If he's making tea, then everything must be okay.

Mohan Lal says, Come here, son.

Where's Mom? asks Siddharth.

Come here, give your father a hug.

He obeys. Thinks, If she were really dead, Dad wouldn't be smiling.

Mohan Lal puts his arms around him. Siddharth squirms. He

doesn't like the scratchy feel of wool on his face. And his father smells bad. Like mothballs.

Mohan Lal says, Arjun has told you?

Arjun says, I told him.

Mohan Lal says, Look at this. No tears from my brave son. What a brave young son I have. The bravest boy in the world.

Siddharth lets go of his father and turns to Arjun, who is standing in the doorway that leads to the family room. Tears are pouring out of his brother's eyes, and he isn't wiping them away. Siddharth thinks, I'm the brave one. I have to be the brave one. In that moment, the fact that he is the brave one makes it all feel okay.

PART I

1

HEAVY SLEEPER

He missed his mother. He ached for her while he watched television during the month of June. He got to watch a lot of television that month, as Mohan Lal had allowed him to miss his final weeks of classes at Robert Treat Elementary School. The pain didn't go away in July, during his hellish trip to Delhi. He felt an especially acute longing as he knelt on the cool marble of his uncle's hot bathroom, puking his guts out into the narrow, too-tall toilet bowl. He had made the mistake of having a Nirula's pizza and milkshake with one of his cousins, things his mother would have counseled him against eating. His father stood over him in that sour, steamy bathroom and said, "Be brave, son," occasionally rubbing Siddharth's back, which made him feel even worse. Afterward, Mohan Lal didn't put a cold cloth on his forehead, like his mother would have done. His father didn't pat his head in just the right way, somewhere between gentle and firm. When Siddharth whined about the pain in his stomach, Mohan Lal said, "You made a choice to have that pizza. Now live with the consequences."

In August, he still longed for his mother. He wished for her to magically reappear while he was brushing his teeth or pouring gasoline into the lawnmower. But he devoted much more of his mental energy to his father, for Mohan Lal was doing so many baffling things. He was drinking. Not like in the movies, but more than before. He drank two or three whiskeys every night, and when he kissed Siddharth goodnight, the bitter odor of alcohol lingered over the bed once he'd left the room. When Mohan Lal kissed Siddharth goodnight, he sometimes said nice things like, "I'm a lucky man to have such good sons," or, "You're a wise boy. A sensitive boy—like your mother." But the things Mohan Lal said could be scary. Once, he said, "Siddharth, my only reason for living is you two. If it weren't for you boys, it might also be my time to leave this earth." The night he said that, Siddharth lay awake tossing and turning. Each time the house creaked, or the rhododendron bush outside his window quivered in the wind, he mistook these noises for the sound of his father committing suicide.

Throughout the autumn of his fifth grade year, his father was having trouble waking up in the morning. In fact, Mohan Lal didn't get out of bed at all on his first day of fifth grade, fifth grade at a brand-new elementary school, so Siddharth had to get ready all by himself. At least Arjun had left out some clothes for him, a pair of corduroys that were too tight now, a striped red T-shirt that was beginning to fray around the collar.

A few weeks later, there was a rainstorm one morning. He tried to wake his father up, so that Mohan Lal could drive him to school. But the man wouldn't budge. Siddharth kept on shaking him, and his father kept on asking for five more minutes. Eventually, Mohan Lal got out of bed, and father and son went out to the driveway. Siddharth made his way to the backseat of their rust-colored Dodge Omni, where he liked to sit in the mornings. He'd always had trouble opening the Omni's doors, but now he was older and could do it all by himself. He lifted the tricky handle, up first and then out. The door opened, but then it quickly slammed shut. Mohan Lal revved the engine, and Siddharth looked on in shock as his father sped down the driveway and up Hilltop Drive. Fortunately, the cleaning woman was there to let him back into the house. He sat in the formal living room with his head pressed into the window, wondering if his father would ever return.

Eleven minutes later, Mohan Lal pulled back into the driveway. He hugged Siddharth tightly and kissed him numerous times. He said, "Don't ever do that again."

"I won't," said Siddharth.

He made sure not to cry, so that his father wouldn't worry about him. He never told Arjun what had happened that morning, because the last thing his brother needed was another reason to hate their father.

The autumn after Siddharth's mother died, Arjun was always angry with Mohan Lal. When Mohan Lal instructed the boys to tell the people who called for him that he wasn't home, Arjun scoffed at him. He said that Mohan Lal needed to stop avoiding people who were trying to help him. When his mother's friends dropped in with CorningWare dishes full of rajma or tuna casserole, Mohan Lal greeted them at the door and said he was running late for a meeting, so that he wouldn't have to invite them in. One time, Mustafa, the manager of Mohan Lal's favorite Italian restaurant, came over with a tray of eggplant parmigiana. As Mustafa stood on the front steps ringing the doorbell, Mohan Lal switched off the television and shushed Siddharth with his finger. Mustafa simply left the food outside the door and drove away. Soon all of these people stopped coming over altogether, and Arjun wasn't happy about it. He told Mohan Lal that he needed to set a better example for Siddharth. Mohan Lal said, "Mind your own business, Arjun. Remember, I'm your father."

A part of Siddharth felt good when he saw his brother taking charge. But he also understood his father's behavior. He could relate to Mohan Lal's need for privacy. The Connor boys kept on calling him to see if he could come over, but he always said no, that he had too much homework. Sometimes they would come by after school and ring the doorbell, and Siddharth would hide in his bedroom closet until they went away. He didn't want to hang out with them anymore and swore that he would never return to their house. Their house was his least favorite place in the entire world.

Though Siddharth understood his father's need for isolation, what worried him was Mohan Lal's temper: The man's fights with Arjun were getting worse and worse. Each day, Mohan Lal returned home from Elm City College with news of another fight with his dean. He was even fighting with Barry Uncle, his distant cousin and best friend. His first fight with Barry Uncle had occurred the day before the funeral. Barry Uncle had been going on about the need for a pandit to preside over some rituals—to say something spiritual for the sake of Siddharth's mother. When two of Siddharth's aunts who had flown in from India agreed, Mohan Lal lost it. His face went red and he started trembling. He said, "Jesus fucking Christ, Barry. Keep your Brahmin charlatans away from my family. Take your fucking Hinduism and shove it up your ass." Siddharth had never heard his father say *fuck* before. Hearing this made him seem like a stranger, like some sort of child abuser. In such moments, Siddharth couldn't help but think that his only real parent was his mother.

The big fight with Barry Uncle had occurred in August, after Siddharth's trip to India with Mohan Lal. Over Little Caesars pizza one night, Barry Uncle said, "Boss, have you thought about the lawsuit?"

"Please, Barry, not now," said Mohan Lal.

Arjun said, "Dad, she was my mother. I deserve to hear this."

When Mohan Lal widened his eyes at Arjun, Siddharth cringed. He knew what those eyes meant. They meant that if Arjun said another thing, Mohan Lal was going to go ape shit. He was going to shout, or raise his hand behind his ear—things he had always done, but with much more frequency now.

Siddharth was relieved when Arjun got up and went to their bedroom. Unfortunately, Barry Uncle kept on going: "Listen, Mohan, we're in America now, and that's the way things work here. That truck driver, he won't pay anything. But this guy's insurance company should pay up."

Siddharth felt it was his responsibility to step in. He said, "Barry Uncle, trust me, it's not like we need the money."

"Boy, your father isn't exactly M.S. Oberoi. He's got mortgage payments. You two boys will go to college one day."

Siddharth wanted Mohan Lal to say something to defend their family's honor. He wanted him to tell Barry Uncle to mind his own business. Mohan Lal seemed strangely calm though. He ate a couple bites of pizza. He downed his whiskey, then sighed. Siddharth didn't see what was coming, and he jumped in his chair when Mohan Lal slammed his fist into the table. The plates shook and the glasses jingled.

Mohan Lal stood up. "Barry, you're an ass," he said.

"Easy there, boss," replied Barry Uncle. "Take it easy."

"Dad!" said Siddharth.

Mohan Lal pointed his finger in the air. "Leave, you bastard. Get out of my house, Barry."

Barry Uncle stood up and placed his hand on Mohan Lal's shoulder. "Come on. Let's change the subject."

Mohan Lal switched into Hindi, or maybe it was Punjabi—Siddharth couldn't tell the difference. All he knew was that he wished his father would stop shouting at his best friend. But Mohan Lal wouldn't stop.

Barry Uncle grabbed his briefcase and rushed toward the front door. He said, "I know you're upset, boss. But you can be a stubborn ass sometimes." He then got into his Honda Accord and sped down the driveway.

After the fight, Barry Uncle tried calling a few times. Mohan Lal either hung up on him or told the boys to say he wasn't home. Soon Barry Uncle stopped calling. One evening Arjun said, "He's, like, your only friend, Dad. You need to talk to him." Mohan Lal called Barry Uncle a swine. He said he wouldn't speak to him for as long as he lived.

Siddharth didn't know what to make of Barry Uncle. There were little things he liked about him. He let Siddharth change the gears of his car, and he let him take little sips of his whiskey. But Siddharth was well aware of his mother's feelings for the man, and he began to wonder if Mohan Lal had banished him out of loyalty to her. In that case, he was definitely on his father's side. He was glad to see the last of Barry Uncle.

2

A JUST WAR

As they drove to Deer Run Elementary School on that chilly February evening, a light snow wetted the windshield of their rust-colored car. His stomach gurgled with dread, which mounted as they approached the town center. Soon they were passing the Carter Family Horse Farm, which was adjacent to South Haven's public library. Over the past few months, Mohan Lal occasionally picked him up from school, and they would get donuts and eat them in the library parking lot. They parked as close to the horses as possible, and Siddharth got out of the car and laced his fingers through the chain-link fence. One of the ponies, which had a blond mane, sometimes came over and licked his fingers, and they started referring to it as Buddy. Whenever they visited Buddy, Mohan Lal remained in the car, sipping coffee from a Styrofoam cup and listening to reports about the aftermath of the Gulf War. Siddharth stood outside alone, inhaling the musky air, staring at the desolate fields and graceful horses. He occasionally looked over his shoulder to check on his father, who responded by blowing him a kiss or just smiling. Siddharth felt good in those moments. He hadn't said a word about them to anyone—not to Arjun, nor to Ms. Farber, his school psychologist. He hadn't even said anything to his only friend at Deer Run, Sharon Nagorski.

It was thanks to Arjun that he had enrolled in Deer Run Elementary back in September. Arjun had said he needed an after-school program now that they were a single-parent family, and

Deer Run was the only South Haven school that had one. That term—*single-parent family*—made him feel like punching a wall. It was a term that should have applied to the people on television, not to real people who he knew and loved.

At first, Mohan Lal was dismissive of Arjun. But he later said that Arjun had a point and instructed him to handle all of the arrangements. Siddharth looked on as his brother pretended to be their father and phoned the principal of Robert Treat Elementary, where he had attended first through fourth grades. Once all the arrangements were finalized, Mohan Lal told Arjun that he was proud of him for sorting everything out. He said that one day Arjun would make a good father.

"Yeah, thanks," said Arjun. "One day you might make one too."

Siddharth said, "Take it easy, Arjun. He was just trying to be nice."

The rest of the summer, Siddharth had dreaded the prospect of beginning at a new school, but once the year actually started, he saw that transferring definitely had an upside. At Deer Run, he was no longer the little brother of the great Arjun Arora, straight-A student and flag bearer. At Deer Run, he was no longer the kid with the dead mom. The problem was that at his new school, he was the new kid, a nobody who people avoided. At his new school, he only had one friend, Sharon Nagorski. The other kids called Sharon a loser. Luca Peroti and Eddie Benson called her "Sharon, the Friendless Wonder."

Mohan Lal pulled into Deer Run five minutes before the PTA meeting was supposed to start, parking beside the derelict tennis courts. For Siddharth, being at school for the second time in one day was a prison sentence. But accompanying his father had still seemed like the best option. Arjun was putting the school newspaper to bed, and Siddharth wasn't in the mood to be alone. More importantly, going with his father meant he could prevent him from doing something stupid.

As they navigated the slushy asphalt, he clutched his father's woolen overcoat. That way, if Mohan Lal slipped, Siddharth could break his fall. When they reached the school's entrance, they dried their winter boots on a large red mat inscribed with the word *Owls*. Owls were the Deer Run mascot.

Mohan Lal muttered, "Owls? This is a place of learning, and owls are the stupidest of birds."

Siddharth rolled his eyes. He saw a sign that read, *PTA Meeting in Cafeteria*, and led his father in that direction. As they walked, he told himself to look on the bright side, just as Arjun was always telling him. His mother used to say the same thing. The bright side was that he would get to show his father where he stood in line for chocolate milk and foot-long hot dogs. The bright side was that he would get to show him where he ate lunch with Sharon Nagorski. To Siddharth's surprise, the positive thinking did the trick, loosening him up.

The cafeteria had dizzyingly tall ceilings, and twenty tables with attached orange benches. One of its walls contained a glass case displaying student artwork and class pictures. Another wall was made almost entirely of windows. It looked out onto a blue Luciani Carting garbage dumpster and two flagpoles, one for the blue state flag and the other for Old Glory. Mohan Lal dashed in front of him and headed to the back of the room, near the spot where you cleared your lunch tray. A little stand had been set up there, with two coffee urns and a tray full of pastries. He made himself a cup with cream and sugar, then picked up a glazed donut. "Eat something," he said. "We'll have dinner later tonight."

"I had a big lunch," said Siddharth. He was waiting for his father to ask him a question about school—about where his classroom was, or which was his lunch table. As soon as his father asked him a question, he would tell him everything.

Mohan Lal chose an empty table, far away from the other people, from the wooden podium that had been set up on the other side of room. Siddharth scanned the cafeteria. He felt stupid when he didn't see any other students. Thankfully, his teacher Miss Kleinberg was also missing. He spotted Mr. Grillo, the mustached school principal. He was wearing a three-piece suit, as usual. Larry, the old janitor, was hunched over a broom and chewing on one of his fat cigars. He always had a cigar in his mouth but never actually lit them. All the other parents were chatting. They seemed to know each other, and they seemed to be having fun. Siddharth wished his father knew how to make small talk with the other parents. Most of them were women, but there were a few men, dressed in jeans and sweatshirts. Mohan Lal had on a cardigan sweater over a ribbed turtleneck. He looked like a dinosaur compared to these other guys.

Mohan Lal tapped him on the shoulder.

"What?" said Siddharth. His voice was harsh, but he was actually relieved. It was happening. His father was finally asking him about school.

"Where is that woman?" asked Mohan Lal.

"Which woman?"

"That shrink lady—that psychologist."

"You mean Ms. Farber? Why would Ms. Farber be here, Dad? This is for parents—parents and teachers."

Mohan Lal shrugged. "She should be here. She was the one who told me I should come."

"You talked to Ms. Farber? When did you talk to Ms. Farber?"

A woman with black hair went up to the podium and said, "Excuse me, everybody. I think it's time we get started."

He poked his father in the arm. "Dad, you talked to Ms. Farber? When did you talk to Ms. Farber?"

Mohan Lal widened his eyes and put a finger to his lips.

Siddharth shook his head and stared up at the pockmarks in the tiled ceiling. He felt like an asshole. He felt like his father had betrayed him.

"Welcome, everybody," said the black-haired woman at the podium. She was wearing a jean jacket. Her curly hair rose upward, not down. She tapped on the microphone, then started speaking. "Most of you know me already. I'm Joe Antonelli, David's mom. And Joey's. And Ricky's. Mindy's too." Everyone let out a snicker, and Mohan Lal laughed as well. Siddharth was glad. At least his father could laugh when he was supposed to.

Mrs. Antonelli thanked John Faruci for the coffee and donuts. "Let me tell you," she said. "Faruci's is the only place in town where my mother would have bought her groceries." She asked everyone to hold off on refreshments until they adjourned, and Mohan Lal took the remaining half of his donut in a single bite, using the collar of his turtleneck to wipe his mouth. Siddharth put a hand to his forehead and peered down. He hoped that no one had noticed his father scarfing his food. He hoped that nobody here knew about his visits to Ms. Farber. He didn't mind visiting her in the "retard room," as Luca Peroti called it. He didn't mind, as long as it was private.

Mrs. Antonelli stared right in their direction. "I'm pleased to see we have a newcomer tonight. Welcome." She flashed a wide smile. "What's your name, sir?"

Siddharth swallowed.

"Greetings, ma'am," said Mohan Lal. "My son is a new student here. I'm Dr. Arora."

"We're so glad you could join us," she said. "Ah, and I see you've brought your boy."

Siddharth shrunk in his seat.

Mrs. Antonelli thanked everyone for last week's baked ziti dinner, then provided the results of December's canned food drive. Everyone clapped, and a man in a checkered shirt and baseball cap stuck his fingers in his mouth and whistled. Siddharth recognized him. He was Eddie Benson's father. Siddharth turned to his own dad, who was sipping coffee and staring into space. Why did he bother coming if he wasn't even going to pay attention?

Mrs. Antonelli cleared her throat. She said that with so many positive things going on, it was easy to ignore the harsher side of life. "I'm sure you all know what I'm referring to. Our boys are making such big sacrifices out in the Persian Gulf. And here we are, living the good life in South Haven. I find myself sitting on the sofa, staring at the television, and wondering what I can do. How can I make a difference?"

Mohan Lal leaned forward. *Crap*, thought Siddharth.

Mrs. Antonelli said she wanted to make a motion to use three hundred dollars of PTA funds to buy each Deer Run student a yellow ribbon. The students could fasten these ribbons to their mailboxes in order to show support for Desert Storm.

Mohan Lal's eyes were now glued to the podium. *Please don't*, thought Siddharth.

A woman with blond bangs raised her hand. She said that Mrs. Antonelli always had such wonderful ideas. The man with the checkered shirt and baseball cap—Eddie Benson's father—was in agreement. "We're all watching it from the couch," he said, "but these kids—they're actually putting their lives on the line for our freedom. Heck, I wish we could do something more—something bigger."

Siddharth noticed his father begin to smile. He nudged Mohan Lal. He wanted to grab him and get out of there. A large woman with glasses stood up and said that the money could be better spent on an extra set of encyclopedias, or color monitors for the computers.

Mrs. Antonelli said, "We're kinda short on time here, Laurie. Let's table the encyclopedias until next time."

It was then that Mohan Lal raised his hand. "Excuse me, Miss Joe?"

A vein in Siddharth's neck started pulsing.

Mrs. Antonelli turned toward him, her eyebrows curved like the wings of a seagull. "Yes?"

"I hope you don't mind, but I would like to add my two cents."

Siddharth bit the inside of his cheek.

Mrs. Antonelli flashed her fake wide smile. "Absolutely. We would love it if you shared."

Mohan Lal handed his empty coffee cup to Siddharth, then stood up. "Good evening, ladies and gentleman. I hope you don't mind, but I wanted to share a few small thoughts." He cleared his throat. "You all seem like such intelligent people. This is why it is all the more urgent for us to really think this through. Before taking action, we must think this through and ask difficult questions." Mohan Lal grinned as he spoke, which infuriated Siddharth. His father was always moping, always fighting off tears.

His voice would even crack when he said goodnight. And now he was smiling. Now? Here?

Mohan Lal kept on going: "Everyone here is an educated person, so you won't mind if I ask you a hard question. Is this war in the Gulf truly just? Is this a war we should be actually be fighting? Because if we buy these ribbons, we are making a statement about this war."

Siddharth dug his fingers into the back of his father's brown trousers.

Mrs. Antonelli interrupted Mohan Lal. "Dr. . . . Arora, right? Dr. Arora, I don't think I know what you mean. We *are* making a statement." Her voice was now sharper.

Mohan Lal continued smiling and said, "Let's review our history, ladies and gentleman. Who gave Saddam his weapons? Who gave him his money? We did. We did these things because it served our interests. Folks, I am a firm believer in the use of force. But if we support this war, what message are we sending to the world? What message are we sending our children?"

The room was totally silent for a moment, one of the longest moments in Siddharth's life. But soon other parents started whispering. Soon people were scowling and yelling, and a chaotic uproar swept over the cafeteria. Siddharth tapped his forehead against the table. When he looked up, his father's eyes were gleaming in a way they hadn't for months.

Mrs. Antonelli banged a gavel.

Eddie Benson's father stood up. He walked up to the podium and pointed at Mohan Lal. "With all due respect to him—Dr. whatever-his-name-is—everything that guy said, it's . . . it's totally baloney." Mr. Benson turned toward Mrs. Antonelli. "Pardon my French, but that's a bunch of crap." The entire audience started clapping, except for the large woman with the glasses who had wanted the encyclopedias. Mr. Benson removed his baseball cap and patted down his hair. "My cousin was in 'Nam, and when he got back, they spat all over him. That's not gonna happen this time—not on my watch."

After some more applause, the blonde with the bangs made

a motion to spend six hundred dollars on the ribbons, not three hundred. That way they could buy two for every student.

Siddharth stood up and yanked his father's arm.

Mohan Lal shrugged him off. "Let go of me," he said.

He released his father and fled the cafeteria. He ran toward the car and wanted to keep on running. He wanted to run all the way home—but to his old home, the one where his mother had lived. For a moment, he wished it were his father who had gone. If he could, he would trade in his father for his mother. But he immediately regretted this line of thinking. He told himself that if his father were to die now, it would be all his fault.

Later that night, Siddharth couldn't keep himself from relating the incident to Arjun. He made Arjun promise not to say anything, but as Mohan Lal was washing dishes, Arjun sat himself at the kitchen counter and started speaking about the Gulf War. "Dad, isn't it America's duty to protect innocent countries from tyranny? My history teacher says that if America hadn't intervened in World War II, we'd all be living in Fascist dictatorships."

"Son, listen," said Mohan Lal. "Youth makes you naive. Yes, the Muslims need handling. But Kuwaitis aren't Jews. And Bush? Your President Bush is no Churchill. He's no Churchill, and he's certainly no FDR."

"Whatever," replied Arjun. "That's not the point."

"Tell me, son," said Mohan Lal, smirking again. "What's the point then?"

Siddharth glared at his brother. "Guys, can we just drop it?"

Arjun said, "Dad, Siddharth told me what you did tonight."

Mohan Lal turned toward Siddharth and raised his eyebrows. "What did he tell you?"

"It doesn't matter what he told me. But you gotta start prioritizing your family. You gotta prioritize your family over all your crazy ideas and conspiracy theories."

Siddharth said, "Arjun, don't say that. Dad isn't crazy."

"Listen, Arjun," said Mohan Lal, "I can do without advice from a child."

"You've got two kids to put through college, Dad," said Arjun. "You've gotta stop being so irrational. You've gotta stop pissing people off and just keep your head down—if not for your sake, then for ours."

Mohan Lal's eyes were now wide with rage. He raised the plate he was rinsing above his head. Siddharth leaped out of his seat and grabbed his father's shoulder. "Dad, please!" he yelled. But Mohan Lal threw the plate into the sink, and it shattered into three big pieces and countless little shards.

Arjun hopped off the counter and kicked one of the iron kitchen chairs, then stomped to the other end of the house. Siddharth's heart was pounding. He wasn't sure what to do. He watched his father pour himself a whiskey and then followed him to the television. Mohan Lal sat down in the armchair and told Siddharth to put on channel thirteen. Siddharth obeyed, then went to check on his brother in their bedroom.

Arjun was sitting up on his bed. His head was resting on his Beatles poster, one in which they had facial hair and little round glasses. Arjun's nose was swollen, and pink lines were now woven into the whites of his eyes. He was sucking on the coin that hung from his gold chain, a coin embossed with the image of King George VI, former ruler of the British Empire. These coins had been a gift from their maternal grandfather. Siddharth thought wearing a chain was too feminine, so his coin was in a safe-deposit box.

"I'm sorry," he said.

Arjun opened his mouth, and the coin softly thumped against his chest. "Why should you be sorry?"

He leaned his head on his brother's knee. "Please don't cry, Arjun."

Arjun used his white undershirt to wipe his eyes. "Did you finish your homework?"

"Yeah. After school."

"Well, you should read then," said Arjun. "You know, every day you don't read, your SAT scores are gonna go down. They'll go down, like, ten full points per day."

Siddharth knew this wasn't possible, that if this were true, he'd end up receiving a negative score on the SATs. But he kept quiet. Arjun got up and grabbed a piece of paper. He wrote down some multiplication problems and handed them to him. Siddharth completed the math at Arjun's tidy wooden desk. Then he left to check on Mohan Lal in the family room.

3

SLUT

Back when she was still Sharon Miller, Sharon Nagorski had lived less than a mile from Siddharth, on Miller Farm. He and Sharon had attended first through fourth grades together, but they didn't speak much during those years. He had his own friends, at least a dozen of them. As for Sharon, she was a loser. She was always staring at pictures of horses, always lugging around a big black case that contained her stupid trumpet. Like Siddharth, Sharon switched to Deer Run Elementary at the beginning of fifth grade. She didn't transfer for the after-school program, but because her mother had gotten divorced. The only rental they could afford was on the other side of South Haven.

During the first days of fifth grade, he had caught Sharon staring at him once or twice, but he refused to meet her eyes. Her social status was definitely a problem, but the big issue was that she knew what had happened to him. She was the only kid in his new school who knew about his mother's accident, and he didn't want her to give him one of those fake sympathy smiles. Those smiles made him feel pathetic, like he was dying of AIDS. Like he was retarded. And he didn't want her to say, *I'm sorry*. He'd heard those words ten thousand times, and they now filled him with loathing. Sorry was something you said for little things—if you cussed at dinner, or coughed without covering your mouth.

One day during the fall of fifth grade, it was pouring out, so they had recess inside. Siddharth was alone at his desk drawing. Without his realizing it, his sketch of a Beverly Hills dream mansion was slowly morphing into one of those ancient Delhi tombs. Those broken-down tombs smelled like piss, and they contained dead people, right there in public parks. But they had arches and domes and were the only pretty buildings in that ugly city. When he had gone to India the previous summer, his aunt's driver showed him a tomb with dozens of rose-beaked parrots perched inside. The driver got one of them to sit on his finger, and Siddharth fed it little bits of fruit. That had been one of the only good moments during the worst summer of his life.

As Siddharth worked on his drawing, Sharon seated herself at the desk next to his and stared. He tried to ignore her, but she wouldn't take the hint. Eventually, she broke the silence: "That's cool. Is it a palace?"

"A palace? Nah, it's just a bunch of lines."

"Well, it's beautiful," said Sharon. "Who taught you how to draw like that?"

"I dunno." Little bullets of blood pounded inside his chest. "I just figured it out."

"Well, you're talented," said Sharon. "You could be an artist—an architect or something—if you wanted."

Over the days that followed, they began eating lunch and doing group work together. They began wandering the field behind the playground during outdoor recess, sometimes catching and releasing tiny quarter-sized toads, sometimes sitting on the grass to play Uno or rummy. Sharon knew how to shuffle the cards fast, so that they sounded like fleeing pigeons. Sometimes they just talked. She told him about her parents' divorce and her mother's new jobs and boyfriends. She explained that her father could lose his temper, but at heart he was a real softie. Sharon's father now lived in North Carolina and worked as a truck driver. He had recently bought her a new trumpet for a recital she'd be attending in New York City, at some famous music school Siddharth had never heard of.

Initially, his stomach burned when Sharon divulged so much personal information. He worried that if she told him so much, he might have to tell her what was going on in his own screwed-up world. But Sharon seemed okay with his silence, and he started allowing himself to sit back and get lost in the details of her complicated life. He listened carefully as she told him about her big brother, who knew how to program computers. Sharon said her brother would probably get a job at NASA one day, and Siddharth imagined him to be like Matthew Broderick in *War Games*. Sharon's eyes lit up when she spoke about her aunt, a paralegal who lived alone in a Manhattan high-rise. Her aunt attended the ballet and the theater, and Sharon had spent four nights with her over the summer, when her parents were finalizing the divorce. She swore she was going to move in with her aunt on her sixteenth birthday.

Sharon also told him fictional stories, and he liked these more than the stories from her actual life. At first, she just related simple things, like the plot of a movie she had seen or a book she'd recently read, but as time went on, she started inventing her own stories. She told him the tale of a teenager who dropped out of high school to become a musician. The girl worked as a waitress in the Plaza Hotel, though she soon got discovered by a big producer. This producer eventually proposed to her, but the girl chose to remain alone. Siddharth objected to this outcome. He asked, "Why can't this story have a happy ending?" Sharon explained that being alone can be the best thing in the world—especially for a woman.

When he listened to these adventures, he managed to forget about Mohan Lal and his mother and the fact that he didn't have friends anymore—except for Sharon. She pushed him to invent some stories of his own, but he shrugged her off every time. He always felt too drained and embarrassed to come up with something. Eventually, she decided that she would be the one to tell the stories, and his job would be to sit down and draw them out.

"What do you mean, draw them out?"

"Duh, it's called illustration," said Sharon. "I'll be the writer and you can illustrate."

He was resistant in the beginning. Something about this game felt too childish—better suited to girls. But Sharon was persistent, and they soon had a smoothly running system. She told him her stories during lunch, and in the afternoon, while their teacher Miss Kleinberg was babbling about multiplication tables or Pilgrims collaborating with Indians, he secretly began his sketches, finishing them off at his boring after-school program. During after-school, most of the other kids played dodgeball or tetherball, and it was a relief to have something fun to occupy his time.

By the end of fifth grade, Sharon's stories got even better. As usual, her characters were runaways, musicians, and farmers. But these people started falling in love. They started fooling around. Men sucked on women's necks, and women licked the earlobes of their boyfriends. In one of her stories, a farmer hooked up with a schoolteacher who had come to buy carrots at his farm stand. Siddharth hoped that this man would bring his hand to the teacher's breast, but he knew better than to say so out loud.

As Sharon narrated her souped-up stories behind the playground, he sometimes found himself developing an erection, and he had to yank his T-shirt toward his knees on the way back into the brick-faced school. But these boners were nice, and he began looking forward to them. He started spending more time on his illustrations, creating characters who could have gone in real comic books. The men he drew wore old-fashioned hats and trench coats, like the actors in his father's black-and-white movies, and the women had beauty marks, bobbed hair, and tight-fitting tops. His mother had once taught him how to make an object seem more spherical, by smudging pencil marks with his finger, and he found that this technique could make a woman's chest leap off the page.

The following year, Sharon Nagorski wasn't in his sixth grade class, and he was both relieved and disappointed. He was relieved because some of the other kids had dubbed him a loser just for being friends with her. But he also knew Sharon was his only real friend at Deer Run Elementary. Without her sitting next to him, his school days would be long and lonely. At least they would still have lunch together. He had Sharon at lunch, and he had her at recess too.

During recess, the pair normally sat as far away from the other kids as possible. On a crisp and cloudy Monday in late September, however, they opted for a small patch of sun that was a mere fifty feet from the baseball diamond, where Luca Peroti and his notorious posse were playing kickball. The ground was moist after a day of hard rain, so Siddharth tore out a few pages from his sketchpad for them to sit on.

Sharon was telling him a story about two kids who had run away from home and were sleeping in the stalls of the New York Public Library bathroom. These kids climbed atop the toilets to conceal their legs when the guards came by early in the morning. They made friends with strangers, who sometimes bought them donuts from a snack bar, or cups of hot chocolate with little marshmallows.

"So these kids," asked Siddharth, "are they, like, boyfriend and girlfriend?"

"They're brother and sister," said Sharon. "Are you even listening?"

He stopped sketching and stared at his overweight sixth grade teacher, Mr. Latella, who was chatting with the principal. Mr. Latella had a whistle around his neck and a short-sleeve shirt despite the unseasonably cool air. "But do they meet anybody?" he asked Sharon. "I mean, maybe one of them is fooling around with a librarian?"

She glared at him. "Do you want me to stop, Siddharth?"

"Chill," he said, avoiding her light-blue eyes. "Keep going."

As she recommenced her tale, he placed his sketchpad on the ground and leaned back, propping himself up with his palms. He stared at the slender oak trees that surrounded the playground; their tall tips were starting to yellow. A group of girls and boys was playing tag, and he was envious of how often they got to touch each other. The kickball boys seemed to be having the most fun. Eddie Benson, the blond-haired pitcher, was laughing hard at Luca, who was at third base and miming some sort of an animal, possibly an orangutan.

He knew that if Eric Connor or Arjun were in his grade, they would be friends with Luca Peroti and Eddie Benson. But he was stuck with Sharon. A couple of weeks earlier, Luca had called her a *ho*, probably because of the short shorts she was wearing. All the girls had been wearing short shorts, but for some reason Luca only picked on Sharon. Sometimes Siddharth wished he could tell Sharon to leave him alone. But he knew she was only partly to blame for his social situation. The real problem was him. The real problem was his personality. It was his defective personality that made Mohan Lal sad all the time. It was his defective personality that had made Arjun move so far away from home.

Arjun was now a freshman at the University of Michigan. He claimed he had chosen Michigan because they were offering him a huge scholarship. He said he couldn't turn down all that money now that the family had only one income to rely on. Siddharth believed this on most days, but sometimes he had the feeling that Arjun was lying. In some moments, he thought Arjun had chosen Michigan because he needed to get away from them. Two days before leaving for college, Arjun had said, "I need to move forward, Siddharth. But Dad—he doesn't want to. What about you? What do you want? I'm not convinced you're committed to your own happiness."

Some withering yellow leaves wafted by his feet. They crackled when he stepped on them. Sharon kept on telling her story, but he wasn't paying her much attention. He tried thinking more positive thoughts, just as Arjun had instructed. He thought about his father, who had seemed a little happier lately. Mohan Lal was waking up earlier. He had begun cooking decent things once or twice a week—lasagnas and his famous tacos—just as he had promised while Siddharth was sobbing on the endless car ride home from Michigan. A few weeks earlier, Mohan Lal had signed a book contract with Walton Publishers. They had read one of his articles on ethics in marketing and commissioned him to write a textbook. Since then, he was still drinking Scotch every night, but a pale yellow glass, not two amber ones. Since then, he had even resumed calling old friends in California and Oklahoma. He complained to them about the bastards in the Congress Party, about the idiocy of the Gulf War. The only person he wouldn't speak to was Barry Uncle. Siddharth still couldn't decide whether this boycott of Barry Uncle was a good thing or a bad one.

Eddie Benson started hollering on the kickball field, which snapped Siddharth out of his trance. "We gotta live one!" Eddie motioned for his fielders to back up. "Dave's a shrimp, but he can kick like a beast!" Eddie rolled the ruby-red kickball toward home plate, where David Marcus was standing poised. David swung his leg back and made contact, and the ball soared toward third base, where Luca Peroti was standing. It flew over Luca's head and bounced in the outfield. Then it rolled by Siddharth and Sharon.

"Great," said Sharon.

Luca charged toward the ball, right in their direction. "Yo, you blind?" he yelled. "Grab that shit!"

Siddharth's heart was thumping, and his mouth was suddenly parched. He sprang up and jogged toward the ball, then bent down to scoop it up. By the time he got back to Sharon, Luca's large frame was casting a shadow over their spot.

"What's up, ladies?" said Luca. He was wearing a hooded sweatshirt and nylon soccer shorts, his boxers sticking out from underneath them. "Planning the wedding, are we?"

"You're hilarious, Luca," said Sharon.

Luca smiled, bouncing a hand off his spiky hair. "A nerd and a loser—it's a match made in heaven." He peered at Siddharth. "Kid, you're giving me that look again. You wanna bang me or something?"

Siddharth tossed him the ball, hoping Mr. Latella would blow the whistle and end recess early.

"Nice throw," said Luca.

He wasn't sure if Luca was being sarcastic or actually paying him a compliment.

The kids on the baseball diamond emitted a series of shouts and whoops, but Luca just stood there smiling.

"They're waiting for you," said Sharon.

Luca started shaking his head, then reached down and lunged for Siddharth's sketchpad.

Sharon leaped to her feet. "Put it down, Luca. Give it back."

Siddharth tried to move, but his legs were frozen. Luca held the sketchpad over his head. Sharon jumped for it but couldn't reach. She kept on hopping, and Luca dodged her hands.

"I'd stay back if I were you," said Luca. "You're gonna wanna stay back." He started thumbing through the pages, and his smile reappeared. Siddharth caught a glimpse of his multicolored braces.

Luca said, "Damn, shit isn't bad."

"That doesn't belong to you," said Sharon.

Luca held one of Siddharth's sketches close to his face. "Nagorski, I always knew you had it in you. I mean, this stuff is kinda kinky. This is kinda hot!"

Siddharth glanced down at his beat-up Nikes, unsure of what to do. Thankfully, Mr. Latella blew his whistle. Luca chucked the sketchpad to the ground and ran toward the baseball diamond, where he was greeted with shrieks and high fives. Siddharth and Sharon lined up by the brick wall in preparation to return to class.

"Jesus Christ, Siddharth," said Sharon.

"What?" he said defensively.

"Why didn't you say anything?"

He scoffed. "What was I supposed to say?"

"You could've stood up for us. You could've told him they were yours."

As Siddharth rode the bus home, it started pouring again. That's the way September had been—days of rain with only glimpses of sunshine. The shouting and laughter of the other kids ricocheted against the vehicle's metal walls, but he was happy to be alone. He hugged his arms and pressed his knees into the veins of the vinyl seat in front of him. He was worried about what would happen if Luca told everybody about the drawings. Being a nobody was one thing; being a freak was an entirely different story. At least it was a Monday, and his father would be home. At least he didn't have to stay at his stupid after-school program, where he had too much time to think bad thoughts.

Soon he was the last one left on the bus, which was barreling toward the blooming cornfields of Miller Farm, with its dilapidated barns and rickety farmhouses. Sharon had lived in one of these houses before her parents' divorce. Siddharth's mother used to say that Miller Farm milk was overpriced, but she'd gone there with an easel and canvas a couple of times. He wondered if Sharon's mother had ever talked with her while she was painting. The bus driver took a left from Miller Avenue onto New England Lane, and Siddharth looked forward to hugging his father and watching some television.

Now they were back in his own neighborhood, where he had lived ever since he was a baby. He knew almost everyone here—the D'Angelos, who lived in a gray Cape Cod and owned a used-car lot, and Mr. Iverson, who rode a Harley and had fought in Vietnam. Mr. Roderick Connor, Timmy and Eric's dad, was a Korean War vet. He lived in the neocolonial right behind the Aroras. Arjun had forced Siddharth to hang out with the Connor boys last fall, but they always ended up doing something that made him feel bad. Timmy once said, "I'm hungry. Maybe we could have those pizza bagels that your mom—I mean your parents—used to make." Siddharth didn't mind this slip-up; it was the way Timmy acted afterward that bothered him. He got all awkward and sweet, and even let him win at checkers.

The bus squeaked to a stop at the top of his street. He hoped his father would be waiting for him so that he wouldn't get drenched on the walk home. The bus driver grunted goodbye, and he stepped out onto the road. All he encountered was a soup of mud and leaves by the sewer grate. A drenched squirrel was cowering on the horizontal branch of a dogwood. Siddharth pulled his hooded Michigan sweatshirt over his head. He loved this sweatshirt. Though he loathed sports, he obsessed over anything involving his brother's Michigan Wolverines. He'd started watching Michigan football games on Sunday, just so that he could discuss Desmond Howard's performance on the phone with Arjun. He plodded down the hill, weaving through an obstacle course of earthworms. He was relieved to see Mohan Lal's vehicle parked in front of the house, the new Dodge minivan that they had bought to deliver Arjun to college.

The Aroras had a four-bedroom, single-story ranch with robin-blue shutters and stained wooden shingles on its exterior walls. The house had small, dark rooms, but his mother had tried to spruce the place up over the years. She'd hired a contractor to install a skylight in the family room and brand-new appliances in the kitchen. She had Mohan Lal and Barry Uncle get rid of the acrylic paneling that lined the corridors. Siddharth had been excited about her plans to tear down the wall between the screened-in porch and the family room. He'd gone with her to look at new carpeting and light fixtures, but then the accident happened.

He pushed open the front door and found that the family room was empty. With his backpack still on, he scurried through the kitchen, passing the laundry room and the guest room to get to his father's office. Ever since Mohan Lal had signed the contract with Walton, he was always in there. Siddharth sometimes woke up in the morning to find his father awake in his office from the night before, typing with two fingers on his new computer, or babbling about Maslow into his microcassette recorder. When Siddharth complained about the situation to his brother, Arjun told him to be more supportive. "You're gonna have to keep Dad on track. Mohan Lal is a lazy man, so you're gonna have to help him focus."

He pushed open the office door, but the room was empty. He scrutinized his father's messy desk. Piles of books and papers formed a small city beside the computer. He was relieved to see a coffee mug next to the keyboard, not a whiskey glass. He picked up the mug and placed it in the kitchen sink, then ran toward the other end of the house, to his father's bedroom. Pushing open the door, he saw a mummy-shaped lump on the bed. That lump was Mohan Lal, and he was almost certain that it wasn't moving—that his father had stopped breathing.

"Dad," he said. He went up to his father and shook him.

"Son," said Mohan Lal, his voice scratchy. He coughed, then propped himself up. "Welcome home, son."

Siddharth was relieved, but irritated. "It's the middle of the afternoon, Dad."

"Your father was up late working last night. He needs to catch up on his sleep."

"Dad, it's not normal to sleep in the middle of the afternoon." He was about to leave, but Mohan Lal called him back. Siddharth paused, wondering if his father was going to ask him about school today. If he asked, Siddharth would tell him all about Luca and Sharon.

Instead, Mohan Lal said, "Son, come back and wake me in another ten minutes."

Jerk, Siddharth thought. He headed to the kitchen and opened a bag of Doritos, then topped them with cheese and microwaved them. He poured out a Coke and sat by the round kitchen table on a wrought-iron chair that had been reupholstered by his mother several years earlier. After he finished his snack, he picked up the cordless phone to call his brother, though as usual, Arjun wasn't home. His roommate said he was at the library, but Siddharth knew he was probably out drinking beer or screwing some girl. That was what people did at college, according to Sharon.

His mind returned to Sharon and what had happened today. She was his friend, and he'd acted like a coward; he would have to make it up to her. His heart was thumping rapidly—he needed to calm down. He needed to watch something. He threw on *The Karate Kid*, one of his favorite movies. He had seen it almost twenty times but still liked anticipating what would happen. He had discovered that rewatching a light movie could allow him to stop imagining certain things over and over, like the image of glass from the windshield piercing his mother's eyeballs, of her seat belt slicing her neck. Movies allowed him to stop thinking about lots of things—if she had thought of him before she died, if she knew that it was all coming to an end.

As he rode the bus to school the next morning, he felt that it was going to be a bad day. Luca was going to say something to them, and then he would have to stick up for Sharon. He would defend his friend, even though Luca would mock him. Even though Luca would call him a faggot. Fortunately, the morning was totally uneventful. Nobody at school said anything to him, and he felt like he was invisible—even to his teacher, Mr. Latella. Sometimes he minded being invisible, but today it was a good thing. As the hours passed, he told himself that he'd blown everything out of proportion. He told himself that everything was totally fine.

He felt calm and contented as he plunked his tray of soggy pizza and chocolate milk onto his lunch table. While Sharon ate one of her peanut butter and marshmallow sandwiches, he asked her about her trumpet lesson, and if her mother and brother had made up yet. But she only responded with nods and one-word answers. He got nervous and started talking about his own life for a change. He told her about Mohan Lal's book contract, explaining that his father would soon be a famous author. He told her that once they were rich, they would probably buy a house in Fairfield or Woodford, that his father would trade in their minivan for a Mercedes.

"Great," said Sharon, arching her dirty-blond eyebrows. "I'm real happy for you."

He finished his pizza and wiped the grease from his lips with a paper napkin. Out of the corner of his eye, he saw someone approaching. His stomach tightened, and he grabbed his neck. *Shit,* he thought. *Fucking shit.* It was Luca Peroti, and Eddie Benson and David Marcus were following behind.

The three boys sat down at an empty table nearby. At first they just sat there snickering, but then Luca started coughing. Siddharth could tell it was a fake cough. He smiled at Sharon and rolled his eyes, but she kept her gaze fixed on her plastic cup of pudding.

Luca mumbled "slut" loud enough for both of them to hear, and the other two boys started coughing too. Eddie coughed and said, "Sharon." Then miniscule David Marcus coughed out the word "Is." Luca kept on going with "slut." "Sharon." Cough. "Is." Cough. "A slut." Cough.

He told himself that everything would be fine, but he couldn't untangle his neck muscles. He turned to Sharon, whose face was bright red. She said, "Get a freaking life, Luca." The three boys chuckled. Siddharth wished she hadn't said anything. He wished she had just remained silent and let the moment pass. He noticed that her lips had begun to quiver and realized that now was the time. The moment for him to act had arrived. But he couldn't move. All he could do was grasp his neck and stare at Sharon. He noticed she was wearing hoop earrings today, not her usual silver studs. His mother had once said that hoop earrings were cheap. He wondered if Luca was right about her. Maybe she was a slut.

Luca and his crew restarted their chanting.

"Just leave us alone," said Sharon. "If you had a life, you would leave us alone."

Eddie removed his baseball cap and started looking around. "I thought I heard something," he said. "Must have been a fly."

Luca said, "Kid, I think you're right. It was that slutty fly over there. I think she was talking about your mom."

Both of Sharon's fists were clenched. "Jesus, Luca. For God's sake, I didn't even do anything."

"Yeah, right," said Luca, still laughing.

"Those drawings," she said. "They aren't even mine."

Siddharth couldn't believe it. Was she betraying him?

"Sure," said Eddie. "They belong to some other slut."

Sharon turned to Siddharth with teary eyes, her lips pursed. He clutched the table and readied himself to speak. Yes, he had to do it. He had to do the right thing. For Sharon.

"Say something," she whispered.

"Yo gaylord," said Luca, "you gonna save your girlfriend?"

"He's not gonna save anyone," said Eddie. "This kid's dad is a commie. That's what my pop told me. I bet Siddharth's a pussy too."

Siddharth swallowed again, and the air went down his throat like little bits of metal. He hated Mohan Lal, but he hated Eddie more.

"Siddharth!" Sharon stood up, her eyes going wide.

"Shit," said Luca, clapping his hands, "I think they're breaking up."

Siddharth gritted his teeth. Those shitty stories and those shitty illustrations—they were all her fucking idea in the first place. He suddenly realized something: he wasn't even twelve years old, and he already had too many people to worry about. He didn't need to worry about someone else. He didn't need to worry about Sharon.

"What?" he said, throwing his hands in the air. "What do you want, Sharon?"

She broke into a jog and headed toward the exit. The lunch monitor yelled after her, but she kept on going.

4

MY FATHER'S TREE HOUSES

Siddharth daydreamed as Mr. Latella droned on about an upcoming independent book project. Students would have to read a novel by themselves, and they would respond to it by creating an art project or a five-page report. Upon hearing this news, the class let out a collective grumble. "This is baby stuff, guys," said Mr. Latella. "They're gonna eat you for breakfast in junior high." Alyssa D. raised her hand. She was one of the hot girls. Her bangs had been sprayed into a blond tidal wave. Alyssa asked the teacher if she could read *To Kill a Mockingbird*, and Mr. Latella said he would be impressed if she could manage such a big book. He gave her a high five, her reward for saying something that pleased him.

Siddharth gave his head an almost imperceptible shake. Alyssa D. was an ass-kisser—what his father called a brown-noser. Mohan Lal had told him to avoid brown-nosers. Siddharth turned toward the window and stared at a few ravens sipping water from a puddle on the crumbling tennis courts. A dream from last night was looping in his mind. In it, his mother had returned from the dead. But she had cancer and would only survive for three more months. When Siddharth started crying, his brother punched him in the arm. "This is objectively good news," said Arjun. "It's good news, and you should be grateful."

Over the past two weeks, Siddharth had had several bad dreams, and his life had become painfully lonely. After the incident with Luca Peroti, Sharon had started sitting at a new lunch table on the other side of the cafeteria, which contained a mixture of girls—girls who seemed younger than their age and talked about horses, and girls with tight shirts and too much hairspray who hooked up with older boys from West Haven. When Mr. Latella noticed Siddharth eating alone, he made him sit at a table with freaks like Bobby Meyers. Bobby was practically a midget and had lots of acne, and he always dressed as if he were attending a dinner party. His grandfather was from Russia, so people called him a commie too.

Siddharth could have hung out with Bobby during recess, but he usually preferred to remain alone. Sometimes he got a special pass for the library so that he could read or draw. Occasionally Mr. Latella let him stay inside and do things around the classroom, like staple portraits of Jackie Robinson and Ronald Reagan to the rear bulletin board. As Siddharth completed these chores, Mr. Latella lectured him. He said that it wasn't healthy for young people to be so solitary, which made Siddharth want to punch him in the face. But he just shrugged, explaining that being alone gave him a chance to think. Mr. Latella told him that a sixth grader shouldn't spend so much time thinking.

The crows outside leaped from the tennis court to a rusty fence that was slowly collapsing. As Mr. Latella babbled on about the independent book project, Siddharth sat at his desk wishing he could go back in time, like in one of his favorite movies. If he could go back in time, he would do the right thing with Sharon. He would tell Luca Peroti the truth about his drawings. A few days earlier, he had tried calling Sharon to apologize. Her brother said, "Hang on a sec," but then came back to say that she wasn't home. As Siddharth recalled the phone call, anger smoldered inside of him and burned away his remorse. *Screw Sharon*, he thought. He decided he was glad about what he had done. He was glad that her parents had gotten divorced. She deserved that—for being such a bitch to him.

A loud bang went off near his right ear.

He jumped in his chair, and his eyes flashed open. Everything was blurry for a second, and he struggled to remember where he was. He turned his head to find Mr. Latella standing a few feet away from him. He had no idea how long he'd zoned out for. He had no idea why his teacher was staring at him. He swallowed, tried to moisten his mouth, but his tongue felt like one of the crinkled leaves outside the window.

Mr. Latella's hairy, ringed fingers were grasping Siddharth's desk, and he was breathing hard. Like an angry bull. "Earth to Siddharth," said Mr. Latella. "Where exactly are you right now, Mr. Arora?"

He shook his head to straighten out his mind. Everyone's eyes were on him, and he needed to do something. He needed to prove that he was normal. What if he pushed Mr. Latella's hand off his desk? What if he said something funny—that there was a girl outside who was so slutty that she was fooling around with a black crow?

"I asked you a question," said Mr. Latella. "Do you have any ideas for a book?"

"A book?" he whispered. Alyssa D. caught his eye. She was smiling. Did she want to help him? No, she was holding her chin. She was holding her chin to keep from laughing.

"For your independent book project?" Mr. Latella wheezed between his words. "The one we've been discussing for the last twenty minutes?"

Come on, he told himself. *Think, you idiot.*

Mr. Latella gripped his fat, red neck and put one of his wingtip shoes on an empty chair. "You're in sixth grade now, Siddharth. Do you really think this type of behavior is appropriate?"

Bastard, thought Siddharth. The classroom was silent for a few seconds—seconds that felt like hours. He closed his eyes, hoping that his teacher would vanish. But when he opened them, Mr. Latella was still glaring at him. His mind returned to the concept of time travel. If time travel were possible, he would go back to last July, when there was no school. When his brother was still at home. No, he would go further back. He would go back to his mother's last day on earth. He would intercept the call from the hospital and say that she wasn't home.

Luca Peroti shouted, "Hey, Mr. Latella!"

"Not now, Luca."

"But I have a question."

"What?"

"What about *Playboy*?" said Luca. "Can I read a *Playboy* for my project?"

Siddharth relaxed for a moment. Was Luca trying to help him?

Mr. Latella's mouth was wide open, but the wall phone buzzed before he could reprimand Luca. He took the call, then pointed at Siddharth and snapped his fingers. "Today's your lucky day, mister. Ms. Farber wants you—on the double."

Luca said, "Yo, Siddharth, have fun in the retard room."

The entire class broke into laughter.

With his eyes fixed on the floor, Siddharth grabbed his backpack and left the classroom.

He sipped some water at the handicap fountain, then grazed his fingers against the smooth cinder-block walls. He palmed the cold steel of a bright red fire extinguisher, wondering what would happen if he pulled a fire alarm. Today he wasn't in the mood for Ms. Farber. He didn't feel like hearing about the different stages of grief. He didn't feel like hearing about the way death changed your relationship with the people you love, so that grieving people have to mourn twice—for the people they lost, and for the people who are still living but will never be the same again. Today he wasn't in the mood for any of that bullshit.

The first time he saw Ms. Farber was at the beginning of fifth grade. Mohan Lal hadn't told anybody at Deer Run Elementary about Siddharth's mother, but his teacher, Miss Kleinberg, sensed there was some sort of problem. She thought he was too quiet, so she referred him to Ms. Farber. Ms. Farber had called him and Mohan Lal into her office, and she asked them if Siddharth's mother was a fluent English speaker. She said, "I know you're a professional, Dr. Arora. But what about your wife? When one parent doesn't speak the language, it can have a serious impact on the child's vocalization."

Despite that dreadful initial encounter, over the past year

Siddharth had actually enjoyed some of his visits to Ms. Farber's office. Since their initial meeting, he had been to her office eleven times. Sometimes they talked about simple things, like his favorite television shows or what he was reading at school. Ms. Farber asked him whether he missed his family in India, about the differences between his two schools. He told her that his old school was better, but that all schools sucked. India was dirty and poor, though his father's older brother was rich. This brother had two drivers and had just gotten cable television. When Ms. Farber asked him how his father was doing, he usually lied. He told her that Mohan Lal was going on three-mile walks every day, that he cooked a three-course dinner every night.

Ms. Farber sometimes asked him to draw pictures. She usually let him draw whatever he wanted, so he made mountains with ponds and evergreen trees, just like his mother had taught him, or he sketched cubes and bowls and then painstakingly shaded them in. One time, she asked him if he would be willing to draw a picture of his family, so he'd made a quick sketch featuring him, Mohan Lal, and Arjun. He thought that their bodies and clothes had come out realistically. Their facial features, however, were the work of a child. Ms. Farber held up his sketch and smiled. She told him he was very talented, and that she also liked to draw. "Honey, do you mind if I ask you something?" He shrugged. She said, "Is someone missing from your picture? You don't have to talk about it, but I think someone might be missing." He had wanted to say, *Duh, what the hell do you think?*—but he just looked down and bit a piece of skin from the inside of his mouth.

He took his time walking down the hallway to her office. He paused outside her door, hypothesizing about what they would talk about. Had she heard about his fight with Sharon? Had she found out about the illustrations he had made for her stories? If she'd been told about them, she would think he was some sort of pervert. When he peeked in through the glass pane above her doorknob, it felt as if someone had kicked him in the groin. His father was right there in Ms. Farber's office.

Mohan Lal was sitting on a tiny student chair at the reading ta-

ble; his knees jutted upward, almost to the level of his thick black
bifocals. Siddharth prayed that he was either dreaming or halluci-
nating. He bit down hard on his tongue but didn't wake up. This
was real. And the fact that his father was at school could only mean
bad things. Either they'd found out he was a pervert or something
was wrong with Arjun.

As he stared into Ms. Farber's office, he was astonished by what
was happening. Ms. Farber was leaning her head back and laughing. He had been imagining the worst, but Mohan Lal was grinning. He was grinning and talking and gesturing with his hands,
the way he used to tell jokes at dinner parties—the way he used to
discuss politics with Barry Uncle when they were drinking. Saliva
flooded Siddharth's mouth. Bitter saliva. It tasted like battery
acid.

He pushed open the door. Mohan Lal turned toward him and
waved.

"Good morning, Siddharth," said Ms. Farber, flashing her
toothy smile. He liked her, but he didn't like that fake smile. She
was wearing a white jacket with puffy shoulders. It looked weird,
or maybe Oriental, and the shiny scarf around her neck seemed
foreign too. Mohan Lal was wearing a tweed jacket with leather
patches on the elbows, and a yellow tie that Siddharth and Arjun
had given him on Father's Day three years earlier. Mohan Lal patted the empty chair beside him, and Siddharth took a seat. He
scrunched up his face and gave his father a look that was supposed
to convey several questions. *What the hell is going on? How could you do
this to me again? Is everything okay with Arjun?* Mohan Lal winked at him,
then turned to Ms. Farber.

"You really said that, Dr. Arora? And they really believed you?
I tell you, you need to write that one down and send it to the *New
Yorker*."

Mohan Lal grinned at her. "If I did, people would think it was
a fiction."

Ms. Farber shook her head and smiled. "Well, thankfully, not
everyone in this country is quite so ignorant."

"Of that I am certain," said Mohan Lal, pointing his right hand toward Ms. Farber. "And you can't blame the people. They only know what they are taught by media."

"Oh, you're being too nice," she replied. "I mean, tree houses? Come on. How could they think that about such a well-spoken man?"

Siddharth breathed deeply to calm himself down. Why couldn't his father talk right? Why couldn't he remember to put the word *the* before *media*?

Ms. Farber said she would love to travel to India at some point. She had always wanted to see the Taj Mahal and Jaipur. Mohan Lal said she could visit anytime, that she would be his family's honored guest.

"That would be lovely. As long as I don't have to stay in one of their tree houses." She let out a laugh, then placed a hand over her mouth. Siddharth hadn't seen her laugh like this before, a dimple appearing on her left cheek.

Mohan Lal smiled for a moment, then grew serious. "Actually, my brother is quite a wealthy man. He has a retinue of servants that would wait on you hand and foot."

Siddharth examined a black-and-white photograph on Ms. Farber's perfectly ordered desk. It showed a lady holding a baby. The photo was ancient, at least from the sixties.

"Oh, yes," said Ms. Farber, "Siddharth has mentioned him." She leaned back in her chair, flicking her auburn curls behind her shoulder. "Don't tell me—is he some sort of maharaja or something?"

Siddharth folded his arms and tried to shoot his father a look. All this India talk was making him sweaty.

Mohan Lal wouldn't meet his eyes though. He said, "Actually, he's in the gun business. But my great-great-grandfather, he was what you could call nobility—the equivalent of your dukes and earls. They hung him on the banks of a river—a wide and beautiful river that is now a cesspool." He paused to rub his chin. "They stripped him of everything—his land, his title. His dignity."

Siddharth didn't actually mind these stories, but his mother had called them exaggerations.

Ms. Farber leaned forward and her chair let out a little whine. "Was it the British?"

"Yes, you're very astute," said Mohan Lal. "Mrs. Farber, my ancestors wouldn't conform to the English tax codes, so they were eliminated."

Siddharth noticed that something green was stuck in the gap between Ms. Farber's yellowed front teeth. Underneath the reading table, her left shoe was off, and her white stockings had a hole near the big toe.

She turned to Siddharth and smiled. "Well, honey, I guess that means you have some royal blood in your veins. Prince Siddharth. It has a nice ring to it."

Mohan Lal patted him on the shoulder.

All of a sudden, Ms. Farber sat upright in her chair. She put on her tortoiseshell reading glasses and opened a folder, then asked Siddharth how things were going.

"Fine, I guess," he said.

She made small talk about school for a minute. Then she asked him if he'd been feeling especially sad lately.

He shrugged.

"His marks have been excellent," said Mohan Lal. "I'm very proud."

Siddharth wanted to elbow his father in the gut.

Ms. Farber explained that Mr. Latella was impressed with Siddharth's intellectual capabilities, but he was concerned about his social situation. He had been a little antisocial lately, and he seemed to be having trouble interacting with boys. As Siddharth absorbed all this bullshit, a bubble of cold air inflated inside his lungs. He decided that Mr. Latella was the biggest bastard in the entire world.

Mohan Lal stared up at the ceiling, then placed his hands underneath his thighs. "Ms. Farber, I don't know what's happened. So many kids used to call my son. Boys, girls—everyone."

She smiled and nodded. "Siddharth has made so much progress over the past year. I'm really quite proud of him. But it's no surprise that he's a little isolated after all he's gone through." She launched into a speech containing terms like *grief* and *depression*, and Siddharth now felt as if someone had him in a chokehold. For the rest of his life, nobody would ever let him just be sad. When he was unhappy, they would always bring it back to his mother.

"Siddharth," said Ms. Farber, "what about sports?"

"What *about* sports?" he said.

She explained that Mr. Latella thought it would be a good idea if he got involved with some sort of team or played some kind of sport.

Smiling, Mohan Lal grasped his shoulder. "His older brother is the sporting man. This one is his father's son."

Shrugging off his father's fingers, he recalled what his brother used to say about sports. If Siddharth didn't play sports, according to Arjun, he would never learn how to be a team player. He would never learn how to be a regular guy and would end up like Mohan Lal.

"What about something else?" said Ms. Farber. "A musical instrument maybe?"

Siddharth needed to defend himself. Music was for losers. Like Sharon. "I like to draw," he said. "I draw all the time."

"I know you do, honey, and you're very good. But tell me, Siddharth, who do you draw with?"

"Nobody, I guess." He thought he liked Ms. Farber. Now he wasn't so sure.

"Exactly. How about something more active? Something a little more interactive?"

He turned to his father for help, but Mohan Lal's eyes were fixed on Ms. Farber.

"I know," she said, thumbing through the pages of her leather planner. "How about karate?"

He wanted to tell her to shut up. But the fact was, karate didn't sound half bad.

Her face was suddenly beaming. "Why didn't I think of it earlier? Dr. Arora, the martial arts can be very good for young people. Tae kwon do has had such a positive impact on my own son."

Mohan Lal said he would have Siddharth search through the yellow pages for a karate class as soon as they got home.

"Oh, we can do better than that," she said. With a bony finger on her planner, Ms. Farber jotted a number onto a yellow square of paper. Her honey-colored eyes gleamed as she handed it over to Siddharth.

As he grasped the note, he felt the tightness in his lungs begin to slacken.

NICE WORK, BODHISATTVA

Siddharth was too excited to fall asleep the night before his first karate class. Over the past few days, he'd watched *The Karate Kid* several more times, and as he lay awake in his bedroom, he fantasized about winning a tournament like the one in the movie. A sea of uniformed fighters would carry him on their shoulders. Arjun would finally be proud, and Luca Peroti would be friends with him. He pictured himself kissing a blonde—a real one, not some slut like Sharon Nagorski.

In school the next day, he couldn't focus on Mr. Latella's booming voice. He was grateful when the teacher gave the class forty-five minutes for silent reading. He wondered if today was somehow lucky for him. He didn't have to take the bus home or stay at his fucking after-school program. He fished out his copy of *Call of the Wild* from his messy desk; Mr. Latella was making him read it for his independent book project. Siddharth predicted the novel would be childish and boring, but after the first couple of pages, he was hooked. He couldn't believe he was actually enjoying something recommended by a teacher.

This story had him riveted, as if it were a movie, and he felt like he had something in common with Buck, the canine protagonist. Both he and the dog had been separated from the people who made them happy. He sat alone on a swing during recess, reading the novel while Luca and his crew played kickball and Sharon played cards with her new gang of hos and losers. Later, when he told his teacher how many pages he'd read, the man said he was impressed. Mr. Latella gave him a high five for the first time all year, and Siddharth found himself smiling. He wondered if he'd been wrong about the guy. After all, if it hadn't been for Mr. Latella, Ms. Farber would never have suggested karate.

Mohan Lal was waiting in the parking lot at three fifteen, and as Siddharth buckled himself into their minivan, his father's appearance squashed some of his cheer and optimism. Mohan Lal was wearing a khaki suit, and Siddharth noticed an ink stain near the lapel. There was a time when his father used to spend half an hour ironing his clothes every night, but today he looked rather wrinkled. His bifocals sat crookedly on his nose, and a few of his wispy gray hairs were sticking straight in the air. He looked old, much older than anyone else's parents. Old people got things like Alzheimer's. Mohan Lal kissed him on the head. He hoped for his father to ask him something about his day, but before they'd even cleared the Deer Run parking lot, Mohan Lal was going off about his latest conflict with his boss, the new dean of Elm City College.

For the past year, his father had become embroiled in an all-out war with the dean, who the college had brought in to save it from bankruptcy. Today, Mohan Lal told him how the dean was now claiming that students were dropping his classes because they had a hard time understanding his accent. "Bloody bastard," said Mohan Lal. "What's wrong with the way I talk? I speak proper English—not like that corporate stooge."

As Mohan Lal steered through the wooded suburban streets, he made Siddharth help him with his pronunciation of certain words. Siddharth struggled to get his father to say *volatility*, not *walletility*, to insert an *r* into the third syllable of *university*. Eventually, he lost his patience, saying, "Jesus, Dad, you're not even trying to sound American." As soon as the words came out, a cold guilt took hold of his stomach. He knew that Mohan Lal was a single parent. He knew that he was supposed to make his father's life easier—not harder. "Anyway," said Siddharth, "the dean obviously feels threatened. He's threatened cause you're smarter." It was Sharon who had taught him that mean people were actually just insecure or threatened. "Trust me, one day they'll be sorry they took you for granted."

Smiling, Mohan Lal squeezed his knee. "Fret not, my son. Those fools will get what's coming. My book's gonna fix them good."

Siddharth turned up the radio now that he had done his duty. He was sick of hearing about the stupid book. Far ahead of the van, the sky was crisp and blue, but charcoal clouds lingered over South Haven's desolate town green and ancient meetinghouse. He told himself that karate was going to change his life. He'd be cool at karate, not the nobody he'd been during his thirteen-month stint at Deer Run. He glanced at the yellow leaves fluttering on the trees in front of the tiny public library. They glowed like gemstones. Most people thought these trees were birch, but he knew they were aspens. His mother had taught him the names of all the trees in South Haven.

They passed the fields where he'd suffered two seasons as an outfielder in the parks-and-recreation baseball league. Last winter, his brother had run special baseball training sessions for him on Sunday mornings. Arjun hit him dozens of grounders and pop flies, and Siddharth had to run and dive for them. When he missed one, he had to drop down on the frosty grass and do five push-ups on his knuckles. If he missed two, he had to sprint around the house four times. If he missed three in a row, he had to stand against a wall and let Arjun pelt him with a tennis ball. The first time Arjun struck him, Siddharth fell to the ground and had to bite down on a clump of clovers to keep from crying. Arjun said, "You're lucky, you know. Nobody was here to do this for me when I was your age."

When they reached Boston Post Road, he got into the backseat to change from his corduroys into navy-blue sweatpants. He had tried to convince Mohan Lal to buy him a karate uniform, which the dojo sold for forty-eight dollars. But his father said he first had to complete an entire month of classes.

As they headed east toward West Haven, the strip malls got grubbier and contained fewer chain stores. Back in the day, his parents used to shop around here. He spotted a pet store where his mother had taken him to buy a ten-gallon fish tank. Beside it, there used to be a smelly Indian shop that sold spices, rice, and daal. The Aroras would laugh at the place's slogan—*So clean you can bring your American friends too*. They were getting closer to their destination. Siddharth needed water, but there was none in the car. He started gnawing on the inside of his mouth, which helped a little, but didn't stop his stomach from twitching and turning.

Mohan Lal took a right turn into the parking lot. "Son?"

"Yeah?" Siddharth wasn't in the mood for nagging of any kind.

"Make me proud, son. I want you to kick some butt."

"So now you're not proud of me? Thanks, Dad. Thanks for always saying the right thing." Then he sighed and grabbed his father's shoulder. "Thanks for bringing me, Dad. Of course I'll make you proud."

He stared at the stores in the shabby, squat plaza. The West Haven Martial Arts Academy sat between a beauty salon and something called a VFW. Mohan Lal parked next to a sleek black Camaro. Arjun had always said that Camaros were cheesy, but Siddharth liked this one. Two thick racing stripes ran along the length of its body, and it had a personalized license plate, *K-Chop*. As they got out of the car, he worried that his father might do something embarrassing. He wished Mohan Lal would just drive off and let him deal on his own.

They walked by some white-haired men who were smoking and drinking coffee out of paper cups. One of them was wearing a cap that looked old-fashioned. European. He tipped it at Mohan Lal, who was holding the door open for Siddharth. Stepping inside the academy, Siddharth was immediately mesmerized by the place's enormous trophy cases, which lined two walls of the slim, rectangular reception area. These cases must have contained at least a hundred trophies, and just as many medals and plaques. He vowed to win a prize for himself one day. He pictured himself bringing it into school and showing it off to Luca Peroti and Eddie Benson. They'd be begging him to join their kickball game. They'd forgive the fact that he'd once been friends with Sharon Nagorski.

Mohan Lal headed toward a window at the far end of the room, and Siddharth followed behind. A young woman was sitting on the other side of the glass. She had silver hoop earrings and was chewing gum. Mohan Lal handed her a check and she told him that he could stay and watch the class.

"No, thank you, miss," said Mohan Lal. "I have to take care of a couple things at the office. You know, I work at Elm City College."

He wondered if his father's accent was especially thick today. Maybe the dean had a point. Mohan Lal signed a few papers, then patted him on the head and walked out the door. Siddharth took a seat on the long wooden bench that lined the room's exterior wall, which was mostly made of windows. When he saw his father's silver minivan pull out of the lot, he started breathing a little easier. A doorway separated the reception area from the actual studio, where a class was taking place. He peered in and saw that most of the students were women. Their instructor was a woman too. He hoped his new teacher wasn't a woman.

With each passing minute, a new boy showed up wearing a karate uniform. Most had white belts, but a few had belts that were green or orange. Some of the boys had gold chains, and a few even had earrings. They greeted each other with high fives or silent nods. Siddharth hunched forward and massaged his crown of black wavy hair. Being here suddenly felt like a bad idea.

A tall boy with an orange belt walked in. He had on a long Sharks parka over his uniform and had a cool haircut, long and floppy on top and shaved on the sides. All the other kids seemed excited to see him. Almost every boy walked up to him and said, "Hey, Marc," or, "What's up, Marc?" either shaking his hand or slapping it five. This Marc kid sauntered over to the secretary's window and said, "Yo, Katie, I was up all night waiting for your call. You doggin' me or something?" Siddharth couldn't make out her words, but he definitely heard laughter.

When the women's class let out, he followed the other boys into the studio. They seated themselves in three neat rows, and he chose a place in the back left corner, close to the doorway. He scoped out the other kids through the mirrors that lined the front wall. They all looked at ease sitting Indian style, so he forced himself to keep his legs crossed even though it hurt. Above the mirrors were two flags, an American one and another that was either Japanese or Korean. Between them was a photograph of a chubby, bearded white man with a black belt. He was bowing down before a somber, gray-haired Oriental.

The other kids sprang to their feet and bowed as soon as the sensei stepped in from the locker room, but it took Siddharth a moment to follow suit. He was shocked: his new karate teacher was black. He had met other black people before, like the woman who had babysat for Arjun and then cleaned the Arora household until he was eight, and he had seen plenty of black people on television. But he had never had a black teacher. The sensei had a rounded three-inch Afro and black freckles, like Morgan Freeman in *Robin Hood*. His black belt had a red stripe running through its middle, which must have meant he was especially hard core.

The instructor said, "Listen up, my young friends. Today we have a new colleague, and I want you to welcome him with open arms." He eyed Siddharth. "Son, I'm Mr. Stone. Why don't you tell us your name?"

Siddharth responded, pronouncing the *d*'s incorrectly, to make it sound more American.

"Ah, a most holy of names," said Mr. Stone. "Perhaps your presence will bring us a step closer to enlightenment."

The first part of the class was disappointing. They had to do a bunch of stretches and punch the air while standing in place. Mr. Stone then led them through some boring "forms," for which the boys completed a series of synchronized movements in different directions. Siddharth tried his best to mimic the others, but he was always a step behind.

Mr. Stone seemed to have a particular fondness for a kid named Gene-Paul, who had spiked hair and a tail that sprouted from his neck, and also for that Marc kid. He referred to Marc by his last name, Kaufman. He said, "Kaufman, my grandmother can punch harder than you," and, "Kaufman, you're supposed to be setting an example for everyone—not showing us what *not* to do." Siddharth wondered if this was *the* Marc Kaufman. Last summer, a Marc Kaufman from Woodford had stolen the family Jeep and taken it for a joyride. He'd crashed it into a mailbox, one of those official blue ones, which made his crime a federal offense. It was Sharon who'd shared these details. Her father's cousin, Randy Miller, had been one of the arresting officers.

With ten minutes left in class, Mr. Stone announced that it was time to spar. The other boys broke into pairs, facing each other in two neat lines. They leaned back on their right feet and brought their fists into fighting position. Siddharth looked down and thought about going to the bathroom or asking to leave early.

Mr. Stone placed his warm, strong fingers on Siddharth's shoulder. "Kaufman, why don't you break in the new guy? But go easy on him."

Marc Kaufman was in a corner putting on padded red gloves. He punched them together and took his place across from Siddharth. Mr. Stone grunted, and all the boys started bouncing on their back legs, making blocks and punches. Marc just stood still and stared him down.

Siddharth definitely regretted being here. Wasn't karate just another sport?

Marc flicked his hair out of his eyes and then made a kick, but Siddharth managed to step back and avoid it.

"Nice work, bodhisattva," said Mr. Stone.

Flicking his hair again, Marc came in closer. He pulled his fist back, then landed a hard punch on Siddharth's chest. He fell backward and hit the rubbery green floor.

For a few moments, he couldn't breathe. He saw Mr. Stone standing over him but couldn't hear what he was saying. Marc held out his hand, and Siddharth used it to pull himself up. He suddenly noticed that the other kids had all stopped fighting and were watching him.

"You okay?" asked Mr. Stone.

"I think so," he said.

Mr. Stone started clapping. All of his students followed suit.

Siddharth wanted to smile but didn't want to seem uncool, so he just kept quiet.

* * *

After class, he sat alone on the curb, using a stick to create a smiley face in the gravel. Only a few cars remained in the parking lot, and he was sitting close to a burgundy Saab 900. A gaggle of five or six boys stood by a green dumpster a few feet away from the black Camaro. They were practicing moves on each other and seemed to be having fun. He wished he were hanging out with them but would only go if they called him over. He grew bored with his gravel drawing and started rating the cars. If he had to drive one, his first choice would definitely be the Camaro, and his number two would be the Saab. Arjun would have chosen the gray Acura in the corner, even though it had a dent in its rear door.

Mohan Lal had told him to bring his jacket, but he'd refused. He rubbed his arms to keep himself warm and stared at the one-story building across the street, a bar called the New Warsaw Café. Above him, the setting sun had streaked the sky with pink and orange, and some seagulls were circling. One of them swooped down, snatching a piece of trash from the dumpster. A kid from karate class picked up a stick and chucked it toward the bird, and the gull leaped back into the air.

Mr. Stone emerged from the academy wearing sunglasses and a leather jacket. He patted Siddharth on the shoulder, saying that he had done well. Then he headed toward the Camaro, pushing a button on his keys that caused the car to squawk, and said, "Boys, if I find even a single scratch on her, what ensues will be unpleasant and nasty."

The boys laughed.

Mr. Stone got in his vehicle and peeled out of the lot.

Cars kept pulling in, and boys kept leaving. Siddharth wondered when his father would get there. He was tired, but not the way he usually was. He felt kind of good actually. Soon the only other kid left was Marc Kaufman, who walked over to him and sat down on the curb.

"What's up?"

Siddharth shrugged. "Pretty good." As soon as he said those words, he bit down on the inside of his cheek again. Only an asshole would say *pretty good* when someone asks *what's up*.

Marc bet Siddharth a dollar that he could hit the insignia on the hood of the Saab with a single stone. He chucked a rock but missed by ten inches. "You try," he said. "Double or nothing."

Siddharth picked up a gray stone that sparkled with mica but couldn't bring himself to do it.

"Don't worry," said Marc, "it's my mom's."

Siddharth took a deep breath and threw the stone, which landed an inch away from the target.

Marc whistled. "Close. Now we're even." He chucked three more stones, and the second two both clanked against the target. "By the way, I'm Marc."

"I know," said Siddharth.

"You know? Why, what did you hear about me?"

Siddharth shrugged.

"Well, don't believe everything they say."

A gull let out a cry and again dove for the dumpster.

Siddharth wanted to say something cool but didn't know what. He threw a stone at the bird, and it soared back to the sky. "My name's Sid."

"No shit." Marc held out his hand. "I know your name. My mother told me all about you."

"Your mother?" Siddharth's brow furrowed as he shook Marc's hand.

Marc smiled, revealing a gap between his two front teeth. "That redhead? The crazy woman from your school?"

"Who?"

"Not too long ago, the famous Ms. Farber used to be Mrs. Kaufman."

Siddharth stared down at his Nikes and noticed the beginnings of a hole near the big toe of his left foot. He felt a surge of loathing for Ms. Farber. She shouldn't have been talking about him to other people. She'd said that everything they discussed was completely confidential.

"She told me what happened to you."

Siddharth knew what he meant. He tossed another pebble at the Saab, this time with much more force.

"That must have really sucked," said Marc.

Siddharth prayed that his father would get there soon. In a little while, he would be back home. He would throw on a movie. He wouldn't have to come back to karate if he didn't want to.

"Let me tell you," said Marc, flicking his bangs out of his eyes, "divorce is no Sunday drive either. It's the second-worst thing that can happen to a kid, after a parent dying."

Siddharth had no idea that Ms. Farber was divorced. The truth was, she knew a lot about him but he barely knew anything about her. This fact seemed totally unfair.

A bell jingled, and he turned to his left. The front door of the beauty salon had opened, and Ms. Farber stepped outside. Siddharth had a rock in his hand; he wished he could throw it at her. Instead, he dropped it and waved.

She looked different, having straightened her normally curly auburn hair. She walked toward them smiling her big toothy smile, and his eyes honed in on the triangle of flat, freckled skin below her neck. She was wearing her gold chain with a star on it, the kind that you drew with two overlapping triangles. "Hi, boys," she said. "Siddharth, how'd it go?"

He shrugged. "Fine. I'm not really that good."

"Oh, come on," said Ms. Farber. "I bet you knocked their socks off, honey." She headed to the Saab and unlocked its front door. "I see you've met my Marc."

"Yup."

She winked at him. "I don't know why, but something tells me you guys might hit it off."

"Oh, yes, mother," said Marc. He got up and dusted off his uniform. "Sid here is a splendid young fellow. We're gonna get along just fine."

6

SLEEPOVER

The phone kept on ringing one Friday night in early December. First it was Arjun. He was calling with flight details for his upcoming trip home, the first one he'd make since moving out to Michigan. Then came a call from Ms. Farber's son Marc. He said, "Yo, Sid, you're spending the night at my house tomorrow." Marc was a seventh grader at the Woodford branch of Eli Whitney Junior High. He was grounded for what he had done to the blue mailbox with his father's Jeep, so he wouldn't be allowed to socialize until summer. But Ms. Farber bent the rules of his grounding for Siddharth, who had already been to their house after karate on several occasions.

These first two calls put Siddharth in a good mood. Then the phone rang for a third time. It was Barry Uncle. Fourteen months had passed since Mohan Lal had had a real conversation with Barry Uncle. Eighteen months had passed since the last time they'd stayed up late drinking Scotch and eating pink pistachios, getting louder with each passing hour, talking trash about Gandhi and Nehru, calling them British stooges. Just the other day, Siddharth had remembered a joke Barry Uncle once told about a Sikh man who didn't know how to use a modern toilet, so he wrapped his shit in a bedsheet and flung it out the window. This joke made Mohan Lal laugh so hard that tears started trickling from his light-brown eyes. Siddharth wanted his father to laugh like that again. He had Marc Kaufman now, and he wanted his father to have someone too.

He tried passing the phone to his father, but Mohan Lal gave him a wide-eyed glare, a look of death usually reserved for Arjun. Siddharth said, "Don't look at me like that." Mohan Lal told him not to stick his nose in other people's business. Siddharth said, "Dad, it's my business if you're all depressed all the time. It's my business if you're gonna be such a loner."

Mohan Lal raised his hand behind his ear. "What did you call me? Listen, it's okay for someone at my stage to keep his own company. You're the one I'm worried about. You're the one who's lost all his friends."

That night, as Siddharth tried to fall asleep, he felt a strong sense of loathing toward his father. He wished the man had actually hit him. Mohan Lal had hit Arjun a few times, and Siddharth thought that something about the pain might make him stronger. As he tossed and turned, he made another wish. He wished that he could disappear for a few days, just so his father could get a small taste of life without him.

Waking up in the middle of the night, he suddenly regretted these horrible thoughts. He regretted saying such horrible things to his father. He imagined Mohan Lal all alone on the sofa, sipping Scotch and staring at the television, his eyes glassy and dazed. Meanwhile, Siddharth would be out having fun with Marc.

In the morning, Siddharth watched cartoons by himself and woke his father up at ten. He served them Pop-Tarts and orange juice for breakfast as a way of making up. As they ate in the dining room, Siddharth declared that he was canceling his sleepover.

"But you've made a commitment," said Mohan Lal. "A man must honor his commitments."

"Just forget it, Dad. You can't force me."

"It's your life, son. If you want to ruin it, it's your decision."

Siddharth grunted. "Fine. But at least put on some real clothes. You're not dropping me off in those stupid sweatpants."

Before they left for Marc's, he flipped through the TV listings and drew little stars next to programs that might interest his father. Mohan Lal told him not to bother. He said he would use the peace and quiet to work on his book. As they headed down Route 114 toward Woodford, Siddharth found comfort in his father's words. Mohan Lal was supposed to be working hard on his book, but he'd barely devoted any time to it lately. Maybe it was a good thing that Siddharth was going out. Maybe he was actually doing his father a favor by hanging out with Marc. The van skirted Foster Farm, the second oldest farm in the country, and his fear and guilt began to fade. He was growing excited for his time with Marc Kaufman. The kid was undeniably cool, and it seemed that he liked him—or at least didn't think he was a total loser.

For almost eight weeks now, the two families had been carpooling. On Tuesdays, Mohan Lal picked up the boys after their karate lesson, dropping Marc off in Woodford so that Ms. Farber could attend a meditation class at the Jewish Community Center. On Thursdays, Ms. Farber drove Siddharth straight from Deer Run to the dojo, picking up Marc from her house en route. Thanks to this arrangement, Siddharth got to spend one less day per week at his hellish after-school program.

He was jittery the first couple of times he walked toward Ms. Farber's Saab in the Deer Run parking lot. What would people say if they saw him cozying up to the school psychologist? Would they think he'd gone crazy? And there were other worries too. It was one thing to talk about his mother in Ms. Farber's office. But what if she brought her up on the way to karate? Fortunately, Ms. Farber just asked him innocent questions about his father's job or his brother's classes, or they drove in silence, listening to a Top Forty station or a boring program on National Public Radio.

When karate class was over on Thursdays, Ms. Farber dropped him off around five thirty, and he watched television and made himself pasta as he waited for his father to return from work. After a couple weeks of this routine, however, Ms. Farber said there was no reason for Siddharth to be spending so much time alone. She insisted that he have dinner with her and Marc when Mohan Lal had evening classes. She wasn't a great cook, but Siddharth began to look forward to Thursday evenings.

In some ways, Marc and Ms. Farber's single-story home was strange. She had started some renovations awhile back but never actually finished them, so parts of their house were in a state of limbo. Their formal living room had new wooden floors, but its walls had a few holes where you could see tangles of wire and copper piping. A bathroom beside the kitchen had a small sauna that wasn't actually functional, and its oversize sink seemed like one that belonged inside a janitor's closet. But Siddharth loved this house so much more than his own ordinary home. It was made of real redbrick, not shabby wooden siding. The place had a grand entrance hallway, with marble floors and an ornate chandelier. The bedrooms had tall ceilings, and most of them had bathrooms—even Marc's. All of the house's light switches were the flat modern kind, and Siddharth felt a small thrill whenever he pressed one.

His favorite part of the house was the basement. Unlike the Aroras' dim concrete basement, this one was finished with parquet floors and gray carpeting. Marc had everything down there—ping-pong, bumper pool, and a floor piano like the one from the movie *Big*. On one of his first visits downstairs, Siddharth spotted the six-foot-long GI Joe aircraft carrier. He had seen thousands of commercials for it when he was younger and had wanted one so badly, but Mohan Lal called it a "made-in-Taiwan piece of crap." His mother simply opposed such violent toys.

He asked Marc if they could play with it, and Marc said, "I guess we could do that. If we were, like, six." Marc then walked over to the aircraft carrier and pulled out a plastic compartment that contained a stash of *Playboys*. From that day on, whenever they went downstairs, they just sat around comparing the breasts of centerfold models. Siddharth knew that his father would kill him for looking at the pictures, but he couldn't get enough of them. He was particularly fond of a blond Miss April from 1984. She was wearing nothing except striped socks and an open pink bathrobe. He started thinking about her before falling asleep at night, pressing his erection into his springy mattress. Marc occasionally loaned Siddharth a magazine, or a picture of a naked woman, and when he got home, he tried copying these images into his sketchpad. Drawing these women was fun. But it also made him wonder if he was some kind of perv.

Usually, when Mohan Lal picked him up from Marc's, Ms. Farber went out to the driveway to chat with him. At first, they just talked about the boys and karate, but much to Siddharth's dismay, Mohan Lal started telling Ms. Farber stories. He told her about his student who had made it to America as a stowaway on an oil tanker, and how the son of the great Igor Sikorsky had once given Arjun violin lessons. Ms. Farber told Mohan Lal about her broken muffler and the junky Greenwich Village apartment she had once rented while struggling to make it as an actress. She discussed her dissatisfaction with the public school system, which piled her up with paperwork that got in the way of her actual work. In a few years, she said, she would quit her job and go into private practice.

"Why wait?" said Mohan Lal.

Ms. Farber folded her arms across her chest. She peered up at the sky. "Well, the bills for one thing. Insurance, taxes."

Mohan Lal told her to make a good business plan and take a calculated risk. He said that it was a proven fact that the universe rewards risk takers. Siddharth was dying to tell his father to mind his own business. But he didn't want Ms. Farber to get the wrong impression about them, so he just bit his lip and stared out the window. He also kept his mouth shut whenever Mohan Lal complained about his own job, which he did with more frequency as autumn turned to winter.

Mohan Lal wouldn't shut up about his dean, and he even bored Ms. Farber with the details of the dean's new book. In this book, the man argued that new advertising specifically designed for children would mold them into more productive citizens. Mohan Lal wanted to publish a paper refuting him, one that exposed the corruption of the FCC under the Reagan administration. "It's the corporations," he said. "The government used to protect youngsters from the Madison Avenue serpents, but then the corporations got into Reagan's bed, and *poof*—everything vanished. Mark my words, Ms. Farber, there will be consequences. These bloody advertisers will undermine the intelligence of an entire generation."

Having heard these diatribes hundreds of times, Siddharth sat there digging his fingers into his temples. Normal people didn't use words like *bloody* or *serpent*. He wished his father would try to be more normal.

They pulled in front of Marc's brick house just before noon, and the mere sight of it filled him with adrenaline. Mohan Lal said he would walk him to the door, but Siddharth told him not to bother. "I'm not five, Dad. Ms. Farber's a busy woman. Leave her alone." Kissing his father on the shoulder, he jogged up Marc's front steps, where a few unread newspapers were stacked in a messy pile. Mohan Lal reversed out of the driveway when Marc came to the door. He gave Siddharth a high five and told him to take off his shoes. "Rachel finally mopped the floors. We don't want her going ape shit on us."

"Where is she?" asked Siddharth.

"My mom? Being a loser."

Marc led him to the family room, which formed one enormous, uninterrupted space with the sleek, modern kitchen. He sat down to finish up a video game, something with guns and jungles. Siddharth didn't mind video games, but there was no point in competing with Marc. So he just sat quietly, swallowed by the plush leather sofa. He stared at his new friend, who was frenetically pressing the controller's buttons while jerking, rocking, and swearing. Marc was wearing sweatpants, but the cool kind with zips down the side. His bangs dangled over his eyes, which today seemed red and small. Had he been crying?

Marc defeated the second level of his game and threw his controller onto the rug. "Yo, let's get the hell out of here," he said. "I need to smoke something."

Siddharth's chest tightened with a mixture of fear and excitement. Marc had talked about smoking before, but he had never actually seen him do it. They walked down the corridor toward the bedrooms. Siddharth sometimes got lost staring at the paintings that lined this wide, carpeted hallway, many of which were Ms. Farber's creations. Some of her paintings contained just a few splotches of color that had clearly been applied with a sponge, and they looked like something a child could have done. He knew that people considered this stuff art, but he'd never understood why. His mother had said that it was a case of the emperor's new clothes. When Marc had once caught him gawking at the artwork, he said, "Yeah, Rachel's a real Picasso. If this stuff starts selling, we're gonna be loaded." Siddharth had cocked his head to one side, unsure if his friend was joking. Marc grabbed his arm and gave him a shake. "I'm just fucking with you," he said. "Dude, you gotta lighten up."

Marc paused in front of Ms. Farber's door and knocked. "What?" she said, her voice gruff and tired. Marc pulled the handle down and stepped inside. Siddharth remained in the hallway, his back up against a small patch of the wall that didn't contain any paintings. He saw Ms. Farber sitting up in bed watching some soap opera. He'd been inside her bedroom a couple of times, when Marc needed money or was looking for a video. It had puffy pink curtains and shiny white furniture. Yet today it was dark. Ms. Farber was usually so neat and tidy, but he glimpsed clothes and papers strewn all over the tan carpeting. The oddest thing was that the room smelled like smoke. He felt like an ass for not having noticed that Ms. Farber was a smoker.

"Twenty bucks, please," said Marc, the palm of his hand hovering near his mother's face.

"For what?" she replied.

"To be a good host," said Marc. "The young fella would like a little ice cream."

She turned toward Siddharth. "Oh, hi honey."

"Hello." He waved and smiled, trying to give the impression that everything was fine.

"You'll have to excuse me today," she said. "I'm just a little under the weather."

"Really, Rachel?" said Marc. He pulled an envelope of bills from her bedside drawer. "What do you got? A cold? A cough? I'm curious about the diagnosis."

Ignoring him, Ms. Farber turned down the volume. "Sid, honey," she said, "I need to rest a little. But help yourself to anything. Please—make yourself at home."

The boys headed out to the garage, which never failed to mesmerize Siddharth. His own garage was disgusting and boring, filled with cobwebs, rusty rakes, and rotting firewood, but this one was spotless and contained numerous cool contraptions. Tools and saw blades hung from the walls, and the ground was filled with neat rows of hockey sticks, volleyball nets, and rollerblades. Marc had two bikes, a fancy BMX that he had built for himself and a ten-speed mountain bike that Siddharth usually rode. Marc started putting air into the mountain bike's tires but after three pumps paused and gave him a look.

"What's up?" said Siddharth. Marc seemed annoyed, and Siddharth wondered if he'd done something wrong. Marc opened his mouth to say something but then resumed his pumping. "What is it?" asked Siddharth.

"Nothing." Marc was shaking his head. "But now you see what I gotta live with."

"What do you mean?"

"I mean my mom. She gets *sick* almost every single week. She should be in the *Guinness Book of World Records*—the only woman who gets her period four times a month."

"Dude," said Siddharth, "she's your mom."

"So? What's your point?"

"My point?" Siddharth wanted to say so many things. He wanted to tell Marc that it was wrong to talk about his own mother like that—that he would regret it when she died one day. He wanted to know if something was really wrong with Ms. Farber. Was she really like this all the time? But he didn't want to ruin his sleepover. "I don't have a point. I just don't wanna hear about her freaking period."

A subtle wind tickled Siddharth's ears as they rode through the sand-covered streets of Woodford. His nose started to run. He wiped it on the sleeve of his quilted blue jacket, which had once belonged to Arjun. It seemed like his day with Marc was going well. He just hoped he hadn't messed things up by saying that thing about Ms. Farber's period. They flew down a steep hill, and the combination of cold and adrenaline slowed his mind. He loved riding through Woodford, which was so much nicer than South Haven. It had more Jews than Italians, and they had much bigger houses. Their yards were the size of entire parks, and they contained trees that were as tall as the Twin Towers. The boys rode by Siddharth's favorite home, which was separated from the street by a stone wall and remote-controlled gate. Its three stories had five large columns that made it look awesome—like the White House, or the mansion from *The Fresh Prince of Bel-Air*. A few minutes later, they arrived at a deli located in a red wooden building at a large but quiet intersection. They got off their bikes, leaning them against a dust-covered freezer in which bags of ice were stored.

Marc told Siddharth to wait with the bikes.

"This is Woodford," said Siddharth. "No one's gonna steal 'em."

"Bro, you look like you're ten. Just stay outside."

Siddharth sat on a boulder at the parking lot's edge, staring at the passing cars and thinking about his father. He hoped Mohan Lal was working on his book and not drinking or moping on the sofa. A disturbing image flashed in his mind. He saw his father lying in pain on the bathroom floor, and nobody was there to help him. Siddharth spotted a pay phone and wondered if he should call home—just to check on things—but by the time he decided this was a good idea, Marc emerged from the squat wooden shop brandishing a pack of five cigars. He lit one with a match, then handed it over. Siddharth had tried a cigarette before, in India, with his cousin, but he had never smoked a cigar. This one had a plastic tip. He brought it to his lips and sucked as hard as he could. The smoke singed his lungs, and he coughed until his eyes watered. Until his throat burned.

Smirking, Marc lit up his own cigar. "Dude, don't inhale that shit. Just taste the smoke—savor it, then blow it out."

Siddharth hunched forward, resting his hands on his thighs. He thought the cough was slowing down, and then it flared up again. He saw a cop drive by and felt a surge of panic. But the cop kept on going.

"Don't waste that shit," said Marc.

His throat still hurt, but he took another drag. This time, he made sure to keep the smoke confined to his mouth. It tasted kind of sweet. Another pull made him light and dizzy. He smiled.

Marc nodded. "That's what I'm talking about. Shit, I needed that."

The boys gave each other a high five. They kept on smoking in silence.

Eventually, Marc spit out a wad of phlegm and said, "That woman is a total maniac. *Marc, I have a headache. Marc, I have a cold. Help me. Help, Marc. Make it all go away.*"

Siddharth giggled at this scratchy, high-pitched imitation of Ms. Farber.

Marc's face suddenly became serious, and he looked Siddharth straight in the eye. "A cold my ass," he said. "Why do you think they got divorced?"

He wasn't sure, but it seemed like his friend wanted an actual answer. "I dunno. Communication problems?"

"Yeah, but why? *Why* didn't they communicate, Sid?"

Siddharth shrugged and puffed on his stogie.

"I'll tell you why: Rachel's a greedy bitch. So my dad got with someone else." Marc smiled, but it wasn't a happy smile. "Honestly, I don't blame him. I'd do the same thing if I were him."

Ms. Farber didn't emerge from her bedroom that evening. For dinner, Marc made them turkey sandwiches, slicing onions and tomatoes and teaching Siddharth how to correctly apply mustard. You had to use the red piece of the plastic container to dab it onto the bread, and whenever possible, the bread had to be rye. Siddharth had never tasted rye before, but these were the best sandwiches he had ever eaten.

Late at night, they went into the guest room, which had a sofa bed, cable TV, and a VCR. Marc put on a porno, and Siddharth couldn't believe what appeared on the screen. People were having actual sex. There were close-ups of men fingering women, of women giving blow jobs. Gigantic penises were thrusting into hairy vaginas. In one scene, four people were having sex at the same time. At first, Siddharth was a little disgusted. Then he started worrying about the size of his own puny dick. Soon all these thoughts vanished, and a strong erection was pressing into the zipper of his jeans.

"Dude," said Marc, "I'm gonna go to the bathroom and take care of my boner." When he got back, he was grasping a minibottle of whiskey, the kind of thing they handed out on airplanes. He cracked it open and held it out to Siddharth.

He shook his head. "Nah, I'm not in the mood."

"Suit yourself," said Marc, downing the whole thing in a long gulp. "Yo, the bathroom's all yours."

"Huh?"

"Don't just sit there with a hard-on all night. Go and relieve yourself."

He walked to Marc's bathroom and turned on the light. He placed his hands on the granite counter and looked in the mirror. All the toothpaste stains on the mirror were nasty, but they reminded him of a sky full of stars. He spotted the beginnings of a pimple on his forehead. The pimple was pleasing; pimples meant he was normal. And his skin was light in tone, just a shade darker than Marc's. He was Indian, but at least he wasn't a dark one. The problem was that he would be twelve in a few weeks, and he barely had any hair on his balls. He put his hand down his pants and grasped his swollen penis. When he'd tried masturbating, it had never really happened—he had stroked and pulled, but nothing came out. He would die if anybody knew that his dick didn't work. He would die if anybody knew that he was a freak who couldn't jerk off.

He tucked his penis up into the waistband of his underwear and pulled his shirt over his crotch, then headed back to the guest room, holding up his hand for a high five.

"Dude," said Marc, "get your cummy fingers away from me."

Siddharth sat back down feeling contented. As far as Marc was concerned, he was normal. As far Marc was concerned, he worked just fine.

* * *

Upon waking up in the morning, Siddharth discovered that Ms. Farber was already in the kitchen. She was listening to classical music and flipping pancakes, and her face looked like it had gone back to normal.

"Morning, boys," she said. "I hope you're hungry."

"Of course we're hungry," said Marc. "I've been living on cold cuts for three days straight."

Smiling, she stacked some pancakes on two plates, which she placed in front of the barstools. Siddharth relished his breakfast. The pancakes contained canned peaches and walnuts, two things he'd never tasted before as far as he could remember. While he shoveled food into his mouth, Ms. Farber asked him if he might want to be a professor like his father. He said no, because professors barely made any money. He wanted to be rich. He wanted to own a DeLorean, Marty McFly's car in *Back to the Future*. He wanted to own more than one mansion, like Donald Trump.

Ms. Farber laughed. "Well, I hope some of your ambition rubs off on my Marc."

"Whatever," said Marc. "I'm gonna work for my father."

"Sorry, Marc," she countered, "I'm afraid you have greater things in store."

"There ain't nothing wrong with scrap metal, Mom. Last time I checked, it pays your bills just fine."

Siddharth didn't know where to look. He gripped the back of his neck and peered down at some leftover gobs of maple syrup. "I better call my dad," he said. "He can come pick me up."

"Pick you up?" said Ms. Farber. "Marc's father's away, and we've got no other plans. You should stay, Siddharth. You boys can have a little fun. And Mohan can get some bonus time with his book." She pulled a packet of green cigarettes out of a drawer. She lit one with a lighter that was meant for the stove. Smoke streamed out of her nose.

Later in the day, while Ms. Farber was reading on the family room sofa, Siddharth and Marc were back on the kitchen barstools, eating one of her bland lentil soups and watching MTV. A video by Bell Biv DeVoe came on, and Siddharth told Marc to turn up the volume. He loved this group's dance moves, and their women had long legs and enormous tits. Marc said, "Screw that. This song is gay." He said that rap was cool, but real hip-hop—not pussies like Bell Biv DeVoe.

Siddharth heard his father's signature honk, one short beep followed by two long ones. He was about to get up, but Ms. Farber rose from the sofa and told him to finish his food in peace. She needed to have a word with his father. Siddharth's stomach tightened. He hoped that she hadn't found the *Playboys*. He hoped there wasn't another problem with Mr. Latella.

She went out to the driveway via the kitchen door and returned a few minutes later with Mohan Lal, who kissed Siddharth on the forehead. He used the sleeve of his Michigan sweatshirt to soak up the saliva and turned to stare at his father, who was wearing a tweed jacket and his especially thick bifocals. This was the first time Mohan Lal had ever been inside Marc's home, and Siddharth felt uneasy. This was his special place now, and he didn't want to share it.

Ms. Farber placed a bowl of lentil soup in the microwave. "Boys, why don't you keep watching somewhere else?"

"I thought TV was bad for you," said Marc. "Should a kid who's grounded really be watching so much television?"

"Scoot," said Ms. Farber. "The adults have to look at some paperwork."

Marc grabbed their dirty bowls and plunked them down in the sink. "What kind of paperwork?"

"My business plan."

"Wait, you're starting a business?" said Marc, walking toward the sofas at the far end of the room.

The microwave chimed, and Ms. Farber removed the soup. "Marc, why don't we stop while we're ahead?" She set the soup down in front of Mohan Lal, who was now on a barstool beside Siddharth.

Marc jumped onto the cushiony brown sofa and turned on

Fox. "I mean, I thought a business had to, like, actually produce something. Last time I checked, psychologists don't really make anything. They just talk. They talk and talk and talk until there's nothing left in your head."

Siddharth laughed, but he wished Marc wouldn't give his mother any attitude in front Mohan Lal.

Ms. Farber slammed the dishwasher shut, rattling some plates inside. "Marc, it's like your father's sitting over there on the sofa. And trust me, I don't mean that in a good way." She walked over to a cardboard box below the kitchen window and started sifting through a stack of papers.

Mohan Lal spooned some soup into his mouth. "Mrs. Farber," he said, "this soup is delicious."

"Really?" She looked up at him over the rims of her reading glasses. "Wow, a compliment. I could get used to that." She went back to her papers but then paused. "By the way, it's *Ms*. Farber. But you need to start calling me Rachel."

Mohan Lal swallowed more lentils in silence.

"Hey," said Ms. Farber, "how about a glass of wine?"

Mohan Lal bit into a piece of bread. "Thank you, but I've been writing all weekend and now have to get to my grading." The bread made his words hard to decipher, and Siddharth elbowed him in the thigh. He hated it when his father spoke with his mouth full. He noticed that Ms. Farber had placed her hand over her own mouth. Was she laughing at him?

"You sure?" she said. "I've got a lovely merlot."

Mohan Lal turned to Siddharth. "Have you finished your homework, son?"

"Definitely."

"Are you sure?"

"Of course I'm sure."

Mohan Lal told Ms. Farber that he would have half a glass of wine.

7

SNOW DAY

Ms. Farber left her job at Deer Run in the first half of January. This turn of events was upsetting. Siddharth wondered what it would mean for him and Marc. But things kept going strong with this new friendship, and Ms. Farber continued the karate carpool. It was upon her suggestion that the four of them made plans to attend a regional martial arts tournament in Springfield, Massachusetts. Marc had been nominated to represent the dojo in a sparring competition for the thirteen-to-fourteen age group, and Ms. Farber arranged for Siddharth to participate in an exhibition forms demonstration.

He was looking forward to a day trip with his friend, and also to the possibility of winning a medal to hang around one of Arjun's many baseball trophies. But as the Sunday of the tournament approached, he began to grow anxious, knowing that he might mess up in front of the other kids, that his father might do something embarrassing. He lay awake remembering the previous year's PTA meeting. It seemed inevitable that Mohan Lal would do something odd again, would say some strange, incomprehensible thing to one of the referees or Ms. Farber.

The morning of the event, the Aroras pulled into Ms. Farber's driveway just after ten. Marc was already outside in his big black parka, waiting beside a dumpster filled with debris from his mother's renewed program of renovations. Ms. Farber came out five minutes later wearing black jeans, a purple coat, and a furry cake-shaped hat. She pulled a steel thermos out of a brown paper bag and poured out a Styrofoam cup of steamy hot chocolate for each of them.

It was a cloudy, windy morning with sporadic flurries. Mohan Lal drove especially slowly, which seemed to annoy Marc, who kept saying he would be glad to lend a hand at the wheel. Siddharth forced himself to laugh. He wondered why his father had to drive like such a fairy. As they headed north, his mind drifted to Arjun. He felt guilty for admitting it, but he was relieved that Christmas break was over and his brother was back at college.

Arjun had definitely changed at Michigan. He had grown a goatee, which Mohan Lal said made him look like a pinko. More importantly, since Arjun had been away, he seemed to have started caring more about his friends than his family. During his two-week stay in South Haven, he was always out with his high school friends, or talking on the phone with some mysterious person from college. Siddharth once asked if he was speaking to his girlfriend, and Arjun told him to shut up and mind his own business.

When Arjun wasn't busy with his social life, he was reading a fat paperback about India called *Midnight's Children*. Siddharth couldn't fathom why his brother would want to waste his time on a book about such a dirty country. This novel was a constant source of tension between Arjun and Mohan Lal. Arjun said that it proved that Hindus and Muslims were actually similar and showed the true tyranny of Indira Gandhi. Mohan Lal called it a bunch of lies. He called its author a British puppet. He said that Arjun should forget about this foolish literature and focus on his grades. Arjun had gotten As in history and English but a C in calculus. He claimed that his math professor had something against immigrants, but Mohan Lal told him not to make excuses for his own errors and imperfections.

Seeking to impress his brother, Siddharth showed him a pile of math quizzes on which he'd gotten 98s and 100s. Arjun, who used to sit around predicting his classmates' grades and future salaries, now said that grades were just numbers and what really mattered was if you were learning. Siddharth then brought him his book report on *Call of the Wild*. He was particularly proud of the cover he had drawn for it, which showed Buck on his haunches by a river. It was one of the greatest things he had ever created. He had used watercolors to render the dog's eyes a light shade of blue, and he had painted some red bloodstains on the animal's muzzle. He had also sketched the feathers of a dead Indian by Buck's paws. He almost cried when Arjun criticized the picture.

Arjun said that Buck was a hero, but Siddharth's drawing had him looking like a savage. After reading Siddharth's actual essay, Arjun decided to reread *Call of the Wild*. He finished it in a single sitting and then declared that Siddharth's thesis was simplistic. Siddharth had argued that the book was a story about undying animal instincts, but Arjun claimed it was a novel about subjugation. The dogs represented workers, or maybe slaves. They had to band together to overcome their oppressors. "And one more thing," he said. "You should have mentioned the book's failings. Look at the way it portrays women. And the way it portrays indigenous people—it's just pathetic."

The absolute low point of Arjun's trip was when he found some of Siddharth's X-rated pictures at the back of their bedroom closet. He started yelling about how these images were disgusting and not even realistic. Siddharth confessed that he'd gotten them from Marc, and Arjun launched into a lecture about Marc seeming too precocious and being a bad influence. "By the way, isn't he the son of your psychologist?"

"She's not *my* psychologist," said Siddharth.

"Whatever," said Arjun. "It's a little weird if you ask me—kind of unethical or something."

Thanks to the snow flurries, Mohan Lal's slow pace, and some bad directions, they didn't make it to the municipal gymnasium in Springfield until three minutes after their designated registration time. Marc was shaking his head and muttering to himself as they scurried through the parking lot, which confirmed Siddharth's prediction that having his father there was a bad idea.

Inside, an overweight woman with gigantic glasses insisted that registration was closed. Siddharth felt an unexpected surge of relief. Maybe they could all just get lunch and head home. Ms. Farber, however, wouldn't take no for an answer. She bent toward the woman and whispered something in her ear, and the woman eventually agreed to make an exception.

Mohan Lal looked on, smiling. Later, he asked, "What did you tell her, Rachel?"

"Top secret," said Ms. Farber, winking at him.

"Rachel, you should forget about psychology and go for politics."

"Oh, I'm fine where I am," she said. Her voice was harsh, but her whole face seemed to be smiling, not just her lips.

Siddharth's forms exhibition was held in a large classroom that had been emptied of its desks and chairs and lined with thin gray matting. Upon seeing the other kids, who looked bigger, stronger, and more American, he bit down on the inside of his cheek and wished he hadn't come. A dozen parents watched as he began making synchronized movements with five other children. He made a huge mistake within the first two minutes, kicking when he was supposed to block during Form IV, which threw the kid in front of him off balance. Siddharth thought he saw a stranger in a baseball cap snicker and shake his head, which made him even more nervous. He made numerous little mistakes for the remainder of his twenty-minute performance. In the end, he got a medal just for participating, and Ms. Farber gave him a hug and told him she was proud. Mohan Lal said, "Son, the world is yours if you want it." Their words didn't make Siddharth feel any better. He knew his medal was pathetic; it wasn't worthy of being displayed alongside Arjun's honors.

Marc sparred with fury, quickly defeating a string of four opponents to qualify for the semifinals. Siddharth yelled and clapped for him, and he was surprised to see his father cheering too. In the semifinal match, Marc received a foul for an illegal hit. He questioned the referee's call and was issued another warning, which prompted him to kick over an empty chair. After that, the referee ejected him from the tournament. Marc hit himself on the head a few times and then walked over to his mother, who kissed him on the head.

"Honey," she said, "what did we say about managing our tempers?"

"Temper?" said Marc. "Who the hell do you think I get it from, Rachel?"

When the foursome headed out to the parking lot, the sky was dark and the snow was coming down harder. Marc grabbed the scraper from Mohan Lal, chiseling ice from the minivan's windshield like an expert. He told Mohan Lal to leave his wipers up in the winter so they wouldn't freeze to the windshield. Siddharth wished his father knew about such things, but he told himself that they didn't have snowstorms in New Delhi.

As the car heated up, Mohan Lal suggested they eat quickly, before the weather got any worse. He said he had noticed a McDonald's by the Basketball Hall of Fame.

"Mr. A," said Marc, "fast food isn't gonna cut it with Rachel. My mom—she likes to be wined and dined."

"Please, Marc," said Ms. Farber. "And it's *Doctor* Arora."

With full bellies, they were soon back in the van heading toward southern Connecticut. The snowflakes were getting smaller and denser, and ghostlike whirlwinds of white were sweeping across the highway. Traffic slowed to thirty miles an hour as they approached the sleek skyscrapers of Hartford. Marc had his hand on his stomach and was complaining that it hurt, and Ms. Farber told him that nobody had forced him to have two hamburgers.

Marc punched Siddharth in the shoulder.

"Ow!"

"Snow day tomorrow," said Marc. "Bet you five bucks."

"Don't count on it," said Ms. Farber. "Seems to be letting up."

"Get your eyes checked," said Marc. "That's ice that's falling."

"He's right," Mohan Lal chimed in. "The roads—they are quite slick, and they seem to be slickening."

Siddharth winced, then peered out the window. The cars were now crawling, and the weather was getting worse. It didn't matter that the traffic was bad, and that his father refused to talk like a normal person. He could have remained in the warm van all night long. He hoped that Marc was right about the snow day. He hated Deer Run, and he would have paid a thousand dollars to miss a single day of school.

Ms. Farber clicked her tongue.

"What's wrong?" asked Mohan Lal.

She clacked one of her burgundy fingernails against the window. "Is that a mosque?"

Siddharth looked to his right and saw a large brick structure capped with a huge purple dome. It reminded him of the tomb in Delhi that he passed on the way to his aunt's house.

"A mosque?" said Mohan Lal. "That building is American like apple pie." He laughed. "It used to be a gun factory—the factory of Samuel Colt." As they inched southward, Mohan Lal embarked on one of his trademark history lessons. The cowboys in the Wild West wanted to defend themselves against wolves and Red Indians, so New England entrepreneurs got rich manufacturing guns. Their factories needed cheap labor, so they brought in immigrants, people from Poland, Germany, and Italy. "These immigrants weren't like people today. They knew how to save. They saved enough to open all your pizza places and pasta restaurants."

Siddharth wished his father would stop talking, but he noticed that Ms. Farber was smiling.

"Think about it, Marc," said Mohan Lal. "Every time you're chewing your Wooster Street pizza, you're actually ingesting the blood of a Red Indian."

"Dad, you're boring everyone," said Siddharth. "And they're called Native Americans."

"Actually," said Marc, "I like a little blood on my pizza."

Traffic started flowing a little faster, and Ms. Farber sighed.

"Penny for your thoughts, Rachel?" said Mohan Lal.

"I was just thinking about my friend Rebecca, Rebecca Rappaport. She was travelling in Israel, and some . . . some Moslem . . . some Moslem blew up her bus."

Marc scoffed at her. "Mom, you barely even knew her."

"The point is, *Marc*, she died for no reason, and now her

daughter's gonna grow up without a mom. All because of some fundamentalist—some crazy Moslem fundamentalist."

Mohan Lal slammed on the brakes, and everyone jerked forward. Siddharth looked out the windshield and saw a Camry skidding out. It banged into the concrete divider at the center of the road, then got back on the highway as if nothing had happened.

Mohan Lal put on his indicator and changed lanes. "The world is only now waking up to it, but India has had this Muslim problem for centuries."

Siddharth couldn't believe how relaxed his father seemed. Mohan Lal was usually a nightmare in traffic or bad weather.

Ms. Farber tilted her head. "Why is it such a . . . such a violent religion?"

Siddharth had heard his father say similar things many times. When Mohan Lal had complained about the Muslims, Siddharth's mother used to get annoyed. She reminded Mohan Lal that some of his best friends had been Muslims, that Muslims had eaten at her parents' dinner table.

"Listen, Rachel," said Mohan Lal, waggling his finger, "there is only one religion in the world that doesn't perpetuate violence."

"And which one is that?"

"Siddharth, tell her which one."

"Buddhism," grumbled Siddharth.

"Good boy," said Mohan Lal.

"And the Hindus too," said Ms. Farber. "Right? I mean, what about Gandhi? He was a Hindu. Wasn't he?"

Siddharth didn't understand why Ms. Farber always had to bring the conversation back to India. She loved to talk about her Israeli meditation instructor who had lived in Kerala for five years. She said she'd love to spend an entire month in an ashram, just focused on being.

"Gandhi?" said Mohan Lal. "That man was a traitor. A traitor and a charlatan."

Twisting a curl of hair around her finger, Ms. Farber explained that she had been to Morocco once, right before she'd met Marc's father. "The people there were so warm—kind of innocent really.

But the way they treated their women—I just couldn't stomach it."

Mohan Lal said, "Name me a country where the women are well-treated."

"Well, for starters, how about this one?"

"Excuse me," said Mohan Lal, "but have we had a female president? Look at India, Britain—even Pakistan—they have all had female leaders."

Marc snickered. "Damn, Rachel, I think you just got told."

Siddharth laughed, but his mind was in another place now. A crisp, clear memory of his mother had formed in his mind. One evening several years earlier, the Aroras had been eating dinner, and she was telling them about one of her patients who was a Vietnam veteran. This patient was addicted to heroin, and he was missing an arm. Siddharth's mother shook her head and said she hoped that human beings would see the truth about war. "Jesus, don't tell me I've married a Gandhian," Mohan Lal muttered. Siddharth wished his father would forget about Gandhi. Mohan Lal had come to America by choice. Nobody forced him to move here.

Marc had fallen asleep and was leaning against Siddharth's shoulder. The weight of his body felt nice. Siddharth stayed as still as possible, mulling over the day. The tournament hadn't been great, but he still felt calm and contented. In fact, he had a smile on his face. Here he was, in a snowstorm with Marc Kaufman, one of the toughest kids around. He wished someone from school could see Marc sitting so close to him, as if they were best friends. Brothers even. He wished Luca Peroti could see him. If Sharon could see him now, she might forget about everything that had happened. Siddharth suddenly felt a pang about Sharon. He wondered how she was doing—if her father had gotten a job closer to home, if her mother had received that promotion.

Mohan Lal turned on the radio, and a cheery voice announced a five-car pileup farther south on 91. Mohan Lal merged onto the Wilbur Cross Parkway, where the traffic wasn't any better. Siddharth's eyes started to flutter, and soon he was asleep too.

When he awoke, the car wasn't moving at all. After rubbing the sleep from his face, he could make out a hazy line of cars extending all the way to the West Rock Tunnel. The windshield was fogging up, and Mohan Lal pressed a button on the dashboard. A wave of hot air washed through the car.

"I think I've strained my neck," said Mohan Lal.

If Siddharth weren't so sleepy, he would have said something. He would have told his father that he needed to do his stretches, the ones he used to do after he'd thrown out his back cleaning the gutters.

Ms. Farber said, "Tell me where. I'm pretty good with knots."

As they exited the tunnel, she reached her hand toward Mohan Lal. Siddharth scowled, unsure if he was really seeing what he was seeing. Ms. Farber gasped all of a sudden, and her hand went to her chest. She said, "Oh my God." The words came out as a whisper.

"Jesus," said Mohan Lal.

Red and blue lights reflected off of Siddharth's white karate uniform. He craned his neck and made out some road flares. Then a police officer came into view. The cop was wearing a trench coat and a cowboy hat. He was using a baton to direct traffic but looked as if he was trying to swat a fly.

After they passed the cop, Siddharth saw a maimed Buick sedan and an ambulance. Then came the deer with immense, intricate antlers. Its mouth was bloody. Its eyes were still open even though it was clearly dead. Siddharth's mouth dried out; it felt like it was lined with sandpaper. "Jesus Christ," he mumbled.

"Siddharth?" said Ms. Farber. She reached back and squeezed his knee. "Look away, honey. Look somewhere else."

"Why look away?" said Mohan Lal. "The kids should see such things. These are the laws of the jungle."

They passed the dead deer and approached another policeman, who was blocking their exit. Ms. Farber rolled down her window and the cop said, "Ramp's closed, ma'am. Get off at 52 and follow signs for the detour."

Exit 52 was where the Aroras got off when coming from the north. Although it was less than two miles away, it took them forty-five minutes to reach it. Once they got off the parkway, the roads in South Haven were treacherous. The van lurched and bucked as they passed the old Foster Farm. When Mohan Lal braked for a red light, the vehicle slid into the middle of the intersection.

"This is just horrible," said Ms. Farber. "There has to be a better way home."

Mohan Lal said something back, but Siddharth was thinking too hard to really listen.

He had seen people die on television, and he'd seen dead fish and dead mice. But he never saw his own mother's dead body. That deer was the largest dead thing he'd ever seen, and the image of its glassy eyes was now seared into his brain. Had his mother had the same ghostly look after the accident? Whenever he'd imagined her dead, her eyes had always been closed. His mind shifted to his father. Mohan Lal would turn fifty-seven in the spring. That was officially old. Siddharth wouldn't be able go through it again. He wouldn't be able to live in a world without his father.

That night, he had a strange dream.

He was walking to Deer Run to practice baseball with Arjun. It was a beautiful spring day, with leaves on the trees and bright blooming forsythia. When he got to the playground, he found his brother's rawhide glove and wooden bat resting against the school's brick wall. He looked around for his brother, but Arjun was nowhere to be found. Siddharth was relieved for a moment, because baseball was never fun. But upon turning toward the backfield, he grew frightened.

At first it seemed the field was occupied by dogs, but upon closer look, the animals revealed themselves to be wolves. Some of them were lying on the ground and panting. Others were on the baseball diamond, grazing like livestock. A particularly large wolf stopped munching grass and stared in his direction. As Siddharth started striding toward the parking lot, the wolf trotted closer to him, so he broke into a run.

"Wait!" said the wolf.

Siddharth suddenly found himself frozen. The wolf approached him and sniffed his leg. It was totally gray except for a white line that ran from its nose to its green eyes. Some red substance, possibly blood, had stained its whiskers.

"Your brother's gone," said the wolf. It sounded familiar, a little like Mr. Iverson from up the street. "You must come with us. There are no other options but to come with us."

Fortunately, the vigorous creaking of the baseboards forced him to open his eyes.

He floated between sleep and wakefulness for a few moments, indulging one of his favorite fantasies. His dream had been so real and yet ended up being fake, which meant everything else—last night and also the past twenty-one months—could have been fiction too. The sight of a breathing body on his brother's bed seemed to confirm this suspicion. Arjun. Maybe he hadn't even left for college yet. The sleeping body kicked off its covers, exposing New York Giants boxers and pale legs covered in hair. But it wasn't ugly hair. It wasn't the Indian kind. These legs belonged to Marc.

Having indulged such delusions before, Siddharth knew what came next. His stomach would buzz and churn, and the only way to feel better would be to watch a movie or some television.

"Marc," said Siddharth.

Marc groaned, placing a pillow over his head.

Siddharth smiled. Marc Kaufman had slept over at his house. Siddharth propped himself up and noticed that his stomach felt fine. He eyed his friend's boxers, which were so much cooler than his own tight white underwear. Marc's back was a little pudgy, but his shoulders were broad and strong. Strands of stringy hair sprouted from the crevices under his shoulders. Siddharth fingered his own armpit. It was totally smooth, the armpit of a child.

He got out of bed and raised one of his curtains. It was sunny out, but the rhododendron bush was buckling under eight inches of snow. He didn't even need to turn on the radio; school would definitely be cancelled. He felt relieved, like he was filled with helium and could float. He put on his Michigan sweatshirt and headed to Mohan Lal's room, but the door was completely shut. Normally, Siddharth would have barged in. But something inside him told him to knock. He got no response and began to worry.

Turning the knob, he peeked inside and couldn't believe what he saw. It had just turned eight, and Mohan Lal's bed was already made. He gripped the back of his neck. It felt thick and numb— foreign, as if it were somebody else's.

He headed to his father's bathroom, where he half-expected to find him sprawled on the vinyl floor. When Siddharth had traveled to Delhi the summer after his mother's death, Mohan Lal tripped while stepping off the plane onto the runway, briefly losing consciousness. Siddharth had been so scared he vomited on the drive to his uncle's home in Greater Kailash 1.

The bathroom was empty and, strangely, Siddharth felt disappointed. He had prepared himself to find his father strewn across the floor—to make the call to 911. If people could read his mind, they would think he was crazy. He stared out the bathroom window. The backyard was an unblemished blanket of white except for some deer tracks. They began at the woods and stopped below the sagging maple, right underneath the rusting, empty bird feeder. His mother used to fill the feeder at least once a week, even during winter. When the temperature fell below zero, she would put out leftovers for the deer and turkey. One time, Mohan Lal had told her to stop, saying that she was interfering with the laws of Darwin. She told him that he was cruel, that she considered herself a part of the animals' evolution.

Siddharth headed to the hallway, passing his mother's framed oil paintings of boats and fruit bowls. She'd won various ribbons for these at the South Haven County Fair. He passed the framed certificate of appreciation from the nurses at the VA hospital, where she'd worked as an attending anesthesiologist for twelve years. He glanced at the black-and-white photo from his parents' wedding, in which his mother was wearing an ugly sari and his father a silly turban, like a real sand nigger. Siddharth didn't know much about their pasts, but he knew the story of their courtship by heart.

After nine years in Manhattan, Mohan Lal had finally returned to India. He spotted Siddharth's mother at a friend's party and immediately knew she was the one. He spent the next two months convincing her to marry him, buying her flowers and taking her out for secret coffee dates on a motorcycle. Mohan Lal had to provide her father letters of recommendation to prove the strength of his character.

Siddharth shook his head and kept walking. As he reached the heart of the house, he could hear Ms. Farber's voice coming from the kitchen. He paused in the family room, turning his attention to the coffee table, where a half-empty jug of Canei wine towered over the usual bills and legal pads. Next to it was a bowl of pink pistachio shells. Taking a few steps into the room, he couldn't see them yet, but he could hear every word they were saying. She was talking about something called a kibbutz until Mohan Lal interrupted her. "You know," he said, "I once managed a farm—in Kashipur, one of the most beautiful places. Let me tell you, the life of a rancher is a good one." Siddharth had heard his father speak about such things before. When his parents used to fight, Mohan Lal would say he was going to run away to this Kashipur.

Siddharth warmed his feet on the family room's thin burgundy carpeting, peering through the sliding glass doors into the porch. It was messy, filled with rickety cane furniture, discarded tools, and deflated balls. His father was dicing tomatoes at the counter. He had on his bulky wire-framed glasses, and his unshaven face was covered with tiny dots of gray.

Ms. Farber told Mohan Lal he had very unconventional perspectives. "Is that why you left India?" she asked. "A man like you—you couldn't have had an easy time in a place that's so traditional."

Mohan Lal cracked a smile. "You could say that." He came down hard on an onion and proceeded to chop it fast, as if he were a machine. "Yes, such a backward place can be stifling."

"For me it was a little different," said Ms. Farber. "I left home to—"

"But ask me why I chose to live *here*," Mohan Lal interrupted.

"Uh, okay. Why here?"

She sounded annoyed, and Siddharth hoped his father hadn't offended her.

"I stayed because this is a great country. Or should I say, it *was* a great country." Mohan Lal turned toward Ms. Farber, and his face hardened as he glimpsed Siddharth. "Son?"

Siddharth stared down at the holes in his tube socks.

"Morning, son. Come here." Mohan Lal sounded very formal, like a stranger.

He entered the kitchen, and Ms. Farber asked him how he'd slept. Her voice was weird too, a little too sweet for his liking.

"Fine," he said. He stared at the white brooch that was pinned below her collar. It depicted two masks, one smiling and the other frowning.

Ms. Farber got up and filled the kettle at the sink, her free hand hovering behind Mohan Lal's back without actually touching it. "Instant coffee takes me back," she said. "My parents—they used to drink it every single morning." Returning to her seat, she paused in front of Siddharth and smiled. Her teeth seemed particularly yellow today. Tiny wrinkles engulfed her honey-colored eyes. The mole on her cheek didn't look like a mole this morning—it looked like a small mountain. "You were fabulous yesterday," she said.

"Yeah, thanks," Siddharth replied. "Dad, I'm gonna watch TV."

"Aren't you forgetting something?" said Mohan Lal.

"Forgetting something?"

"Sunday morning rules. Pour yourself some milk and take a seat."

"Sunday morning rules?" He had no idea what his father was talking about. But something odd was in the air, so he sat down.

Ms. Farber stared at the photographs and magazine cutouts on the fridge, which had been up there for ages. "So you were saying?"

"Pardon me?" said Mohan Lal.

"This country *used* to be great? If it used to be great, then why stay? It's not like you don't have other options."

Mohan Lal beat some eggs with an electric mixer. He said, "Siddharth, please tell me—what is the definition of wealth?"

"Dad, come on—I haven't even had breakfast yet."

"Just say it," said Mohan Lal.

Siddharth explained that a wealthy country was one that had the ability to manufacture, a phrase his father had uttered thousands of times.

"Very impressive," said Ms. Farber.

"You see, Rachel, when I came to this country in 1959, the Eastern seaboard was the manufacturing capital of the world. They made clocks and tools—such products of high quality, I tell you. Right here in Connecticut, the ball-bearing industry was the greatest in the world."

"So what happened?"

"Greed—greedy politicians and greedy businessmen." Mohan Lal launched into an explanation of how American ball-bearing manufacturers started helping the Japanese set up more cost-effective factories. "Yes, a few barons got rich. But the country—the people? No. They lost a genuine source of wealth."

"But that's capitalism," said Ms. Farber. "Show me a better system and I'll give you a million bucks."

"True, there is no better system than capitalism. But what I have described isn't capitalism. Tell me, where's your free market if the Japanese government is subsidizing production? And what about our own government? It must provide conditions in which business can prosper."

The kettle whistled, and Ms. Farber got up to finish making her coffee. Mohan Lal started sautéing some spices, and Siddharth cringed as the odor of Indian food filled the kitchen.

"That smells wonderful," said Ms. Farber. "I'd love to learn a few dishes."

"Anytime," said Mohan Lal, dumping the onions into his wok. "Siddharth, set the table and put in some English muffins."

Siddharth begrudgingly got four white plates out of the cabinet, and then some forks and knives. Ms. Farber was back at the table, pressing her mug against her cheek and staring out the window.

"Rachel?" said Mohan Lal.

She didn't respond. Siddharth had seen her look this way before. Her mind was in some far-off place now.

"Rachel?" Mohan Lal repeated.

Siddharth glared at him.

She shuddered, then faked a smile. "I'm so sorry. I'm used to a little more sleep, I guess."

Mohan Lal turned down the burner and dumped in the tomatoes. "I hope I haven't offended you."

"Offended me?"

"Dad," said Siddharth, "how many muffins do you want?"

Mohan Lal ignored him. "If you were a jingo, my words may have been offensive."

Ms. Farber laughed, then grasped her mug with her long, bony fingers. "No, not at all. I was just thinking about my father. He had a factory in New Jersey. They made some sort of widget that went into fluorescent lightbulbs. He was always complaining about Japan—Japan, Taiwan, and, of course, the Germans." She paused and shook her head. "To be honest, I always thought it was all a bunch of excuses."

"Dad?" said Siddharth. "Hello? I asked you a question."

"Put in three," said Mohan Lal. "We'll make a fresh one for Marc when he wakes up." He poured in the eggs. "Let me tell you, this country's greatest asset was its entrepreneurs—amazing men who we took for granted."

"Amazing?" said Ms. Farber. "I would have settled for functional." She arched her eyebrows. "My mother, she died a few weeks after my sixteenth birthday. Dad—he wasn't like you. He fell apart, into a million little pieces."

PART II

1

POND HOCKEY AND OTHER TUESDAY-THURSDAY AFFAIRS

In the spring semester, Mohan Lal taught late classes on both Tuesdays and Thursdays, but Ms. Farber picked Siddharth up from school so that he could continue with karate. He loved these afternoons. All the other kids had to remain in their seats until their buses got called over the loudspeaker, but he enjoyed a solitary stroll down the corridor at 3:13, two minutes before dismissal. Marc was often waiting for him outside. He'd be leaning against the pay phone and listening to his Walkman, his lower lip puffy with tobacco, the asphalt around him splotched with tiny pools of brown. The boys would slap hands and walk over to Ms. Farber's ailing Saab, Marc spitting out his pouch before they got there. Siddharth knew people stared at them—the gym teacher, the bus drivers, the principal—but for once he didn't mind the attention. He would look straight ahead, not down at the laces of his imitation Keds, which he had bought because Marc had gotten a pair of real ones. He was still a faggot according to Luca Peroti, still the ex-friend of slutty Sharon Nagorski. But that didn't matter anymore. It didn't matter that he spent recess alone and ate lunch with Bobby Meyers.

It was a cold month, with carrot-shaped icicles dangling from the roofs and drainpipes. The boys spent a lot of time indoors. Marc's father bought him a new video game every weekend, and Marc wouldn't relinquish the controller until he'd conquered it, which usually took forty-eight hours. Siddharth preferred it when they watched movies. Marc continued introducing him to the world of pornography, and he in turn introduced Marc to the joy of seeing a single film multiple times. They watched these films in Ms. Farber's basement, where they'd been spending much more time because the guest room had been turned into her home office.

Marc said that building an office was easy when someone else was footing the bill.

"What do you mean?" asked Siddharth.

"Who do you think paid for this shit? Shelly did. My dad's busting his ass so Rachel can play doctor."

"Fucking ridiculous," said Siddharth. But he didn't actually think it was ridiculous. He'd met Marc's father two times, and the man was grumpy. Too quiet. Marc sometimes said that he wished he could go live with his father full-time, but Siddharth didn't think that would be a wise idea.

It took Ms. Farber more than a month to complete her home office, and she'd hired a team of three carpenters for the job. First they wrapped up the renovations that had ceased during her divorce, and then they put in a door that led directly from the guest room to the outside world. This door was essential, she claimed, for it would make her clients feel that they were in a real office. It would allow her to maintain healthy boundaries between work and home. Siddharth had watched the builders as they sawed and hammered, and he even helped a worker named Sean sand down some new oak shelving.

Three weeks after the Springfield karate tournament, he and his father went on another outing with Marc and Ms. Farber, this time to get her a new desk. They honed in on a hefty modern one that was on sale at the Post Road furniture warehouse where Siddharth's parents had done a lot of shopping. But then Ms. Farber fell in love with something called a "secretary's desk" at an antique shop in Westville, which cost twelve hundred dollars. Mohan Lal said that spending so much on a secondhand piece of furniture didn't make sense considering the financial strain of starting a new business. But Ms. Farber was adamant. She explained that the antique desk reminded her of one that had belonged to her mother.

Her father had left it out on the street when they moved out of their Victorian home and into their horrible apartment.

Marc bargained the antique dealer down to nine fifty, and Siddharth tried to help him load it into the back of his father's minivan. He wasn't strong enough, so Mohan Lal stepped in. Siddharth was proud to see his father heaving and lifting. Mohan Lal looked like a real man, not some crazed sand nigger from *Indiana Jones*. But the way he panted afterward embarrassed Siddharth. It also scared him.

Ms. Farber started complaining that the boys were spending too much time in front of the television. She gave Siddharth a pair of Marc's old ice skates and began ferrying them to Foster Pond, which was on the border of Woodford and South Haven. Siddharth had never skated before, so Marc had to teach him.

During their first day on the ice, Marc skated backward and pulled him from one end of the pond to the other with a hockey stick. They did this for twenty minutes, then lit a fire in the woods and shared a cigar. On their second day, Siddharth managed to skate into his turns, crossing one foot over the other. Marc told him he was bending his ankles, and that ankle-benders were girls. By their third day, Siddharth had learned how to skate backward, and Marc clapped for him. "Atta girl," he said, sticking his fingers into his mouth and whistling.

"Screw you," said Siddharth, but he was smiling; he knew that Marc wasn't serious.

Marc was still grounded for what he had done to the mailbox, and he would remain grounded until the summer, so the boys' Foster Pond trips were often an excuse for him to get around the rules of his punishment and meet up with a Woodford eighth grader named Dinetta Luciani. Dinetta always showed up with her best friend, Liza Kim. The girls wore miniskirts and stockings, even with howling winds and temperatures in the teens. Dinetta's grandfather owned Luciani Carting, but her father owned a liquor store, and she usually brought a few tiny bottles of vodka or rum. Siddharth only pretended to sip from them. If his father caught him with booze on his breath, his days with Marc would be numbered.

The four kids avoided the main pond, instead heading into the frozen labyrinth of swamps and trees behind it. This area mesmerized Siddharth. It seemed like a portal to a secret world, like the setting of one of his fantasy books. But he knew better than to share such observations out loud. Marc and Dinetta usually seated themselves on a fallen tree trunk and French-kissed the whole time, so Siddharth ended up spending a lot of time with Liza. She told him that junior high was awesome, that even though Marc was only a seventh grader, he was one of the cutest kids in their whole school. She asked Siddharth if he had a girlfriend.

"Used to," he said. "But we, like, broke up."

"You're lying," said Liza. "I can tell when people are lying."

"Why would I lie? I even got to first base with her—second, over the shirt."

"So what was her name then?"

"Sharon," he said. "Sharon Nagorski."

Marc later told Siddharth that Liza thought he was cute, but Siddharth said he wasn't into Orientals.

"Pussy's pussy," said Marc. "I'd go for it if I were you."

"We'll see," said Siddharth. He was thrilled that a girl actually liked him, but also petrified. He didn't know how to kiss. And he would die if she saw his penis, which was probably the smallest dick in the world.

On weekends, fifteen or twenty kids showed up to Foster Pond for pickup hockey games. Everybody had to plunk their sticks in the middle of the ice. One boy would chuck the sticks into two separate piles, and the spot where your stick landed determined which team you were on. Siddharth was the smallest and most inexperienced player, and since nobody thought he was worth defending, he was usually left wide open. If his teammates were in a jam, they'd see him standing all alone and send the puck sailing in his direction. The sight of the approaching puck would make Siddharth want to gag. As soon as it would reach him, he'd smack it as hard as he could at nothing in a particular with his brand-new hockey stick, which was a gift from Marc and his father. Once in a rare while, one of these wild shots actually scored a goal, but most of the time they just went out of bounds, eliciting grumbles and ridicule from the other players. One of these slap shots accidentally pelted a tenth grade football player named Dennis Bolzano, and Dennis told Siddharth to watch it.

That same afternoon, another one of Siddharth's frantic shots hit Dennis in the groin, and Dennis started cursing. He flew over to Siddharth, hooking his stick into the blade of his skate and yanking him onto the ice. Siddharth fell hard on his shoulder, but he didn't care about the pain. He just hoped that nobody had seen what had happened. Marc, who was playing goalie, skated over and helped him up. Marc then jetted over to Dennis and shoved him hard from behind.

Dennis stumbled but didn't fall, and when he turned around, he looked pissed. He was wearing hockey gloves, which he cast onto the ice the way the pros did on television.

"Hit me," said Marc, raising his stick in the air. "Hit me, and I'll crack your fucking skull."

Siddharth was drenched in sweat despite the numbing cold. He wanted Marc to do it.

"Fucking midgets," said Dennis, grabbing his gloves and skating away.

Siddharth laughed. He felt safe with Marc, like nothing bad could happen when he was around. He hated to admit it, but he would choose hockey with Marc over baseball with Arjun any day of the week.

After his evening classes, Mohan Lal made it to Ms. Farber's by eight thirty. She microwaved him a plate of food, and as he ate, Siddharth and Marc would devour bowls of frozen yogurt alongside him. Ms. Farber usually steered the conversation toward her favorite topics, like "self-actualization" or "everyday enlightenment," or the adults discussed books they had exchanged. Ms. Farber had given Mohan Lal a paperback by Ram Das, who Siddharth discovered was actually American. Mohan Lal had lent her something called *The Autobiography of a Yogi*, a book that particularly bothered Siddharth, for the holy man on its cover was too feminine and foreign-looking.

Siddharth liked it best when Ms. Farber swore them to secrecy and provided updates on her clients' progress, making sure not to use their actual names. By the end of February, three clients were attending regular sessions at her clinical psychology practice. All of them had been referred to her by the rabbi at her new synagogue. There was the Polish woman who had lost most of her family in the Holocaust. She'd immigrated to America when she was six and later went to a Methodist university, but she dropped out to marry one of her professors. Her husband turned out to be an abusive alcoholic, and they eventually got divorced. Now she was dating a Jewish lawyer with a heroin problem.

"The truth is," said Mohan Lal one night, "most people lack the capacity for introspection. For most people, genuine change is an impossibility."

"Hell yeah," said Marc. "Once a loser, always a loser."

"That's awful," said Ms. Farber. "I actually don't think there's a grain of truth to what you're saying. I mean, if she can get to the bottom of that trauma—if she can articulate it—then she can definitely stop being so . . . so . . ."

"So retarded?" said Marc.

"So self-destructive," said Ms. Farber.

"Well, I think people can change," said Siddharth. "Look at Arjun."

"How interesting, honey," said Ms. Farber. "And just how did your brother change?"

"Just look at the way he dresses. First it was heavy metal T-shirts, and then everything had to be preppie. Now all his clothes are torn up. He'll only wear a shirt if it's made of—"

"Let me tell you about the problem with the West," Mohan Lal cut in. "The Western mind always wants to blame everything on the past—the past and the parents."

Siddharth shot his father a look, partially because Mohan Lal had interrupted him, but mainly because he didn't want him to go off on some ridiculous tangent. If Mohan Lal got political, everything could go to shit.

Ms. Farber placed her hands over her ears. "I don't want to hear it."

Siddharth closed his eyes and swallowed.

Mohan Lal began to speak again, but Ms. Farber started shaking her head back and forth, her hands still cupping her ears. "I'm not listening . . . I'm not listening." She kept shaking her head, but soon let out a muffled laugh.

Mohan Lal started chuckling, which made her laugh even louder. Siddharth felt relieved and started laughing too.

Marc said, "What freaking cornballs." But Siddharth was pleased to see that he was also smiling.

Marc was sleeping over at his father's on a Thursday in early March, so Siddharth had to spend a few hours alone with Ms. Farber. He tried to concentrate on the television, but she insisted on making small talk. She asked him if things were getting any better with Mr. Latella. He lied and said everything was going great at school. She then told him about her charity work at the Jewish Community Center. She was running a clothing drive for struggling settlers in a place called the West Bank. All this talk bored Siddharth, and he was relieved when his father showed up early.

But Mohan Lal had dark pouches under his eyes. His tie was already off, and the two top buttons of his shirt were open, exposing the top of his worn, ribbed banyan. Siddharth asked him what was wrong, then fastened one of his father's buttons.

"Get your things," said Mohan Lal. "We have troubled Rachel enough for today."

"No way," said Ms. Farber. "First, you're gonna have some dinner."

She was about to place three slices of white clam pizza in the microwave, but Siddharth grabbed the plate and put the pizza in the toaster oven. His father hated microwaved pizza.

Ms. Farber asked if Mohan Lal wanted a glass of wine, and he said he wouldn't mind a Scotch.

"Bourbon?" said Ms. Farber. "That's what you-know-who used to drink."

"Fine, a bourbon with ice and water."

Mohan Lal devoured an entire slice in just two bites. He took a large gulp of bourbon and immediately started in on his second slice, but then started coughing until his cheeks turned red.

"Dad!" said Siddharth. He wished his father wouldn't eat like an animal in front of Marc's mom.

Ms. Farber placed her hand on Mohan Lal's back and gave it a rub. Once his breathing went back to normal, she said, "Okay, time to spill it, mister."

"Beg your pardon?" said Mohan Lal.

"You're not going anywhere until you tell us what's up."

Mohan Lal cleared his throat. "It's nothing. I just had a very unsatisfying meeting."

"What?" Siddharth sat down next to his father. "But you said there was nothing to worry about."

"Well, I was wrong. The dean said the university would be making a decision about my position next year. I told him, *Fine, no problem, all my paperwork's in order.*" Mohan Lal paused to crunch an ice cube. "The bastard, he tells me my paperwork isn't the problem—it's my track record."

"What does that even mean?" asked Ms. Farber.

"Your students love you," said Siddharth.

Mohan Lal sighed. "He was referring to my publications."

"He's a fool," said Siddharth. "You did, like, two articles last year."

"And I edited that idiotic journal," said Mohan Lal. "But that's not enough these days. Nobody gives a damn about education. The dean said he wants a world-class program, and in a world-class program, everyone must have a book."

"Loser," said Siddharth. He watched Ms. Farber pour Mohan Lal more bourbon, fighting the urge to tell her to stop. *She's a psychologist*, he reasoned. *She knows what she's doing.*

Ms. Farber said, "Mohan, I fail to see the problem. You're working on a book. I mean, you even have a contract."

A memory flashed in Siddharth's mind of the day Mohan Lal had actually signed his contract with Walton Publishers. They had gone out to an Italian restaurant in West Haven, one next to a costume store that no longer existed. Arjun raised his glass and said, "To new beginnings." Mohan Lal had replied, "Son, you don't get new beginnings at my age. Only endings." Recalling that evening, Siddharth felt grateful for all the new things he had—karate and Marc. Even Ms. Farber.

Mohan Lal began shaking his head. He explained that Walton wanted a complete draft by September. Between teaching and everything else, there wouldn't be enough time to turn in anything worthwhile.

Ms. Farber dabbed his chin with a paper towel. "That's plenty of time," she said. "Especially if you have some help."

"Rachel, what can you do? Teach my classes?"

She placed both of her hands on his wrist. "Of course not. But I can do other things. I can help with Siddharth."

Siddharth cleared his throat. "Thanks, but I'm pretty sure I can take care of myself."

The adults didn't respond. They had goofy smiles on their faces and were having some sort of staring contest.

Siddharth cleared his throat more loudly. "Let's go, Dad. It's time to go home."

Mohan Lal stood up and brushed the crumbs from his blazer.

2

CONSPICUOUS CONSUMPTION

On a foggy Saturday morning, Siddharth was sitting on the shabby white armchair in front of the television, eating cereal alone off the three-legged Indian end table. When his father woke up, Siddharth asked him if they could watch something together, or go somewhere—just the two of them. Mohan Lal told him he had to work. He grabbed a paperback from the bookshelf behind the portable television stand and headed to the kitchen. Siddharth got up and followed him. "But I thought you needed a break," he said. "I thought you couldn't write another word."

"This is other work," said Mohan Lal.

Siddharth snatched the book out of his father's hands. It was called *Taj Mahal: The True Tale of a Ruined Temple*, and published by some company called Satya. He shook his head. His father used to go on about the Taj Mahal all the time. He called it an "emblem of decadence," an "ostentatious graveyard." Siddharth flipped through the pages of the slim paperback. "Looks fun . . . Are you kidding me?"

Mohan Lal handed him a glass of apple juice. "Son, I am reading about the destruction of our heritage."

Siddharth took a sip. "Who destroyed it?"

"The Mohammedans first, and then the Britishers. But Hindus only have themselves to blame."

"This cover," said Siddharth, thumping the book against his chest. "A five-year-old could have done it. Looks like they printed this crap on a photocopier."

"Have more respect for knowledge, son." Mohan Lal put an English muffin in the toaster. "This book was a gift from your Barry Uncle."

"What?" Siddharth's smile disappeared. "You saw Barry Uncle? Why didn't you tell me you saw him?"

Mohan Lal opened his mouth to speak, but the phone rang and he lunged for it.

Siddharth could tell it was Ms. Farber by the way his father's voice got all sweet and formal. During their three-minute conversation, Mohan Lal kept on saying, "Simply wonderful, Rachel," and, "Congratulations, I'm so impressed." When he put down the phone, he told Siddharth to get ready. They were going out to a celebratory lunch because Ms. Farber had just signed up her seventh patient.

"Wait, what about Barry Uncle?" asked Siddharth.

"Mind your own business, son. And hurry up!"

Ms. Farber picked them up at 11:43. Nobody said much as they drove, and Siddharth sat in the backseat of the Saab stewing. He knew that his father's seeing Barry Uncle was a good thing. It was further proof that things were going back to normal. But Mohan Lal should have consulted him first. He should have asked for his advice.

When they got to the mall, the lot was crammed with cars. Ms. Farber parked near the rear exit, beside a lingering bank of blackened snow. They first went to Filene's, where she bought Marc a pair of baggy Guess jeans and then picked out a striped designer button-down for Siddharth. He had never heard of the brand, which was displayed on the shirt's abdomen. Marc said it was cool, so he tried it on.

"Very handsome," said Ms. Faber. "Your eyes—they have little flecks of green in them."

Siddharth couldn't stifle his smile.

"Handsome or not," said Mohan Lal, "take it off."

"Mohan, I'd like to buy it for him," said Ms. Farber.

"Don't waste your money, Rachel. These things will be too small by summer."

"It's my money." She was smiling, but her voice was firm. "If I feel like being generous, then that's what I'm gonna do."

She paid for their things, and the group left the store. Siddharth felt contented as he clutched his shopping bag and stared at the throngs of weekend shoppers. A hunched-over, wrinkled white man stood behind his walker and picked out a watch strap. Two black couples giggled as they struggled to fit inside a single photo booth. Bands of familiar-looking teenagers squabbled and flirted.

Normally, if Siddharth had been there alone with his father, these kids would have made him nervous. But today he was able to gawk at them with confidence. He fell behind his companions, and when he looked up, they were fifteen or twenty feet ahead. Ms. Farber was standing between his friend and his father. She was gripping Marc's wrist, and her other hand was clasping Mohan Lal's elbow. They looked right together, almost natural. With these people by his side, Mohan Lal could have been a Jew, or even an Italian.

They went from the mall to Pasta Palace, Mohan Lal's favorite South Haven restaurant. The Aroras had been dining there for years. The portions they served were huge, and each meal came with a free salad. The restaurant was packed today, but Mustafa, the place's Pakistani manager, still took the time to personally greet them. He clapped Mohan Lal on the back, then patted Siddharth on the head. He said, "Look at him. This one's gonna be shaving soon." Siddharth's face got hot, and he peered down. But he didn't mind Mustafa. Even though the man was Pakistani—even though he referred to Mohan Lal as *Chacha-ji*—Siddharth thought he was funny. Mustafa spoke English with a perfect guido accent, like the Mafia goons from the movies. He said things like, "The spinach raviolis? Fugget about it—best raviolis this side a da Bronx."

For lunch, Marc and Siddharth ordered meatball subs. Mohan Lal got veal parmigiana, and Ms. Farber asked for a Caesar salad with the dressing on the side. When both adults ordered wine, Marc said, "Rachel, boozing in the daytime? What are the lawyers gonna say about that one?"

Ms. Farber smiled, but her nostrils were flaring. She said, "Marc, put your napkin on your lap. And watch it, or no Coke."

Marc craned his neck toward the bar to catch a basketball game. Siddharth couldn't care less about sports again, now that Michigan's Fab Five had lost in the finals. He half-listened to Ms. Farber blabbing about the art therapy class she was taking a local community college. Her professor was also a hypnotherapist, and he performed something called past-life regressive hypnosis. She wondered if Mohan Lal might be interested in a consultation.

"I'm interested, yes," said Mohan Lal. "But I wouldn't trust some amateur—some Western quack."

"Oh, Mohan, you're all bark," Ms. Farber responded. "I know you don't really think like that."

Marc buttered a roll and bit into it. "What's regressive hypnocrap?"

"Don't be crude, Marc," said Ms. Farber. "And don't talk with your mouth full." She paused to sip some wine. "Honey, I'm sorry. Do you really wanna know?"

"Totally," said Marc. "I'm always interested in your thoughts and ideas, Rachel."

Ms. Farber sat up straight and explained how according to the Hindus, a person's soul lived multiple lives in multiple bodies. "What a person experiences in his past lives affects him in his present one. But the thing is, we don't have any conscious memories of these past lives, and that's where hypnosis comes in. With regressive hypnosis, a person can reconnect with the people they were in previous lifetimes. And once you unlock all those experiences, they say you feel a deep sense of freedom. Your soul is finally unburdened from centuries' worth of guilt—from centuries' worth of suffering."

"Well put, Rachel," said Mohan Lal.

She raised her glass, then gulped more wine.

"Wait, Dad," said Siddharth. "I know you don't really believe this stuff." He liked Ms. Farber, but why did she have to encourage all this Hindu bullshit?

"What's so strange, son? Half the world thinks there's a red man with little horns at the center of the earth." As Mohan Lal was speaking, Mustafa came with their appetizers. "Even Mustafa here believes in reincarnation. Don't you, chief?"

Siddharth stared at the manager. He was wearing a white collared shirt with too many buttons open, so that you could see his black chest hairs and gold chain. Mustafa may have been Pakistani, but he looked just like an Indian. The most Indian thing about him was his ugly mustache. It was so thick, as if black rope was spilling from his nostrils.

Mustafa smiled, and his mustache turned into an ugly upside-down V. "Reincarnation? When I was growing up in Pakistan, we believed in it all." He said *Pakistan* the way Americans do, so that it rhymed with *can*—not the way Mohan Lal pronounced the word. "We believed in everything, and we celebrated everything— Christmas, Holi, Eid. Anyway, buon appetito, folks." He then nodded at them and walked over to another table.

Mohan Lal said, "Boys, wouldn't you like to know who you were in a past life? Marc, wouldn't you like to know if you were an officer in Napoleon's army? What if you were Roman senators, or Julius Caesar himself?"

Siddharth sucked down some Sprite. "I'd only wanna know if I was, like, Cornelius Vanderbilt or J.D. Rockefeller or something."

"I'd be Michael Jordan," said Marc. "Or maybe Donald Trump."

"Dude, they're not dead," said Siddharth.

Marc smirked.

"What now?" asked Ms. Farber.

"Nothing," said Marc. "But last time around, I musta been some sort of serial killer or something."

Siddharth laughed, but tensed upon noticing his father staring out the window.

Mohan Lal was grinning to himself. "Siddharth," he said after a moment, "tell me—what happens to a caterpillar as it grows?"

"What? Dad, I have no idea what you're saying."

"A caterpillar," said Mohan Lal. "How does it grow?"

Marc grabbed a second roll. "It becomes a butterfly. What's going on with the food? It's like they're flying in the subs from Italy or something."

Mohan Lal's eyes were gleaming. "Kids, answer me this: Do you think a butterfly can remember his life as a caterpillar? Does it have any recollection of what things were like before it could fly?"

Siddharth began to answer the question, but Ms. Farber cut him off: "Oh, I see what you're saying. That's quite an analogy."

Marc said, "I have no freaking clue what any of you are talking about."

"Honey, think of the caterpillar as our soul," said Ms. Farber. "Its metamorphosis is like our rebirth into a new body."

Siddharth glanced up at the ceiling. He had never noticed how high it was, but today it seemed a hundred feet tall. The ceiling was lined with wooden beams and heavy, tubular piping. He wondered what would happen if one of these ventilation pipes were to fall. Would it kill somebody? Or just wound them?

Mohan Lal took a sip of wine. "Yes, we could be like the caterpillar," he said. "Death could just be our cocoon." He let out a sigh of satisfaction. "The ancient Hindus, they understood some truths. They knew about maths—even love."

Marc crunched on an ice cube. "If they were so smart, then why are they all so poor now?"

"Jesus, Marc!" snapped Ms. Farber.

"What? Haven't you seen those commercials? The kids all got those big bellies. They got all those flies buzzing around their heads."

Siddharth forced himself to cackle.

"He's right, Rachel," said Mohan Lal. "What can I tell you, son? If you aren't a forward thinker, then it's easy for others to destroy you."

When the food finally arrived, Mohan Lal proposed a toast. He called Ms. Farber a wise entrepreneur. He said they felt grateful to her, and were lucky to call her a friend. It dawned on Siddharth that his father had never proposed a toast to him. He tried to remember if the man had ever toasted his mother.

He lay in bed that night wondering if he and Marc had been friends in a previous lifetime. Then he fell asleep and had another strange dream. In this dream, he got home from school and the house was completely empty. Everything felt eerie and looked the way it did when he was much younger. The family room had no skylight, the fake wooden paneling still lined the hallway that led to the bedrooms, and the old National Parks wallpaper covered the wall behind the leather sofas. Staring out the kitchen window, he found that the backyard was occupied by big machines—yellow backhoes and bulldozers and a couple of smaller orange ones. There were nine of them in total, just sitting there like giant, lazy animals. He felt relieved upon spotting Mohan Lal, who was standing beside a dozer, his hand resting on one of its enormous fanged tires. Mr. Iverson from up the street was standing next to Mohan Lal. He still had a ponytail and a thick beard. He was wearing a Red Sox cap. Siddharth jogged toward the men, and Mr. Iverson picked him up, raising him into the air so that he could peer inside the machine. A baby was lying on the driver's seat sucking on a bottle. It was a girl, and she had brown skin and a big crown of curls. Siddharth felt as if he knew this child, and a jolt of electricity pulsed through his bones.

And then he woke up.

He stared at the ceiling, his father's muffled snores echoing through the wall. His waist felt moist, so he ran a hand under his sheets. They were wet, as was his underwear. He felt hopeful. He might have just had a wet dream. He touched the wet patches again, then smelled his fingers. They were sour. Realizing what had actually happened, he went to the bathroom and stepped into the shower. As he soaped himself, the image of the curly haired baby lingered in his mind. It was her. He closed his eyes, allowing the hot water to pour over his face. He had previously told himself that dead meant the opposite of infinity. Like infinity, it was something human beings couldn't truly understand, so there was no point in thinking too hard about it. But if all that caterpillar bullshit were real, then she might be alive.

She could be in a zillion possible towns or countries, and if they ever passed each other on the street, they wouldn't even recognize one another. But it didn't seem to matter. She would have a new family who loved her, and he wouldn't have to feel bad each time he offered up his forehead to Ms. Farber. He could stop feeling tense whenever Ms. Farber grasped Mohan Lal's hand, for his mother would one day love another person too.

Siddharth dried himself in his bedroom, then stuffed his soiled sheets into his closet. Sunlight streaked his worn, stained mattress. He heard a dull rumble overhead, squirrels scuttling across the roof. Some blue jays were squawking. His mother hadn't liked these birds. They had ugly calls, and they bullied the other birds that frequented her feeder. He wasn't thinking straight and needed to talk to somebody. He didn't want Marc to think he was a freak, and he didn't want to worry his father. Besides, Mohan Lal was clearly confused. One minute he was an atheist, and then he was a Buddhist. Now he wouldn't shut up about the ancient Hindus. Siddharth picked up the family room phone and punched in Arjun's eleven-digit number.

His brother answered after five rings, and his voice was tired and scratchy. Siddharth suspected he had a hangover. He started rehashing what had happened with Michigan in the NCAA finals, saying how Weber had really blown it.

"Are you serious?" said Arjun. "This is why you're calling me at eight in the morning? Siddharth, we've been over it, like, five times already."

"Jesus, shoot me for caring."

"Siddharth, what's going on?"

"Nothing's going on. Can't I just call my big brother?"

"You better tell me," said Arjun. "Now."

"Well, it's kind of a weird question."

"Just talk. You can tell me anything."

Siddharth took a deep breath. "Like, reincarnation and all that stuff—do you believe in it?"

Arjun sighed. "You know, I wish Dad wouldn't burden you with all of his fundamentalist crap."

"It wasn't Dad, I swear."

"Look, you're still young, but you're mature—so I'll be honest. I used to believe a lot of things, but the more I read, I just can't anymore. Religion, it's just meant to control people—to make them feel better. But it's all a total fiction."

"Dad used to say the same thing."

"*Used to* being the operative words here. If you ask me—and you are asking me—reincarnation was something cooked up by people in power. They just wanted to justify their lives. They wanted to suppress the people who were below them in the caste system."

"What's the caste system?"

"Siddharth, you should know that. Look it up."

He swallowed hard. "Arjun?"

"What?"

"There's something I need to tell you."

"Say it, then."

He paused, unsure of why he hadn't said anything before— unsure of why he was saying something now. "I think Dad has a girlfriend, Arjun."

"What did you say?"

"You heard me. Dad—he has a girlfriend."

"A what?"

Siddharth told him about the karate tournament. He told him about the books they exchanged and the business plan—all the dinners, goodbye kisses, and hand-holding. As he spoke, he knew he was betraying Mohan Lal. He might have even been betraying Marc. But he couldn't hold back. He couldn't hold back even though he might be ruining things for himself.

Upon completing his narration, he was breathless. "You still there?" he asked.

"I'm here." Arjun's voice sounded higher. "I just don't understand why this is the first time I'm hearing about this." Nobody spoke for a while, but eventually Arjun broke the silence. "It's just selfish. Dad is so fucking selfish."

Siddharth bit the inside of his cheek, removing a sizable chunk of skin. He knew that he'd messed up. Why was he always messing up?

3

HAPPY BIRTHDAY, BOBBY

During his twenty-month career at Deer Run, Siddharth had been invited to a total of seven birthday parties. He had only attended one of them, Sharon Nagorski's, back when they were still friends. The other invitations had either come from popular kids whose parents made them invite everybody, or those who were desperate for friends. As soon as any invitations arrived, he normally threw them in the compactor. Unfortunately, Ms. Farber was over the day the invitation from Bobby Meyers arrived. As he was eyeing the envelope, which had been penned in fine calligraphy, she said, "Ooh, what's that, honey? Why don't you open it up?"

He tore it open, noting that the card inside looked like a poster Arjun had once owned, back before he'd put up the ones of Bob Dylan and the Beatles. It depicted a bikini-clad blonde atop a Ferrari, and she was coaxing invitees with a curled finger.

Ms. Farber snatched it out of his hands. "Bobby Meyers . . . Marc, isn't that Jocelyn Meyers's boy?"

"Who?" said Marc.

"She's an architect, I think. Her husband is definitely a podiatrist. This is good, if you ask me."

"Good?" said Marc. "Dealing with other people's nasty-ass foot fungus is good?"

Siddharth let out a laugh and slapped him five.

Later that week, Ms. Farber called Bobby's mother, RSVPing for him and soliciting an invitation for Marc. She said she was letting Marc go despite his grounding since he'd been so positive lately. "If you keep it up, Marc," she said, "you might just drive before the age of twenty-five."

The party was at Amity Rec, an arcade on the Woodford–New Haven border. Mohan Lal and Ms. Farber drove the boys there the following Saturday. As the adults listened to a report about the Democratic presidential primaries, Siddharth grew nervous. He dreaded the idea of Marc seeing him among his classmates. If Luca were to say something, Marc might find out the truth about him. He might stop talking to him, and then Siddharth would go back to being alone. He'd been especially anxious about their friendship over the past couple of weeks. Marc had quit karate because he couldn't juggle it with baseball. Without karate to link them, Siddharth worried that that their connection might start to dissolve.

Fortunately, they were still seeing a lot of each other, and they spoke on the phone as well. In fact, not much had changed at all. Siddharth had decided to take a break from karate too, but Ms. Farber was still picking him up from school, even when Marc had practice. Sometimes she brought him back to her house. Other times, she brought him straight to his own home, and together they waited for Mohan Lal to return from work. When Mohan Lal finally arrived, he cooked them delicious dinners—Indian food, but also his lasagnas and eggplant parmigiana.

Before reaching the arcade, they stopped at a record store to buy Bobby a birthday present. Mohan Lal insisted they get him a cassette and not a CD. He said, "I'm fifty-eight years old, and I've yet to indulge in such extravagances." Marc picked out a tape by NWA, but Ms. Farber said she didn't like the looks of it. "Those men on the front," she said, "they look like criminals."

Marc said, "Mom, I thought you used to be an artist."

"I *am* an artist. But something tells me this doesn't qualify as art."

They ended up opting for Siddharth's choice, an album by EMF, and then Ms. Farber used some newspaper and Marc's new Swiss Army knife to wrap it. Her wrapping job failed to impress Siddharth, whose mother had been an expert at such chores. By the time they pulled into the parking lot, the party had already started. Mohan Lal handed Siddharth a quarter and told him to call them at Ms. Farber's twenty minutes before they were ready to come home.

"Marc, I'm trusting you," said Ms. Farber. "Siddharth, make sure he stays out of trouble."

"Mom, I'm trusting *you*," replied Marc.

The boys strode past gaggles of smoking adolescents, Puerto Ricans with flattops and gang beads, and ponytailed white kids with jean jackets and pimples. They went straight to the food court and found the tables with the balloons. None of the other guests were around, but Bobby Meyers was there in a blue blazer and jeans. He was carrying a clipboard and had a leather fanny pack around his waist. "Welcome," he said, jotting something down before holding out his hand. "Thanks for coming."

"Thanks," said Siddharth. "This is Marc. Your mom said he could come."

"Oh, I know this guy." Bobby grinned, revealing a dimple. "We go way back."

Marc shook his hand and clapped him on the back. "What up? Happy birthday, Bobby."

"Everyone's having a great time." Bobby pulled out two rolls of tokens from his fanny pack. "These are for you—spend 'em any way you want." He winked, then handed them over. "Oh, and please keep an eye on the clock. Pizza will be served in precisely forty-three minutes."

"Thanks," said Siddharth.

"Wait," said Marc, "should we synchronize our watches?"

Bobby's face became stony for a second, but then he broke into a smile. "Guy, you're hysterical. That's funny stuff."

After a few games of pinball, Marc led Siddharth toward a video game that simulated the experience of piloting a real military helicopter. Marc inserted five tokens into it, and the game rattled and shook as he gunned down enemy aircraft. He played so well that a group of ponytailers started hovering around. When he finally lost, the ponytailers clapped, and a screen prompted him to enter his initials into a top-scorers chart.

Siddharth patted him on the shoulder. "You should be a pilot someday."

"My cousin Brian," said Marc, "he's in the Israeli air force—only twenty-two, and the kid flies an F-15."

As they headed back to the food court, Siddharth felt someone flick him in the ear. He turned around and saw Luca Peroti. *Shit*, he thought. Siddharth had just seen him a day earlier, but Luca looked different. He'd pierced his left ear, and his hair had changed too. It was shaved on the sides and floppy on top, just like Marc's.

"What up?" said Luca. "No hug, kid?"

"Hey, Luca." Siddharth wanted to flee.

"Sid, who's your friend here?" said Marc.

"Yo, Marc," said Luca, "it's Luca. Luca P.? From basketball? Holy Infant basketball?"

"Rings a bell," said Marc.

Luca smiled, revealing his multicolored braces. "You're a jokester, kid. We were in the same league for a whole freaking season."

Squinting, Marc tilted his head to one side. "Wait, you were, like, fatter back then. Right?"

Luca's face turned red, and he glanced down at his black Adidas. "Yo, Marc, why you hanging out with this tool?"

Siddharth swallowed. He wished Ms. Farber hadn't made them come.

"You mean Sidney?" Marc placed a hand on Siddharth's shoulder. "Are you calling him a tool? Because he's, like, one of my best friends. So if you're calling him a tool, you're kind of calling me a tool too."

"Yo, I was just kidding," said Luca.

"You sure?" said Marc, puffing out his chest.

"Siddharth and I go way back," said Luca. "We've been friends for, like, years."

Marc smiled. "You know, Siddharth here just ran out of tokens. You got any left? I'm sure he'd appreciate a few."

Luca stuffed his hands into the pockets of his acid-washed jeans. He pulled out some candy wrappers and two rust-colored tokens, which he offered to Siddharth.

"Thanks," he said, suppressing a smile.

"That was extremely kind," said Marc. "You know, it's important to be respectful to this kid. He's, like, royalty."

"What?" said Luca.

Siddharth furrowed his brow. He had no idea where Marc was going with this.

A PA announcement interrupted them, requesting all members of the Meyers birthday party to proceed to the food court.

"His great-great-grandfather?" said Marc. "He was, like, an Indian prince—with a castle and elephants and shit. He even had people to wipe his ass for him."

Siddharth figured it out: Marc was referring to something Mohan Lal had said to Ms. Farber ages ago, way back in the fall.

Marc's eyes were gleaming. "I guess that means you should probably bow down—or kiss his hand or something."

Luca let out a nervous laugh.

"Go on," said Marc.

Luca flicked his hair out of his eyes. "Are you for real, man?"

Marc let out a cackle, then punched Luca in the shoulder. "Nah, I'm just fucking with you."

The three boys headed to the food court, which had purple carpeting and wallpaper with multicolored lasers. As Siddharth ate his soggy pizza and french fries, he felt uneasy. On one hand, he was sitting between Marc Kaufman and Luca Peroti, and so many of his classmates were there to witness this triumph. Then again, good things never lasted, and Luca couldn't be trusted.

Marc asked questions about the other kids in their grade, and Luca told him who was who. Eddie B. was a good soccer player and really funny. Alyssa D. was hot but really prude—that's why he'd dumped her. "She thinks she's great because her father owns a couple car washes, but he's a freaking guido—just like my pops."

"And what about her?" asked Marc, pointing at Sharon Nagorski.

Siddharth stared at Sharon, who was sitting at the loser table, the one with Bobby's grandparents and siblings—the one where he would have had to sit just a couple of months earlier. Sharon was laughing at something Bobby's older sister was saying. Her dimples made her look cute. Not pretty.

"That dog?" said Luca. "She's the biggest tool in our school."

"But those lips," said Marc. "Those lips gotta be good for something."

Siddharth forced himself to laugh, slapping his knee as he chuckled. He pretended that he was still following Marc and Luca's conversation, but in actuality he continued to watch Sharon out of the corner of his eye. She was wearing boyish jeans and a gray full-sleeve T-shirt. Her dirty blond hair looked particularly plain and stringy, as if she hadn't washed it in a couple days. All of a sudden, she got up and walked toward the bathroom. He wondered if she knew they'd been talking about her. He wondered if he should get up too—if he should wait for her by the cigarette machines and have a talk with her. He wouldn't say sorry. Just hello. They could start being friendly to each other, if not friends. Then he recalled something Sharon had once said about one of his drawings.

The previous year, she had said that a woman Siddharth had drawn—the singer from one of her stories—looked like his mother. Siddharth had grabbed his picture back and realized Sharon was right. The woman's nose was hooked like a bird's beak, just like his mother's. The woman was wearing a string of black beads around her neck, like his mom used to do. And she had a large mole on her neck, just like his mother's mole. Sharon said, "Relax, Siddharth. It was a compliment. You know, my mom always said your mother was beautiful." Siddharth erupted. He told her that she needed to learn how to shut up. He told her that Luca was right—she could be a real loser when she wanted to. Sharon said, "I may be a loser, but at least I'm not an asshole." The next day, he couldn't go to school because he had a fever, and his father had to cancel his classes in order to care for him.

Luca said something and Marc laughed. Siddharth laughed too, even though he didn't know what they were talking about. He dipped a fry in some ketchup and stuffed it into his mouth. He knew he couldn't do it. He couldn't talk to Sharon. They were never even supposed to be friends in the first place. And as Arjun said, things happened for a reason. If he hadn't fallen out with Sharon, he never would have gone to karate. If he hadn't gone to karate, he never would have become friends with Marc. This line of thinking soothed him for a second. But if life really worked that way, what did this mean about his mother? Had she died for a reason? In that moment, he could see the mole on her neck so clearly. It used to fascinate him. He used to flick it sometimes, as if it were a toy. He felt a surge of loathing for his own achy neck. It was all healthy and fine while hers had been mangled and broken.

He heard fingers snap by his left ear. He looked over to find Marc squinting at him. "Yo, where the fuck are you, homey?"

"Me?" Siddharth licked his lips. "I barely slept last night."

Luca said, "I bet he was up late petting his pussy."

"Screw you, Luca," said Siddharth. "I was up petting your mom's pussy."

Marc cracked up, and whacked him on the back. Siddharth pretended that it didn't hurt.

After lunch, the trio ambled through the room with the air hockey and pool tables toward the one with the Skee-Ball machines. Beside these machines was a glass counter containing prizes—cap guns, candy bars, and key chains with pictures of marijuana leaves and sunbathing models, all of which were up for grabs if you could win enough tickets playing Skee-Ball. Luca explained that he knew a way to get thousands of tickets for free. There was a button on the back of the machines, and if you held it down, they kept on spitting out balls, even if you didn't put in any tokens.

"So that's free balls," said Siddharth. "Not tickets."

"No shit, Sherlock. But if *you* go back there and press the button, *I'll* stuff the balls right into the bull's-eye. All Marc's gotta do is keep a lookout."

"But who's gonna grab the tickets?" asked Siddharth, already sweating.

"Me," said Marc.

"Guys, this sounds stupid," said Siddharth.

"You're right," said Marc. "But it just might work. Sid, you're small. Crawl back there and check it out."

Sighing, Siddharth crouched down and headed behind the machine on all fours. The carpet was smelly and moist, but he found a red plastic button and pressed it down. A bell sounded, and he heard a set of Skee-Balls descend and clack against each other.

"Sweet, Sidney," said Marc. "Nice work."

Siddharth was slightly trembling, but he cracked a smile. He liked when Marc used this moniker.

"Grab 'em," said Luca. "Grab the fucking tickets."

"I got it, I got it," said Marc.

"Siddharth, press it again," said Luca. "Keep on pressing it until I tell you to stop."

Siddharth remained crouched in the corner and did as he was told, but then he heard a voice—a new voice.

"What do you think you're doing?" The voice was deep. Pissed off.

Siddharth gritted his teeth. He pressed his hot face into the cold steel of the machine.

Marc told the man that the machine had eaten their tokens and they were trying to fix it, but the man said they were going to have to come with him. Siddharth's whole body felt heavy, as if mud were running through his veins.

"You little shit!" the man suddenly yelled. "That freaking hurt!"

"Run, Sid!" said Marc. "Get the fuck outta there."

Siddharth crawled out and saw a tall, bearded man limping around in a circle. Marc and Luca were charging toward the pool tables, and Siddharth sprinted to catch up with them. They reached a stairwell and descended one flight, then burst through a set of emergency doors leading to the parking lot.

Siddharth had to shield his eyes from the sun. Marc grabbed his sleeve, and they started running even faster. They fled across Amity Road, taking refuge behind a Luciani Carting dumpster in the parking lot behind a Greek diner. They were all panting, and Siddharth's brain was pounding against his skull.

"That was freaking awesome," said Luca. "You missed it, Sidney. He wrecked that guy. He fucking wasted him."

"I had no choice," said Marc. "He was all grabbing me and shit."

Marc looked at Siddharth, who in turn looked down at his fake Keds. He thought about Mr. Stone, their karate teacher. He would have been disappointed. Arjun would have been disappointed too, but he didn't know about Marc's good sides.

"Let's go to Wendy's," said Marc. "Call your dad from there, Sid. It'll be safer."

"Screw that," said Luca. "My moms'll be here in, like, ten. She can take you home. Wait, there she is right now." He pointed to the busy road. "That's her shitter, right there at the traffic light."

Mrs. Peroti's station wagon had wooden paneling on its exterior and smelled like an ashtray inside. Luca sat shotgun, and Siddharth sat next to Luca's little brother, who was sucking on his fingers.

"What the heck's going on here?" asked Mrs. Peroti.

"Just step on it," said Luca. "Get the hell out of here, Ma."

Mrs. Peroti pulled out of the parking lot. "And who are they?"

"My friends," said Luca. "We gotta take 'em home."

"Hi, friends." She had a strawberry-blond perm. "Something's wrong here, and I'm gonna find out what. You I know," she said to Siddharth. "But who are you?"

"I'm Marc. Nice to meet you."

"Marc who?"

"Marc Kaufman."

"Never heard of you."

"My mother's Rachel Farber."

"You mean the psychologist?"

"Yup."

"Oh."

Siddharth detected some sort of secret meaning in her tone— like she looked down upon Ms. Farber or something.

As Marc gave Mrs. Peroti directions, Siddharth's whole body continued to throb. But he didn't feel entirely rotten. A part of him was exhilarated. A part of him was numb. He noticed that Luca's little brother was staring at him; the kid's eyes were bright blue and strangely large.

"Hello," said Siddharth.

The kid just giggled. He started making a buzzing sound with his lips, and little drops of spittle landed on Siddharth.

"Danny," yelled Luca, "quit it or I'll knock you out!"

"Don't talk to him like that," said Mrs. Peroti.

"Just ignore my brother," said Luca. "He's a 'tard."

Mrs. Peroti gave Luca a hard slap on the back of the head, and he stuck his hand out the window and flashed his middle finger at the passing cars.

When they pulled into Marc's driveway, Siddharth saw his father's minivan parked underneath the hoop. He and Marc said thanks and headed to the front door.

"Yo, what's up with your friend?" Marc asked.

"Luca? He's okay sometimes."

"Okay? He's a total lunatic."

"Yeah, he's freaking nuts."

The door wouldn't open, so Marc rang the bell.

Mrs. Peroti rolled down her window. "You can come home with us if nobody's home."

"Oh, they're definitely home," Marc called back to her. "Thanks though." He pounded on the door.

The Perotis reversed out of the driveway. A few moments later, Siddharth heard the sound of footsteps. When the door swung open, he couldn't help but frown. His father was standing there, but he didn't look right. His hair was out of place, and his face was sweaty.

"I told you to call," said Mohan Lal.

Marc walked inside and tugged at Mohan Lal's checkered shirt, which was untucked in the back. "I love the look, Dr. A. Very gangsta."

Mohan Lal smiled and patted Marc's arm.

Siddharth clenched his jaw and squeezed his temples. "Jesus, Dad, tuck in your damn shirt."

Ms. Farber emerged from her bedroom with her hair wrapped in a towel. "Oh, boys," she said. "How was the party?"

"A real blast," replied Marc.

Siddharth wanted to say something. He wanted to say, *The party was fine, but what the fuck were you two doing?* Yet he couldn't bring himself to open his mouth. He sat down on the sofa, took several deep breaths, and forced himself to think positive thoughts. It only looked like something weird was going on, but everything was actually fine. Mohan Lal had probably forgotten to tuck in his shirt after taking a shit. He'd probably gotten all sweaty because they'd taken a long walk.

Ms. Farber walked up to Mohan Lal and kissed him on the shoulder. "Marc, what did we say about sarcasm?" She removed a carton of milk from the fridge. "Boys, we could do a movie tonight. Doesn't that sound nice?"

"Mom," said Marc, "Dad's gonna be here in an hour."

She served the boys milk. "What about you two? What do you think, Mohan?"

Siddharth glared at his father.

Mohan Lal said, "We should go home, Rachel."

"Home?" she said. "Why home?"

Siddharth needed to do something. "Dad, what about the epilogue? I thought you wanted to get started on your epilogue."

"Yes, that's right," said Mohan Lal. "This book won't write itself. And then there's piles and piles of grading."

4

PRINCE SIDDHARTH

After the Pledge of Allegiance two days later, Mr. Latella said that the class would be reading Mark Twain's *The Prince and the Pauper*, passing out a copy of the book to each student. "These books stay here," he instructed. "Bring 'em home at your own peril."

Siddharth wrote his name inside the cover, where ten years of students had done the same thing. One of them was Brad Horowitz, who Arjun had been friends with in high school. Leafing through the novel, he realized that it was an illustrated and abridged edition. He was sick of this kiddie crap. He began drawing a caricature of his teacher on a loose sheet of paper.

Mr. Latella asked the kids to define the words in the novel's title. Megan S. raised her hand, explaining that a pauper was someone who experienced hardship. The teacher gave her a high five, then said, "But what about *prince*, guys?"

"Duh," said Luca. "We're not, like, five."

"Okay, Mr. Smarty Pants," said Mr. Latella. "Tell us what it means then."

"A prince?" Luca snorted. "He's, like, the son of a queen."

"But what's a queen? Words that seem easy can actually be pretty tough."

Siddharth focused on his drawing, penciling in the man's hefty torso. He drew the little horse that was stitched into the breast of his short-sleeve shirt. It wasn't a real Polo horse, but one with wings, which reinforced the fact that Mr. Latella was lame.

The teacher clicked his tongue. "Come on, guys, what's a prince? This is baby stuff."

"Yo," said Luca, "why don't you ask Siddharth?"

"Luca, let's quit while we're ahead," said Mr. Latella.

"I'm serious," said Luca. "He should know."

"And you shouldn't?"

"Well, I'm not, like, royalty."

A few sets of eyes turned to Siddharth. He put down his yellow pencil and turned to Luca, who separated his lips and flicked out his tongue. Siddharth had no idea where this was going, though he knew it wouldn't end well. He had hoped that things would change between him and Luca after Bobby's party, but the kid had barely glanced in his direction since Sunday.

Mr. Latella slammed his chalk down on the ledge of the blackboard, generating a tiny cloud of dust. "Can you keep your mouth shut, Mr. Peroti?"

"I didn't even do anything," said Luca, throwing his hands in the air.

Mr. Latella's forehead went red. "You're a real wise guy, Luca. You know that?"

"But I'm not kidding. Just ask him. Ask Siddharth."

"You're gonna be sorry, Luca."

"Hit me," said Luca. "I'll sue."

Mr. Latella walked over to Siddharth and thumped his hand down on his desk.

Siddharth winced. He placed his wrists over his drawing and stared at them in anticipation of what would follow.

"So, Siddharth," said Mr. Latella, "your new friend back there is making some claims about you. He's saying something about your family. Are you gonna sit there and let him do that? Isn't there something you wanna say to him?"

"Tell him," said Luca.

Siddharth took a deep breath and kept his eyes fixed on his desk. He reread the words a previous occupant had etched into it: *Kiss Rules.* His brother used to like Kiss. He wished Arjun would barge into the room at that very moment and save him.

"Siddharth, you need to look at me when I'm talking to you."

He met his teacher's angry eyes, green slits in his pudgy, bearded face. "What do you want?"

"What do I want? I want to be able to move on with class, if that's not too much to ask."

Each student was now looking at him, and his face burned.

"So?" said the teacher.

Siddharth turned toward the window. It didn't matter that a hard rain was falling, or that water had turned the asphalt paths into little rivers—he would rather have been outside getting drenched.

"You want me to wait all day?" said Mr. Latella. He placed a hand on one of his flabby hips. "Because I can, you know."

Siddharth put his pencil in his mouth and started chewing it, keeping his eyes fixed on the rain. "My great-grandfather . . ." He peeked down to make sure his rendition of his teacher's bulbous gut was still obscured by his arms. "Well, my dad . . . he says my great-grandfather was royalty."

"I can't hear you with that pencil in your mouth. Lead poisoning is a serious thing, you know."

He removed the pencil. "My great-grandfather was royalty, but that was a real long time ago."

"Is this some kind of joke? Did you and Luca plan this or something?"

Siddharth shook his head, and his teacher wheezed deeply.

"You're telling me you're serious?" said Mr. Latella.

"I told you so," said Luca.

Mr. Latella shifted his weight to his other leg, and his stomach jiggled. "So what? He was, like, a maharaja or something?"

"He was a prince," said Siddharth.

"A prince?" Mr. Latella gripped his beard. "Wait, was he, like, nobility?" His eyes suddenly widened. "Was he English?"

The next sentences came out before Siddharth could pause to consider them. "My great-grandfather went to study in England—at Oxford. That's a famous college."

"Thanks, I know what Oxford is."

"He married this, uh, woman there—my great-grandmother—and she was, like, a real distant relative of the king."

"Which king?"

"King George."

"How distant?"

"I don't know. The king and my great-grandmother were fifth cousins or something."

"Really?" Mr. Latella put his foot on an empty seat, and the keys on his belt loop jingled. He stared into the air and smiled. "You know, I always wondered if you were mixed."

The teacher's words made Siddharth feel bolder. "That's why my skin's light. And my eyes—in the right light, they have little flecks of green in them."

"Go figure," Mr. Latella snickered. "Your great-grandmother was British nobility."

Siddharth nodded. In that moment, the lie he had told felt right. It didn't feel like a lie.

Luca started pounding on his desk and chanting. "*Prince Siddharth, Prince Sidd-harth.*" The rest of the class joined in too: "*Prince Sidd-harth, Prince Sidd-harth . . .*"

Mr. Latella shook his head, but he was still smiling. "Okay, okay. Settle down." He gave Siddharth a high five for the second time that year. "Take a bow, Prince Siddharth. Take a bow, and let's move on."

5

LAND OF THE ARAB-HATERS AND NYMPHOMANIACS

Siddharth was pretending to do math homework but was really watching television. He heard his father call for him. "What is it?" he yelled back. He wasn't in the mood to get his father a glass of water. He wasn't in the mood to tell him if the clothes he was wearing looked good or not. Mohan Lal kept on calling, and Siddharth begrudgingly peeled himself off the sofa.

He found his father in the bathroom wearing a pair of tan pants and a ribbed banyan—what Marc called a wifebeater. He was on his knees scrubbing the floor of the shower.

"Dad, what do you want?"

Mohan Lal told to him to clean up the house. He said Siddharth had turned their home into a pigsty.

"I turned it into a pigsty? Me?" Siddharth was about to shoot back with something mean—that Mohan Lal was worse than a pig, he was like a dirty Indian beggar who lived in a slum. That the house got so dirty because Mohan Lal was too cheap to pay the Polish cleaning lady to come more than once a month. But as he looked down at the glistening gray hairs of his father's shoulders, he realized something strange was happening. Mohan Lal did clean from time to time. He blued the toilet bowls with that gel, vacuumed the floors in the family room and kitchen. But he rarely got down and dirty like this.

"Go clean your room," said Mohan Lal. "Rachel and Marc will be here soon."

"They're coming over? Again?"

"Hurry up. Thanks to you, she'll think we are animals."

"Yeah, thanks to me," Siddharth muttered. "I'm the one who has seven dirty coffee mugs on my desk. I keep the catalogs on the dining table for five months but never actually cut the coupons." He reluctantly headed to his bedroom with an empty garbage bag and the vacuum cleaner. He sifted through the chaotic assortment of school papers on his desk, chucking a blackened banana peel and a paper plate full of Dorito crumbs into the garbage. Two weeks of dirty clothes were strewn across the patterned carpet. He stuffed his sweaters and sweatshirts into a drawer, then dumped his pants and T-shirts into the laundry basket in the linen closet outside the main bathroom, where Mohan Lal was now ringing out a mop.

Siddharth said, "So what are we doing tonight?"

"*We* are not doing anything. Rachel and I have an appointment."

"An appointment? What does that mean?"

"Nothing that concerns you."

Fuck off, thought Siddharth. At least Marc was coming over. As long as he had Marc, the adults could do whatever they wanted.

The electronic doorbell rang just after five, and it sounded particularly off-key, like a dying bird. Ms. Farber walked into the house before he or his father could get there. She kissed Mohan Lal first on the cheek and then on the lips. She said, "I think those batteries need a-changing."

"I've been telling Siddharth," said Mohan Lal, who was now wearing a tie and blazer.

"I'll take care of it right now," she said. "Marc, get me a chair."

"Leave it," said Mohan Lal.

Marc slapped Siddharth five, then plunked himself down on the frayed love seat. Siddharth sat beside him and stared at Ms. Farber. Today she was wearing lots of black—black stockings and a black ribbed shirt. But her skirt was gray, and it stopped at her knees. He thought she looked good tonight—sort of elegant.

Mohan Lal handed her a recent letter from his publisher, which Siddharth had already read aloud to his father multiple times. Mohan Lal had sent in the first four chapters of his manuscript to

Walton, and they were pleased with his progress. According to Ronald Wasserman, an assistant editor, Mohan Lal's "perspectives on the field of marketing are not only impressive, but often innovative." Although the book wasn't due for another four months, Wasserman suggested that Mohan Lal rush to finish it by June. That way, they might be able to publish it as early as February.

After reading the letter, Ms. Farber dropped it to the floor and threw her arms around Mohan Lal's neck. "Absolutely amazing! See, what did I tell you about positive thinking?"

Mohan Lal grinned. "Well, perhaps my discipline also played a role—my innovative ideas."

She gave his neck a long smooch, and Siddharth had to look away.

Mohan Lal tapped his wristwatch. "We should be leaving."

Siddharth stood up and removed the letter from the floor. "Would somebody please tell me where you guys are going tonight?" he asked sharply.

Ms. Farber winked at him. "Honey, we're going to your school."

"You're joking." Siddharth's stomach tightened.

"I'm not." She pulled out a brochure from her purse and used it to swat him on the head. "There's an event in the gymnasium."

He grabbed the pamphlet. Upon reading it, he felt relieved. They were going to some dumb-ass meeting about something called Dianetics, which could help people "unlock their true potential." He threw the pamphlet onto the coffee table, which was neat and tidy for a change, then watched Ms. Farber apply lipstick to her contorted mouth. She pulled Mohan Lal toward the door and said, "Be good, boys. We're trusting you."

Once the adults had pulled out of the driveway, Siddharth followed Marc to the dining room and watched him kneel down on the orange carpet. "What do you think you're doing?"

"What am I doing?" said Marc. "I'm gonna get us happy."

Siddharth watched Marc open a cabinet that contained stacks of china, teacups, and glasses. The next cabinet held piles of old Indian and Pakistani periodicals, and Christmas cards people had sent the Aroras in the eighties.

Marc asked, "Where the hell did the booze go?"

Siddharth pointed to a third cabinet door. Marc yanked it open, and the boys stared at Mohan Lal's sizable stash of alcohol. Most of it consisted of unopened bottles of whiskey, a few of which looked fancy. Mohan Lal used to buy these from duty-free airport shops on his way back from India. Barry Uncle had given him a couple as birthday presents.

Marc reached into a corner and pulled out a bottle of brown liquid called Old Monk XXX, unscrewing its cap and sniffing it. "Shit looks Indian," he said. "Smells good, but he might notice." He pulled out a half-empty bottle of Gilbey's Gin, then took a swig and sighed. "This'll do just fine." He gulped some more, and a few beads of sweat appeared on the bridge of his freckled nose. He wiped them away with the bottom of one of his shirts. He was wearing a red short-sleeve T-shirt, and a black full-sleeve shirt underneath it. "I could get used to this." He took out a glass and poured some gin, then handed the drink to Siddharth. "Bottoms up," he said. "Before they get back from their retard festival."

Siddharth accepted the glass. It was crystal and had an intricate, heavy base. Holding it in his hands, he felt guilty. And a little sad. His father hadn't touched these glasses since his mother had died, and even back then he would only use them on special occasions.

"Go for it," said Marc. "I promise you're not gonna die."

Siddharth brought the vessel to his lips and sipped. The fiery liquid got stuck in his throat, and he sprayed it all over Marc's shirt.

"Dumb-ass," said Marc, but he was smiling. He took another swig from the bottle.

Siddharth wiped his mouth and cleared his throat. "You think it's retarded?"

"You're not retarded—just a little goofy sometimes."

"Shut up. I mean this thing they went to—that stuff."

"What stuff?"

"You know: visualizing things, being born again—*that* stuff."

Marc tucked his bangs behind his ear. "Yo, I think I can already feel it."

Siddharth drank some gin and managed to get it down this time. "I've been in a plane hundreds of times, and there's definitely no heaven up there. I mean, it kind of makes sense really."

Marc squinted at him. "What makes sense? What the hell are you talking about?"

"You know, reincarnation—that kind of shit."

"Oh God, not you too." Marc shook his head. "All this shit is getting on my freaking nerves. Listen, when you're dead, you're dead, and that's it. Hell, they don't even believe half of the crap they're saying."

"What's that supposed to mean?"

"Believe me, it's like a code language or something. They'd rather be screwing each other twenty-four seven, but they can't do that—not with us around, anyway. All this philosophical mumbo-jumbo, it's just bullshit they talk about to get their mind off fucking each other's brains out."

Siddharth forced another sip of liquor down his throat and winced.

Marc laughed. "There you go." He poured more gin into Siddharth's crystal glass.

Siddharth took another long swig. "What do you mean, fucking each other?" He had his suspicions about his father's sex life. He knew that Mohan Lal and Ms. Farber had kissed, but maybe they had done a bit more.

"You know, sexual intercourse?" said Marc. "When a man inserts his penis into a vagina?"

"Yeah, thanks. You really think they're doing it?"

"We're sleeping over at your house tonight. They're gonna sleep in the same freaking bed. What do you think they're gonna do? Tickle each other?"

"What?" Siddharth felt his lip begin to tremble. "You're sleeping over?"

"What do you think's in my bag? Toys?"

Siddharth finished his drink and tried to tell himself that Marc was lying, but knew this wasn't true. Mohan Lal had been acting strange. He had been acting strange because he was keeping something from him. How could his father have done this? Arjun had called him selfish, and their mother had said the same thing. Once, his parents had been fighting because her sister was supposed to visit for two whole months. Mohan Lal didn't want her there for such a long time, and Siddharth's mother called him egotistical. She said that his ego would get in the way of their family's happiness, and Mohan Lal got into his shitty Dodge Omni and sped down the driveway.

Staring at Marc, Siddharth now saw his father for the selfish man he was. He liked to talk but not listen. He was only nice to people who were nice to him. Siddharth had always thought that Mohan Lal had become friends with Ms. Farber to make things easier for his son. But maybe he was only in it for himself—for the sex. This thought made him actually shudder.

Marc poured him some more booze. "I didn't think you were that stupid, Sidney. Look, at least somebody's getting some."

Siddharth couldn't calm his frenzied nerves. "Yo, you don't know what you're talking about."

"Oh, but I do. Our parents are doing it, Siddharth. They're having sex. They've done it at my house, and tonight they're gonna do it here—right in your father's bed. Maybe they'll even make us a little brother."

Siddharth's stomach began to lurch. He gave Marc a shove.

Marc laughed. "Are you serious? Try doing that again."

Siddharth froze for a second. He wanted to kick his friend in the balls or bite his face off, but instead he ran toward the bathroom and locked himself inside. With his back against the door, he took some deep breaths. The breathing failed to settle his stomach; it failed to still his mind. He wondered if he was drunk—if he might puke. His body felt hot, so he cupped some water into his mouth. Doing so only exacerbated his nausea.

He wondered what they did together. Was it regular sex? Or the stuff he had seen in the movies? Had Ms. Farber sucked his father's dick? Had Mohan Lal stuck his penis between her tits? Licked her pussy? The man suddenly seemed like a stranger, a sex addict who would do anything for a naked body. Betray his wife.

Betray his kids. But it wasn't his fault. Mohan Lal was sad and confused, and Ms. Farber was a slut. She was the one who had led him in this disgusting direction.

Siddharth began to burp up a mixture of garlic and gin. He felt himself starting to shiver. He walked over to the toilet bowl and raised the lid. When he opened his mouth, nothing came out, so he shoved his index finger toward his tonsils and gagged. An acidic liquid singed his larynx but then retreated. He poured the rest of his drink into the toilet bowl and flushed.

When he got out of the bathroom, Marc was on the love seat thumbing through one of Mohan Lal's books. "Yo, you done with your little hissy fit?"

"Shut up," said Siddharth. "I'm not feeling good. I think I ate something bad at school."

Marc waved Mohan Lal's book in the air. "Funny shit. It's like all sci-fi—like *Total Recall* or something." .

Siddharth snatched the book out of his hands and examined the cover. It was called *Am I a Hindu?* He had never seen it before.

"You know what my dad says?" said Marc. He put a stick of gum in his mouth and handed one to Siddharth. "He says Hindus and Jews, they only got two things in common: they're both really bad tippers—and they hate the Arabs, and the Arabs hate them too."

Siddharth threw the book on the table and suggested they watch a movie. He recommended *Planet of the Apes*, but Marc said it was too old. After some back and forth, they eventually opted for *Back to School*. Marc was laughing out loud the whole time, but Siddharth's mind was elsewhere. He couldn't believe his father was fucking Ms. Farber. He couldn't believe the man had already forgotten about his dead wife. *Dead, dead—when you're dead, you're dead.* Siddharth's brain burned with these words. He could feel a big, heavy sob building in his body. Dead was dead. You weren't reincarnated, and you didn't go to heaven. Arjun had pretty much said the same thing. Siddharth imagined the flames licking at his mother's body. They had cremated her and left him with nothing— not even a strand of hair or a gravestone where he could say hello.

A key rattled in the front door.

Mohan Lal and Ms. Farber walked in, though they remained in the entrance hall. Marc didn't seem to notice, but Siddharth peered at the adults from the darkened family room. Ms. Farber removed her coat and hung it up in the closet. She was saying something about being individuals—about not having to like the same things.

"It is not a question of liking," said Mohan Lal. He loosened his tie and stuffed it into his blazer pocket. "Aren't you the one always telling people to be more open?"

"Listen, it's just not for me," she said, grasping Mohan Lal's lapels. "But that doesn't mean it can't be for you."

Mohan Lal stepped away from her. "What? So I'm a fool? My judgment can't be trusted?"

Ms. Farber tied her hair into a bun. "Look, we just went over this. Paying thousands of dollars to learn how to be happy—it just doesn't seem right. For Christ's sake, normally you're the skeptic. You're the one who would call it consumeristic."

Siddharth noticed that her boots made her look almost as tall as Mohan Lal. These boots were tall, black, and leather. He couldn't stop himself from imagining her naked, wearing nothing else besides them. Did she keep them on while they were screwing? He shook his head to rid it of this perverted image.

Mohan Lal stepped into the family room. "As if you're one who should talk of consumerism," he muttered.

"What's that supposed to mean?" She then noticed the boys behind her. "Why are you guys sitting in the dark?"

Marc brought a finger to his lips and shushed her.

She kissed him on the forehead. Her curls appeared eerily orange in the light cast by the television. Siddharth hoped she wouldn't kiss him but then cursed her in his mind when she didn't. Mohan Lal turned off the VCR and put on CNN, then seated himself beside Siddharth. Marc clicked his tongue. Ms. Farber sat down next to her son.

"What about dinner?" she suggested. "One of my famous stews maybe?"

"There are leftovers in the fridge," said Mohan Lal.

"But what about your news?" said Ms. Farber. "We should celebrate."

"Celebrating would be premature."

Siddharth grasped his father's knee. "Dad, I don't feel so good."

"What's wrong?" Mohan Lal's eyes were fixed on the television.

"My stomach hurts."

Mohan Lal didn't respond.

"Dad, I vomited."

"What?" Mohan Lal grabbed his wrist. "Yes, you're warm."

Siddharth caught Marc smirking out of the corner of his eye. He didn't care though.

Ms. Farber stood up and placed her fingers on Siddharth's forehead. "How about I make him some soup?"

"I just wanna go to bed," said Siddharth. "If I eat, I'm definitely gonna puke again."

Mohan Lal said he would boil some fennel water that Siddharth could drink in his bedroom. He took him by the hand and began to lead him away.

"Mohan . . ." said Ms. Farber.

"What?"

"Mohan, hang on a sec." She sounded annoyed.

"What is it?" said Mohan Lal.

"Everybody else needs to eat, right? Why don't I go ahead and make something for the rest of us?"

Don't you get it? thought Siddharth. *He doesn't want your fucking food.*

Mohan Lal glanced down, and when he raised his head, his eyes were wide with anger. "Tonight's not the night, Rachel."

She placed a hand on her hip. "What do you mean?"

"What I mean is, my son is unwell."

"Are you saying we should leave? Because if that's what you mean, just say so."

Mohan Lal sighed. "We'll be seeing each other in just two days' time."

Ms. Farber's chest was heaving. Her nostrils began to flare. "That'll be perfect, right? I'll watch the boys, and you can get down to work. I mean, Mohan, we talked about this. I packed a freaking bag."

Siddharth groaned, then squeezed his father's hand. "Dad, my stomach's killing me."

Later that night, after Marc and Ms. Farber were gone, Siddharth lay in bed on the verge of sleep. His stomach felt better now. He was alone in the house with his father, and everything was totally fine. The ringing phone startled him, and he got out of bed and crept down the hallway. He seated himself on the floor, right by the doorway that led to the family room. That way his father wouldn't see him.

Mohan Lal was on the sofa wearing pink shorts and an untucked striped shirt that had once belonged to Arjun. A glass of whiskey stood on the coffee table, and the receiver was sandwiched between his ear and shoulder. He was frowning silently as somebody spoke on the other end of the line. One of his hands held a slice of mango, and the other wielded the serrated Ginsu knife he had ordered from the television.

Siddharth could almost make out Ms. Farber's angry words all the way from where he was sitting, but more than a minute passed before he heard his father say anything. When Mohan Lal finally spoke, his mouth was full of mango. "I never said that. Why would I think we're doing anything wrong?"

Siddharth wished he could hear Ms. Farber's words.

"Look," said Mohan Lal, agitated, "it sounds like you're giving me an ultimatum."

. . .

"Well, to me it sounds like an ultimatum."

. . .

"So you're the boss then?" said Mohan Lal. "If you think something is right, then that's the final word?"

. . .

"What if I said the same thing about you?"

. . .

"I don't give a damn what you meant."

. . .

"Frankly, I've also had more than enough!"

Mohan Lal slammed down the phone and took a long sip of whiskey. Then he used his free hand to suck on the heart of his mango. He devoured it like a savage, like someone who hadn't eaten in ages.

Siddharth wondered what his father was feeling in that moment. Was he angry? Lonely? Did he miss Ms. Farber? No, Mohan Lal didn't really care about her. He missed his wife, and she was dead now. Both of them missed the same person, and she was dead. Normally, Siddharth would have gotten up and wrapped his arms around him. But he didn't feel like it tonight. Tonight he just wanted to go to sleep. As he tiptoed toward his bedroom, a small part of him felt guilty. But mostly he was filled with a deep sense of relief.

BUFF BLUE GOD

For the next two days, Mohan Lal didn't let Siddharth answer the phone, instead sending all calls to the new answering machine. Ms. Farber stopped trying after she'd left a few unreturned messages.

Siddharth and Mohan Lal resumed their dinners together in front of the television, laughing along with their favorite sitcoms. Mohan Lal made him turkey burgers and a special vat of rajma, enough to eat all week. He asked Siddharth to check his manuscript for typos and then to read certain chapters out loud. Once or twice, Siddharth even got up in the morning and crawled into his father's bed like he used to when he was younger. He brushed his teeth in his father's bathroom while Mohan Lal shaved, the man dumping his mug of murky shaving water out the window for the sake of the septic system.

By the end of the week, however, Mohan Lal started to seem distant and distracted. He stayed in his office straight through dinner and resumed old habits like falling asleep in front of the television or not sleeping at all to work on his book.

Things at school weren't much better. Even though Luca had invited him to sit at his lunch table and play kickball, he still felt on edge around these kids. One day in the cafeteria, when he was reluctantly eating the brown Indian beans his father had packed for him, Eddie Benson started sniffing the air and grimacing. "Yo," he said, "your lunch smells like my dirty stinkhole." For the rest of the afternoon, Eddie and Luca referred to Siddharth as the Prince of Poop.

Without Ms. Farber to collect him from school, he found himself on the bus more often, and these long rides felt quieter and lonelier than he'd remembered. One evening, his father made him come to Elm City College and sit in on his graduate-level management course so that he wouldn't have to spend the entire evening alone. Mohan Lal showed his students a clip from a movie in which an ape picks up a bone and starts smashing the ground. The scene seemed weird and totally irrelevant, but the students kept raising their hands to make different comments—that the movie was "criticizing the inherent savagery of progress," or that it "depicted mankind's innate animalistic nature."

On the ride home that night, Mohan Lal asked Siddharth what he had thought of his teaching.

"It was fine," said Siddharth, who had spent much of the class squirming in his seat, embarrassed by his father's accent and constantly gesticulating hands. To Siddharth, Mohan Lal actually resembled the ape from the movie.

"Just fine?"

He turned to face his father. The man looked particularly exhausted in that moment, vulnerable. Siddharth's embarrassment and frustration suddenly evaporated. He wondered how Mohan Lal could make it in the world if even his own son were so cruel to him. "Dad, your students totally love you."

"They do?"

"Come on—you're one of the greatest teachers in the world."

Mohan Lal grinned, the glow returning to his tired face.

After almost a full week without Marc or Ms. Farber, Siddharth felt himself falling into a dark place. Even his favorite movies weren't distracting him. He needed someone to talk to, but his brother was flaky these days, and also rather annoying. First Arjun had hated Ms. Farber and ranted about their father's selfishness, and then, out of the blue, he called to say that he thought their relationship was a great idea. "Dad's finally moving on. You need to be mature and let him."

Siddharth wished he could talk to Marc. Two days earlier, he'd left a message on his friend's answering machine, but Marc hadn't called back. At the time, he told himself it didn't matter, that he had other friends now and was doing just fine. But he'd come to see how this was bullshit. Maybe Arjun was right. Maybe he needed to stop living in the past. His life would probably be better if his father and Ms. Farber just did whatever they wanted. He felt like an ass for the way he had acted that night—for exaggerating about his stomach.

On Saturday morning—eight days after the adults had fought— he decided to give Marc another try. He took the cordless phone into the bathroom and dialed his number. The machine picked up again, so he called Ms. Farber's office line. She answered after three rings.

"Hi. May I please speak with Marc?"

"Siddharth? Is everything okay?"

"Can I talk to him, please?"

"He's out, Siddharth." Her voice was deeper than usual, and raspy. "He's been at his father's for the past few days."

"Really? Why?" He heard her light a cigarette.

"What do you mean, *why*? It's his father."

Neither of them spoke for a moment. He stared at himself in the mirror and tugged at his bangs, which came down to the middle of his nose. Soon his hair would be long enough to get it cut right—long on top and shaved on the sides.

"Siddharth, is there something you'd like to say?"

"Nope."

"Are you sure? How's your dad?"

Oh God, he thought. She never knew when to shut up. "He's fine—great, actually."

"Has he mentioned anything?"

"About what?"

"About me, Siddharth."

He swallowed hard, wondering if he should make something up. "No."

She scoffed. "He's a stubborn man, your father."

Siddharth gritted his teeth.

She took a long, audible drag. "Honey, it's fair to say that the four of us were getting along—right?"

"I guess so."

"You guess so? You mean you didn't like hanging out with Marc? You boys have gotten pretty close. That's a good thing—right?"

"Yeah."

"Yeah, what?"

"Yeah, right. That's a good thing, I guess."

"Remember that, honey. Keep that in mind."

Rain poured on and off for the next few days. It stopped on a Tuesday, and when Siddharth was walking to the bus stop that morning, he noticed that the trunks of the nearby pine trees had started oozing an orange slime. He thought about the awful afternoon that lay ahead of him. His father was insisting that he attend his idiotic after-school program. A part of Siddharth had wanted to say, *Call Ms. Farber and tell her you're sorry.* But the pissed-off part of him won out, so he kept his mouth shut.

The school day was fine. During recess, he played a board game with Luca and Eddie, and then came math. Once that was over, Mr. Latella started going on about Memorial Day, which was only a couple of weeks away. He wanted to know if anybody's father had ever served in the military. Siddharth thought about mentioning Mr. Iverson, his neighbor who rode a Harley-Davidson. Mr. Iverson had fought in Vietnam, and he and Mohan Lal were always talking about how that war was a disgrace to the nation. Siddharth wished he could bring up Marc's uncle, who was wounded in basic training before actually shipping out to Vietnam, or Marc's grandfather, who had been in one of the World Wars. He stayed quiet though. These people weren't family; they were strangers.

Samantha R. raised her hand and said that her father had fought in Grenada. John G. said his grandfather had gone to Korea.

"That's wonderful," said Mr. Latella. "We should all be grateful to these men. Do you know that? Do you know why?"

Nobody raised a hand.

Mr. Latella scanned the room, then let out a sigh of exasperation. "You guys are really still babies. I'll say it again—they're gonna eat you for breakfast in junior high."

Siddharth looked up at the clock. There were only fourteen minutes remaining in this crappy day, but even Mr. Latella was better than his stupid after-school program. Even though he had only stayed after school three times in the last six months, when he did so, it was like he was a pathetic little fifth grader again. He would wander around the playground alone, time passing like a broken clock.

Mr. Latella pointed up at the American flag. "Let me tell you," he said, "if it wasn't for guys like John's grandfather, we might not have *that* anymore. To be frank, you and me might not even be here today. We might not be able to vote, and we probably wouldn't be free." Mr. Latella explained that the next day they were going to make cards for Samantha's father and John's grandfather, and also for a battalion of soldiers who had fought in the Gulf War.

Siddharth wished he could be teleported to his sofa, and if that weren't possible, he would rather just disappear—just evaporate into nothing. If only Marc would be waiting for him by the pay phone like he used to. Siddharth started making promises to God. If Marc showed up today, he swore to watch less TV and be nicer to his father. He swore to stop watching pornos, touching his penis, and smoking cigars. And then it happened: the phone on the cinder-block wall began to buzz.

Mr. Latella took the call and then told Siddharth to gather his things and go to the office. Siddharth smiled. He wanted to take back all his negative thoughts about religion and God.

With his backpack over his shoulder and Marc's old hoodie dangling over his wrist, he walked down the hallway feeling relieved but also anxious. Who would be there for him? Ms. Farber? Marc? Both of them? He paused before entering the office and caught a glimpse of black denim through the windowed wall. *It must be her,* he thought. *When it comes down to it, she's really not that bad.* He opened the door. The school secretary was standing behind the counter that separated the office from the reception area. She had short silver hair and was smiling. "All set, hon?" She peered at Siddharth over her tiny rimless reading glasses. "Aren't you gonna say hi?"

Siddharth couldn't speak. All he could do was stare at the man standing a few feet away from him. This man was wearing black jeans and a rugby shirt with fat yellow stripes. The man smiled, and his capped teeth gleamed in the fluorescent light.

The secretary cocked her head to one side. "Hon, you know this gentleman, right?"

The man took a step toward Siddharth. "Of course he knows me." He had a booming, raspy drawl. "Known me since the day he was born."

Siddharth wanted to turn around and run. He glanced down at a gummy black stain on the worn blue carpet.

The secretary scowled. "What's his name, honey? Can you tell me his name?"

"Hi, Barry Uncle," said Siddharth. He knew something really bad must have happened. His father had had a heart attack. He'd been carjacked. Bloody bits of his brain were splattered all over Boston Post Road.

The secretary brushed her forehead and recommenced her smiling. "Well, go on then," she said. "Don't be shy, honey."

Barry Uncle opened his arms widely. "Come on, squirt. Give your uncle a hug."

But Siddharth just stood there and stared. Barry Uncle's hair used to be gray, but now it was jet black. His face had always been mottled, but today it was looser. His chest seemed thick and strong, and so did his shoulders. Though his stomach bulged like a basketball, and it rested on a leather fanny pack that was strapped around his waist.

Barry Uncle stepped toward him. He engulfed Siddharth in his arms and gave his head a vigorous rub, then leaned forward and kissed him on the cheek.

Siddharth clicked his tongue and used Marc's sweatshirt to dry his wet face.

As they walked through the jam-packed parking lot, Siddharth parted his hair with his fingers. He noticed a few blue fissures forming in the dark sky. Some light-blue eggshells were lying in a clump of pachysandra, and he guessed they'd belonged to a family of robins. He asked, "Where's my father?" He didn't understand how his father could have done this to him. First he had made up with Barry Uncle without even saying anything, and now he'd sent the man to his school unannounced. Mohan Lal could be a real dick when he wanted to. He could be a negligent father.

"Working," said Barry Uncle. "He asked me to take you for a little ride." He pressed his keychain, and a burgundy Integra flashed its lights.

Siddharth seated himself in the car's passenger seat and whistled as the electronic seat belt clicked into place automatically.

"It's an old car," said Barry Uncle. He started the engine and revved it. "I'm looking at a Beamer now."

But Siddharth wasn't in the mood to talk about cars. He wanted to know what was going on with his father.

"Or what do you think about a Porsche?"

"Beats me," said Siddharth. "Get a Porsche. Go for a 911."

Barry Uncle chuckled. "Good taste, kiddo. The Germans, they know engineering. They know lots of things. I dunno why your dad insists on that American junk."

Despite his discomfort, Siddharth found himself smiling.

"I'll work on him for you." Barry Uncle unzipped his fanny pack and pulled out a tiny blue sachet, emptying its contents into his mouth, and the car suddenly smelled like mint and pepper—like Delhi. "We'll get him driving something more appropriate."

Barry Uncle drove fast, taking a right turn where he should have gone left. They didn't pass the old white church or town hall like they were supposed to. A nervy roller-coaster feeling churned in Siddharth's stomach, but it was better than the unabating deadness of the past few days. He was too stunned to talk. He just sat there absorbing his surroundings. An actual car phone rested behind the gearshift. Did it work? Could he use it to call his father?

From the rearview mirror dangled a cardboard cutout of a blue Hindu god. It somehow looked different from the deities that had once rested on Arjun's nightstand. This god had chiseled pecs and a six-pack, and it didn't seem all tranquil and girly.

Barry Uncle, still masticating the contents of his blue sachet, touched the god and brought his fingers to his forehead. "You like him?"

"Huh?"

"Who's that? Can you tell me his name?"

Siddharth shook his head. He could only identify the gods that resembled animals.

Barry Uncle pressed a button to lower his window and then hawked a glob of phlegm. "Ain't your fault. Your father's a busy man. Believe me, women take up a lot of energy."

Siddharth clenched his jaw and stared out the window. They were paused at the intersection of Center Road and Route 1. To the right was a bank that could have been a suburban home. When he was six, Mohan Lal had taken him there to open his first savings account.

The light changed, and Barry Uncle made a left. "So what do you think of her?"

"Who?"

"Of what's-her-name."

"Ms. Farber?"

"That's it." Barry Uncle snapped his fingers. "She pretty?"

He shrugged. *No,* he wanted to say, *she's a fucking dog.* He punched some of the buttons on the car phone.

"Easy," said Barry Uncle. "Emergency use only."

They drove in silence to the next light, passing by the road that led to the dump, then the pancake house where Arjun had once worked as a dishwasher.

"He should watch out, you know," said Barry Uncle. "My ex-wife was a gori—what a terrible storm." As Siddharth listened to these words, a surge of optimism pulsed through his veins. Maybe Barry Uncle's return was the sign he'd been waiting for—a sign that things were really and truly returning to normal.

Barry Uncle said, "At least Dad's got himself a Jew. With them we have something in common."

"I know, I know. Bad tipping and hating Arabs."

Barry Uncle turned into a plaza containing a bridal shop and a Subway, parking next to a Jeep Wrangler. "Good man," he said. "Yes, we both have the same problem with the Mohammedans." He shut off the engine, and the seat belts slid forward on their own. "Listen, kid, this all must be strange for you. But your father's a smart man. And we all gotta look to the future."

Inside Subway, the radio was playing "More than Words," one of Luca's favorite songs. Barry Uncle explained that the turkey here was better than the roast beef, and that pickles went well with the peppers. He called the Latina cashier "sweetheart," telling her she had gorgeous eyes. Siddharth wondered if Barry Uncle could knock some sense into Mohan Lal—if he could keep him from doing something stupid, like marrying Ms. Farber.

They sidled up to a booth by the window, and Siddharth asked when he would see his father.

"Don't worry," said Barry Uncle, his mouth full of turkey, "I'm not gonna kidnap you." He devoured his sub, then tapped his hairy fingers against the acrylic tabletop, the two of them going quiet.

Siddharth struggled to finish his sandwich, breaking the silence by asking, "You're a lawyer, right?"

"Me? I'm an entrepreneur—got a gas station and half a liquor store. I actually *do* the things that your dad teaches." He slurped some ginger ale through a straw. "You could say this place—America—has allowed me to live with some dignity. But things are changing over there too."

"Over where?"

"In India, boy. I keep telling your father, but he doesn't wanna listen."

They took an odd route home, a tape with some wailing Indians playing on the stereo. Barry Uncle asked if Mohan Lal still listened to this stuff, and Siddharth shrugged. To him, all Indian music sounded the same. Barry Uncle said, "This is Rafi Sahib. Mohammed Rafi. Real music, not like your McHammer."

Siddharth struggled to contain his laughter.

"What's so funny, kid?"

"Nothing."

"Say it."

"It's MC Hammer, not McHammer. And he's lame."

"Boy, all your music's lame. Same with your cinema. Your movies are nothing compared with the classics. Me and your Dad, we used to go to the movies once a week. Your father, he was a Guru Dutt man. But me, I loved Raj Kapoor."

"I should know these people?"

"Don't tell me—you don't know Raj Kapoor?"

He shrugged. "I saw *Gandhi* once."

"That trash? That's not a movie—it's bloody propaganda."

Once they were home, Barry Uncle poured himself some of Mohan Lal's whiskey. He sipped it on the armchair while reading an Indian magazine that he'd pulled out of his briefcase. Siddharth sat on the sofa, and as he watched TV, he wondered if being here with Barry Uncle was better or worse than his after-school program. Maybe the best thing would be if things could just go back to the way they were a few weeks earlier. He took the cordless phone to the bathroom and dialed Marc's number. There was still no answer.

He recalled a time when Barry Uncle had really pissed off his mother. They were eating a standard weekday meal of daal, vegetables, and frozen pita, and Barry Uncle declared that the food was nice, but that nothing was better than piping-hot, homemade chapattis. Siddharth's mother had slammed down her glass. She took the man's pita from his plate and threw it in the trash compactor.

Mohan Lal's van pulled in a few minutes after eight, and Siddharth ran to the front door to greet him. As Mohan Lal hung his blazer over a kitchen chair, Barry Uncle removed an expensive-looking bottle of alcohol from a plastic bag.

Mohan Lal held the bottle up to the light. "Wow. Rocks and soda, chief?"

"Boss, that's the good stuff," said Barry Uncle. "We gotta have it neat."

The men poured the whiskey into Mohan Lal's special crystal

glasses, sipping it on the family room sofas as they munched cashews flavored with Indian spices. Siddharth sat on the armchair,
eating a plate of rajma on his three-legged Indian table. He tried to
concentrate on a sitcom, but Barry Uncle kept interrupting him. At
one point, he told Siddharth that his table was gorgeous.

"Thanks," he replied. "I made it all by myself—from scratch."

"I bet you don't even know where it's from," said Barry Uncle.

He scrutinized the wooden table, as if seeing it for the first
time. It was only a foot tall and had a round top carved with intricate
floral patterns.

"Kashmir, boy," said Barry Uncle, who then turned to Mohan
Lal. "I bet he doesn't even know where that is."

Of course he knew where it was. Kashmir was in India, the
goddamned country that nobody would shut up about.

"Why would he know?" replied Mohan Lal. "All kids know
today is television."

"But it's his grandmother's place. It's one of the most beautiful
places on this earth. Sid, listen up. You must visit Kashmir one day.
But your father can't take you there now. He can't take you thanks
to these bloody Pakistanis."

Siddharth got up to raise the volume.

Barry Uncle poured a second round and grew even louder, yelling over the television. He went into great detail about his new
business. He had invested in an Indian company that would print
American textbooks for a quarter of the price and then ship them
back to America.

"Chief," said Mohan Lal, "I wish you all the best, but you
couldn't pay me enough to do business in that cesspool of a
country."

Siddharth was relieved to hear these words. The last thing he
needed was another trip to India. If he went to India, he'd get al-
lergies from the all the dust and smog. If he went to India, he'd
have to see his mother's little sister, who wrote him letters once
in a while and called him on his birthday every year. She had the
same nose as his mother, and she bought him sweets and took him
to temples. He wanted to see her again—someday. Just not now.

"Boss, I'm gonna make a killing," said Barry Uncle. "There's a new mindset over there." He started going on about something called the BJP, which would revolutionize things, and a place called Ayodhya, where justice would be done. He would soon be traveling to Delhi, where he planned on meeting a man named Advani.

Mohan Lal grunted. "I've heard it all before, chief. If I recall, you once had an appointment with Indira Gandhi."

"This time it's different."

"Different? Politics don't change, Barry."

"They do. They change when you call on someone with a suitcase full of greenbacks."

They drank another round, and Barry Uncle asked Mohan Lal why his son was watching shit like *Gandhi*. Mohan Lal said that the kids here did what they wanted. They were individuals, not like in Barry Uncle's beloved India. Siddharth was taken aback by the fact that his father was swearing, and that he'd begun to slur his words. But more than anything else, the men's loud voices made him happy. Such boisterous conversation hadn't filled the family room in a long time.

Barry Uncle said, "But he should learn. He should know the truth."

"Oh, he'll learn."

"Learn what?" asked Siddharth.

Mohan Lal burped, then took another sip of whiskey. "The truth about that traitor."

"He was a homo," said Barry Uncle.

"A British agent," said Mohan Lal.

The men clinked their glasses together.

"Boss, you've always spoken the truth," said Barry Uncle. "It's time to share your opinions with a wider audience—to put them down in print."

"My book's almost finished, chief—four months ahead of schedule."

"Yaar, that marketing nonsense is useless. Focus your talents on something important."

Siddharth tensed up. He'd have to say something if Barry Uncle kept criticizing his father. But Mohan Lal was smiling, so Siddharth settled down.

"Okay, sir," said Mohan Lal. "And what would you have me do?"

Barry Uncle tried to take a sip but missed his mouth, the whiskey dribbling down his chin. "You must create something you're passionate about. Something that's gonna make a difference." He wiped his chin with the cuff of his shirt.

"Like what?" asked Mohan Lal.

"How about a book on Partition? A book about independence by someone who actually saw it."

"Maybe in another lifetime," said Mohan Lal.

"Dad, what's Partition?"

His father ignored him.

Barry Uncle finished the last of the cashews. "You know, I've been telling Vineet about you. He's very interested in your perspectives. If you wrote something, I bet he would print it."

"Forget your Vineet," said Mohan Lal, batting the air with his hand. "Forget your Satya Publishers. That Taj book was shit. Not at all respectable scholarship."

"Why, boss? Tell me why."

Siddharth remembered seeing the book—the one that looked like it had been made on a photocopier. Yeah, it was definitely a piece of shit.

"For starters, whatever you may say about the Muslims, at least they knew engineering. The Hindus couldn't build a proper doghouse."

"Well, that's your perspective," said Barry Uncle. He walked over to the entranceway and opened up his briefcase, returning to the sofa with a paperback. "Here's his latest baby. Actually, it's *our* baby. Trust me, this one you're gonna love."

Mohan Lal examined the book, then placed it on the coffee table.

Siddharth grabbed it. The volume was called *Islam and the Infidel: What the World Should Know about Muslims but Is Afraid to Ask.* The cover depicted several bearded strongmen breaking apart a temple with swords and daggers. This drawing was impressive. The men's muscles were nicely shaded, and the carvings on the temple showed a lot of detail. Siddharth hadn't sketched in a while. He would try to copy it later on.

7

SHAKESPEARE SUCKS

As they drove to Woodford that Friday, Siddharth tugged at his uncomfortable formal clothing. His father had made him wear one of Arjun's old blue blazers. It had gold buttons with little anchors on the cuffs. Mohan Lal was wearing a similar coat. Earlier in the week, Ms. Farber had taken Mohan Lal to lunch and given him a pair of bamboo wind chimes, which were now hanging from the maple beside the old bird feeder. She told him that she had bought some theater tickets as a surprise for his birthday and that it would be a shame for them to go to waste. Mohan Lal mulled over her invitation for a couple of days before saying yes. Siddharth had been dreading the thought of the adults going back to their sex, along with the idea of his father being so busy again—of Mohan Lal devoting too much of his energy to Ms. Farber. And yet he also appreciated that he would have his friend back. He wouldn't have to stay after school or spend more lame afternoons with Barry Uncle.

Once they got to her house, Marc greeted him with a high five but barely said hello, which made Siddharth's stomach tighten even further. Ms. Farber gave Mohan Lal a loose hug and no kisses. She then wrapped her arms tightly around Siddharth, whispering that he looked great and that she was sorry. He wondered why she was apologizing—for screwing his father, or for being such a freak on the phone?

The foursome drove to New Haven in relative silence, parking in a private, multistoried lot. Siddharth felt alone and wished he hadn't come. The play, Shakespeare's *Richard III*, was sold out, and throngs of glamorous people were chatting and drinking from plastic cups in the lobby. The women wore long dresses and flashy jewelry. Most were gray-haired and plump, but he nudged Marc and pointed out a few "bangable" ones. Marc cracked a smile but remained quiet. Siddharth felt that familiar emptiness swelling in his chest. It was official: his best friend hated him.

A suited usher seated them, and the enormous, opulent theater made him a little dizzy. Gigantic chandeliers shimmered on the ceiling, and complex patterns were carved into the walls. Just sitting there made him feel older, more mature. Once the performance started, the audience started snickering, but he didn't see what was so funny. At first he thought the English accents were getting in the way, but once he got the hang of them, he decided it was the jokes. They were childish and dumb.

During the excruciating second act, the boys got up to go to the bathroom. Marc slammed his body into a vending machine, which spat out a free pack of Camels. They went outside and stood beneath a tree with bright pink blossoms. Siddharth's mother used to beg his father to drive them downtown to admire these flowers, but Mohan Lal usually said no, making some excuse about parking. Siddharth shook these thoughts out of his mind and focused on Marc, who looked like a full-grown man as he pulled on his cigarette. Only a couple of weeks had passed, but Marc had changed. For one thing, his hair was growing out. It fell over his ears and reached down to his neck. He seemed taller too. Wider.

Marc handed him the cigarette and said, "Yo, why haven't you called?"

Siddharth took a drag and coughed. "What?" Water sprang from his eyes. He spit up some mucous, wiping his mouth on the sleeve of his blazer. "I called, like, a hundred freaking times."

"You're messing with me," said Marc.

A campus police car sped past, splashing oily water on Siddharth's loafers. Had Marc really not gotten his messages? Or was he lying?

Marc took another drag. "I mean, you're, like, one of my best friends. That means we're supposed to keep in touch."

Best friends. That made him feel a little better, lighter. They passed the cigarette back and forth until a homeless man appeared. The guy wore a leather jacket that said *Vietnam Veteran* and was pushing a shopping cart filled with various pieces of junk: a lamp, a tennis racket, some bottles. "Gentleman, I'm very hungry. Can you spare a dollar for some food?"

"Food?" said Marc. "Or a needle and a spoon?"

The man tilted his head to one side, staring at some faraway thing, and gave his torso a thorough scratching. Marc fished his cigarettes from his blazer pocket and handed three of them to the homeless man, who smiled and said, "Your parents—they raised you well."

"My parents?" Marc lit one of the man's smokes. "Dude, my parents are worse off than you."

The man ambled away, the wheels of his shopping cart creaking loudly in the darkness.

Staring down at his soiled loafers, Siddharth mulled over the evening. He was glad that his friend was opening up, but he'd never understand the harsh way Marc spoke about his parents.

"What is it?" said Marc, pushing him on the shoulder. "What's on your mind?"

"Nothing."

"Say it," said Marc.

"Say what?"

"Whatever little thought you're thinking."

"It's nothing."

"Don't be a pussy."

Siddharth sighed. "I need to know something."

"Know what?"

"Were you being serious before? You really didn't get any of my messages?"

Marc held the stubby cigarette between his thumb and forefinger. He sucked a final drag then flicked it into a puddle. "That bitch—she must have forgotten to tell me you called." He stuck a piece of gum in his mouth. "Rachel, she's not like your dad. She's nuts. For the past week, she's been sitting around doing nothing and jabbering like a madwoman. Every night she calls my dad and just starts yelling at him."

"About what?"

"Money and shit. And then he gets on the phone and does the same thing to me. And then one night—one night she smacked me."

"You're joking."

"I'm not fucking joking. She hit me right in the face. I said, *Rachel, I know you're a chick—and you're my mother and stuff—but try that again, I'll give you a beating.*"

After the play, the foursome began the five-block walk to the parking lot, for which Mohan Lal had a special coupon. Ms. Farber had a pleasant but tight-lipped smile on her face. She slipped her hand through Mohan Lal's arm and asked him what he'd thought. He said it had been an invigorating experience. *What a suck-up*, thought Siddharth. He knew that his father hated Shakespeare.

Marc started shaking his head.

"What is it?" said Ms. Farber.

"Nothing."

"Spill it, dear."

"Nah, you wouldn't be interested."

"Marc, I'm always interested in what my son has to say."

Siddharth thought about what Marc had said while they were smoking. If he'd been telling the truth, then she was a really good actress.

"Listen," said Marc, "I know those tickets were worth a bundle, but let me tell you, that play sucked. It was a total piece of crap."

"Language, dear."

Marc was smirking now. "I mean, I thought about jumping off the balcony—just so something interesting would happen."

"Me too," said Siddharth. "I wish I'd had some tomatoes."

"Tomatoes?" said Marc. "What the hell would you do with a tomato?"

"When you see something boring, that's what you do. You throw tomatoes at the stage." He saw Ms. Farber clutch his father's arm more tightly.

She said, "Boys, you're talking about one of the greatest artists to ever live."

"Whatever, I don't see why he's so hyped up," said Marc. "If you ask me, the play was like one of your stupid soap operas—except the chicks were total dogs."

"Cute, Marc," replied Ms. Farber. "But for your information, I don't watch soap operas." She turned to Mohan Lal and poked him in the belly. "And you, mister. Just what's so funny?"

Mohan Lal broke into a grin. "Nothing, but you've raised a smart young man, Rachel. The world lacks people who are willing to speak the truth."

As they walked down the desolate sidewalk, Marc announced that he was hungry. Ms. Farber said she had Ben & Jerry's at home, but he said he needed real food. Mohan Lal suggested they go out somewhere, telling Marc to choose the place. Siddharth was pleasantly surprised by his father's attitude. Mohan Lal was more easygoing around Ms. Farber. That was definitely a good thing.

"We can walk it to Paulie's," suggested Marc. "It's the only decent thing that'll be open."

"I'm not sure about sticking downtown at this hour," said Ms. Farber. "How about somewhere in Woodford?"

"Fret not, dear Rachel," said Mohan Lal. "You have three strong men to protect you."

Siddharth had never been to a place like Paulie's before. It was a squat wooden building that looked more like a cabin than a restaurant. Stepping inside, he found no neon signs, no milkshake machines. He saw no pictures of the toys that could accompany your food for an extra charge.

"Get stoked," said Marc. "This is the best shit you're ever gonna eat."

The place was dimly lit and contained lots of wood. The wooden tables and chairs were oddly shaped and built directly into the walls, and long wooden beams lined the ceiling. Thousands of customers had chiseled their names into every square inch of this wood. Some had even made declarations of love. Marc pointed out a spot below a fire extinguisher where his father had carved the name of the family business, *State Street Scrap*. "That's where I'm gonna work someday," he declared. "Not in some pussy-ass law firm."

Siddharth laughed. He noticed a pair of cops sitting on bar-stools in front of a wooden counter, on the other side of which was the place's rustic kitchen. Standing in the kitchen was a young man with a red mustache and a grease-stained apron. His bright green eyes were focused on a tiny TV mounted above the entrance.

One of the cops, a short, squat guy, addressed the redhead: "What do you think, Ronny? How's about I put a bill on Philly?"

Ronny squeezed his temples. "There's fifteen minutes left in the game, Sam. It's not a bet if you already know what's gonna happen." He extracted a metal cage filled with glistening hamburger patties from an upright iron oven. Actual flames were flickering. This oven seemed strange. Ancient. For some reason, it reminded Siddharth of India.

Ronny served the cops their hamburgers, which came on toast, and the second cop, a tall guy with a shaved head, complained that his was too bloody. Ronny pointed to a sign above the cash register. *This isn't Burger King. We don't do it your way, and we take our time.* Then the redhead finally turned to Marc. "Long time no see, kid." He wiped a hand on his apron and extended it. "Where's the old man?"

Marc shook Ronny's hand. "Somebody's gotta pay the bills."

Ronny nodded at Ms. Farber, who flashed a perfunctory smile and put a hand on Marc's back. Marc ordered a cream soda and a burger, and then Ronny turned to Siddharth. "What about you, kid?"

Siddharth had no idea what to order here, but Marc stepped in and saved him: "Same again for him, Ronny."

Mohan Lal approached the counter and asked for a cheese toast.

"A what?" said Ronny.

"A grilled cheese," explained Siddharth.

"Sorry, sir, we got hamburgers, cheeseburgers, chips, and blueberry pie. Oh, and Monday through Wednesday there's Mother's potato salad."

"You're kidding," said Ms. Farber with a scowl. "People get grilled cheese all the time."

Mohan Lal clasped her elbow. "I think chips would be fine."

Siddharth bent down and peeled a candy wrapper from the bottom of his loafers. He wished his father would just have a burger. But then he remembered what the doctor had said about his cholesterol.

"Junior!" a voice called from behind the kitchen. A few seconds later, an old man walked into the dining area carrying a box of onions. He dropped it on the counter, wiping his hands on his jeans. "Junior, I don't see a big crowd here. We don't have a rush. Would you please give this gentleman what he wants?"

The old man was wearing thick glasses and a plaid flannel shirt. Siddharth wasn't accustomed to the elderly looking so robust. His father's mother had always been shrouded in white and liked to complain a lot. His mother's father had worn a three-piece suit every day, and he was so skinny and old that it looked like the wind might blow him away.

"Welcome, folks," said the old man. "Is it your first time?"

"Me?" said Marc. "I've been here like a hundred times."

The old man squinted at Marc and nodded. "That's right. I know your father—knew your grandfather too."

Mohan Lal took off his blazer and sat on a bench. "Sir, are you Paulie?"

"Me? No. Paulie was my grandfather. Moved here from Ireland and worked the gun factories. Started this place up back in 1892—exactly a hundred years ago." He winked at Siddharth. "So where you folks from?"

Siddharth's pulse quickened; he hated that question.

Ms. Farber sat down next to Mohan Lal. "Oh, we're from the area."

"Actually," said Mohan Lal, "before Connecticut I was a New Yorker."

The old man rolled down his sleeves and buttoned them. "Ah, the melting pot." He sat on the only empty barstool, patting the tall cop on the back. "Used to deliver groceries for my uncle in the Bronx. But where are you *from*—I mean your people."

Ms. Farber placed a hand on Mohan Lal's knee. Siddharth wished she wouldn't touch him like that in front of strangers.

"Me?" said Mohan Lal, pointing at himself. "By birth I am an Indian."

"Thought so." The old man snapped his fingers. His smile widened, revealing a silver-capped incisor. "I spent more than a year of my life in your country. Was stationed in Karachi during the war, and once it was all over, I traveled around with my buddies—some of the best months of my life."

Ms. Farber tilted her head. "You mean World War II? My father—"

"What a country! You've got everything over there. Deserts, mountains. And those cities—they're something else." The old man spread his arms to convey the grandness of these things, winking at Siddharth again.

Mohan Lal was grinning. "Why, thank you."

Siddharth sipped his cream soda, wishing the old guy would leave them alone. He was glad Marc was watching the game, not listening.

"Kashmir," said the man. "That place had the most beautiful ladies. Bet you a hamburger that's where your people are."

"I had some family there." Mohan Lal loosened his tie. "But you could call us Punjabis."

The man shook his finger at Mohan Lal. "My second guess. I swear it was gonna be my second guess. The Punjab—Golden Temple—Amritsar. I bet that's your city."

"Actually, I'm from a small place near a city called Peshawar."

Siddharth was confused; these places were totally unfamiliar to him.

"Which town?" asked the man.

"Abbottabad."

The man snapped his fingers a second time. "Oh, I've been there. Been everywhere in Pakistan." He cocked his head to one side. "Muslim?"

"I'm a Hindu—from a Hindu family, that is."

"So you were a refugee?"

Mohan Lal stroked the stubble that had started to shadow his cheeks. "Yes, we had to move."

The old man puffed up his cheeks and sighed. "It's just awful what they did to each other. Saw the photographs in *Time* magazine. So much bloodshed in such a holy place. I tell you—brought tears to my eyes."

Mohan Lal shook his head. "Well, the Britishers, they threw stones at a hornet's nest. It was a deviant course of action."

"But they left you with so much. That railroad—it's just spectacular. And your army? One of the largest in the world."

"Sir, your sense of history is most impressive," said Mohan Lal.

The old man chuckled. "Well, they actually used to teach you something back when I was a kid." He got up abruptly and disappeared back behind the kitchen.

Ronny handed the boys their sandwiches atop tiny paper plates. Siddharth grasped his burger. It didn't look like much; it had no lettuce or mayo, and there were no pickles or onions. He squeezed the patty, and the toast it was served on turned purple.

"Mine's all dry," said Marc. "I wanted you to have the good one."

Siddharth brought the burger to his mouth. He took a deep breath, then bit down. The meat was moist, but he couldn't stop thinking about the source of this moisture. It was blood from an actual living thing, an animal with parents and children. He could see his own mother's blood splattered across the vinyl seats of her Chrysler LeBaron. As he suffered his meat in silence, the old man returned and started sorting through bags of plastic cutlery. After completing this task, he walked over to Mohan Lal and placed a mole-ridden hand on his shoulder. Siddharth clenched his teeth. He wanted this guy to leave them alone. He wanted to eat in peace.

The old man said, "Can I show you something?"

Mohan Lal was finishing up his grilled cheese. "Please."

Siddharth followed the man's fingers, which were pointing toward a spot close to the ceiling, one of the only brick-laden sections of the restaurant. Amid these bricks were several pieces of stone. Some of the stones were green, and two of them were blue. Only one was white, and the man was pointing at the white one. "Guess where it's from."

"No idea," said Mohan Lal.

"Here's a story for you," said the man. "When I was in Karachi, I made good friends with a nawab. He was a captain in the British Indian Army. Well, we cabled him and said we were going to visit the Taj Mahal, and guess what he did?"

Siddharth prayed that his father wouldn't go off about the Taj Mahal, about how much he hated the Muslims.

"He arranged a special tour," said the old man. "And you'll never guess what they did for us . . . They hung thick ropes from the top of one of those pillars—"

"The minarets," said Mohan Lal.

"That's the word. They hung rope from the top of a minaret, and we put on harnesses and climbed the thing as if it were a mountain. That rock right there—the white one—I took a chisel and carved it out myself. That building is just gorgeous—makes Lady Liberty look like child's play."

Mohan Lal had a wide grin on his lips. "Very true, sir. I couldn't agree with you more."

Siddharth didn't get it. What the hell was his father talking about?

Back in the car, Ms. Farber told everyone to lock their doors. Siddharth watched her pull a cassette from her purple purse. She inserted it into the minivan's stereo, and he resisted the urge to say, *Hey, you should ask first.* The cassette began to play, and an American man started chanting the name *Sitaram* over and over.

Marc snickered, "Cool music."

"Dear," said Ms. Farber, "don't be such a philistine."

"I'm serious," said Marc. "It's kind of trippy."

Ms. Farber said, "Marc, you're too young to know that word."

Mohan Lal turned up the volume. "Where did you get this, Rachel?"

"You like?"

"It's wonderful."

"Mo, let's plan a trip to India," she said. "I would love to see the Taj Mahal."

This nickname—Mo—was new to Siddharth. It wasn't that bad.

"We can go to many places," said Mohan Lal. "But not that one."

"What do you mean?" Ms. Farber turned the music down.

"That's a conversation for another day." Mohan Lal turned onto Chapel Street, passing a herd of drunken students. Siddharth spotted a police checkpoint a couple of blocks ahead.

Ms. Farber clicked her tongue. "I mean, is it a special place for you?"

"No," said Mohan Lal, who was grinning again.

"If it is, that's okay. We all have our pasts."

Siddharth could tell she was growing sullen. "Ms. Farber, don't take it personally. He hates the Taj Mahal."

"What?" she said. "Why's that?"

He told her how the building was a symbol of decadence—how it used to be a Hindu temple until the Muslims came and destroyed it.

"Mo," she asked, "could that really be true?"

"There are grains of truth in every story," said Mohan Lal.

Ms. Farber sighed. "Well, I wish I could say I was surprised."

They were getting closer to South Haven, passing through endless streets of old Victorian homes. Siddharth knew that this neighborhood was bad, and yet some of the houses were large and pretty, if a little run-down. He hadn't realized poor people could live in such nice houses. Mohan Lal slowed down near Saint Rafael's Hospital, pointing out an old brick building where he'd once had a third-floor apartment.

"You mean you lived there with your wife?" asked Ms. Farber.

Siddharth gritted his teeth. When he had visited her office in school, they sometimes spoke about his mother—but it didn't seem right anymore.

"That was in my bachelor days," said Mohan Lal.

"There's just so much I don't know about you. I mean, you were born in Pakistan? I should know that."

"It was India then," said Mohan Lal.

"Well, I should know that too."

Marc leaned forward. "Mom, you're ignorant. I still love you though."

She placed a hand on Mohan Lal's thigh. "Mo, why did he call you a refugee?"

"Nothing is to be achieved by dwelling on such things. Aren't you the one always telling us to be more mindful of the present?"

She started fiddling with her hair. "But I also say that if you've experienced something traumatic, you need to tell that story. You need to talk about it."

"Well, I could say the same thing to you."

They were back on familiar suburban turf. Siddharth gazed at the ancient Yale Bowl, then the pastoral reservoirs of South Haven. He found himself agreeing with Ms. Farber. His father needed to talk more. About his feelings. His past. Siddharth's mother used to say the same thing.

"Marc's grandfather," said Ms. Farber, "he was in the war too."

"Yes, I know," said Mohan Lal.

"Did I ever tell you how he met my mother?"

"Which war?" interrupted Siddharth.

"The Second World War," said Mohan Lal. "Boys, who fought in World War II?"

"*We* did," answered Siddharth.

"And on the other side?" asked Mohan Lal.

"The Russians," said Siddharth.

"You're retarded," said Marc. "It was us against Hitler—the Nazis and the Japs."

"You're the 'tard," said Siddharth. "The Russians are the freaking enemy."

"Oh well," Ms. Farber sighed, "I guess no one wants to hear my story."

"I do." Siddharth reached between the front seats to turn down the volume even more.

* * *

"My parents met in London," she explained. "It was 1945."

"Your mother was a Britisher?" said Mohan Lal

"She was born in Germany, but her parents were from Russia. And when the war started, they shipped her off to England. Can you believe it? She was fourteen years old."

"Too bad her parents didn't go too," said Marc. "Then Hitler wouldn't have gassed 'em."

"Marc!" snapped Ms. Farber. "Not another word."

They took a right toward Woodford, and Ms. Farber continued narrating her mother's story. After arriving in England, she'd studied to become a nurse and got a job in a place called Croydon, and in the hospital there she came upon an American soldier who was totally unconscious. "He'd literally just gotten in from the African front. He was a driver there, and the other troops called him Lucky."

"Lucky?" said Marc. "That's not what I heard."

Ms. Farber shot him a look. Marc drew a finger across his lips to indicate that he was shutting up, then nudged Siddharth and gave her the middle finger behind her seat.

"He was *very* lucky," Ms. Farber went on. "Men sitting right next to him got shot. The truck right in front of him would get destroyed by a landmine, but somehow—somehow—he always made it through without a scratch." She paused to tie back her hair. "But when he was two weeks away from discharge, they put him on a plane out of Egypt. Halfway through the flight, he came down with this crazy fever. They diagnosed him with malaria once he got to London. When he finally came to, he couldn't hear anything, but the first face he saw was my mother's. For some reason, Mom felt something special for him. There was something about his voice. She started bringing him soup from home—she had a room in a boardinghouse—and she gave him sponge baths. She read him books all the time, even when she was off duty."

"What books?" asked Marc.

"Marc, what did I tell you?"

"Jeez, shoot me for caring."

"Do these little details really matter, Marc? She read him Kipling—your grandfather loved Rudyard Kipling. Can I move on? . . . So when Dad was strong enough to fly, he went home to New Jersey and wrote the nurse every single week. Then it became every day. Eventually, he proposed to her in one of these letters."

"And she said yes?" asked Siddharth. He wished his own family had done such interesting things. He wished they'd lived in such interesting places. But the Aroras were boring.

"No, but she did get on a boat and come to America. She moved in with some friends in Brooklyn, other Jews. Mom and Dad dated for two years until she had no choice but to marry him."

"Immigration?" asked Mohan Lal.

"Nope," said Ms. Farber, laughing. "She was pregnant with my big brother."

Mohan Lal held out his hand to her. "You should write this all down and publish it."

She grazed his hand but then started fixing her hair again. "You'll love this, Mo. One time, my father actually got to drive Eisenhower."

"Really?" Mohan turned right onto Ms. Farber's street. "Ike's driver—his main driver—was a woman. Kay. They were lovers." He took a left into her driveway and parked underneath the hoop.

The engine idled, and nobody said anything. Siddharth felt cozy and warm and wished they could just stay right there in the driveway, but Marc shattered the cozy silence: "Listen, story time was great, but I've got to excuse myself—unless you want me to take a dump in the backseat." He stepped out of the van and let himself into the house through the garage.

Ms. Farber took a long, deep breath. "Mohan, this has been . . . Really good. I was thinking . . ." She let out a breathy laugh. "No, forget it."

"What? What is it?" Mohan Lal shut off the motor.

"No, it's all a little too raw still."

"Please, Rachel." He held out his hand.

She didn't touch it. "Not now. It's not the right time."

Siddharth shrunk in his seat, worried that she was referring to him, then Mohan Lal restarted the engine.

Ms. Farber reached for his wrist and took another deep breath. "Okay, I'm done holding things back." She paused before continuing. "Mohan, I want you to come inside. You can have some coffee and go home, and that'll be okay. But you could also stay till tomorrow. That would be fine too . . . What am I talking about? It would be more than fine. I would love it if you both spent the night."

Mohan Lal started rubbing his neck. He stared into the rearview mirror with raised eyebrows, and Siddharth met his eyes. *These people are fucking crazy*, he thought. It was almost as if they were waiting for him to decide. Well, he was done. He didn't care anymore. He had seen what happened when he got in the way. They could do all the screwing they wanted.

He hopped out of the car and jogged toward the house. Marc was in the family room watching *Saturday Night Live*. Siddharth sat down beside him, sinking into the plush leather sofa. He laughed hard, forgetting all about the adults and their love life for a little while.

PART III

1

A WORLD OF SHEEP

The doorbell chimed. Siddharth sighed as he extricated himself from the leather sofa. At the front door, he encountered the whirring of weed-whackers and the bearded postman, who was wearing his summer outfit—gray shorts and a light-blue short-sleeve shirt.

The postman said, "Summer break, kid?"

"Yup."

"I'm gonna need a signature." The postman held up a clipboard, then said, "You're eighteen." He winked. "Right?"

Siddharth forced himself to smile as he signed a pink form. "Thanks," he said, accepting a small envelope from Walton Publishers. He returned to the family room, where a rap video was blaring, then picked up the remote control to mute it. The best thing about Ms. Farber was the fact that she had forced his father to get a real cable box, one with thirty new channels and an actual remote control. He turned on the Indian brass lamp that stood between the two leather sofas and held the envelope to the light. Mohan Lal had sent in his completed manuscript three weeks earlier, and Siddharth was curious about Walton's reaction. A few words were clear—*June 1992, Dear Dr. Arora*—but before he could discern anything else, he felt her hand clutching his shoulder.

"What's that you got there?" asked Ms. Farber. She was wearing an apron with red-and-white checks. It had once belonged to his mother.

"It's for my dad."

She snatched the envelope from his hands. "Sid, how do you like it when Dad goes into your room without asking?"

"Trust me, he likes me to sort the mail."

"Honey, we're all eager, but you need to learn to respect other people's privacy." She strode back to the kitchen, the letter sandwiched between her torso and the skin of her jiggly forearm.

He returned his attention to the television. A Nirvana video was on, so he unmuted it. Arjun had recently sent him a package from Michigan containing a Wolverines keychain and a Nirvana album. In the accompanying card, he wrote that today's pop music was materialistic and superficial, but this group was reinventing old traditions. Marc disagreed—he said that Nirvana was a bunch of pussy-ass posers. As the video played, Ms. Farber's words kept echoing in his head. *How do you like it when Dad goes into your room without asking?* At some point over the past few weeks, she'd stopped using the word *your* before *dad*.

Since *Richard III*, Siddharth had counted that Mohan Lal and Ms. Farber had spent twenty-two nights in the same bed, usually at the Aroras' home. Back in June, when school was winding down, Siddharth had forced himself to forget the fact that his father was now sleeping with Ms. Farber and enjoy the agreeable aspects of this new arrangement. He and Marc were able to stay up late talking in bed or flicking through a *Playboy* together, and in the mornings they brushed their teeth in unison. During the first days of summer, the boys had biked to the playground behind town hall, where they would meet up with other kids, including Luca Peroti. They'd ride down a bumpy, wooded path to a nearby convenience store, where they got candy, lottery tickets, and chewing tobacco. One afternoon, Siddharth and Marc met up with Dinetta Luciani and Liza Kim at a Post Road pool hall. While they played eight-ball, Liza kept touching Siddharth's arm. He told himself that she was begging for a kiss, that next time he would make his move.

But now Marc was in Florida visiting his grandparents with his father and his father's new girlfriend. When he got back, he would have football camp. A full year would have passed since he had gotten arrested, and his grounding would finally be over.

Siddharth wasn't sure whether Marc would hang out with him once he could do anything he wanted.

In the kitchen, Ms. Farber started the noisy blender, the television shimmering in the background. She was at it again, making another dish from her brand-new vegetarian cookbook. He hated to admit it, but she was getting better at cooking. Her meals were rarely delicious, but at least they were a break from Indian food. And he appreciated her concern for Mohan Lal's diet. She made them use sea salt in their food—not table salt—because it would be better for his blood pressure.

"Siddharth!" she called. "Honey, I need you to taste something."

"I'm kind of in the middle of something."

"It'll only take a second. I promise."

He lumbered to the kitchen and found her staring out the window with a goofy smile.

"Look over there," she said, pointing at the backyard.

He saw two turkeys pecking at the ground underneath the maple. "So?"

"Aren't they just beautiful?" She dipped a teaspoon in the blender and handed it to him.

He swallowed her green concoction, then coughed.

"What do you think?"

"It's okay."

"Just okay?"

He tasted another bite. "No, it's good. Add a little salt maybe."

She clapped to herself, then kissed him on the forehead.

He smiled and looked down, slightly embarrassed on her behalf.

As he repositioned himself in front of the television, he thought about the evening that lay ahead of him. The three of them would have dinner together and then maybe watch a movie. It didn't actually sound all that bad. If Ms. Farber weren't there, he and Mohan Lal might not exchange a single word over dinner. Or Mohan Lal would read all night, or babble to Barry Uncle about the BJP on the telephone. The truth was, even though there were many negative things about her—the most obvious one being that she was fucking his father—she brought many good things into their lives, at least when she wasn't in a mood. Thanks to her, they went to the mall, the movies. One time, they had even gone to an art museum in downtown New Haven. At dinner, Ms. Farber asked him about his day, about the books he was reading. At dinner, they had conversations about the cruelty of the death penalty, or why it was important that abortion was legal. When the four of them had dinner together, he sometimes felt as if he had a real family again.

Mohan Lal got home around four and yelled for Siddharth to help him with the groceries.

"Five minutes," said Siddharth.

"With you it's always five minutes," his father said, but he was smiling.

Mohan Lal walked through the family room cradling two paper bags brimming with hairy ears of corn. He had on new khaki shorts, with extra pockets on the side. He also had on new suede running sneakers and a pair of tan dress socks, which were pulled up way too high. He was wearing a collarless green T-shirt, and Siddharth wondered if he had ever seen his father leave the house in a T-shirt before. This one depicted a hotel in Martha's Vineyard, a place that nobody in the Arora family had ever visited.

Siddharth went outside and stretched his arms. He'd been avoiding the outdoors lately, as all the freshly cut grass made his eyes itchy, but he was glad for a break from the sofa. A breeze sliced through the sticky air and cooled his skin. He looped some bloated plastic bags around his fingers and lugged them inside, then froze before entering the kitchen. His father and Ms. Farber were in front of the sink with their arms around each other. Her lips were near Mohan Lal's ear. Siddharth couldn't tell if she was kissing it, or just whispering.

He stepped toward them, dumping his bags on the table. "Did you give it to him?"

"Give me what?" asked Mohan Lal. He slackened his embrace, but his bulging belly remained pressed against her apron.

Ms. Farber playfully smacked herself on the head, then slid open a kitchen drawer. She pulled out the letter and handed it to Mohan Lal. He unsuccessfully attempted to open the envelope with his fingernails, then removed a letter opener from the bottom drawer of the family room bookcase. Years ago, Siddharth had used it as a toy; it resembled a samurai sword.

Mohan Lal sliced open the envelope and read the letter on the family room armchair.

"Come on, already," said Ms. Farber, who was leaning against the kitchen doorway. "Give us the good news."

Mohan Lal removed his glasses and pinched the bridge of his nose.

Siddharth grabbed the letter from him. It was signed by Reginald Feldman, senior editor, and not Mr. Wasserman, the assistant editor who'd previously written.

"Read it out loud," said Mohan Lal.

"Huh?"

"Are you deaf? I said read it aloud."

Siddharth seated himself on the love seat. "*Dear Dr. Arora, this letter is regarding your manuscript entitled* Marketing for the Twenty-First Century: A New Paradigm, *which we received on June 12, 1992.*"

"Louder," said Mohan Lal.

"*While I applaud your efforts to push the boundaries of your field and raise interesting ethical questions, our editorial team—*"

"Stop," said Mohan Lal. "Skip to the next paragraph."

Siddharth cleared his throat. "*Though I personally appreciate your approach, your manuscript, in its current form, might be considered too eso—*" He was unfamiliar with this last word and hesitated.

"Esoteric," said Mohan Lal. "You should know that."

". . . *might be considered too esoteric. Some readers might be repelled by its partisan nature,*" continued Siddharth. "*However, if you can rework your project along the lines we've previously discussed and resubmit in December—*"

"Enough!" snapped Mohan Lal, pounding his fist onto the chair's wooden arm. He shot up and stomped to the dining room. Still holding the letter, Siddharth followed behind, looking on as his father poured himself a tall glass of whiskey, the fancy stuff Barry Uncle had brought over.

"Mo, honey, hang on a sec," said Ms. Farber.

"Leave me," said Mohan Lal.

"We need to talk this through." She put a hand on his shoulder. "There's definitely a silver lining here. Actually, that's an understatement. If you ask me, this is encouraging news."

"She's right, Dad," said Siddharth.

Ms. Farber started rubbing Mohan Lal's back, and Siddharth turned his head toward the window. Outside, a hummingbird was hovering over a withering pink blossom.

Mohan Lal sipped some whiskey. "Listen. Ours is a world of sheep, and this man is the biggest sheep of them all. He's a bullshitter—a coward." He grabbed the letter from Siddharth and crumpled it into a little ball. He chucked it at the window, and the hummingbird fled. "I'm in a useless profession—a useless profession in a useless country."

"Oh, Mo." Ms. Farber brought his fingers to her mouth and kissed them. "They want you to make a few small changes. Just some minor alterations."

"You see, publishing is a business, and businesses exist to make money. Books that sell are written by stooges—people who are willing to uphold prevailing ideas, not challenge them." Mohan Lal scowled. "The dean. He has a long arm now. His fingerprints are all over this affair."

"The dean, Dad?" said Siddharth. "Are you for real?"

Ms. Farber retrieved the letter and placed it on the counter, smoothing it down with the palm of her hand. "I know you're upset, Mohan. But is that really rational? Do you *honestly* think the dean had something to do with this?"

Mohan Lal slammed his glass down. "What do you know about it, Rachel? What do you know about anything?"

"Chill, Dad," said Siddharth. "We're just trying to help."

Siddharth sat in front of the television, feverishly flipping through the channels, regretting that he hadn't thrown the letter in the garbage as soon as it had arrived. He wished that his father hadn't lost it in front of Ms. Farber. She entered the family room and flashed a nervous smile, then went out to the porch and lit a cigarette. He wondered if Mohan Lal had told her she could smoke out there. He wondered if Walton was right about the book. What if it was too esoteric?—whatever that meant. Arjun had once said that their father was addicted to his freakish opinions because he felt so small inside. *Poor Dad*, Siddharth mused, *the man is a genius, but people never appreciate him.*

He plodded down the hallway to his parents' bedroom, where Mohan Lal had holed himself up. The door was locked. Siddharth knocked, but nobody answered. He picked the lock with a tiny screwdriver meant for repairing eyeglasses, something he hadn't done in years. Hearing the shower running, he entered the bathroom. Mohan Lal's dirty undergarments were draped on the toilet seat, and Siddharth brushed them onto the pink vinyl floor.

"Rachel?" said Mohan Lal.

"No, it's me," said Siddharth.

The bathroom was dark and steamy, and he found it peaceful. Mohan Lal shut off the water and started soaping himself. He then turned the tap on to rinse off the suds, muttering a Buddhist prayer to himself. After shutting off the shower a second and final time, Mohan Lal reached for his rough yellow towel. "Son," he said, "your old man can be a fool sometimes." He wiped himself down slowly and meticulously, then exited the bathroom and threw his towel on the patchwork bedspread.

Siddharth hadn't seen his father naked in a long while. The tufts of hair on his ass were totally white now, and his wrinkly penis seemed smaller than before. It was darker too, darker than any other part of his body. He shifted his eyes to the black lacquer nightstand that used to belong to Mohan Lal. It now contained Ms. Farber's things—her reading glasses, a psychology journal, and a couple of orange bottles of pills. On top of his father's dresser sat a stone statue of a blue Indian god playing a metal flute. He had never seen this statue before and wondered where it had come from.

Mohan Lal put on a fresh pair of underwear. He sat himself on the edge of his bed and began clipping his fingernails. Siddharth scrutinized the scar on his father's chest, a hairless depression between his nipples that resembled a map of Florida. A few weeks ago, Mohan Lal had been trying to repair Ms. Farber's busted dryer wearing nothing but an undershirt. She asked him how he had gotten that scar, and he told a story that Siddharth had never heard.

When Mohan Lal was just a baby, he had suffered from various respiratory problems. As a last resort, a Buddhist monk took Mohan Lal up into the mountains and performed surgery on his lungs. But the wound from the operation got infected, and it smelled so badly that Mohan Lal's mother wouldn't hold him. She didn't hold him for an entire year.

When Mohan Lal finished his story, Ms. Farber said that nobody could be crueler than a person's own parents. Mohan Lal insisted that it was no big deal, that it was wrong of Western psychologists to always blame the parents. The thing that really mattered, he said, was that he was still alive thanks to that monk.

Mohan Lal finished with his fingernails and put the nail cutter in a drawer. He threw on sweatpants, then a new pair of beige dress socks. "Son," he said, "will you do your father a favor?"

"Of course."

"Put some ointment on my back? Today it is very sore."

Siddharth grabbed a blue plastic bottle from atop the cistern and squirted the gelatinous substance onto his fingers. It smelled like peppermint, only much stronger. He sat beside Mohan Lal and began applying the cool gunk to the skin of his back, which was soft and warm. Mohan Lal emitted little moans of relief. "Good boy," he said. "I don't know what I have done to deserve such a son."

2

COMMUNAL DINNER

Siddharth was sitting on his bed drawing for the first time in a while, attempting a sketch of a Michigan basketball player taking a jump shot. He planned on turning it into a birthday card for Arjun. Mohan Lal was making a racket in the kitchen, preparing a huge Indian spread for Barry Uncle. The thought of daal and rice turned Siddharth's stomach.

When Marc got home from football camp, he barged into the room and started rummaging through the closet.

Siddharth looked up from his drawing. "What's the plan?"

"The plan?" said Marc. "The plan is, *I'm* sleeping at Andy's." He fished out a flask of Southern Comfort from one of Siddharth's winter boots, and then a can of spray paint from inside a board game.

Siddharth had no idea that either of these things were in his closet. He said, "You're kidding me—graffiti?"

Marc gave the can a rattle. "Nah, makes a good blowtorch." He cocked his head to one side and cracked a smile. "You know what?"

"What?" said Siddharth, feeling hopeful.

"I got a bottle of Bacardi in there—up top, behind that old camera. I think it'll do you some good."

Soon Marc left with his mother, and Siddharth tried to return to his drawing. He wondered how he could make things go back to the way they were with him and Marc. When Marc had first gotten back from Florida, everything seemed fine. He'd even invited

Siddharth to the mall one day and helped him pick out clothes, telling him what would be cool for junior high. After swearing him to secrecy, Marc confessed that his father's girlfriend, Madeline, was pregnant.

"Congratulations," said Siddharth.

"Congratulations? This is bad, Sidney. Very fucking bad."

"Why?"

"Cuz Rachel and my dad—they're past the point of no return."

Once Marc's grounding was officially over, he'd started spending all of his time with Andy Wurtzel, a fourteen-year-old from his junior high school. Marc invited Siddharth out a few times with them, but Siddharth couldn't understand why Marc was so fond of Andy. The kid seemed dumb, and he looked like a bulldog.

When Andy and Marc were together, they talked about stupid things like football, or whether pussy tasted better in the morning or at night. The pair had a penchant for shoplifting, swiping clothes or compact discs or bottles of perfume that Marc later gave to Dinetta Luciani. Siddharth wished he could be more like them, but stealing made him nervous. When he tried to talk like them, the words got stuck in his throat, and he felt they could see right through him.

Sometimes Marc and Andy met up with kids who he suspected were drug dealers, like Corey Thompson, a grubby ninth grader who attended the South Haven branch of Eli Whitney, Siddharth's future junior high. One day, Corey stole a Gamecocks cap from the mall, which he later planted on Siddharth's head. He told him it fit like a glove and that he should keep it. Siddharth started wearing it every day, but he was always uneasy that someone might know it was stolen.

As he struggled to sketch the biceps of his basketball player, Mohan Lal knocked on the door.

"What?"

"Dinner," said his father.

"I'm not hungry," he lied.

"I made you something special. Come and eat."

As usual, Siddharth ate his spaghetti and garlic bread on his three-legged Kashmiri table. Ms. Farber got home around seven thirty wearing a summer dress that made her breasts look bigger than they actually were. She said, "Siddharth, honey, how about putting some newspaper down? I just cleaned the carpet yesterday."

Barry Uncle let himself in twenty minutes later. "Greetings, good evening!" he shouted. He shook Mohan Lal's hand and then gave Ms. Farber a kiss on each cheek. "Rachel, you look especially lovely tonight. I still can't figure out why you're settling for my plump friend over there."

She turned to Mohan Lal and winked at him, then pinched the sleeve of Barry Uncle's burgundy shirt. "This color, Barry, it's just so you."

Siddharth snorted. Barry Uncle's shirt was too shiny, and the sight of his chest hairs peeking through the open top buttons made him want to hurl. And as for Ms. Farber, she could be a real hypocrite sometimes. When Barry Uncle wasn't around, she called him a chauvinist, or a know-it-all. But she kissed his ass in person, asking him all sorts of questions about Mohan Lal's family, about India. Barry Uncle had told her about Mohan Lal's big-shot brother, the one who bribed government ministers and slept with flight attendants. But she was more interested in family history. She once asked him if he had been a refugee, like Mohan Lal.

"Yes, indeed," Barry Uncle responded. "You wouldn't believe the things we saw—the things those Muslims did to our people."

"Chief, you were in diapers," said Mohan Lal.

"Boss, you may be the intellectual, but I have a photographic memory." Barry Uncle grew serious. "And even a baby can remember what they did to Chacha-ji."

"Enough," said Mohan Lal. "Now's not the time for such talk."

Upon Mohan Lal's suggestion, the adults seated themselves in the family room. Siddharth considered heading to the guest room, where Marc had set up a ten-inch TV that he'd salvaged from his father's scrapyard, but there was no cable there, and he wasn't in the mood to be alone.

After a little small talk about Ross Perot and Bill Clinton, the conversation returned to India. Barry Uncle said that the country's main problem was its astronomical population growth, for which the Muslims were to blame. "These Mussulman breed like rabbits," he said. "They have no loyalty to any nation—just to their bloody prophet."

"Forget it, yaar," replied Mohan Lal. "The real problem is the Congress and those bloody Nehrus. They're the ones who let the Muslims get away with everything—just for their bloody votes. They're a bunch of dictators—the reason why India is a sham democracy."

"You said it, boss," said Barry Uncle. "And that's why we gotta get together and support a new party. I'm telling you, the BJP is gonna get India out of the Stone Age. They'll make India a land where people can be proud to call themselves Hindus."

Ms. Farber had been looking on in silence and smiling, but she finally chimed in: "It's like I'm always telling Marc—if you really want success, you've got to love yourself, and that means loving your roots. Embracing your religion, your ethnicity."

"Smart lady," said Barry Uncle. "Rachel, hopefully some of your wisdom will rub off on your man over there."

Your man. The words rang in Siddharth's ears.

Ms. Farber was beaming. "Oh, he's doing just fine in the wisdom department."

Barry Uncle said Mohan Lal wasn't dumb, just tight-fisted. "I've been asking him for a little cash—to get things rolling back home. But this man, he's a Bania—that's our version of the Jews."

"I'll pretend I didn't hear that," said Ms. Farber. She turned to Mohan Lal. "Mo, Shelly and I—that's my ex-husband, Barry—we used to give to a charity in Israel. Let me tell you, when we cut that check every year, it felt so good—like I was really making a difference."

When Barry Uncle asked how Mohan Lal's book was progressing, Siddharth lowered the volume. Since the last letter from Walton, Mohan Lal had been working in the yard and cooking, but he hadn't written a single word. Siddharth knew this wasn't a good thing. When his father wasn't writing, he got grumpy. He became mean.

Mohan Lal told Barry Uncle that things were going fine, which caused Ms. Farber to speak up: "Mo, he's your best friend. You should tell him."

Siddharth furrowed his brow. *What about his privacy?* he thought.

Ms. Farber retrieved the letter for Barry Uncle, who put on his reading glasses. He examined the letter, mumbling to himself as he read.

Mohan Lal leaned forward, grasping his chin. "So, what do you think, chief?"

"You wanna know what I think?" Barry Uncle tapped on his empty wineglass. "I think I need something stronger." He went to the dining room and came back with two tumblers and a bottle of whiskey. He poured out two tall drinks and topped off Ms. Farber's glass with wine. "All I can say is, I'm not surprised. Look, these American publishers are lackeys. Corporate stooges, nothing more."

Ms. Farber took a deep breath and said, "Barry, you can't be serious. I mean, this country has produced some of the greatest literature in the world."

Siddharth sipped his Coke. "She's right," he said. "What about *The Call of the Wild*? It's one of the greatest books, and it's definitely American."

Ms. Farber flashed Siddharth a fake smile as he turned the television back up.

Barry Uncle leaned in closer to her. "Darling, here's what I'm saying: I'm saying that this man . . ." He pointed at Mohan Lal. "This Indian man—he shouldn't be putting all his eggs in a Western basket. He wasn't born into their establishment, so the only way he'll be successful here is if he totes their line."

"You mean *toes*?" said Ms. Farber.

"Whatever," said Barry Uncle. "I'm not the writer."

"You're right, chief," said Mohan Lal. He sipped some whiskey. "Such is the nature of power."

Ms. Farber shook her head. "That's just too cynical. Look at you, Barry. You've been so successful here. Both of you have."

Barry Uncle laughed, then downed his whiskey. "Successful at what? Pumping gasoline? Teaching at subpar colleges staffed by nincompoops?"

Siddharth felt a surge of gratitude for Ms. Farber. Barry Uncle didn't understand America. This was a country where everyone was equal, where everyone could be happy if they wanted—where everyone could get rich. And he didn't like what Barry Uncle was implying about Elm City College. It may not have been in the Ivy League, but it wasn't some half-assed institute in a dusty country where people shat outside.

Ms. Farber grasped Mohan Lal's arm. "Well, I think we need to be encouraging. I think that if Mo puts in the time—if he just bends a little—everything will turn out fine."

"And how can you be so sure?" asked Barry Uncle.

She clasped her hands to her chest. "Because I can feel it right here."

Barry Uncle poured out more whiskey. "Maybe you're right. But I've got a better idea. I've told you all about my publisher friend, Vineet. He's begging for Mohan Lal to sign on the dotted line." He downed some more whiskey and sighed, then launched into a familiar speech about the need to take Nehru and Gandhi to task, to make a tangible impact on actual people and places.

When he was finished, Ms. Farber said, "Barry, that's really very exciting—very interesting. But I still have some reservations. I mean, Mo's a marketing man. How would a book about India affect his tenure?"

Barry Uncle scowled, swatting the air with his fingers. "A book's a book," he said. "And once it's out, you're not gonna have to worry about this tenure-shenure. He'll be into bigger things."

Ms. Farber tilted her head to one side. "But the same thing could happen again. How can we trust your friend, Barry?"

"Yeah, Dad," said Siddharth. "I bet this Vineet guy is just another sheep."

Barry Uncle jammed his fist into the palm of his other hand. "Impossible," he said. "One hundred and fifty percent impossible.

Vineet's a personal friend. And once we win the elections, he'll be a giant in the Indian media. Satya Publishers will be big-time."

Mohan Lal instructed Siddharth to go get his copy of *Islam and the Infidel*, one of Vineet's books. He protested but then trudged over to his father's office. He found the volume in between hardcovers by Peter Drucker and M. Scott Peck, recognizing it by its well-drawn cover—the one with the muscly Muslims destroying a temple. He returned to the family room and handed it to Ms. Farber.

After studying the book, she pinched the bridge of her nose and said, "Mo, this is exciting. This could be a serious opportunity for us."

For us? thought Siddharth. What did his father's writing career have to do with her?

Ms. Farber draped her arm around Mohan Lal and drew him close. "I mean, isn't this what we've been talking about? Isn't this what they call synchronicity?"

"Imagine that," said Mohan Lal. "This foolish old man might finally get a break."

Barry Uncle nodded. "Boss, what can I say? You've found yourself a perfect woman." He raised his whiskey glass in the air. "I think a toast is in order. To the future—to old friends and new beginnings."

The three adults clinked glasses.

Siddharth got up from the armchair to toast with the remnants of his Coke.

3

THE PINKO RETURNS
AS A MULLAH

The morning Arjun was scheduled to arrive, Ms. Farber had her hair straightened at the salon beside the West Haven Martial Arts studio. Siddharth told her it looked nice, and he wasn't lying. She seemed more sophisticated with straight hair, possibly even sexy. Mohan Lal disagreed. He told her she'd wasted her money. "Darling, you look much better in a natural state."

She said, "I know there's a compliment in there somewhere." She had a shopping bag in her hand, from which she pulled a brand-new metal picture frame. She then put a photo of the four of them in the frame, one from the tournament in Springfield in which both boys were wearing their karate uniforms. Siddharth helped her find a place for the photo, and he decided the best location was on the dining room counter, where his mother used to showcase Christmas cards.

When Mohan Lal said it was time to leave for the airport, Siddharth prayed for Ms. Farber to change her mind and stay at home, but she went to Mohan Lal's bedroom and put on a flowing white skirt, then yelled for Marc to get off the sofa and change his clothes.

"I'm not coming," said Marc.

"And why's that?" asked Ms. Farber.

"Because he's not my brother. We're not even related."

She groaned. "Fine, Marc, you can be rude—but don't think there won't be any consequences."

Mohan Lal honked the horn from the driveway, and she dashed

outside. As Siddharth was putting on his sneakers, Marc grabbed him by the wrist. He pulled a condom from his sweatpants pocket and dangled it in front of Siddharth's nose.

"So?" said Siddharth.

"Dinetta's coming over. I'm finally gonna bang her."

"Dude, we're gonna be back in, like, two hours," he said, imagining Dinetta underneath Marc's pale body.

"Two hours? If my dad were driving, it would take, like, three. With Mo behind the wheel, we're talking at least four."

Soon they were on the Merritt Parkway, a Clinton campaign speech blaring on the radio. It was a hazy, humid day, and the air-conditioning struggled to cool the car. He sat there wondering what he could do to make Marc happier about their new living arrangements. He wondered if Marc would ever be like a real brother to him, like on a television show. He wouldn't mind having a Jewish stepbrother. He swallowed. At least Arjun was coming home now.

As they merged onto I-91, Mohan Lal was telling Ms. Farber about a recent conversation he'd had with his new editor. Half-listening, Siddharth recalled the day that his father had signed the contract with Satya Publishers. He'd been at Luca's all day, and when he walked through the front door, Mohan Lal and Ms. Farber were sitting with Barry Uncle and the famous Vineet in the dining room. Siddharth asked what was going on, and his father told him it was an adult conversation. "Go watch some TV," said Mohan Lal. "And keep the noise down." Siddharth asked why *she* was allowed to be there under his breath. Either nobody heard his words, or they chose to ignore him.

Thanks to a traffic jam near Hartford, it took them more than two hours to reach Bradley Airport. They drove though the arrivals area twice without spotting Arjun. Mohan Lal said he would keep on circling while the other two looked for him, but Ms. Farber insisted that he park, and that all three of them go inside and greet him together. They eventually found Arjun on a bench outside near a car rental booth. He was reading a copy of *Harper's* and carrying a green backpack, the kind you would use for camping. His goatee was still there, but there was also a lot of stubble high on his cheeks—as if he hadn't shaved in a couple of days.

Mohan Lal greeted him first with a trademark side hug, his face beaming. "Welcome home, son. What happened to your beard?" he asked, grasping Arjun's chin. "Has my pinko turned into a bloody mullah?"

Smiling, Arjun clapped him on the back. "Oh, Dad," he said. "Maybe it's good that some things never change."

Ms. Farber placed both of her hands on Arjun's shoulders. She was wearing heels, and was almost as tall as him. "Let me have a look at you. You're so handsome—just like Dad." She kissed him once on each of his cheeks.

Finally, it was Siddharth's turn to say hello, but he found that he was frozen. He just stared at his brother, a lump forming in his throat.

"You're huge," said Arjun. "I bet I can't even pick you up anymore."

Arjun bent down and embraced him, and the sound of the screeching cars and chattering travelers suddenly disappeared. In that moment, it was as if he and his brother were the only people at the airport—the only living people in the world. Arjun's strong arms were the best thing he had felt in ages.

As they cleared the airport, Arjun asked if they could turn off the air-conditioning, as it aggravated his breathing. He told them about his bumpy flight, which had arrived forty minutes early, and how he had sat next to a state senator, talking to him about reproductive rights for the entire time. Siddharth couldn't take his eyes off his brother's Indian sandals, which were made of leather and exposed his bristly toes. He hoped Arjun would take off these faggy shoes before meeting Marc.

Ms. Farber asked Arjun for his thoughts on the upcoming election, but before he could respond, Siddharth said that voting for a third party was the best thing for the health of a nation, mimicking one of his father's current talking points.

"Good man," said Mohan Lal.

"Unlike my brother," said Arjun, "I can't say that I share my father's views. A vote for Perot is basically a vote for Bush."

They passed the Colt factory, the one that looked like a mosque, and then a bright billboard advertising an alternative rock station that Siddharth had started waking up to on his clock radio. While he stared out the window, resting his thigh against his brother's, Arjun went on about the inner-city poor. He said that the government needed to give these people tools to live with dignity, and that Clinton was the only candidate who might do this.

"Oh, you're so articulate," said Ms. Farber. "I guess it runs in the family. My only worry about Clinton is Israel. I'm just not convinced he'll prioritize the Jewish people."

Arjun nudged him and arched his eyebrows. Siddharth smirked, though he had no idea what his brother was getting at.

"The point is," said Arjun, "Bush led this country into a ridiculous war. Thousands of innocent people are dead, including some Americans."

"What about the Kuwaitis?" asked Ms. Farber. "Didn't someone have to stand up for Kuwaitis?"

"Exactly, Rachel," said Mohan Lal. "If you ask me, the world should be thanking Bush." Siddharth wasn't surprised by Mohan Lal's words—he was used to his father changing his mind. "Say what you will," Mohan Lal continued, "but this man has done a great thing."

"Great?" Arjun responded. "Invading a country for oil is now a mark of greatness?"

"Why do we revere the kings of antiquity?" said Mohan Lal. "Not for making peace, but because they secured resources."

Arjun pulled at his whiskers. "You're kidding me, Dad."

"Why would I be kidding? Son, Bush has shown the world how to stand up to these Muslims. For that I admire him."

"I know you know better," said Arjun. "I know you're not that dumb."

Siddharth shot his brother a look.

"Yes, son," said Mohan Lal, "your father is a very—"

"Arjun," interrupted Ms. Farber, "I hope you're hungry. Your father has prepared quite a feast for you."

When they got home, Marc greeted Arjun at the door and shook his hand. Arjun said he had heard that Marc was a big Yankees fan. Marc said, "The Mets. I think you mean the Mets." Siddharth knew this was a lie, that his friend really loved the Yankees. But he didn't say anything. Ms. Farber showed Arjun to the guest room and brought him a bath towel, and Siddharth found this whole interaction unsettling. She seemed to be treating his brother like a guest even though this was his house, not hers. But Arjun didn't seem to mind the attention. Before getting into the shower, he told Ms. Farber that the place felt so alive with her and Marc around. These words wounded Siddharth. He wondered what it had seemed like before. Was it too depressing? Or just really boring?

As Mohan Lal heated up their dinner—rajma, bharta, chicken, and paneer—Ms. Farber set the table and plied Arjun with questions about Michigan. He told her that balancing his part-time job with schoolwork was challenging but doable. In May, he had moved into a co-op, where everyone shared the household chores and threw parties together. He explained that over the summer, he had been taking an intensive Hindi course.

Mohan Lal started coughing. "Hindi? You should be focusing on your premed."

"Oh, Mo," said Ms. Farber, "you should be proud. Gents, how about a little wine?"

"I'd love a glass," said Arjun.

"Wine?" said Mohan Lal. "He's only nineteen."

Arjun laughed, but it wasn't a pleasant laugh. "If I'm old enough to pay the rent, I think I can have a little wine."

"Come on, Mo," said Ms. Farber, "one glass isn't gonna hurt."

"Wait," said Marc, "if he gets to break the law, then I'm gonna too."

"Yeah, me too," said Siddharth.

When they were all seated at the kitchen table, Mohan Lal uncorked a bottle of red wine and poured out three glasses. "To what shall we toast?"

"Hang on." Arjun got two small brandy glasses from the dining room cabinet and poured out a little wine for Siddharth and Marc. "In France, kids drink wine all the time. The Europeans have a much healthier relationship with alcohol."

"Let's move to France," said Marc.

Siddharth chuckled. "Yeah, I wanna live in France."

"How about we toast *us*?" said Ms. Farber. "To new beginnings— to the five of us finally being together."

"To us," said Mohan Lal.

Looking around the table, Siddharth felt a surge of contentment. This was his new family, and they were finally all together.

Later that night, when Mohan Lal and Ms. Farber were in bed and Marc was watching a repeat of *The Tonight Show*, Siddharth knocked on the door of the guest room.

"Come in," said Arjun.

He entered.

Arjun was reading a book. "Give me a sec," he said. "I gotta finish my page."

His brother was reading yet another book about India. It was written by someone named Romila, an ugly name. It reminded him of Attila, or Brunehilda. Siddharth sat on the edge of the bed and stared at his brother. Arjun had on boxer shorts with little sail-boats, and he wasn't wearing a shirt. The downy hair on his belly had gotten thicker, and so had the tuft at the center of his chest. As usual, Arjun had on the gold chain that he'd worn every day for the last five years, but he'd taken off the gold King George coin that their grandfather had given them. Siddharth wondered why Arjun had removed it. Had he sold it for drugs?

Eventually, Arjun rested the paperback on his chest. "What's up?"

"Why are you reading *that*?"

"What do you mean?"

"I mean, you're American. Why don't you read about America?"

"Jesus," said Arjun, "I gotta get you out of here."

Siddharth lay down, leaning his back against the wall. He placed his left leg across his brother's waist. Arjun was staring at something, and Siddharth followed his gaze to the far corner of the room, to the family portrait above a dingy love seat. The picture was held in an intricately carved Indian frame. He must have been around four, and he was wearing a red sweater that had been a birthday gift.

Arjun rested his wrists on Siddharth's leg. "I can remember the day it was taken," he said. "Mom had one of her migraines. I think she even puked."

"So why did we go then?"

"Go where?" asked Arjun.

"To get the picture taken. Why did we go if she was sick?"

"She probably didn't want to piss off Dad. Everybody lived in perpetual fear of pissing him off—everybody except for you."

Arjun got up and went to the bathroom, and Siddharth lay there thinking about their mother. Arjun had so many memories of her, which was good, but also a reminder of all that Siddharth would never know. He looked around the guest room and noticed how cluttered it had gotten. Discarded luggage and old furniture lined every wall, and the dressing table was crammed with all kinds of knickknacks. He spotted the brass fisherman they had bought on a family trip to Maine. When you wound him up, he started to spin, and a little music box played "Moon River." Mohan Lal had invented his own nonsensical Hindi lyrics to go along with the tune. Siddharth couldn't imagine him doing something like that anymore.

He started thumbing through the pages of Arjun's book, and a photo fell out. He grasped it by the edges, just as his mother had taught him. The picture was of a girl, about nineteen or twenty years old. She was standing in a room with white marble floors, bending forward and blowing a kiss. She was trying to look glamorous but was clearly also kidding around. Siddharth's breathing quickened. He had suspected that Arjun had a secret love life for some time now. A few months earlier, he had phoned his brother's room, and Arjun's roommate answered. The roommate said that Arjun was out with his girlfriend. When Siddharth later followed up with his brother, Arjun said that his roommate was crazy, then quickly changed the subject to college basketball.

Now he knew why Arjun had been so sketchy. The girl in the photo—his girlfriend—had hips that were too wide. Her hair was floppy and short, and a portion of her bangs were painted pink. But none of that was a big deal. The real problem was that she had a nose ring. The real problem was that she had brown skin. The real problem was that Arjun's girlfriend was Indian.

Hearing a noise, Siddharth placed the photo back inside the book and quickly closed it.

Arjun walked in and gave him a curious look. "What are you up to?"

"What does it look like?"

"I dunno, but I can tell you're up to something."

Siddharth needed to change the subject. "So?"

"So what?"

"So what do you think of her?"

Arjun reached his arms up to the ceiling and then bent down to touch his toes. "You mean Ms. Farber?" He took a few deep breaths while his fingers hovered over the blue carpet, then stood upright again. "To be honest, I like her. She's a little naive—a little conservative. But who isn't around here? And she's attractive—for her age, I mean. And ambitious. Dad needs that. I just hope he doesn't fuck it up."

4

THE CONDITIONING
OF WHITE GIRLS

Ms. Farber cooked everyone breakfast the next morning, and then Arjun drove Siddharth to the Blue Trail in Woodford, where they hiked to some waterfalls. Despite the savage mosquitoes and his itchy eyes, he was happy to have his brother all to himself. He wished he could ask Arjun about his Indian girlfriend, or tell him about the freakish parts of Ms. Farber's personality, but he knew that this was all sensitive terrain. He knew that like Mohan Lal, Arjun could be explosive.

Later, as they were driving to Post Road to do some shopping, he told Arjun how much Barry Uncle had been around lately. Arjun told him that Barry Uncle was tasteless and uncouth—that it was inappropriate of him to try to convince Mohan Lal to sue the truck driver who had rear-ended their mother. As Siddharth listened to his brother talk about their mother's death, he again felt claustrophobic. Arjun spoke about her so openly—so calmly—as if he were referring to some random thing that had happened to a stranger, as if he were recapping highlights from the evening news. How could he be so cold? Didn't he care about them?

"I don't get it," Siddharth said. "I thought you'd be happy about Dad and Barry Uncle. I thought you were the one who didn't want Dad to be isolated."

"Look," Arjun replied, "I don't really care about any of that lawsuit garbage. But I do think Barry's an imbecile. He's an idiot. He's even more simplistic than Dad."

"Dad's not simplistic."

"They're both freaking simplistic—simplistic fascists."

He hated hearing his brother use such cruel words about their father. But they only had a few days together, and he didn't want to waste a second fighting. He needed to change the subject, so he told Arjun that he was anxious about starting junior high. "I'm worried about all the homework. What if I don't make any friends?"

Arjun told him to relax. Seventh grade was a big step, but junior high school students were more mature. "I know you have your thing against sports," he said, "but if I were you, I would definitely run track. The track kids are cool, but they're also smart. And you should definitely run for student council. It's a good way to get noticed. And remember, the coolest kids are the ones with the best sense of humor. Make sure you laugh at other people's jokes."

Soon they were at the mall, and they headed to a shoe store. After Arjun tried on a couple pairs of running sneakers, he picked out some suede bucks for Siddharth's first day of school.

"I'm not sure," said Siddharth.

"Trust me," said Arjun. "They're cool."

On their way home, they passed through the center of town, skirting the annual South Haven County Fair, where their mother had won ribbons for her paintings. From the car, Siddharth was able to catch a glimpse of the fair's antique auto show, with ancient plows and tractors.

Arjun sneered. "This place is really so freaking hickish."

Siddharth frowned. "It's not that bad."

"Trust me—it is."

"Okay, so where would you rather live?"

"A million places. London. Bombay. New York."

"Bombay?" He gritted his teeth. "That'll be perfect. My big brother's gonna live in *India* with his *Indian* girlfriend."

Arjun slowed the car. "What was that?"

"Nothing." Siddharth realized he'd made a mistake.

"Don't be a child. Tell me what you said."

"Honestly, I was just joking around."

"No you weren't. Siddharth, we're gonna have a problem if you don't start talking."

They paused at a stop sign, and he sighed. "I saw a picture of your girlfriend."

"Which picture?"

"The one in your book."

Arjun glared at him, then proceeded across Route 114. "You're still snooping through my stuff. What are you, five?"

"I wasn't snooping . . . It just fell out."

"Of what?"

"Your goddamn book."

"Yeah, right. Grow up, Sid. You're almost a teenager. You gotta stop acting like a child."

"Yeah, I'm the child." He stared out at the beige-colored fields of Miller Farm, where a few fat cows were lazing about. "I'm not the one who's going out with an Indian girl. Who would do that? That's disgusting."

Arjun pulled over close to the old Miller farmhouse, where Sharon Nagorski's great-uncle still lived. "What did you say?"

"You heard me. Who the hell would want an Indian girlfriend?"

"You don't know how stupid you sound." Arjun shifted into park, then turned off the engine. "But I suppose it isn't your fault." He grunted. "You're so brainwashed. And for your information, she's not even Indian."

"Right. I guess she's Polish. Chinese maybe?"

"Just drop it." Arjun started up the car.

"Is she from Siberia? Where was she born? Oh, I know—Mars?"

"Stop, Siddharth. You're making a fool of yourself."

"I'm a fool? You're the one who's screwing a freaking Indian."

"You're an idiot," Arjun said, twisting up his lips. "And she's definitely not Indian."

"So where's she from then?"

"None of your business."

"Tell me."

"She's from Michigan, alright?" Arjun was gripping the steering wheel so hard that his knuckles turned white. "And her parents—they're from Pakistan."

"You're joking."

"Would you just shut up? And not a word to Dad."

"What are you gonna do about it? Beat me up?"

Arjun reached over and grabbed the back of Siddharth's neck.

"Ow!"

"No, but if you say anything, it's over between us. I won't even look in your direction."

On the final night of Arjun's visit, the plan was for everyone to go out to dinner and a movie. Siddharth was dreading the evening. He and his brother had made up, but since they had wasted some precious time fighting, he wanted to be alone with Arjun—or at least have it be a family affair, just the two of them and Mohan Lal. An hour before they were scheduled to leave, Marc claimed to have a stomachache and said he wasn't coming, which eased some of Siddharth's tension. At seven p.m., everyone else piled into the minivan and headed toward Pasta Palace. Ms. Farber had decided she didn't care for the place, calling it loud and garish. But Siddharth still liked it, and it remained Mohan Lal's favorite restaurant.

As they approached the center of South Haven, Mohan Lal told Arjun about the shady land deal that had led to the destruction of the Carter Family Horse Farm, which had been turned into a new complex of large luxury homes. Converting this type of agricultural land into commercial property was illegal, but Mrs. Carter, the town treasurer, was friendly with the South Haven mayor, Bob Swirsky. Swirsky had the town charter amended so that she could sell the land quickly, and for lots of money. Within a few months, Mrs. Carter had bought a brand-new six-bedroom home in Woodford. Bob Swirsky was driving around South Haven in an S-class Mercedes.

Mohan Lal said, "What a marvelous place that farm was. But corruption has a way of spoiling beauty."

"Bob Swirsky?" said Arjun. "I think he used to be my bus driver. Always seemed kind of sleazy."

"Ah, small-town politics," said Ms. Farber. "Aren't they just charming?"

Siddharth stared out the window at the new luxury mansions, which were still empty, not even up for sale yet. He didn't miss the Carter Farm. He barely ever thought about those afternoons with his father and the horses. As far as he was concerned, they could destroy every single farm in town. If there were more mansions in South Haven, then they would be cheaper, and the Aroras would be able to afford one.

When they got to Pasta Palace, the restaurant was crowded as usual. The hostess, who had abundant cleavage and lots of hair spray, told them they would have to wait for at least twenty-five minutes. But Mustafa, the Pakistani manager, came over and said, "Sweetheart, these are my oldest customers. I think we can squeeze 'em in Beth's section." He slapped her on the ass, then kissed another customer on each of her cheeks.

Ten minutes later, they were seated at a cushioned booth. The clamor of conversation and clanking silverware had a calming effect on Siddharth, who made sure that his knee was touching his brother's thigh. Arjun would be gone tomorrow, and he wanted to remain as close to him as possible for the next eighteen hours. Their waitress, Beth, had spiky hair and called everyone "honey." Siddharth told her he wanted his usual, baked spinach ravioli, and Ms. Farber ordered soup and salad. She shot Mohan Lal a look when he ordered the veal parmigiana, and he changed his order to broiled scrod. She told Arjun that he was young still, and that he should try the veal.

"I'll have the eggplant," said Arjun. "Eating veal's a tad uncivilized."

As they ate bread and salad, Ms. Farber told Arjun that studying premed was admirable. "I'm sure your mother would have been very proud."

Siddharth coughed, then downed some ice water.

"Actually," said Arjun, "I've been meaning to mention it. I'm not really sure medicine is for me anymore."

"What?" said Mohan Lal, crunching a piece of lettuce.

"Let me guess," said Ms. Farber. "Law school?"

Arjun started fiddling with his facial hair. "Actually, I find the humanities very inspiring. I'm thinking about becoming a history major."

Ms. Farber smiled. "You'll be a professor, just like Dad." She patted Mohan Lal on the shoulder.

"No, not like my father," said Arjun.

Mohan Lal took a swig from his bottle of Becks. A pimply busboy dropped off a fresh basket of bread. Siddharth knew the busboy's little brother, who was a fifth grader at Deer Run.

"History," said Ms. Farber. "Are we talking Potsdam? Or Napoleon?"

"More like South Asia," said Arjun.

Ms. Farber squinted. "You mean Vietnam?"

Mohan Lal scoffed at her. "*South Asia* is a term invented by the CIA," he said. "It refers to the region that was once British India."

Arjun shook his head. "Why do you always have to be so cynical?"

Siddharth nudged his brother.

The waitress arrived to clear their salad bowls. "We all set with drinks here?"

"I'll have another beer," said Mohan Lal.

"I'll have one too," said Arjun.

Ms. Farber told Arjun that he would make a great history professor. She told him that he would be a big help with the book Mohan Lal was writing about India.

"I highly doubt it," said Arjun.

Siddharth didn't like the way his brother was smiling, sensing trouble.

The waitress arrived with their beers, and Mohan Lal took a long sip. "You doubt it?" he said. "Son, what is it that you doubt?"

"Forget it," Arjun responded.

"Be a man," said Mohan Lal. "Speak your mind."

"You want me to be a man? What does that even mean?"

Ms. Farber squeezed Mohan Lal's wrist. "Arjun, I think your father just wants you to communicate a little more clearly."

Arjun drank from his green bottle, then shook his head. "What I'm saying is that I want no part of that thing. I'm saying that I could never work with someone like him."

Siddharth gave his brother a light kick on the shin. Arjun then stomped on his toes, and he had to bite his own wrist to keep from yelping.

"You're a hater, Dad." Arjun said Mohan Lal had taught them how to hate since they were children—hate Gandhi, hate Nehru, hate the Muslims. "I guess I shouldn't blame you. You were programmed by the British. They programmed your whole generation so they could control you."

"The British?" Mohan Lal thumped his hand on the table.

"Guys, let's keep it down," said Ms. Farber.

Siddharth had been about to say the same thing, but it didn't sound right coming from her. She wasn't family, and she shouldn't have butted in.

Mohan Lal leaned in toward Arjun. "Let me tell you something about the Britishers. If it wasn't for them, we'd still be shitting in the trees. And as for your Nehru and Gandhi, these fools were British agents. Look what they did to your beloved Muslims. Look what they did to Jinnah."

"That was politics," said Arjun.

"Politics? What about Abdul Ghaffar Khan?"

"Who?" said Arjun.

Mohan Lal smirked. "You're the one in chains, my son. The chains of a pseudointellectual."

Arjun opened his mouth to speak. Siddharth knew that he was about to say something bad, something he wouldn't be able to take back. Fortunately, just at that moment, Mustafa and the pimpled busboy arrived with their meals.

"Wow, what a feast," said Mohan Lal.

"Buon appetito," said Mustafa.

Mohan Lal said, "Mustafa, tell me what to do."

"Why, what's wrong?" asked Mustafa.

Mohan Lal grinned. "What's wrong? What's wrong is that my son is a bloody pinko."

Siddharth watched Mustafa chuckle, and the combination of his smile and his thick mustache made him resemble Bugs Bunny.

Mustafa said, "Oh, I wouldn't worry about it. He's just an intellectual, like his pops."

"Please," Mohan Lal replied, "speak some sense into him. Tell him the truth about Gandhi."

"Gandhi?" said Mustafa. "That guy was a crook. My pops, back in Pakistan, he said they were all a bunch of crooks. Gandhi, Nehru—Jinnah too." He pawed his jet-black hair. "It's the same with all the politicians. We work, and they stuff our money in their pockets. Only good one was Reagan. He locked up the crooks. He did something about all the welfare."

After Mohan Lal paid the bill, they agreed to skip the movie and go straight home. Nobody said a word as they drove through the darkened streets of South Haven. Arjun put a hand on Siddharth's knee, but he stared straight ahead at the pale hairs of Ms. Farber's neck. For a moment, he wondered if he hated Arjun. He contemplated telling Mohan Lal about Arjun's Pakistani girlfriend. But then he realized something: His mother would have wanted him to prevent Mohan Lal and Arjun from fighting. She would have wanted to keep them together. He swore that he would never tell his father about Arjun's girlfriend, not for as long as he lived. He thought about Mustafa, which made him hopeful. If Mustafa could be so nice—so normal—then maybe Arjun's Pakistani girlfriend would be normal too. If Mohan Lal could get along with Mustafa, then maybe he wouldn't go ballistic about Arjun's girlfriend.

When they walked into the house, the television was on, but the sofas were empty.

"Marc!" yelled Ms. Farber, peeking into the kitchen.

Siddharth found the remote control and started flipping through the channels.

Mohan Lal headed for the dining room; Siddharth knew it was for a whiskey.

"I hear music playing," said Arjun. He walked toward the guest room and was soon yelling at the top of his lungs: "Dad, Rachel! You better get over here!"

Siddharth sprang up and sprinted through the kitchen, passing his brother, who was walking in the opposite direction and smiling. Somehow, Ms. Farber made it to the guest room before him. She was standing in the doorway, her bony fingers covering her mouth.

"Oh, Marc," she said. "Marc, what the hell is going on?"

Siddharth was now behind her, and when he peered inside the room, his knees buckled.

Marc was on the guest room bed fastening his belt. Dinetta was next to him, buttoning up her checkered shirt. On the pink love seat, underneath the family portrait, sat Andy Wurtzel and Liza Kim. Andy was wearing plaid boxers, holding his face in his hands. Liza was swathed in a green blanket, one that Mohan Lal liked when watching late-night television. Various articles of Liza's clothing were in a pile by her feet. There was a black bra, a pair of jeans, and a peach-colored T-shirt. Siddharth glared at Marc. How could he have done this? Liza was supposed to be for him.

Dinetta was bawling and babbling, saying, "I'm so sorry, Mrs. Kaufman, I'm so sorry."

"That's not my goddamn name, Dinetta." Ms. Farber's teeth were clenched, and her nostrils were flaring. "I expected this from you, Marc—but not you, Andy. What am I gonna tell your mother?"

Marc stood up, his face red and sweaty. "Chill, Rachel. What? You and Mo are the only ones who get to have any fun?"

"Shut up, Marc," said Ms. Farber. "For once, can you just shut up?"

Siddharth felt a hand on his shoulder. He turned to find his father standing there with a drink in his hand.

"Jesus," said Mohan Lal.

"Just go, Mo," said Ms. Farber. "Girls, put on your freaking clothes."

Mohan Lal whistled. "What's going on?" He stepped forward, his eyes wide and furious.

"Mo, you need to leave right now," said Ms. Farber. "You need to let me handle this."

Siddharth stared at Marc, who was gesturing at him and jerking his head toward the floor. He followed his friend's movements and noticed Mohan Lal's bottle of Old Monk rum on its side.

"Kick it," whispered Marc.

He moved closer to the bottle. He knew that if he gave it a light tap, it would roll under the bed and might go undiscovered—but he couldn't bring himself to do it.

That night, Siddharth's AC wasn't working, so he went to bed with the window open. It was hot, and the cicadas were loud and relentless. He found it difficult to sleep. He stared up at an old hook that was screwed into the ceiling. His mother had put it there to hang a pole, from which his stuffed animals used to dangle. Had she done that for his birthday? Or was it just for the sake of it? He couldn't remember, which made his chest feel even heavier. It was hard to think coherent thoughts with all that had happened. Ms. Farber and Marc had left with Marc's friends. Mohan Lal had raised his hand behind his ear, the way he did when he was really pissed.

"Mo, take it easy," she'd said.

"You want that I feel easy?" replied Mohan Lal. "This *go easy* mentality is the bloody problem."

"The problem?" said Ms. Farber. "And what problem is that?"

"The problem, Rachel, is you. The problem is that you cannot control your son."

"Right, you're an angel," Ms. Farber had said angrily, dabbing her eyes. "You're parent of the fucking year."

As Siddharth lay in his room, he wondered if this was the beginning of the end. If it were, would that be good or bad? His clock flashed 11:42. He wished his brother would come and check on him. He wished his brother wouldn't give their father such a hard time. Mohan Lal had done so much for them both despite all that he had been through. But it wasn't like things had been easy for Arjun either. He would be leaving tomorrow, and Siddharth felt horrible that his trip had gone so badly.

He got up out of bed and made his way down the hallway, scraping his fingernails against the wallpaper. His shoulder bumped one of his mother's paintings, but he didn't pause to straighten it. Mohan Lal was slouching on the sofa, a whiskey glass resting on his bulging belly. Siddharth rushed past him to the guest room.

Arjun was on the bed, shirtless, reading his India book—the one by Romila, or Brunehilda, or whatever her name was. His eyes were a little red, and Siddharth knew he'd been crying. Nothing made him feel more hollow inside than seeing his brother cry. He seated himself beside Arjun, resting his head on his thigh. He listened to the soft crackle of his brother turning his pages, to the cries of the ceaseless cicadas.

Arjun closed his book. "So I take it your friend has a girlfriend."

"Kind of."

"What about you?"

Siddharth shrugged. "That Korean girl—Liza—I hooked up with her once."

"What do you mean, *hooked up*?"

"I mean I kissed her."

"You're lying," said Arjun.

"I swear to God."

"I don't believe in God," said Arjun. "Swear on my life."

"Look, we French-kissed. At least she's not a Pakistani."

Arjun returned to his book, underlining a passage in pencil.

Siddharth cocked his head to one side and examined his brother's beard. It looked neater now. Arjun had shaved his neck. A few bristles on his hairy chin were red, which Siddharth thought was a good thing. Perhaps some English blood cells flowed through their veins after all.

Arjun cleared his throat. "I just want you to remember that it's not your fault."

"What's not my fault?"

"This whole thing with girls."

"What whole thing with girls?"

"Listen, when the time comes, you might find it hard to get a girlfriend."

"But I already told you—I hooked up with Liza."

"It was hard for me too, you know." Arjun smiled. "The white girls, they wouldn't give me a second look. But that's the way they've been conditioned. They're attracted to guys who remind them of their fathers."

"You don't know everything, you know," Siddharth muttered.

Arjun returned to his book once again. Siddharth lay down beside him and stared up at the white swirls on the ceiling. He remembered a day many years ago when Barry Uncle and Mohan Lal had painted the entire guest room. His mother had made them fresh puris, and everyone had seemed happy. He fought to keep his eyes open but was soon asleep.

He woke up to Arjun's gentle snores and the singing of a bird. The lights were off, but morning was softly glowing outside the window. His elbow grazed the flesh of his brother's back. Arjun's skin felt nice, so he touched it with the tips of his fingers. He was dreading the day ahead of him. He was dreading the entire school year.

PART IV

1

PUSSY MAN

Eli Whitney Junior High was a drab single-story building, a part of which seemed much taller due to the vaulted ceilings of the gymnasium. A concrete slab in the school's foundation announced that it had been built in 1958. Arjun had gone here six years earlier, and the trophy case in the lobby still contained two of his photos.

In one photo, Arjun was standing with his cross-country track team, which had come in second place at the regional finals that year. The other photo was of him, Iris Chang, and William Evans, all three of them with braces and glasses. They had just won a statewide science olympiad for ninth graders. During Siddharth's first days of school, he occasionally paused to stare at these photos on his way to the bathroom. But he never mentioned them to any of his friends.

The school combined kids from three different elementary schools—Deer Run, Lower Housatonic, and Rolling Ridge. Siddharth had attended two of these schools in his short academic career, so there was no dearth of familiar faces in his seventh grade class. But during the first days of junior high, he dreaded reconnecting with the students from Rolling Ridge, where he had spent first through fourth grades. Those kids would always talk to him in that irritating formal tone, which said it all: *We feel bad for you, you single-parent loser.* To those kids, his friendship with Luca Peroti or Marc Kaufman would never matter. He would always be the boy with the dead mom.

He dreaded seeing his neighbor, Timmy Connor, who was now an eighth grader at Eli Whitney. Siddharth had successfully avoided the Connor boys over the past couple of years, ducking down in Mohan Lal's minivan when they passed them on the road, or staying out of the backyard when Timmy and Eric were cutting the grass. But now he was on the same bus as Timmy, so it would be almost impossible to escape him.

During the first two days of school, he timed it so that he was a solid five hundred feet behind Timmy on the three-quarter-mile trek to his new bus stop in front of the rickety Miller farmhouse that belonged to Sharon Nagorski's great-uncle. When he got to the top of his street on the third day of school, however, he found Timmy waiting for him. He was standing there with his faithful mutt, Naomi, wearing white jean shorts and a black tank top. His hair was spiked, with little lines shaved into the sides of his head.

They greeted each other with a handshake and walked in silence, kicking a gray stone back and forth to each other. As they neared the farmhouse, Timmy finally spoke: "Yo, what's up with those people who are always over at your house?"

"Which people?"

"That woman. The one who's always with that tall kid."

"Marc Kaufman? He's my best friend. She's his mom."

"Kaufman?" said Timmy. "Wait, I've heard of Marc Kaufman. Isn't he, like, nuts?"

"Nuts? He's really nice, actually—really cool." He tensed up, preparing for an avalanche of further questioning.

Fortunately, Timmy changed the subject, telling him that his brother Eric was dating a hot senior. "They haven't done it yet, but he's doing her up the butt."

"Gross," said Siddharth.

"Why, you gay or something?"

"Nah. I'm just more of a pussy man myself." He looked over at Timmy and was relieved to see he was smiling.

"Yeah, me too. But he doesn't wanna get her pregnant."

Even though things were going smoothly with Timmy, Siddharth still dreaded seeing his ex–best friend, Chris Pizzolorusso. He had slept over at Chris's house at least a dozen times when he was younger, and his mother had been friendly with Chris's mom. After the accident, Chris had tried to be nice. Every time he called, he said, "I'm here if you wanna talk." Siddharth had found that shit suffocating, so he cut himself off.

For the first week of seventh grade, he glanced down whenever he passed Chris in the hall, or took refuge in the lavatory upon spotting him at lunch. One day, as he was squirting ketchup onto his fries in the cafeteria, he felt someone touch his shoulder. He turned to find Chris standing there with a smile on his face. He had braces now, and was much lankier.

When Chris started going on about a summer fishing trip to Lake George, Siddharth loosened up. He even made a couple of jokes, saying how their new English teacher must do her hair in the morning by sticking her finger in a light socket.

Chris laughed, but then suddenly got serious. "Yo, I gotta ask you something."

"What?" said Siddharth, grinding his teeth.

"Those shoes—are they, like, suede?"

"Yeah. Yeah, they are." He breathed out in relief. "Of course they're suede. I don't wear that fake-ass shit."

"Dude," said Chris, "I gotta get me some of those."

The person he most dreaded seeing was Sharon Nagorski, and when he spotted her in the back corner of his first-period English class, he made a plan: he would have his father call up his guidance counselor and get him transferred to another class.

His English teacher, Mrs. Wadsworth, was a tiny elderly woman with a bloated belly, which made her appear pregnant. She had a crown of jet-black permed hair, but her curls were so thin that the purple dye stains on her scalp were visible underneath the flickering tube lights. On the first day of school, Mrs. Wadsworth recognized his surname while taking attendance. "Arora?" she said. "I have fond memories of an Arjun Arora. Would you by chance be his son?"

"His son?" said Siddharth. "Uh, he's my brother." Several students laughed. He wasn't sure if they were laughing at him or with him. He recalled Arjun's observation: *The funniest kids are the coolest ones.* "If he was my father," Siddharth continued, "he would have had me when he was, like, seven. They'd probably put him in *The Guinness Book of World Records* or something."

The class erupted with laughter.

"Well, he was a beautiful writer," said Mrs. Wadsworth. "I'll be expecting great things from you, Mr. Arora. And no funny business, because I know your mother too. My husband was a veteran of the Second World War—God rest his soul—so I had the privilege of making her acquaintance."

Siddharth stared down at his desk, telling himself that most of the other kids didn't know a thing about him or his family. And the ones who had known probably didn't remember. But he felt a pair of eyes on him and turned to find Sharon looking in his direction. Her hair was much shorter, and a little darker, and pimples now marred her cheeks. She offered him a faint smile, but he ignored it, returning his attention to the front of the classroom.

Later that week, they were going over their first reading assignment in English class, Jack London's "To Build a Fire," which Siddharth hadn't liked as much as *Call of the Wild.* He stared out the window during the classroom discussion, and Mrs. Wadsworth slammed her book on her table to get his attention. She demanded that he tell her about the story's principle theme. Siddharth said, "The theme? I dunno—like, winter sucks." Various students snickered, which made him feel good, but when he saw Sharon covering her mouth and grinning, he felt a real rush. He didn't know why, but he liked making her laugh. He wanted to make her laugh even harder.

Another time, they were reading a short story by Kipling, and Mrs. Wadsworth singled him out to ask if the story rang true. He said, "Ring true? I don't even know what that means."

"What I mean is, does this story's description of India seem authentic to you?"

"Authentic? How am I supposed to know?"

"I'm quite certain you've been to India before. At least your brother was a well-traveled young man."

He turned to Sharon, who was smirking, which made his chest tingle. Sharon's smile made him feel gutsy. Strong. "If this was really India," he said, "then the characters would be complaining about how bad it smells. They'd probably say something about their stomach hurting, because if you eat anything there, you get really bad diarrhea." He turned to Sharon, who was laughing so hard that she snorted. He felt like he had won some sort of victory.

The pair also had fifth-period science together, and during the second week of school, when their teacher, Mr. Polanski, told the students to pick a permanent lab partner, Sharon asked him to work with her. He didn't really know anybody else in the class and said yes. By the end of the month, they were speaking on the phone at least once a week to complete their lab reports.

At first he dreaded these phone conversations, fearing that she would bring up what had happened between them. But Sharon never mentioned their fight. She didn't mention Luca Peroti, and talking on the phone with her—an actual girl—began to make him feel good, even if she was still a pariah who had lugged around that stupid trumpet case. In some ways, Sharon had changed a lot since sixth grade. The most noticeable thing was that she was quieter now—more serious. She never wore skirts or dresses anymore, just black jeans or black tights, and baggy sweatshirts that fell below her waist. But he could tell that her breasts had gotten bigger, and he liked the way she decorated her eyes. They were always outlined in black, and her eyelashes seemed longer. They seemed wetter than everyone else's. He occasionally wondered if she'd be more game to put out for him than the popular girls, but he always repented this line of thinking. Luca wouldn't let him live it down if he hooked up with a freak like Sharon Nagorski.

During their phone conversations, he and Sharon soon began talking about topics unrelated to English or earth science. At first, he preferred to keep focused on simple things, like their teachers, music, or the latest season of *Beverly Hills 90210*, a program Arjun said was indicative of America's postwar decline. But Sharon, just as before, liked to get more personal. She told him about her weekends, which were surprisingly exciting. He had imagined that she sat in her bedroom alone on weekends playing trumpet and reading, but she usually hung out with her older brother's friends, some of whom had dropped out of high school. These kids were often at Sharon's house, drinking beer and playing bumper pool while her mother was at work. Sharon said she didn't like booze, but she smoked cigarettes, one a day and more on weekends. She said, "Drinking's lame. It turns people into jerks. Cigarettes are different though. They help you think more. They make all the annoying shit in life a little bit better."

He told her about his weekends, though he was careful to censor these conversations and leave out any details involving Luca. He also avoided mentioning Mohan Lal and Ms. Farber. But as the weeks passed, he found himself opening up about other parts of his life; Sharon was the only person he told about Arjun's Pakistani girlfriend.

"I don't get it," she said. "What's the big deal?"

He tried to explain that Pakistanis were bad people.

"But why?" she asked. "What did they ever do to *you*?"

"It's complicated. They've just always been cruel to Indians, for like thousands of years. And if my dad finds out, he'll go ape shit."

"I think it's romantic," said Sharon. "Very *Romeo and Juliet*."

"That's Shakespeare, isn't it?"

"Duh."

"Shakespeare fucking sucks."

"Siddharth, you sound stupid when you say things like that. You sound like such a typical guy."

"What's wrong with that? I *am* a typical guy."

"No you're not."

Sharon told him about her parents' legal battles over alimony and their fight over their large collection of LPs. Her father now lived on a lake in North Carolina and sometimes played harmonica in a band. She hadn't yet visited his new house, as he was usually driving his truck, moving freight between Florida and Kentucky.

Her mother worked the night shift at the phone company, and on Fridays as a waitress at a Tex-Mex restaurant; she spent Saturday evenings with her new boyfriend, who Sharon said was dopey but fine. On the phone one night, Siddharth asked her if her mother was going to marry him.

"I hope not," she said. "What about your dad?"

"What about my dad?"

"Him and Ms. Farber—are they gonna tie the knot?"

"What are you even talking about?"

"Come on, Sid. Don't be so immature."

"I'm not being immature."

"So answer my question. How serious are they?"

"How the hell am I supposed to know?"

"You're not stupid," said Sharon. "I mean, they're sleeping together—right?"

"Gross. No way." He needed to change the subject. "What about you?"

"What about me?"

"Have you ever done it?"

"I just turned thirteen, for Christ's sake."

"Well, how far have you gotten?"

"Siddharth, what I do with my boyfriend is none of your business."

"Boyfriend? You have a boyfriend?"

"It's no big deal. He's just a friend of my brother's."

"You're lying."

"I'm not lying. He's from East Haven."

"Sharon, I can tell when people are lying."

"Don't believe me. What do I care?"

2

SOME SORT OF ZIONIST

Whenever Arjun called to check on Siddharth during the first days of September, he refused to say hello to Mohan Lal. Arjun said he didn't have time to rehash a bunch of bullshit with a closed-minded bigot. The situation frustrated Siddharth, especially because his mother would have wanted him to fix it. He pleaded with Arjun to make up with their father, and Arjun eventually relented.

By the first week of October, Arjun and Mohan Lal were talking once a week. This truce pleased Siddharth, at least at first. But soon they were speaking several times a week, causing him to feel pangs of jealousy. He began listening in on their calls, to find out if they were exchanging declarations of love or secrets about his progress at school. He needed to know if Mohan Lal was telling Arjun about a covert plan to marry Ms. Farber.

Each time he eavesdropped, he was relieved—and also annoyed— to discover that they were just going on about India. Mohan Lal called Gandhi a "traitorous homo," a stooge who had "let the British chop India in two," whereas Arjun said that "the Mahatma altered the course of modern politics." Arjun said, "Don't you get it? If you fight force with force, then the violence never ends." When he called the Indian Congress Party a "truly progressive political party," Mohan Lal said, "Bullshit. It's a criminal organization. How can a party be progressive when it murders innocent Sikhs?"

"So it's okay to kill Muslims?"

"Did I say that?" asked Mohan Lal.

"It's what you're implying, Dad. You're starting to sound like some sort of Zionist."

"What's wrong with that? Son, the Israelis have done quite well for themselves. Thanks to the Jews, an impoverished desert is now a blooming civilization."

"I'd talk to a couple of Palestinians about that. I'd look up the word *oppression* in the dictionary."

Many of their debates led back to Israel, and Siddharth couldn't fathom why his brother had such a problem with that country. Andy Wurtzel had gone there the previous summer, and he got to drink in bars and go spelunking. Andy had also reported that Israeli girls gave good blow jobs. When Siddharth tried to ask his father about Israel, Mohan Lal was dismissive. He said, "For now, just focus on your studies. One leftist son is enough."

Mohan Lal was in his own world as summer faded into fall. He was always working on his new India book, or reading some paperback or magazine from India. He had taken to pacing around the house with an old tape recorder, sometimes listening to cassettes of motivational speakers provided to him by Ms. Farber, but usually studying recorded political speeches in Hindi. Barry Uncle acquired these for him on his frequent business trips to Delhi.

Mohan Lal kept listening to one particular politician over and over again, a woman who sounded rather manly. Ms. Farber said the woman sounded so passionate, and Mohan Lal explained that her life was truly inspiring. She had been born a pauper, but thanks to the BJP, she had managed to make a success of herself in one of the most backward places on earth. Siddharth hated these tapes, which he found scratchy and whiney.

Mohan Lal sometimes went to meetings with Barry Uncle and other BJP supporters, and one time, Barry Uncle said it would be a good idea if Siddharth came along. Siddharth protested at first but gave in upon finding out that the meeting was being held in a Fairfield home whose owner possessed an actual Lamborghini. When they finally made it to the place, it turned out the Lamborghini was in the shop, and Siddharth had to spend two hours sitting around while some hairy-eared Indians drank cans of Coors Light and droned on in Hindi about politics. They talked about the same things over and over—Ayodhya and Advani, and Hindus being proud to call themselves Hindus. Once the political discussions were over, they all sang a song in Hindi—or maybe it was a prayer. Siddharth wasn't sure, but hearing the men sing together made him want to vomit.

On the car ride home, he said, "Dad, this BJP crap is so stupid."

"Son, this stupid crap just might change the world."

"I thought Hindus were weak, Dad. I thought Hindus didn't have backbones."

"Precisely, son. That's what I'm trying to change. I am being the change that I want to see." Upon uttering this sentence, Mohan Lal chuckled to himself.

Siddharth didn't get what was so funny. All he knew was that his father was a hypocrite.

When Mohan Lal wasn't working on his book, he was preoccupied with finishing up his application for tenure at Elm City College. Everything about the application put him in a bad mood, like using a typewriter to fill out countless lengthy forms. The most difficult part of the tenure process was getting original copies of his Indian degrees, which resulted in several calls to Delhi University, and even a phone consultation with an Indian lawyer. After these phone conversations, Mohan Lal snapped at Siddharth about cleaning up his room or doing his homework, about turning down the television so that he could focus on his work. Eventually, Barry Uncle stepped in, placing a call to a politician friend in India. A few days later, Mohan Lal's degrees arrived via DHL. Siddharth was impressed with Barry Uncle. Yet he was anything but pleased with his father.

Even though Mohan Lal was stressed all the time, staying up late and sleeping in, he still managed to be such a kiss-ass with Ms. Farber. Whenever she cooked something, even if it was horrible—like her salmon cakes—Mohan Lal told her that dinner was delicious before locking himself in his office. Mohan Lal, who hated "brownnosers," was himself being a brownnoser, and Siddharth knew why: his father was being a brownnoser because he was addicted to Ms. Farber's pussy.

Siddharth wanted to remind his father that he was more important than a piece of pussy. He tried doing small things to demonstrate that he was the most valuable person in Mohan Lal's life. But when he offered to type up his dad's handwritten pages, Ms. Farber said she could type much faster. When he checked Mohan Lal's manuscript for spelling mistakes, Ms. Farber rechecked the pages afterward, even though he had done a fine job on his own.

Ms. Farber went way too far with her editing. She not only made comments about Mohan Lal's writing style and vocabulary, she also told him to rearrange sentences about Stafford Cripps and Lord Mountbatten. Siddharth thought this was ridiculous, since she hadn't even been to India before, but when she made these suggestions, Mohan Lal beamed. He told her that she was a genius. He told her that she should leave psychotherapy and go into publishing. All this gushing nauseated Siddharth.

He started keeping a written tally of the annoying things that she did in one of his old sketchpads that he rarely used for actual drawing anymore. Thanks to Ms. Farber, anyone who entered the house had to remove their shoes in the entranceway. The sandwiches she prepared for his lunch were served on dark-brown bread that tasted like cardboard, and she stuffed them with disgusting things like sprouts and hummus—pussy-ass poser food, according to Marc.

An especially annoying thing about Ms. Farber was the way she took pleasure in meddling in his personal life. Once, when Siddharth had gotten off the phone with Sharon, Ms. Farber said something about Sharon not being the right type of friend. Siddharth said, "What's that supposed to mean?"

"Things are pretty complicated for Sharon," replied Ms. Farber. "I'm not at liberty to divulge the details—just trust me on this. Sharon has a difficult situation."

"Maybe I'm the one with the problem. Sharon should watch out for *me*. My home life is pretty damn complicated." He looked to his father for a reaction, but Mohan Lal was lost in a book, unaware that he was even speaking.

But the single most irritating thing about Ms. Farber was that she made both he and Marc do chores. One week, Siddharth had to do the vacuuming, while Marc had to place the recycling bin at the end of the driveway, and then they switched jobs on the following week. They also had to help with the dishes. On a Wednesday evening, when the four of them were finishing one of Mohan Lal's Indian meals, Ms. Farber said it was Marc's turn to help clean up. Marc, who was in the middle of football season, complained that he was tired.

"Don't worry," said Mohan Lal, patting him on the shoulder. "Marc, go and rest."

"Oh no," said Ms. Farber. "Mo, he's gotta learn. If he's gonna reap the benefits of this household, then he's gotta give something back."

Marc muttered something under his breath.

"I didn't hear that, honey," said Ms. Farber. "If you have something to say, speak up."

Marc said, "Rachel, can you give a man some peace?"

"Marc, my parents would have whacked me if I spoke that way."

"So whack me then," said Marc. "I know you want to." He was smiling, but his eyes looked deranged. "And for your information, I don't give a shit about this household." As he spoke this final word, he flexed his fingers to mime quotation marks. "If it was up to me, I'd be back in my own freaking household."

She took a long sip of water and then grasped the top of her head. "Jesus, why doesn't anyone want me to be happy? Nobody has ever wanted me to be happy."

"Mom, there are these things called psychologists," said Marc. "Maybe you should go and see one."

A part of Siddharth enjoyed watching his friend stand up to his mother, but he hated hearing him talk about their life together like that. He wanted Marc to be his second brother. Brothers fought, but at the end of the day, they were family. They were there when you needed them. In some moments, it was painfully obvious that Marc didn't feel the same way. He had been distant and cold ever since the August incident with Dinetta. After that night, he'd been grounded for a second time. But this grounding was brief. Now he was free again, and out all the time. When he was home, he watched TV in silence or lay on Arjun's bed listening to his new Discman, a recent gift from his father. He only seemed to get animated when speaking on the phone, or getting ready for a football game.

Siddharth blamed himself. He should have kicked that rum bottle under the bed. He tried doing things to get Marc to like him again, such as taking an interest in baseball, but Marc would only talk sports with Andy or his father. Siddharth even pilfered some expensive whiskey from Mohan Lal's dining room stash. The boys drank it down together, but the alcohol didn't bring them any closer.

Fights between Marc and Ms. Farber became more frequent, and they gave rise to slightly revised living arrangements. Marc had been spending one night a week at his father's Hamden condo, but he soon began spending two. And he and Ms. Farber started staying at their own home at least two nights a week, usually without the Aroras. These changes meant even less time with Marc, and Siddharth began to wonder if Marc hated him.

But the new routines had an upside. With Ms. Farber and Marc spending more time at their own house, he had his father all to himself some days. When Ms. Farber wasn't around, he didn't have to eat lentils or tofu steaks. He got to order pizzas with extra cheese and pepperoni, and they ate their meals in front of the television for the first time in months. When Ms. Farber wasn't there, Mohan Lal sometimes asked him to read passages from his manuscript out loud, claiming that hearing the rhythm of the words made his sentences stronger. Even though Siddharth was so sick of Gandhi and all that shit, he showered praise upon his father's writing. He said that his book would make them rich, but Mohan Lal told him that real intellectuals weren't in it for the money.

On a Thursday night in October, Marc and Ms. Farber left to attend a function at their synagogue, and they planned on sleeping in Woodford. This would be Marc's third night away that week, which irritated Siddharth. What was the point of putting up with Ms. Farber if it didn't mean more time with Marc? What was the point of letting her fuck his father? He shed some of his anger when Mohan Lal declared that he was treating him and Barry Uncle to dinner at Pasta Palace.

The place was packed that night, with dozens of cops. They were in uniform, laughing, shouting, and drinking. Mohan Lal told the hostess to get Mustafa, but she said he was busy in the kitchen. It took them twenty minutes to get a table, and once they were seated, the waitress took ages to gather their orders. Barry Uncle thumped Mohan Lal on the back. "Boss, if this is how they treat VIPs here, I'd hate to be an ordinary customer."

Siddharth was starving by this point, and he thought Barry Uncle was right. But he needed to stick up for his father. "Trust me, Barry Uncle. The wait is worth it."

Mustafa eventually showed up with a complimentary round of drinks—more whiskey for the men, and a Coke for Siddharth. He also brought over a free order of fried mozzarella.

Barry Uncle had a weird smile on his face. "Mustafa-ji, I've heard a lot about you, boss."

Mustafa laughed, stroking his thick moustache. "Well, Arora sahib here is one of our best customers. His wife, she was such a fine lady."

Siddharth coughed on his Coke and the table fell silent. After an uncomfortable pause, Barry Uncle asked, "So what about you? You married, Mustafa?"

Mustafa broke into a big smile. "Oh, very happily married indeed. I'm very blessed, actually. I got two daughters—twin girls." He pulled his wallet out and handed Barry Uncle a picture. Siddharth glanced over and saw two baby girls wearing little dresses. He had to admit they were cute despite their very dark skin.

"Girls, eh?" said Barry Uncle. He handed the photo back and finished his whiskey in a single gulp. Then he took a long sip of the other one that had come for free. "Tell me something. You gonna make those little darlings cover up their heads?"

Mustafa's lips gaped but no words came out.

"Because those kids are sweet," continued Barry Uncle, "and it would be a shame to cover up their little heads."

Siddharth knew that Barry Uncle shouldn't have said this, but a part of him was glad—for in that moment, he loathed Mustafa for bringing up his mother. Staring at Mustafa, he saw anger flash in his eyes—a cold, hard look. But then it vanished, and Mustafa was his usual smiley self again. He said, "Well, folks, I better be going. A lotta work to do tonight. The PBA's here—annual function. Don't wanna tick off the coppers. Am I right?"

Mustafa started walking away, but Barry Uncle grabbed his wrist. "Hang on, man. Let's finish our little conversation. Your wife—you make her cover her head too?"

Siddharth now realized that Barry Uncle had crossed a line, and he wanted his father to intervene. But Mohan Lal was gobbling a saucy bite of fried mozzarella, which dripped onto the tablecloth. He swiped it with his finger and lobbed it onto his tongue. Siddharth winced at his father's dining manners.

Mustafa dusted off his shirt and gazed around the restaurant. "You know what, gentlemen? Dinner's on me tonight. The service is gonna be slow, so consider it an early Christmas present."

Siddharth said, "Wow, Mustafa, that's really nice of you."

"Mustafa mia," said Barry Uncle, "one more question for you."

"Barry Uncle," said Siddharth, glaring in his direction.

"Your wife—she's your cousin, right? You people still do that, right?"

Chewing his fried mozzarella, Mohan Lal mumbled, "Enough, Barry. Let Mustafa get back to work."

Mustafa definitely wasn't smiling anymore. He was rubbing his neck and looked as if he might hit someone. Siddharth made a plan: If Mustafa hit Barry Uncle, he would grab Mohan Lal and run. If he hit Mohan Lal, however, then he would have to retaliate. He would give him a sharp kick—right to the balls.

Barry Uncle said, "Wait . . . don't tell you married your own sister. Mustafa, that that would be too much. That's when we get into problems."

Mustafa put both of his hands on their green tablecloth and leaned forward. He said something sharp in Hindi that Siddharth couldn't understand.

Siddharth prayed for Barry Uncle to apologize.

"Mustafa-ji." Barry Uncle emptied his whiskey into his mouth, then slammed the glass down on the table. "Mustafa-ji, how many thumbs do your little girls have? How many toes? Because if you married your sister, you better count those toes."

Mustafa switched back to his guido English: "You know what, guys? We're gonna need this table sooner than I thought. Why don't I get your food wrapped up tonight? Why don't you eat it at home?"

Mohan Lal stood up, dabbing his face with his napkin. "Good idea. That's a very good idea."

Siddharth glanced to the right and saw a gaggle of police officers staring in their direction.

Mustafa placed a hand Mohan Lal's shoulder. "Arora sahib," he said, "see you again—soon, I hope. But I'd lose the friend if I were you."

Mohan Lal cocked his head to one side. "What was that?"

"Yous are always welcome in my restaurant. Always. Just not him."

Shit, Siddharth thought. Mohan Lal was going to say something stupid. Something that could get them arrested.

Mohan Lal clasped Siddharth's arm and yanked him out of his seat. "Come, son. Get away from that bloody mullah."

3

TRICK OR TREAT

For the first time in his life, Siddharth found himself actually looking forward to school. In junior high, he felt a new sense of freedom. He got to walk by himself to his classes, not like the primary-school drones with their regimented routines and single-file lines. He tried to plan his routes so that he could use the breezeway, an open-air corridor with a roof but no walls. The breezeway reminded him that he could flee the premises any time he wanted, and he used it even when it was raining.

Having his own locker that he could decorate any way he chose was another source of simple but constant pleasure. He put up a picture of Kurt Cobain that he'd ripped out of one of Marc's copies of *Rolling Stone,* and a photo of a television actress in a sports bra from one of Sharon's teen magazines. Luca gave him a magnetic mirror from his father's beauty salon, and Siddharth used it at least twice a day to brush his hair, which was now long on top and shaved on the sides.

In some ways, Luca had changed over the summer. He was taller and had lost some weight. He dressed better, wearing brown moccasins and tucking in his shirts. A little stubble now shadowed his cheeks, and he had long, stylish sideburns, like the actors in *90210.* He even acted fairly normally around other people, talking about sports with boys and listening to girls as if he really liked hearing about their summer breaks. But he would then do something to remind Siddharth that he was the same old Luca, like telling a joke about Mrs. Wadsworth sitting on someone's face.

Luca liked to say good morning to the dorks in a voice that sounded retarded. He often snapped Carol Corcoran's bra as she opened her locker, but strangely, Carol didn't seem to mind. In fact, Luca and Siddharth were getting close to Carol, one of the pretty girls from Lower Housatonic Elementary. She and her friends were good at sports, but also liked to smoke cigarettes and drink wine coolers. Even though these girls had older boyfriends, they hugged Siddharth in the hallways or gave him a squeeze on the waist.

Each morning, he met Luca at his locker, and the pair combed the hallways together before the first bell, talking shit and joking around. Eddie Benson usually joined them, and by the second week of October, a whole squad of seventh graders was following them around. Random wiggers and metalheads who Siddharth knew through Marc—grubbers, as Luca called them—nodded their heads as they passed him by, and Marc's friend Corey Thompson always stopped Siddharth to shake his hand. Sometimes Corey asked him if he could borrow twenty bucks, so he would steal a bit of extra cash from his father's wallet. Corey always paid him back, occasionally with a buck or two of interest or a miniature bottle of rum.

Siddharth was developing a reputation for being smart and funny, and he didn't want to ruin this, which was why he was perpetually anxious about being seen with Sharon Nagorski outside of class. If Luca saw them together, there would be trouble. Fortunately, she didn't pay Siddharth any attention in the hallways, and in the morning, when everyone else was roving and socializing, she went to the band room to practice her trumpet. She did the same thing at lunch, and, thankfully, she only mentioned Luca a single time during the fall semester.

It had happened on a Monday morning in science class. Sharon said that Siddharth seemed upset, and he told her that he was just tired after a crazy weekend.

"Why, what did you do?" she asked.

"Nothing. Just hung out with a couple friends."

"Friends? Oh, you mean Luca—Mr. Asshole?"

"Take it easy. Once you get to know him, he's not that bad."

"Sure," said Sharon, blowing her bangs out of her eyes.

"Hey, it takes two to tango, you know."

"What's that supposed to mean?"

"It means you just sit there and take it. If you want him to respect you, you should say something back."

"Whatever," said Sharon. "I've got bigger things to worry about."

"You mean your boyfriend?"

She smiled, revealing a dimple. "He took me out to Pasta Palace on Sunday. The bill was, like, forty dollars."

By the end of October, Siddharth was going over to Luca's on most Saturdays. The house was dark and old-fashioned. Luca's family room had a La-Z-Boy recliner, which was great for watching movies. It had thick brown carpets and a wallpaper mural of the Grand Canyon. This wallpaper reminded Siddharth of the mural that had once adorned his own family room, back when his mother was still around—before Ms. Farber had taken over his father's life.

Mrs. Peroti had grown fond of Siddharth. She cooked him fresh manicotti or ravioli, always sending him home with some. She said, "I got plenty of pasta for you. Just keep my Luca outta trouble."

Luca would mutter the strangest things in front of his mother. One time, when she was cooking and watching television, he said, "Ma, do you like pussy better, or cock?"

When she turned around, her blue eyes were blazing, and her ringed fingers were clasping one of her ample hips. "Did you just say what I think you did?"

Luca threw his hands in the air. "Jeez, Ma, I asked you a simple question—are you a Pepsi woman, or are you into Coke?"

In moments like these, Siddharth's heart beat quickly, and yet he couldn't help but grin. Luca was definitely one of the funniest people he'd ever met, and Siddharth was pretty sure that Arjun would like him.

Initially, he avoided spending the night at Luca's, as he had heard about the crazy things that Luca and Eddie did during sleepovers. They went out shitting houses, which had once consisted of spray-painting dirty words on people's driveways but had evolved into more serious acts of vandalism, like burning mailboxes and shattering windows. Sometimes Luca and Eddie sat in the woods by the edge of the Merritt Parkway and chucked stones at passing cars.

When Siddharth finally decided it was time to spend the night at his new friend's house, it was because he was sure Eddie wasn't going to be there. He ended up having a good time. He and Luca just sat around listening to music and talking, and they also taught Luca's little brother how to ride a bicycle with training wheels. At night, over a game of Monopoly, Luca said he'd heard that Marc was smoking reefer.

"Smoking what?" said Siddharth.

"You know—grass."

"I haven't heard anything about that." But he knew Marc was getting stoned, and the truth was, he was nicer high. When Marc came home stoned, they stayed up late talking, and he asked Siddharth interesting questions: "If the world was ending and you could only save one person—would it be your dad? Or the president?" "If you had to kill yourself, would you do it with a gun, or by jumping off a bridge? Keep in mind that I hear drowning yourself is the most painless way to die." These conversations made Siddharth feel older. They made him feel that his special connection with Marc wasn't totally dead.

Luca said, "Yo, weed's fucked up, kid."

"Why's it fucked up? You're always talking about getting hammered."

"Yeah, but that's different."

"If anyone can take care of himself, it's Marc."

"All I'm saying is that reefer's for porch monkeys."

"For what?"

"For jigaboos," said Luca.

These were new terms for Siddharth. But he knew they were racist, and that made him nervous. Racism was definitely bad. His father had called racists the biggest cowards.

All of a sudden, there was a knock at the door, and Mr. Peroti barged in. He was a beanpole of a man with a thick Italian accent who put in twelve-hour days at his Howard Avenue beauty salon.

"Boys," announced Mr. Peroti, "time for dinner."

"Dad," said Luca, "this kid doesn't know what a porch monkey is."

"Enough porch monkey talk," said Mr. Peroti. "I get enough of that at work."

"One question, Dad: how do you get all that nigger sweat off you—all those pointy little Negro hairs?"

Siddharth's stomach tightened. He counted his Monopoly money to avoid making eye contact with either of them. He had heard the N-word said in movies and on Marc's rap tapes. But this was the first time he was hearing it said in real life—the first time he was hearing it said by a regular person. He told himself that his friend was joking, that he needed to lighten up.

"You're bad," said Mr. Peroti, who was shaking his head but smiling. "Hurry up, Luca. Your mom's gonna chop off your hands."

Halloween was on a Sunday that year. Luca invited him and Eddie to come straight over to his house from school. The plan was to go trick-or-treating in his neighborhood and then have a sleepover. Siddharth was excited, but anxious. The thought of ending up in handcuffs just two months before his thirteenth birthday wasn't appealing. Not to mention, Luca was on the same bus route as Sharon Nagorski. Luca had told him about the things he said to her on the way home from school—that she was a slut, a loser, a wild boar. When Luca gloated over his cruelty, a part of Siddharth wanted to say that Sharon had changed—that she was cool once you got to know her. But he would always just laugh before changing the subject.

As Halloween approached, Siddharth tried to figure out an alternate way of getting to Luca's. But Ms. Farber wouldn't be around that afternoon, and his father had an evening class. Mohan Lal said he could drop off Siddharth at nine, but that wouldn't work because then he would miss the best part of the evening.

On Halloween morning, it started drizzling as Siddharth and

Timmy Connor made their way to the Miller farmhouse, passing smiling jack-o-lanterns and garbage bags bursting with decomposing brown leaves. Timmy told him about a new pellet gun that his father had gotten him for his fourteenth birthday, and how he had used it to kill a squirrel. Siddharth was too worked up to listen. He had a note in his pocket that gave him permission to take the bus home with Luca. He wondered if he should crumple it up and throw it into the sewer.

For some reason, Sharon wasn't in English class, and he felt a deep sense of relief. Maybe she was absent. But when he walked into science, she was standing at their station, preparing materials for the day's lab. She was wearing a strange homemade costume, which consisted of a yellow T-shirt with pieces of cardboard attached on the side. There was also a disc-shaped piece of golden cardboard on her head. He said, "What the hell are you supposed to be?"

Sharon told him that the entire band had dressed up as their instruments. "What about you?" she asked. "Too cool for costumes?"

"I didn't feel like dressing up," said Siddharth.

"Are you going out tonight?"

He responded with silence.

She poked him in the chest. "Hey, is everything okay?"

"Everything's fine. I gotta go to the bathroom."

Siddharth grabbed the lav pass and headed down the hallway. He was glad that that the bathroom was empty. He placed his hands on the sink and stared at himself in the mirror, noting that the little hairs above his lip were getting thicker. If he could only hang out with Marc tonight, then he wouldn't be worrying about any of this. But Marc was going out with Andy Wurtzel, and that was the way things were now. Siddharth recalled a conversation he'd had with his father, after their last dinner at Pasta Palace. He had asked Mohan Lal why he hadn't stood up for Mustafa when the man was always so nice to them. Mohan Lal said, "Son, you'll understand once you're my age. One has to be true to his values. And there is no greater virtue than loyalty."

Siddharth gave the paper towel dispenser a solid punch with

the top two knuckles of his right hand, just as he had learned in karate. As usual, his father's words were of no help to him. He had no idea which one of his friends was more deserving of his loyalty.

When the last bell of the day sounded, he found Luca at his locker with Eddie whispering into his ear.

"Yo, what's up?" said Siddharth.

"We're just doing some planning," said Eddie.

"What's the plan?" asked Siddharth.

"The plan?" said Eddie. "Tonight we're gonna pop your cherry. Tonight we're gonna get you a freaking mailbox."

"Pop your cherry," repeated Luca, shaking his head and smiling.

Luca and Eddie boarded the school bus first, and Siddharth followed behind. He handed his note to the driver, who was wearing a mesh baseball cap. Siddharth spotted Sharon in the sixth row. Fortunately, she was staring out the window. Holding his breath, he kept his eyes glued to the ribbed rubber walkway and scurried past her. Luca and Eddie were seated in the second-to-last row, and Siddharth sat alone in the seat before theirs. The bus pulled out of the lot, and a ninth grade girl in the back lifted a live rabbit from her backpack. Everyone cooed over it for most of the ride. At one point, Eddie grabbed the animal and held it up to his face, miming that he was giving it cunnilingus. Siddharth chuckled, but he tried to keep himself from laughing too hard. As the bus navigated the quiet, soggy streets of South Haven, he occasionally stole furtive glances at Sharon. Maybe she hadn't even realized he was there. Twenty-five minutes into the ride, he saw her gather her things and prepare to leave. He was grateful that the journey had passed without any incident.

The bus stopped, and Sharon exited along with four other kids. Siddharth watched as she walked toward her house, weighed down by her bursting backpack and clunky trumpet case. This was the first time he was seeing the house that her mother had rented. It was a tiny ranch, with chipping paint and overgrown grass. On the front lawn sat an old sofa and a rusty, broken-down jeep. The sunless sky made it all seem especially dreary. In that moment,

Siddharth realized something: Sharon was poor. In that moment, he felt worse for her than he ever had before. But he also felt like he barely knew her. He felt uneasy about letting her back into his life.

He turned back to Luca, who was sliding down his window. "Yo Niggerski," shouted Luca, "you look hot today! Would you be my girlfriend?"

From her driveway, Sharon glanced up at the bus and scowled, then stuck up her middle finger.

Siddharth crouched down, focusing his gaze on the worn knees of his blue jeans.

"Freaking dyke," said Eddie. "Her mailbox is mine."

Luckily, the rain picked up, and by six o'clock, loud booms of thunder were rattling the windows of the Peroti household, causing Luca's little brother to howl. Mrs. Peroti said she would drive them from house to house to get some candy, but Luca said that would be lame. Mrs. Peroti served them tortellini for dinner, and the boys watched a movie called *Re-Animator*, which Mohan Lal had rented for Siddharth. After reading the back of the case, Mohan Lal had said it was a work of science fiction, and science fiction taught young people to think critically.

The movie ended up being about a scientist who developed an injection that could bring dead things back to life. In Siddharth's favorite scene, a decapitated body grasped its own head and performed oral sex on a woman. Siddharth ended up having a great evening and wondered if the universe was finally on his side.

Mrs. Peroti drove them to school in the morning, which meant that he avoided another encounter with Sharon. But the thought of facing her in class made his stomach churn. During English, he tried smiling at her, but she wouldn't meet his eyes. As he walked to science later that day, he thought about visiting the nurse to see if he could go home early. But it was Thursday, and Ms. Farber was usually home on Thursdays. He stopped in the bathroom to cup some water into his mouth and ended up arriving three minutes late to class. Mr. Polanski said he would give him a detention if it happened again.

Today they were going to do an experiment that involved comparing the masses of various liquids. By the time Siddharth got to his lab station, Sharon had gathered most of their materials—goggles, glass beakers, and a triple-beam balance. She looked up at him and said, "Is something wrong?"

"Wrong? Why would something be wrong?"

She yawned and stretched her arms. "Well, I'm pretty exhausted."

He strapped his goggles onto his head. "Why, what did you do last night?"

"Jake came over. We were watching scary movies until three in the morning."

"You mean he slept over?"

"What did you do?" asked Sharon, ignoring his question.

"Your mother let him sleep over?" Siddharth didn't know why, but he felt himself growing hard. He felt disgusted with himself, and with Sharon too.

Smiling, she wrote their names on their lab sheet. "Come on, Siddharth. Why do you always gotta make such a big deal about everything?"

4

SHARON'S BLUES

As the temperatures dipped toward freezing, Siddharth started daydreaming about his brother's holiday visit. Once Arjun was back, it wouldn't matter that Marc didn't have any time for him. Arjun would take him to the mall. They would stay up late talking. Siddharth would show him off to Luca Peroti and Eddie Benson. He would show off Eddie and Luca to Arjun. He would prove to Arjun that he was definitely a regular guy—so what if he didn't play sports?

On a mid-December evening, Arjun called to say he had a change of plans. Instead of flying to Connecticut for winter break, he was getting a ride in a van to rural Tennessee, where he would spend Christmas with other college students building houses for poor people. Siddharth was hurt. Angry. He couldn't fathom why his brother would want to do something so lame and taxing.

"Let me guess," he told Arjun, locking himself in the bathroom with the new cordless phone, Ms. Farber's most recent purchase. "You're doing this to impress your girlfriend."

"Don't be a child," said Arjun. "I'm doing this because I believe in justice. Look, I have a week off in February. I'll definitely see you then."

"Whatever."

"Siddharth, what did I tell you about trusting people? You gotta trust me. I'll see you in February."

Over dinner that night, Mohan Lal said he was glad Arjun was putting his money where his mouth was, but that he hoped this charity nonsense wouldn't interfere with his studies. Ms. Farber said that Arjun was setting a great example, and she thought that the four of them should plan something similar for the summer.

"Fabulous," said Marc, who then made a gagging sound.

"Siddharth, honey," said Ms. Farber, "I know this is disappointing, but it actually might be for the best."

"The best for who?"

Ms. Farber explained that an old friend from her Manhattan days was finally getting married, and that the wedding was being held in Atlantic City on the final weekend of Arjun's February vacation. "Mo," she said, "Arjun could watch the boys. We could turn it into a little vacation."

"Vacation?" said Mohan Lal. "You think my book will write itself?"

"Jeez, Mohan," she replied. "God forbid we spend a night alone."

A few days later, Ms. Farber booked a two-night February package at a boardwalk hotel, which included four meals, a live show, and thirty dollars of tokens for the slot machines. Siddharth cringed at the idea of her and Mohan Lal being alone together in a hotel room, but he calmed himself with the thought of having his brother all to himself. Besides, February vacation was still two months away. A lot could happen between now and then. Ms. Farber could be hit by a bus, or perhaps move to Indonesia. No, that would be bad. That would be bad because Mohan Lal would have to grieve for another woman.

The next morning was the second-to-last day of school before Christmas vacation. The sky was bright blue, but the temperature hovered around freezing. As Siddharth headed to the bus stop, he couldn't free his mind from thoughts of Atlantic City. He had once gone there when he was seven or eight, for one of Mohan Lal's marketing conferences. On the first night there, they went out to a fancy restaurant, where the waiters pulled out their chairs and brushed away their crumbs. He had loved all the luxury and attention. He ordered mussels for dinner, even though his mother said he wouldn't like them. She was right, but to prove a point he had eaten every last one and said they were great.

Siddharth reached the top of his street, pausing in the middle of the quiet intersection to wait for Timmy Connor. He placed his foot on a frozen puddle, causing it to shatter. When they were small, this area would often freeze over completely, and he and the Connor brothers used this ever-present patch of ice as a makeshift skating rink. Surrounded by sand and salt, the puddle now looked like a miniature ocean, complete with its own beach. During the Atlantic City trip, while Arjun had bathed in the ocean, Siddharth remained on the shore building a sand castle. As he stood there now, waiting for Timmy, the memory was still so vivid in his mind. He could taste the bitter mussels. He could see his Velcro sneakers, the silk scarf his mother tied around her neck when it was windy. But what was the point of these memories? That weekend was gone forever.

Looking up, he saw Naomi, Timmy's mutt, trotting toward him. Siddharth's mother used to keep a water bowl for Naomi by the Aroras' front steps. The dog nuzzled up against him, and he scratched below her jaw. The tip of her left ear was oozing blood; a few gnats were swarming around it. "What's wrong?" asked Siddharth. "Where's Timmy?"

The dog wagged her tail and offered him a paw.

If he waited any longer, he would miss the bus, so he started walking. Naomi remained by his side. He saw that many of his neighbors had placed Christmas candles in their windows, and a few had put up menorahs. This year, Ms. Farber would light a menorah at the Aroras', and she would buy him a compact disc player for Hanukkah. His neighbors' lawns were blotched with snow, so he stuck to the street to avoid ruining his suede shoes. As the road curved to his left, he passed an enormous oak. The tree stood in front of a tiny brick house, which a family of Jehovah's Witnesses had recently purchased. Naomi abruptly halted and started barking.

"It's just a tree," said Siddharth, patting her head.

The dog's ears pointed outward, and her tail shot up in the air. She started pacing back and forth, growling.

"Naomi, you're gonna make me late."

But her barks got louder and sharper.

Suddenly, a large falcon leaped from the oak and shot upward. As Siddharth watched the bird fly circles above their heads, another image from Atlantic City surfaced. During the trip, his mother had visited a boardwalk psychic who claimed that his dead grand-mother was always watching over them—manifesting itself in birds. The psychic said that the presence of any unusual avian life might actually be a sign from Siddharth's grandmother, and at the time, this notion gave him chills.

He resumed his journey, but with his eyes glued to the winged missile hovering in the clear blue sky. Yes, his mother might have sent the falcon. She might actually be inside of it, he thought. If the bird were actually her, he would apologize to it for so many things—for not drawing regularly or thinking of her more often. He would say sorry for that time she had wanted him to spend a night with his grandfather and he told her that his grandfather was old and boring and smelly. Naomi started barking again. The falcon nosedived toward the earth and grazed the grass, then shot back to the sky. It was now clutching something in its talons.

As it flew toward the main road, the bird released whatever it had hunted. The object crashed on the hood of a parked burgundy Taurus, then bounced to the ground. Siddharth anxiously jogged over to the car and was dismayed to discover that what had fallen was nothing but a crunched-up can of beer. "You're fucking kid-ding me," he mumbled. He stuffed the can down a sewer drain, and it made a plopping sound upon hitting the sooty water. Naomi approached him, once again wagging her tail and panting.

"Go home," said Siddharth. She wouldn't budge, so he threw a stick at her. He recalled what his father had said on the ride home from Atlantic City: birds were just birds, and the psychic was a goddamned liar.

During homeroom, the principal got on the PA system and told ev-eryone to make their way to the gymnasium in an orderly fashion. Today was the band's annual winter concert, which meant that

Sharon would be performing. Siddharth had a vague recollection of her complaining about her mother not being able to attend the event.

He walked down the hall with his only homeroom friend, David Marcus, who was telling him about an upcoming ice-fishing trip. Siddharth was only half-paying attention. He still couldn't get over the fact that David was shorter than him and not as funny, and yet he had somehow managed to bag a decent girlfriend.

By the time they reached the gym, it was already abuzz with the animated chatter of several hundred students. The basketball hoops had been cranked up, and the bleachers were out, behind a dozen rows of metal folding chairs. Mrs. Oliver, his blond math teacher, directed him and David to these chairs. He turned around and spotted Luca on the bleachers, sitting beside his skinny new girlfriend, Jeanette Horiuchi, who was part Japanese and part Italian. He had lost many hours counseling Luca about this volatile relationship, doling out advice he'd gleaned from the television.

Principal Moser, a short woman with huge glasses, got up onstage and stood in front of the closed curtain. She issued warnings about the consequences of disruptive behavior, smiling in spite of her stern tone. She said she wouldn't be averse to issuing Christmas Day detentions, which made a few people laugh. "That's no idle threat," she added. "Right, Corey?"

Corey Thompson sat in the front row of chairs, flanked by a teacher on each side. He was smiling like a child who had been caught stealing candy. It struck Siddharth that the world was more fond of troublemakers than the kids who actually did what they were told.

When the curtain rose, the parents in attendance approached the stage to snap pictures. Siddharth spotted Sharon to the right, with all the other horn players. The entire band was wearing black pants and white shirts, except for Sharon, who was wearing a black turtleneck. She sat beside Kenny Hong, a Korean kid with golden glasses and spiked hair. Kenny seemed to be having a problem with his trombone, so he handed it to Sharon, who made some quick adjustments and then handed it back. He gave her a thumbs-up, and she nodded her head and cracked her knuckles.

As the band went through a series of screechy classical pieces, Siddharth's mind wandered. He thought about how Arjun would have laughed at the idea of their mother communicating with them through a bird. He thought about how most of the other kids would soon be away with their families. Marc was flying to Florida, and Luca would be driving to Maryland. Even Sharon was spending Christmas with her father. All he had to look forward to were ten nonstop days of the Mohan Lal and Ms. Farber show.

Suddenly, the entire audience began clapping. Onstage, there was a huge commotion. Most of the band members cleared out, with just a few kids remaining. They brought out a full drum set, then wheeled out a wooden piano. Mr. Donahue, the ninth grade biology teacher, leaped onto the stage. He grabbed a microphone and told everyone to settle down. "People, you're in for a real treat," he said. He had a crew cut, and his thick eyebrows seemed as if they'd been drawn with permanent marker. "I and some talented musicians—all of whom are significantly more talented than myself—have formed a little jazz quartet. We call ourselves the Cotton Gins." He put the microphone back, then brought an enormous guitar-like instrument over to the piano, where the eighth grade social studies teacher was sifting through some sheet music. A ninth grader named Keith Liaci seated himself at the drums.

"That's my cousin," said David Marcus. "Go, Keith!" He whistled. "Rock out!"

Siddharth stared at the drummer, who had a butterfly collar and large silver glasses, the kind that were tinted. Keith looked more like someone who had gone to junior high in Arjun's day. From the bleachers, someone shouted, "I love nerds!"

He wondered if it had been Luca, but he could no longer see him. Turning back to the stage, he was surprised to see Sharon walking on with her trumpet. He hoped Luca wouldn't say anything—not today. Not when she was about to do her thing.

Mr. Donahue introduced the members of the band, then said, "We're going to play a song of Ms. Nagorski's choosing. It's a song of great beauty, of great importance. Unfortunately, it's a song that most of you have never heard." He slipped the mic back into its holster, and a few people clapped, mainly parents and teachers.

David kept whistling, which made Siddharth uncomfortable. He wondered why David wasn't embarrassed about Keith. He wondered if he should be cheering for Sharon too.

Mr. Donahue snapped his fingers and counted to four in a firm whisper. He then started plucking the strings of his large instrument, which stood vertically, like a dance partner or a high-rise building. It emitted one of the deepest sounds Siddharth had ever heard.

After a few beats, the piano chimed in with two solid chords, and the pair went back and forth like this for a couple of minutes, as if they were having a conversation. When the drums kicked in, Siddharth started tapping his suede shoes against the shiny wooden floor. Keith held brush-like batons in his hands, not actual sticks. His shoulders bounced while he played, as if he were dancing in his seat. His head was turned to the side, and he looked peaceful and contented.

As for Sharon, she was just standing there, bobbing her head and tapping her hip. He couldn't imagine her keeping up with these skilled musicians, but as soon as she started playing, he knew he was wrong. Her fingers pumped the trumpet's keys like the pistons of a perfect machine. The sound her instrument emitted was sweet but serious, and it lodged itself deep into his bones. At first his insides were icy, but then he felt as if he were floating in bathwater. He could tell that Sharon was making up the notes as she went along, and he wondered how someone so young could play so well and why he had never known that his weird friend could do something so beautiful. In that moment, he was proud of her. In that moment, he wanted to be like Sharon.

After the song was over, the whole gym seemed to be cheering and shouting, as if they were at a rock concert, not inside a school gymnasium. He clapped his hands more frenetically with each passing moment. The musicians bowed, and Sharon's face turned bright red. As he looked on, his father's words popped into his mind: *There is no greater virtue than loyalty.* He decided he was going to do it. When the commotion died down, he would get up and give her a hug.

The principal rose and made some announcements, and the students started mingling in little circles. David Marcus charged toward the stage, and Keith grabbed his hand and pulled him onto it. Siddharth remained seated, watching the two cousins exchange enthusiastic greetings. His heart thumped loudly when he saw Sharon wipe down her instrument. She placed it in its case and then hugged some girl, another band loser.

As he was finally about to offer congratulations, he paused upon seeing Eddie out of the corner of his eye. Eddie was miming that he was playing an instrument, a clarinet or a saxophone. Luca punched him on the shoulder and broke into laughter. Siddharth got up and rushed to the exit. He headed toward his next class, stopping on a concrete bench in the breezeway. The frigid air cooled his fevered face, and he felt calmer. He told himself that he had been loyal—to Luca, not Sharon.

5

TERRORIST ATTACK

It was New Year's Eve. Siddharth was on the love seat, sipping a mixture of pink wine and Coca-Cola. *Stand By Me* was on cable as he flipped through an old issue of *Playboy* from the late seventies. The centerfold was a brunette who was smiling and wearing sunglasses on a beach chair. She was totally naked, but the picture failed to arouse him.

Marc was still in Florida, and Mohan Lal and Ms. Farber were out to dinner with some of her friends and Barry Uncle, who had just gotten back from Delhi. Siddharth was relieved to be alone after the past couple of weeks. Christmas break had been a haze of microwave french fries, snow shoveling, and general boredom. Ms. Farber had been up to her usual crap, rearranging the furniture and putting up pictures of the four of them. One evening a few days earlier, she had really pissed him off.

He had been in the middle of a *Facts of Life* episode when his father emerged from his office for the first time in hours. Mohan Lal was wearing stupid kurta pajamas, which he had always refused to wear until one day Ms. Farber said they were handsome. He seated himself on the sofa and asked what was happening in the show. Siddharth explained that a character named Natalie had almost been sexually assaulted.

"Natalie?" said Mohan Lal. "You mean the black?"

"No, the fat one."

Ms. Farber clicked her tongue from the armchair, where she was reading. "What did you just call her?"

"Call who?" he said.

"Natalie."

"Natalie? You mean *fat*?"

Ms. Farber's lips pursed with indignation, and she peered at him over the rims of her reading glasses.

"What's wrong?" he asked.

"Nothing. I just thought you would have a little more empathy—you'd be a little more sensitive after all you've been through."

"All I've been through? What's your freaking problem?"

"Siddharth!" said Mohan Lal, his voice stern and menacing. "Don't you dare speak that way to Rachel."

"Are you kidding me?" said Siddharth. "What ever happened to loyalty, Dad? I thought loyalty was the greatest virtue."

Now Siddharth put down his *Playboy* and picked up his glass. As he finished off his purple concoction, he recalled the strange thing his father had said a couple of days after the Natalie incident. Mohan Lal had needed some salt for the driveway and rechargeable batteries for Marc's old Walkman, which Mohan Lal had begun using, and he'd made Siddharth accompany him to the store. On the way home, Mohan Lal grasped Siddharth's knee and told him he wanted to say something. Siddharth said, "I'm listening," feeling hopeful. Maybe his father wanted to apologize. Maybe he would finally admit the truth about Ms. Farber—that she was a bossy bitch who talked too much.

Mohan Lal paused to let out a sigh. "Son, I want you to know something."

"What is it?"

"Son, I want you to know that not once—not a single time—was I unfaithful to your mother."

Siddharth groaned, then grabbed his head and stared out the window.

"And it's not that there weren't opportunities," said Mohan Lal. "But I couldn't hurt you. I couldn't hurt my family."

Siddharth went to the kitchen with his empty glass and dirty dinner plate, which he loaded into the dishwasher. He needed to talk to someone, but Arjun was in the middle of nowhere building fucking houses with his stupid Pakistani girlfriend. When Siddharth felt angry, he thought about telling Mohan Lal the truth about this girlfriend, but he never ended up going through with it. He suddenly felt a strong urge to speak with Luca, but Luca was still in Maryland. At least he had called a few days earlier, telling Siddharth that he had cheated on Jeanette with his hot second cousin. Siddharth was relieved to hear that Luca's voice was back to normal—that he seemed to have forgotten about what had happened on the day before vacation. Luca had walked into his science class to deliver a note to the teacher, and that same night he phoned to say that Siddharth and Sharon had looked pretty cozy together.

"Gimme a break," said Siddharth. "She's my freaking lab partner."

"Face it," said Luca. "You're best friends with a freaking dyke."

"Well, you're an asshole. Anyway, she has a boyfriend."

"Sure, and I'm banging Kim Basinger," said Luca.

"It's true. I think they're even screwing."

At the time, saying this about Sharon had felt like the right thing to do—a way of actually protecting her—but now he felt guilty for having lied. He decided he would make up for it by being especially nice to her. He decided he would call her right now. He picked up the phone and dialed her number, and she picked up after five rings.

"Hello?"

"You're back," he said.

"Siddharth?"

"No, Ronald Reagan."

"I never left," she said. "My dad—he had to work."

"Fucking blows."

"Are you okay?"

"Why wouldn't I be?"

"I can tell when something's up," she said.

"Sorry for calling. I just wanted to say Happy New Year."

"Happy New Year, Siddharth—but I really can't talk right now."

"Oh, let me guess: you're with your boyfriend."

"Siddharth, I have to go."

When he put down the phone, he realized he was a little tipsy. *Fuck Sharon*, he thought. He told himself that she had a wild imagination—that her boyfriend probably wasn't even real. He picked up his *Playboy* and examined a cigarette ad with a weather-beaten cowboy. On the following page was a photo that awakened his crotch. It depicted a brunette dancing in a smoky room, possibly a nightclub. She had on leather pants, but nothing on top except for a string of pearls. Her hands were running through her head of wild curls. He brought the magazine to the bathroom and locked himself inside. He had just turned thirteen, and his "cock curse" had been over for several months now. He could now get his penis to perform whenever he wanted. He imagined standing behind this woman and dancing. He imagined wrapping his arms around her waist, then moving them up to her nipples. But as he got closer to coming, images of Sharon invaded his mind. A scruffy older kid was kissing her neck, and she seemed to be really enjoying it. This was the picture he focused on as he ejaculated into the bathtub.

When it was over, he ran the shower, sending the evidence of his misdeed down the drain. As he washed his hands, he heard the sound of voices. *Oh shit*, he thought. He shoved the magazine underneath some towels, then patted down his hair and tucked in his shirt. He was moving so quickly that he knocked his toothbrush into the trash bin.

Ms. Farber was taking off her boots in the hallway. She smiled without looking up. "Having fun?" she said. She kissed him on the head, then asked if Marc had called. She had asked this question twice a day for the past ten days, but Marc had only called once from Florida.

Siddharth stepped into the family room before speaking, so that she wouldn't smell his breath. "He called, like, forty times," he said. "I stacked all the messages in the closet." He headed to the kitchen and pulled a piece of gum from the drawer with the scissors and coupons. Thanks to Ms. Farber, this drawer now always contained a little candy or chocolate. There were a few good things about her. Just a few. As he popped the peppermint stick into his mouth, he noticed Barry Uncle pouring drinks in the dining room.

"Boy!" said Barry Uncle. "I missed you, boy." Barry Uncle walked into the kitchen with two whiskeys, which he placed on the counter, then pulled Siddharth into his armpit and kissed him.

Siddharth winced at the feel of his sandpaper cheeks, at the noxious smell of Old Spice, betel nut, and booze.

"I brought you a present," said Barry Uncle.

"You did?"

"Yes sir."

He followed Barry Uncle to the family room. Barry Uncle placed his drinks on the Kashmiri table and then picked up a plastic duty-free bag from the carpet. Just then, Mohan Lal walked in. He had already removed his shirt and tie and put on his peach-colored kurta. After giving Siddharth a hug, he asked Barry Uncle if he wanted a whiskey.

"Three steps ahead of you, boss." Barry Uncle nodded toward the little round table. He reached into his bag and pulled out a videocassette, then handed it to Mohan Lal. "Boss, this is for you." Next he pulled out a large, fork-like object with an intricately carved wooden handle. He turned to Siddharth. "Now what do you think of that, boy?"

Siddharth grasped the gift. It had two metal prongs. A slack length of rubber was connected to each of them, and at the center of this cord was a quarter-sized piece of leather.

"You know what it is?" asked Barry Uncle.

He nodded. "Of course."

"A real weapon for a real man." Barry Uncle snatched it back, then pulled and released the rubber, which gave off a dull twang. "With a good rock, you can kill a bird—a rabbit maybe, or even a squirrel."

Siddharth took hold of it, pulling and releasing the cord as Barry Uncle had done. The Connor brothers had a slingshot, though theirs was much sleeker, with a special fiberglass attachment for extra leverage. But this slingshot wasn't bad. It was definitely better than a crappy snake-charmer's flute, or some other shitty toy from India.

"Thanks a lot," he said.

"Pleasure, boy. You and me can do a little hunting come spring. Your father—he was a great one for hunting."

Ms. Farber walked in carrying a glass of her pink wine. "Mo used to hunt? How awful. Why is this the first time I'm hearing this?"

"I could write a whole book about him," said Barry Uncle. "But I'm not the writer."

Grinning, Mohan Lal seated himself on the love seat. He picked up a whiskey and raised it in the air. "Cheers, chief. Chalo, let's watch your little video."

Barry Uncle and Ms. Farber sat down, and the trio clinked glasses.

"Siddharth," said Mohan Lal, waving his new tape in the air, "put this in and press play."

Siddharth sighed but did as he was told. He was about to flee to the guest room when Barry Uncle said, "Stay, boy—this is important. You should know about your culture."

Static shimmered on the screen, but soon the words *Jain & Son Productions* were streaming across a blue background. Siddharth let out a muffled laugh. These graphics looked cheap, the work of amateurs. Blowing a bubble, he realized that his gum had already lost its flavor. That was the thing with Ms. Farber's sugar-free stuff—it tasted like crap and never lasted.

The camera focused on a gloomy, vacant prison cell. Suddenly, a little blue boy with a bow and arrow flashed on the screen. He kept on flashing on and off, as if he were a ghost. He then multiplied into four distinct boy-gods, which started rotating in a kaleidoscopic fashion.

A narrator started speaking in Hindi.

Ms. Farber leaned forward, squinting and grasping her chin. "What are they saying?"

"That is the god Ram," said Barry Uncle. He explained that Ram used to have an important temple in a place called Ayodhya, but a Muslim king came and destroyed it. "And then—surprise, surprise—that bastard invader erected a bloody mosque."

Ms. Farber was riveted. "Jeez, it's always the same story, isn't it?"

Siddharth sat down beside Barry Uncle, who squeezed his knee. Barry Uncle said that some years ago, Ram had appeared in the dream of a Hindu holy man. The god urged the Hindus to demolish the mosque and rebuild their forsaken temple. Soon, little statues of Ram mysteriously appeared in the mosque, and these were further proof of Ram's wishes.

"Don't worry," said Mohan Lal, draping his arm around Ms. Farber, "he doesn't actually believe this drivel."

"Call it what you want," said Barry Uncle. "All movements need myths to mobilize the masses." He poked Siddharth in the thigh. "Boy, fast-forward a bit."

He begrudgingly got up and pressed the forward button. It was 11:23, and he didn't want to miss the festivities in Times Square.

"Stop, stop, stop," said Barry Uncle. "This is it. This is what we need to see."

When he pressed play, the screen was much shakier.

"This is my own handiwork," said Barry Uncle. "Shot it all myself."

"Forgive me, Barry," said Ms. Farber, "but I wouldn't quit your day job."

Mohan Lal chuckled, then kissed her on the shoulder.

"Hah," said Barry Uncle. "We'll see who laughs last."

Siddharth remained standing, spitting his gum into an old receipt that he found in his pocket. The screen now showed a dusty Indian square with some sort of religious structure in the background.

"That's it," said Barry Uncle. "That's the mosque."

"You mean the temple?" asked Ms. Farber.

"Bright bird," said Barry Uncle, snapping his fingers.

Thousands of men were gathered in front of the mosque. A few of them were cops with perfect mustaches, and some were grubby holy men with painted foreheads. But most were ordinary Indians—

not the kind who spoke English, like Siddharth's relatives, but the ones who rode around on mopeds with their entire families, the ones who worked as cooks and drivers. These men were wielding sticks and shouting slogans.

As Siddharth rolled his gum into a perfect ball, the men on the screen were getting angrier. A few of them jumped over a fence and bolted toward the mosque. They started hurling things at it, mainly stones, but also bricks and bottles.

The camera zoomed in on the huge dome that capped the building. It reminded Siddharth of the Colt factory near Hartford—and of that nice park with the parrots near his uncle's Delhi home. He picked up his new slingshot, grazing its cold metal prongs against his warm cheeks.

"Boss, I hope you're paying attention," said Barry Uncle. "Isn't that something?"

"Amazing," said Mohan Lal. "I never thought I would live to see it. The Hindus have finally grown a spine."

Several men standing atop the dome began battering it with pipes. Others kept pelting it with bricks from afar. The thing began to crumble. This video was the first decent one Siddharth had seen about India. Something actually happened in it. He placed his pellet of gum into the slingshot's leather holster, then aimed at the screen. He knew his father would get upset, but he needed to test out his weapon.

6

I-95 TO THE BJP HOSPITAL

The weather had been strange lately. On Siddharth's thirteenth birthday, it had hit fifty-three degrees. Then, during the first week of January, a record-breaking nor'easter pummeled the East Coast with two feet of snow. Now, as he dozed in the family room, freezing rain clicked and crackled against the skylight.

Marc walked through the front door and started unlacing his tan work boots, a recent gift from his father.

"Hey," said Siddharth, "I thought you were staying at your dad's."

"Things change, young Sidney. Get used to it." Marc grabbed the cordless phone and headed toward the bedroom.

Ms. Farber entered the house carrying the small black suitcase she used to transport personal items between her home and the Aroras'. She patted him on the head on her way to the love seat. "Honey," she said, "what did Dad say about straightening up the coffee table?" She organized the chaotic swamp of bills and catalogs into three tidy towers, then proceeded to the kitchen. A few minutes later, she called for Siddharth.

"What is it?" he yelled back, shaking his head.

"Could you turn on the outside lights?"

He groaned, then got up and walked to his bedroom.

Marc was on the phone, examining one of Siddharth's old model cars, a die-cast Mercedes SSK that Siddharth and his mother had built together. "Hang on, Andy," said Marc. He turned to Siddharth and squinted. "What?"

"You wanna do something?"

"I *am* doing something," said Marc.

Siddharth returned to the family room and pressed his forehead into the cold glass of the sliding doors, wishing he could go back in time to those afternoons on Foster Pond. He eyed a broken hedge trimmer, the porch's musty cane furniture that had been there since he was born. He couldn't see into the backyard but heard the maple's branches scratching against the house. The wind chimes Ms. Farber had gotten Mohan Lal batted against each other, producing notes that were hollow and spooky.

A loud noise jolted him out of his trance. It had come from the front of the house and sounded like an explosion. He rushed to the living room and looked out the window.

His father was back. He had crashed the minivan into the front steps, bending the cast-iron railing forward. Mohan Lal reversed a few feet, then pulled into the car's usual spot. He cracked open his door, and the car's overhead light illuminated his disheveled hair. He tapped his head against the steering wheel two times before emerging from the vehicle.

Siddharth hurried to the entrance hall, where Ms. Farber was already standing, one of her bony fingers on the waist of her burgundy dress. She threw her arms around Mohan Lal as soon as he entered, but he pushed her away.

"What happened?" asked Siddharth.

"*What happened?*" replied Mohan Lal. He placed his overcoat on its special wooden hanger. "What happened is that I live among foolish people."

"What?"

Mohan Lal glared at Siddharth. "I ask you people one goddamned thing—to turn on the outside lights when I'm gone. But you're useless."

"Mo, it was my fault," said Ms. Farber, flashing Siddharth a crooked smile.

He couldn't tell if she was trying to make him feel better or express her irritation. Assuming it was the latter, he responded with a glare, then looked down at the old, cracked stones of the corridor floor.

"Thanks," said Mohan Lal. "Your forgetfulness will cost me a thousand dollars."

"So I'll pay for it," she said.

Mohan Lal placed his hat on the closet's messy tool shelf. Siddharth thought that the furry, elliptical hat made him resemble the worst kind of person: a cross between an Arab and a commie. Mohan Lal stormed toward the dining room, Ms. Farber and Siddharth in tow. He took out his most expensive bottle of whiskey, the blue one he only opened on special occasions, finishing half of a tall drink in a single gulp. Siddharth knew it was something serious. Either something had happened to Arjun or his father had cancer.

"Mo, what's wrong?" asked Ms. Farber. "You have to tell me what's wrong."

Pulling a handkerchief from his blazer pocket, Mohan Lal wiped the back of his neck. "Rachel, I don't have to tell you anything."

"Dad, what the hell is going on?"

Mohan Lal's lips formed a tight, bitter smile. "Son, your father has some news."

"What?" said Siddharth, swallowing hard.

"That bastard did it."

"Did what?" asked Ms. Farber.

"The dean," said Mohan Lal. "He has denied my tenure."

"What—why?" said Siddharth.

Mohan Lal finished his drink without responding.

Ms. Farber placed her hand on Mohan Lal's shoulder. "I'm so sorry, Mo. But you gotta talk about—"

"Talk, talk, talk!" Mohan Lal raised his palms in the air and stomped off to the family room, seating himself on the armchair and turning on the news. Siddharth sat down on the love seat and placed a hand on his father's knee. Ms. Farber walked in a little while later carrying a glass of her pink wine. She stood beside the television, partially blocking the screen.

Mohan Lal said, "You weren't made in a glass factory."

"What?"

"I can't see!"

She stepped toward him. "I'm your friend, Mo."

"Everyone's your friend in times of bounty. Drought is a different story altogether."

She took a sip of wine. "Mo, it's hard to see sometimes, but trust me, this is still gonna be our year." She combed his stray gray hairs with her fingers. "This tenure thing, you can appeal it."

He shifted, evading her hands. "Believe me, there is no future for me at Elm City College."

"Mo, it's that pessimism that's holding you back. I know it feels really bad right now, but it's not gonna feel that way tomorrow."

Siddharth thought about telling her to shut up, but he just said, "Jeez, let him feel bad if he wants to."

"No, they will never offer me tenure, Rachel." Mohan Lal stood up and tossed the remote control at the large sofa. It bounced off the leather and landed on the carpet.

"And why's that?" she asked.

"Because I've left them. I've quit my job."

Siddharth gasped. "You're joking."

Ms. Farber stared up at the skylight. Siddharth could tell she was really pissed because of the way her nostrils were flaring. After a moment, she said, "I don't know what to tell you, Mo. You didn't wanna discuss this first?"

"So I needed your approval?" Mohan Lal had a fiendish grin on his face. "Shall I ask your permission before taking a shower?" He stormed off to his bedroom, his dress shoes clomping loudly on the corridor floor.

Later that evening, Siddharth tried to open his father's door, but it was still locked. "Dad!" he called out, banging on the door and rattling the knob.

"Go away," said Mohan Lal.

He kept knocking. "Open up, Dad. We need to talk."

"Are you deaf? Leave me alone."

Siddharth rested his forehead on the door. A few moments later, he felt her thin, cold fingers on his shoulder. She gave him a pat and tried to nudge him away. But he wouldn't budge. He said, "My dad doesn't wanna talk right now."

She flashed a fake smile, then tapped on the door.

"Jesus, Siddharth!" said Mohan Lal, furious now. "Don't you listen?"

"It's me, Mo," said Ms. Farber. "Come on, love. Let's sort this out."

Siddharth heard the sound of footsteps. Then the door cracked open. Ms. Farber slipped inside, locking it behind her.

Siddharth bounded to the main bathroom and sealed himself inside it, then punched the bathroom door. His knuckles struck an old nailhead, and one of them started bleeding. He sucked on his wound, soothed by the sour red trickle. He then went to his room and dove onto his bed.

Marc was lying down, listening to his Discman and staring into space. "What the hell's going on?"

"Nothing."

"Bullshit," said Marc. He removed his headphones and walked over to Siddharth, giving him a light smack on the leg. "Don't be a bitch. What's wrong?"

"Everything's fine. Actually, everything's fucking great."

Marc shook his head. "Yeah, everything's fucking great. Sure. Your mom's dead, and your dad's fucking a crazy Jewish lady. I can tell you feel great about that."

"Leave me alone," said Siddharth.

"You sure know how to open up about your feelings. It's a real talent, Sidney." Marc left the room.

Siddharth tried to close his eyes and empty his mind, but his body was pulsing with nervous energy. He got out of bed and paced around in circles. He picked up one of Arjun's baseball trophies, then hurled it at the floor. He eyed his old *Call of the Wild* report, which was thumbtacked to the bulletin board on the backside of the door. The dog's eyes had once seemed so perfect, but they now looked like the work of a toddler. He ripped the report down and tore it in two, then walked over to Marc's nightstand and picked up the cordless phone. Underneath it was a copy of *GQ* and a brochure for a teen tour to Jerusalem. Marc had never said anything about going to Jerusalem. Siddharth punched in Luca's number, and his friend answered after three rings.

"Hey, kid," said Siddharth.

"Yo, I was about to call you," said Luca. "You're not gonna believe what Jeanette just said."

"Man, I got some news."

"What is it?"

"It's my dad," said Siddharth. "He got laid off."

"Shit, kid, that really sucks. You know I know how bad that sucks."

"Yeah, that's why I'm telling you."

"Look on the bright side," said Luca. "My mother—she got another job in, like, three or four months."

"Totally." Siddharth wished he hadn't said anything at all. He didn't want anyone to get the wrong idea about his father. "Hey, what happened with Jeanette?"

"Yo, that bitch is off the hook."

After listening to the story of Luca's latest fight with his girl-friend, Siddharth felt calmer. He buried his face in his pillow and decided to wait for someone to come check on him. If Ms. Farber came knocking, he would forgive her. If she didn't, he would show her. He would show both of them. He would tell his brother how freakish they'd become.

Twenty minutes later, the sound of footsteps made him hope-ful, but there was no ensuing knock. If Arjun were still home, he definitely would have knocked by now. His mother would definitely have knocked.

He wondered if Arjun and his girlfriend were having sex, or if she'd ever given him a blow job. No, probably not. She was a Paki-stani, and though Pakistanis were the archenemies of Indians, they were probably just as prude. He wondered how it must feel to eat dinner with a girl after she'd sucked your dick. Was it strange to see her lips on a piece of pizza knowing where they'd been?

He thought about his brother. Mohan Lal's news would defi-nitely anger Arjun, who would probably get into a fight with their father, or at least say something mean to him. A couple of years ago, Arjun had predicted that this would happen. Maybe he had been right about other things too. Maybe their father was a closed-minded bigot. Selfish. After all, he had quit his job without even considering his sons. He was choosing to remain with a fool like Ms. Farber.

It was as if Mohan Lal was afraid of her. He let her decide what they watched and what they ate. He listened to each word of her advice about his manuscript, even though she didn't have the slightest clue about India. And she was making him get a five-hundred-dollar suit for Atlantic City, something the old Mohan Lal would have thought was ridiculous. Even Marc had commented on Mohan Lal's sheepishness. He said that Mohan Lal needed to grow a pair—that Rachel needed a man who knew how to handle her.

Eventually, Siddharth fell into a deep sleep, and when he next glanced at his clock, it was 3:14 a.m. To his left lay Marc, under the covers and snoring. Siddharth had fallen asleep in his cargo pants, and he was still wearing socks. No one had woken him up or wondered if he was hungry. *What a skank*, he thought. *She's a skank, and he's a fucking asshole.*

He fell asleep again and had strange, vivid dreams.

He dreamed that he was riding his bicycle through the streets of South Haven. It was an old bike from when he was six, with only a single training wheel. He was trying to get to the hospital to see his father but kept getting lost. He was on a street that resembled Boston Post Road, but among the strip malls and chain restaurants were Indian men hawking vegetables, yelling that they had the greenest peas in town. He overtook a dirty Indian beggar, who had no legs and was navigating the road in a tiny wooden cart, like the one Eddie Murphy uses at the beginning of *Trading Places*. A car pulled up beside Siddharth. It was Mrs. Peroti; she asked where he was going.

"To the hospital," he said.

"The BJP hospital?"

He nodded.

She told him to put his bike in the back. "We can take 95," she said. "I'll get you there in a jiffy."

7

FEBRUARY VACATION

The first weekend of February vacation was boring. Marc was around since his father had gone to Syracuse, where his girlfriend would have their baby, but Marc remained holed up in Siddharth's bedroom most of the time, talking on the phone. Sometimes he read a Polish Holocaust novel or listened to hip-hop, but he didn't utter more than twenty words. Siddharth didn't care anymore. He no longer needed Marc. His real brother was finally coming home.

This year, Arjun's break coincided with Siddharth's February vacation, and Arjun planned on borrowing a car from a friend and driving all the way from Michigan. He would leave Ann Arbor early Monday morning and drop off his housemate in Pennsylvania. He planned on making it to South Haven by dinnertime. The five of them would spend the next few days together, and on Friday, Mohan Lal and Ms. Farber would leave for Atlantic City. They would return home on Sunday night, and Arjun would set out for Michigan the following morning.

The night before Arjun's scheduled arrival, Siddharth lay awake making plans for his visit. They would see movies together; they would go to the mall or just drive around. He had a feeling that this time Arjun would finally see the truth about Ms. Farber—that she was totally fucked up. She was constantly nagging her son and putting him down. She had even hit Marc, which meant that one day she would probably hit Siddharth.

And look what she had done to their father: Mohan Lal had

fallen apart in her company. Just the other day, Siddharth woke up and found his father asleep at the kitchen table. His head was resting on his hairy arms, and his India manuscript was beside him, marked up with zillions of red squiggles. He hadn't dyed his hair in a while, which made him look particularly old, as did the uneven patches of gray stubble sprouting from his cheeks. He woke up with a start, then declared that he needed to say something.

"I'm late," said Siddharth.

"Just listen a second," said Mohan Lal.

"I'm listening."

Mohan Lal sighed. "Son, listen up carefully. Do whatever you want in life. Become a lawyer, a banker, a doctor. But whatever you choose, don't turn out like your old man."

Siddharth knew what his father wanted him to say—that Mohan Lal was brilliant, the greatest father in the world. This was their old song and dance. But he left the house without uttering a word.

Arjun would know how to handle their father. He would tell him to get more sleep, to apologize to the dean and get his job back. Since Mohan Lal had quit, Siddharth had begun to worry about the family's financial situation. If they ran out of money, he feared, they would have to move to a poorer town, or a city like New Haven. He imagined them living in a scruffy Victorian with old-fashioned radiators, or worse still, a grimy, multistoried apartment complex. He would have to go to some inner-city school where the students were crack babies or gave birth to crack babies—a school where the kids' parents collected welfare and carjacked Yalies.

He comforted himself with the knowledge that Ms. Farber had a big empty house in which all of them could comfortably fit. But if they moved in with her, she would have won. Other times, he imagined the riches that would pour in from his father's book. Authors like John Grisham made tons of money. Maybe once Mohan Lal got published, they would be set for life. That's what Barry Uncle thought; Ms. Farber thought so too.

Siddharth woke up out of pure excitement on Monday morning. He got up and made sure the guest room was ready for his brother, placing back issues of Marc's music magazines on the nightstand and a clean towel on the dresser. Recently, he had found a three-by-five picture of him and Arjun with their mother's family, which had been taken outside of their grandfather's Chandigarh home. Siddharth leaned it against a white bottle of aftershave that had been sitting there for as long as he could remember.

It started snowing around ten a.m., and two hours later Arjun called to say that the roads were getting dicey. He would spend the night in Pennsylvania and make it to South Haven the next afternoon. Siddharth slammed down the phone, wondering if his brother was lying. He wondered if Arjun was still under the fucking sheets with his Pakistani girlfriend.

The next morning, four or five inches of fresh powder covered the cars, and a slender crest of ice lined the telephone wires. His brother pulled into the driveway around eleven. By the time Siddharth reached the front door, Arjun was already inside, giving Ms. Farber a tight hug. Arjun said, "Rachel, I hope you don't mind my saying so, but have you been working out?"

She smiled. "Actually, I *am* paying a little more attention to what I put in my body. In fact, Arjun, I'd like to have a word about your diet."

Siddharth hadn't realized that she and Arjun were on a first-name basis. He hated the way she said his brother's name, as if the *j* were French, like in *Jacques*.

Marc was suddenly lumbering down the hallway. He cut in front of Siddharth and gave Arjun a halfhearted hug and a handshake. "Nice beard," said Marc. "I bet they're just lining up to sit next to you at the airport."

Marc was right. Arjun's facial hair was longer, and thicker too. He looked like a real foreigner, like one of the bad guys from *Die Hard*.

Arjun finally stepped toward Siddharth and hugged him, but they were interrupted by their father, who appeared in the entryway wearing nothing but a pink towel.

"That was fast," said Mohan Lal.

"You were right. The Tappan Zee was totally empty."

Mohan Lal embraced Arjun, then patted him on the cheek. "Son, do me one favor."

"What?" asked Arjun.

Mohan Lal smirked. "Cut your damn beard."

"Dad, please," said Siddharth.

Ms. Farber gripped Mohan Lal's naked shoulder. "Go put some clothes on, dear." She turned to Arjun. "Hon, you must be starving."

Arjun brought gifts for everyone. He gave Siddharth a fitted Michigan baseball cap with Jalen Rose's number stitched into the back, and handed a Michigan hockey T-shirt to Marc, who said, "Thanks, I guess," but then immediately put it on. Arjun got Ms. Farber an expensive-looking set of candles and their father a Michigan pen that required special cartridges. Mohan Lal put on his reading glasses to examine it, then uttered a faint thank you.

"You don't like it?" said Arjun.

"Your father loves it," said Ms. Farber.

Arjun then presented Mohan Lal with a stack of essays he had written that semester. As Mohan Lal thumbed through them, Siddharth saw him genuinely smile for the first time in days. Siddharth peered over his father's shoulder and read the strange titles of these papers—*Elusive Truths in the Zen Koan*, *Woodrow Wilson: Liberator or Racist*? Not surprisingly, Arjun had gotten As on all of them.

"Proud of you, son," said Mohan Lal, grasping Arjun's shoulder. "Next month, when my book is done, you will lend me your expertise."

"Uh-huh, sure," said Arjun.

As evening fell, Arjun told them about the treacherous drive on Interstate 80, and how the rural people of Tennessee were poor but inspiring. Ms. Farber and Mohan Lal were hanging on his every word. Siddharth thought about how they barely even listened to what he had to say anymore, but he was ready to drop that for today. It felt good to have Arjun home, and that's all he wanted to think about.

Ms. Farber made paneer that night, using tofu instead of actual cheese. Mohan Lal and Arjun were complimentary, but Siddharth stayed quiet. Marc said she should stick to pancakes and leave the curry to the Indians. She quickly changed the subject, bringing up the Honda Civic Arjun had driven home from Michigan. "It's very generous of your friend to lend out his car like that. It must be a thousand miles here and back."

"Fourteen hundred, actually," said Arjun. "But we don't really look at things like that."

"Like what?" Ms. Farber scrunched up her nose.

"With real friends, it's not about quantifying things," said Arjun. "It's not about miles or money."

Mohan Lal said that next year, Arjun wouldn't have to borrow anybody else's car. He could buy him his own vehicle.

"That's a nice idea," replied Arjun, "but it's not exactly an ideal time for frivolous expenditures."

Mohan Lal coughed midbite, then took a gulp of water.

Ms. Farber rubbed Mohan Lal's back. "Arjun, this time next year, your father's book'll be out. It'll be a whole new ball game."

"If you say so," said Arjun, giving her a tight-lipped smile.

Ms. Farber told the boys to clear the table and then brought out a lemon meringue pie that one of her clients had given her. She placed it in front of Mohan Lal, who served each person a slice, giving himself a particularly wide one. Siddharth struggled to eat his pie, but Marc quickly finished his and took seconds.

"My question is," said Marc, "who's gonna wanna read a book about India? If you haven't noticed, Americans don't really give a crap about much. They really only care about themselves."

"Marc, I've had enough for today," said Ms. Farber.

"Okay, lemme grab my muzzle."

She pulled his pie away and placed it on the kitchen counter. "Arjun, if you had a car, you'd be able to get away from campus—do a little grocery shopping on weekends."

"Honestly," said Arjun, "I'd like to do without a car for as long as possible."

Ms. Farber dabbed her mouth with a napkin. "Oh, and why's that?"

Arjun commenced a long speech about the pointlessness of

automobiles, which had made Americans lazy and dependent on autocratic governments. "They created *this*," he said, spreading his arms wide apart.

"This what?" asked Siddharth.

"This sprawl. It's just . . . disgusting. Americans are so isolated, so lonely. You ever wonder why?"

"Heavy," said Ms. Farber. "Interesting."

"But Mom," said Marc, "I just said the same exact thing."

Mohan Lal served himself more pie. "Son, what about your beloved workers? Didn't Henry Ford give them jobs? Automobile factories have given the working class of this country some dignity."

"Dignity?" countered Arjun. "Dad, Henry Ford was a racist."

"Jesus," said Mohan Lal. "What kind of pinkos are teaching you at the University of Michigan?"

Arjun cleared his throat. "I take it you won't be applying for a job there. They'll be devastated, I'm sure."

After dinner, Siddharth was finally alone with his brother in the guest room, where Arjun carefully unpacked the contents of his worn backpack. He pulled out a wool sweater with little animals on it, then a hairbrush and several books. He placed these items in the dresser before picking up the photograph from Chandigarh that Siddharth had left for him.

"I heard they're selling Nana-ji's house," said Arjun. "I wanna go back there this summer—see it one last time."

"Great," said Siddharth. "Have fun."

"What's the matter with you?"

"Nothing." He didn't know where to begin.

"I can tell something's up—so talk."

Siddharth shrugged. "You know Dad's book?"

"Unfortunately."

"Come on, Arjun. Don't be like that. I've got a serious question."

"So ask your question."

"Well, I wanna know if Dad's book is gonna be a hit. You think it'll make us rich?"

Arjun snorted. "You're kidding, right? Siddharth, it takes years to write a real book, not a few months. Dad, he's writing more of a pamphlet—a silly piece of propaganda."

"Propaganda?" Siddharth's throat was now scratchy.

"Yeah, fascist propaganda."

"You mean like the Nazis?"

"Not the Nazis. More like Hindu fascism."

"That's not even a real thing, Arjun."

Arjun sat on the bed and placed a hand on Siddharth's shoulder. "Listen, as long as I'm alive—and I plan on being here for a while—you don't have to worry about anything, especially not money. Dad's gonna find another job. And he has some money to fall back on."

"He does?"

"Yeah, he does."

"What money?"

"I really shouldn't talk about it."

"Come on," said Siddharth. "I'm a teenager now."

After some coaxing, Arjun explained that when their mother had died, their father received money from a life insurance policy. "It's not a lot, but enough for a couple of years."

As Siddharth lay in bed that night, the thought of this life insurance money made him feel lighter, but then he was overwhelmed by a wave of disgust. The only reason they had this money was because she was gone. Did that mean he was happy she was gone? *You're a freak*, he told himself. *A cruel and demented freak.*

8

PARTITION

On the Thursday morning of February vacation, Ms. Farber dropped Marc off at Dinetta's on her way to see clients at her place. Siddharth sat in front of the television, waiting for his real family to awaken. Arjun had been out late last night. He'd gone drinking with Derrick Rodgers, a roofer, and Sam Palmieri, who had taken over his father's landscaping business. Siddharth couldn't understand why his brother wanted to go out with people who weren't in college. He wondered if Arjun was doing so to buy drugs.

Mohan Lal emerged first, just after ten, wearing sweatpants and a flannel robe. Siddharth made them pizza bagels, and while they were eating, Arjun walked into the kitchen wearing jeans and a sweatshirt. He gave Siddharth's shoulders a brief massage and then downed a glass of water.

"You want one?" asked Siddharth.

"I'll grab something when I'm out. The car needs an oil change."

"I'll come," said Siddharth.

"We'll both go with you," said Mohan Lal.

Arjun grabbed Siddharth's bagel from his plate and ate half of it in a single bite. "You'll get bored," he said, still chewing. "I have to run a bunch of errands, actually."

"Which errands?" asked Mohan Lal.

"I need a new comforter. I need a copy of the *Times*."

Mohan Lal started grinning.

"Don't start, Dad." Arjun took a banana from the counter and peeled it open. "I'm not in the mood for one of your conspiracy theories."

"What conspiracy theories?"

Siddharth knew all about his father's conspiracy theories. Mohan Lal had always said that the *Times* was a State Department mouthpiece. It "bad-mouthed India" but "glossed over the fundamentalists in Pakistan."

"Whatever, Dad," said Arjun. "The *Times* is one of the most respected newspapers in the world. And my professor has an editorial coming out—about the riots."

"Good for him," said Mohan Lal, wiping his mouth.

"You should read it. Professor Sengupta's pretty amazing. They say he's gonna get a Nobel Prize."

Mohan Lal plunked his dirty napkin onto his empty plate. "I know all about these Professor Senguptas. They're sycophants. Pseudosecularists. Babbling Bengali Brahmins."

"You know what, Dad?"

"Tell me."

Arjun threw his peel into the trash compactor. "It's just the way you operate—your way of controlling other people. You criticize everybody else because of your own insecurities."

"Arjun," muttered Siddharth, looking at him with narrowed eyes.

"Wonderful," said Mohan Lal. "Now my son is also a psychologist."

"Come on, Siddharth," said Arjun.

"What?"

"Come with me—that is, if you want to."

Siddharth felt bad admitting it, but he did want to go with his brother. And he was glad their father wasn't coming with them.

Mohan Lal went to the sink and started doing dishes. He said, "Son, if I had insulted my father like that, he would have given me a thrashing."

They got into Arjun's borrowed Civic, and Arjun put in a cassette that sounded crackly and faded. He said it was a live performance by the Grateful Dead, a name that was vaguely familiar to Siddharth. For some reason he associated it with drugs—drugs and motorcycles. The music was surprisingly gentle, though, even a little babyish—the kind of thing they made him sing in the fourth grade.

Arjun took a right onto Post Road, where mountains of plowed snow were glimmering in the strip mall parking lots. Siddharth squinted, and his brother put on a pair of aviator sunglasses.

"Where'd you get those?" asked Siddharth.

"A friend. I'll get you some when you're older."

The road was so clogged with cars that they had to wait six minutes to clear a single light. "Where the hell is everybody going?" said Arjun, lighting a cigarette. It was the third time he had done so in front of Siddharth. "It's like, if they don't buy something, they'll go crazy—they won't feel like good Americans."

Siddharth's stomach tingled. He wasn't sure if he wanted to ask Arjun for a drag of his cigarette, or to make him promise to quit smoking. Neither option would go over well, so he just kept his mouth shut.

Arjun ashed his cigarette out the window. "How long has Dad been like this?"

"Like what?"

"Depressed."

"He's not depressed, Arjun. He's just focusing on his book."

Arjun stopped at another light. He glanced at Siddharth and smiled. "Don't be so serious all the time. What's wrong?"

"Nothing." Then, after a long pause, he said, "Well, lots of things."

"Name one."

Siddharth chewed a chunk of skin from the inside of his mouth. "I don't know. Money."

"We already talked about that. I thought that was all settled."

"Yeah, but Rachel, she spends way too much money."

"What?"

"She's always buying such pointless stuff—shampoo and make-up. And she makes Dad spend his money on stupid things. His suit—it cost, like, a thousand dollars. And the new shoes? They were at least a hundred bucks."

Arjun wove the car through the congested thoroughfare. "That doesn't sound like him. Dad's too cheap to spend that kind of money on shoes."

"Yeah, well, things change. You don't know the real Ms. Farber, Arjun. All she cares about is money. That's why she got divorced in the first place."

"She has her own money," said Arjun, smoke trickling out of his nostrils. "It's not really your place to judge."

"You don't get it. Why do you think she's sticking around?"

Arjun took a hard drag off his cigarette and then chucked it out the window. "Why?"

"I bet she wants the life insurance money."

Arjun cracked a smile, then slapped Siddharth on the knee. "Sometimes I forget."

"Forget what?"

"That you're just a kid." He pulled into a gas station, parking beside a beat-up tow truck. "Siddharth, you really need to try to be more honest with yourself. Otherwise you're gonna end up like Dad."

Arjun stepped out of the car, leaving Siddharth sitting there stewing. His brother was just as big of a pain as his father.

In the morning, when Siddharth walked to the bathroom to pee and brush his teeth, he spotted their luggage at the end of the hallway—Ms. Farber's black suitcase and the rolling duffel she had given Mohan Lal for Hanukkah. A bag containing Mohan Lal's new suit was draped over the luggage. *They'll be gone soon*, he thought. *Thank God.*

When he got to the kitchen, Ms. Farber was at the table clipping coupons while Mohan Lal cracked eggs at the counter. Mohan Lal was wearing a sleeveless wool sweater and a tucked-in button-down shirt. Siddharth was pleased to see him so crisp. His father seemed alert for a change, strong in a way that he hadn't in months.

Mohan Lal told him they would be leaving before noon and then offered him an omelet.

"Sure," said Siddharth, who headed toward the guest room. Arjun wasn't there, and his bed was already made. Siddharth dashed back to the kitchen, where Ms. Farber explained that his brother had gone for a jog.

"But it's freezing out," said Siddharth.

"It's forty-eight degrees," she said. "You boys should take note and follow suit."

You should shut the fuck up, thought Siddharth. He poured himself a glass of orange juice and moved toward the family room, but Mohan Lal told him to wait.

"What?" said Siddharth.

"Today we shall have a family breakfast."

Siddharth contemplated saying a couple of things—that he didn't like breakfast, and not everyone here was actual family—but he seated himself in the kitchen, staring down at the newspaper Arjun had bought from the gas station. An advertisement announced a special offer on a tour of Mallorca, which he assumed was in Mexico.

Ms. Farber offered Siddharth a bowl of fruit from the fridge, and he spooned the mixture into a quarter plate. He noticed that it contained bananas. His mother had always said that bananas were a big mistake in a fruit salad. They turned all the other fruit brown.

Ms. Farber brought her planner to the table and flipped through its pages. "Lots to do this morning, I better hurry."

"There's plenty of time," said Mohan Lal. "Spend five minutes with the mirror, not fifty."

"Really, Mo?" said Mr. Farber. "Now?"

Siddharth heard the front door open, and moments later, Arjun walked into the kitchen sweating and panting. Before greeting anyone, he downed two glasses of water.

"Arjun," said Mohan Lal, "what kind of omelet will you have?"

"I'll just have fruit," said Arjun. He seated himself beside Siddharth and ate some grapes and bananas directly from the bowl. Mohan Lal placed a steaming omelet in front of him. Siddharth knew this one had been intended for him but chose not to say anything.

"I read your little article," said Mohan Lal.

"Great," said Arjun, shaking salt over his eggs.

"You don't want my opinion?"

"I have an idea," said Arjun. "Why don't you write one of your *little* letters to the editor?"

"I want cheese in mine," said Siddharth. "And no onions." He turned the page and found the article in question: "Shattered Dreams of Democracy" by Arup Sengupta.

Ms. Farber tore out a check. "Honey, what did we say about the cheese?"

Mohan Lal beat some more eggs, and soon they were sizzling on the stove. "This professor of yours—I know his type. He's nothing but a lefty—a leftist Muslim-lover. Such people only write half the truth."

"Thanks for the input, Dad. Can I get some toast?"

"Let your professor have his opinions," said Mohan Lal. "My only problem is that he has converted my son."

Arjun slammed down his glass, and Siddharth jumped in his seat. "If I remember correctly," said Arjun, "weren't some of your best friends Muslims?"

"What rubbish are you speaking?" said Mohan Lal, placing an omelet in front of Siddharth.

"Mahmood?" said Arjun. "Shamim?"

"Those were your mother's friends."

"Bullshit. You went on vacation with them. You let them babysit your son."

"I have no recollection of those events."

"That's worrying," said Arjun. "I hope you're not going senile."

Ms. Farber peered at them over the rims of her reading glasses. "Guys, you know what my mother used to say? She said there's no point in hurting someone you love over politics."

"That's the problem with this country," said Arjun. "Everyone is so damn apolitical. That's why our government can do whatever it wants, wherever it wants."

Siddharth said, "If you hate America so much, then why don't you go to India—or maybe Pakistan?"

Ignoring Siddharth, Arjun glared at Mohan Lal, who turned off the exhaust fan and brought an especially large omelet to the table. He gave a third of it to Ms. Farber and saved the rest for himself.

"Listen, son," said Mohan Lal. "You don't know what I saw—what I lived through. If you did, you'd be singing a different song."

"How *could* I know? You've repressed it all. You can't even remember what actually happened."

Ms. Farber put away her planner and let her reading glasses dangle around her neck. "I'm always telling you the same thing, Mo." She scrutinized her omelet. "Are those hot peppers?"

"Coriander," said Mohan Lal, seating himself beside her. "Listen, your professor is crying about crimes against Muslims, but what about the Mussulman? Haven't they raped? Haven't they murdered?"

"This is different," said Arjun, his fingers twisting the bristles of his beard.

"Different? You're telling me a murder isn't a murder? What strange leftist notions you've acquired at college."

"Dad, when a government inflicts violence on a specific group of people—for no apparent reason—they have a name for it in the civilized world. They call it genocide. Rachel, can't you talk any sense into him?"

In that moment, Siddharth saw his older brother for what he was: a traitor. He loved Muslims, and he hated America. He was more loyal to Ms. Farber than to their own father.

Ms. Farber closed her planner with a thump. "Arjun, your father's a very learned man. And last I heard, this is a democracy."

That'll teach him, thought Siddharth.

Arjun stood up, his chair squeaking against the wooden floor.

"Sit down," said Mohan Lal.

"Don't tell me what to do. Rachel, you of all people should understand. The Muslims, they're just like the Jews."

She gave him a hard stare. "That's hard to believe, Arjun. And a little insensitive."

Arjun yanked the newspaper from Siddharth. "Here, read it for yourself."

"Hey, I was reading that," said Siddharth.

Ms. Farber placed her reading glasses back on her freckled nose. "Is this the one?"

Arjun was pacing around the kitchen. "No, it's the other one about Hindu-Muslim violence."

She clicked her tongue, then started reading to herself. Arjun interrupted and told her to read the piece out loud. "Siddharth should hear this," he said. "He should know what his family is really all about."

"You know, you and your father are actually quite similar." Ms. Farber cleared her throat. "'Shattered Dreams of Democracy' by Arup Sengupta. *During the first weeks of the year, the journalist Tiliptuma Sharma Sengupta—my daughter-in-law—was covering the so-called "Bombay Riots," which have claimed the lives of thousands of individuals, some Hindus, but mostly Muslims. On the evening of January 18, she was looking on as a Hindu mob gathered in a busy commercial locality, home to printing presses and cloth-ing stores. These shops were owned by Hindus, Muslims, Christians, and Parsis, an unsurprisingly eclectic mixture of people in one of the world's most historically cosmopolitan metropolises.*"

Siddharth was listening, but he couldn't make much sense of what was being read. He had never been to Bombay. His relatives had told him that it was even dirtier than Delhi.

"*The Hindu mob started chanting slogans about their motherland. A few men broke away, entering certain stores and pulling out various shopkeepers. Each of the stores they targeted had a Muslim proprietor, and the men who were pulled onto the street were also Muslims, though you wouldn't have been able to know this by looking at them. They were wearing western—*"

"Skip to the next paragraph," said Arjun.

"*Three Hindu men proceeded to throw tires around one of these Muslims, a young man named Hassan Khan, and they doused him in petroleum. My daughter-in-law struggled to get in front of the assailants, but the mob thwarted her efforts. The Hindu rioters then lit Mr. Khan on fire. As he burned to death, he begged for mercy, but not a single person came to his rescue.*"

As Ms. Farber read, Siddharth found himself intrigued. The things she was reading seemed like something from a movie—not events that could happen in real life.

"My daughter-in-law ran toward a group of loitering policemen standing five hundred feet away. She implored them to intervene, but they ignored her, even after she had flashed her press credentials. Later, she tried to print an account of what she had witnessed in a major Indian newspaper, but her editor—"

"Enough!" snapped Mohan Lal. "Christ, I've heard enough."

"Let her finish," said Arjun. He seated himself on the kitchen counter.

"No," said Mohan Lal. "We are having a family breakfast, not a seminar of your leftist propaganda."

Ms. Farber removed her reading glasses and pinched the bridge of her nose. "This . . . Mo, did this really happen?"

"Of course it happened," said Arjun. "It's right there in the *Times.*"

"Yah, yah, yah," said Mohan Lal, standing up. "That bloody paper is the gospel. Jesus, I can't believe it—I've raised a bloody Congress-wallah."

Arjun jumped off the counter and stood a foot away from his father. "Why does everything have to be so black or white with you? And for your information, Dad, you didn't raise me."

Siddharth could see spit fly from his brother's mouth. He could see his father's lips quivering. He wanted to intervene but remained frozen.

"Yes," said Mohan Lal, "I just sat there and watched."

"You said it," said Arjun. "You know, Mom was right about you. Face it, you weren't cut out for parenting."

Ms. Farber reached for Mohan Lal's wrist. "Arjun, I know you don't mean that."

"Oh, I do," said Arjun. "But actually, I'm grateful. Thanks to my mother, I'm not a fascist. If it wasn't for her, I might actually believe that people should die because of their religion. Who knows, I might even believe that a person should die because of the color of their skin."

"Now Arjun, your father doesn't think any of those things," said Ms. Farber.

Mohan Lal stepped closer toward Arjun. "No, my son understands me quite well. Arjun, I have learned one truth in my life."

"And what's that, Dad? Please—share your wisdom."

"What I've learned is that a Muslim can't be trusted. The only good Muslim is a dead one."

Arjun gritted his teeth. He clenched his fist and raised it behind his ear.

"Arjun . . ." said Siddharth. Tears dripped from his eyes.

Mohan Lal smirked. "Yes, my Gandhian son. Go ahead, hit your father."

Arjun glanced at him, then clasped his hands behind his head. "It's funny," he said, his voice cracking, "you spend your whole life reading, Dad, and yet you're still like a child. You're still so fucking ignorant."

"Then why remain in my presence?" asked Mohan Lal. "Why remain in my home?"

"Finally, we're on the same page about something."

"Talking like a man is one thing. Acting the part is another."

Arjun stormed to the guest room and slammed the door. Siddharth let himself in and watched as his brother hurriedly packed his duffel. Arjun then ran through the house and out the front door. He stowed his bag in the trunk of his borrowed Honda. As he got into the car, Siddharth literally clung to him. "Where are you going?"

"Home," said Arjun, buckling his seat belt.

"But you are home."

"No I'm not. This isn't my home anymore."

"If you go, I'll tell him about your girlfriend."

"You think I give a shit?" said Arjun.

"I'll tell him you're on drugs."

Arjun lit a cigarette. He started the engine and rolled down the driveway. His tires squeaked as he charged up the hill.

Siddharth sat down on the front steps, allowing his salty tears to coat his tongue. He remained outside for fifteen minutes, but his brother didn't return. The only vehicle that appeared belonged to the postman.

9

RIOT

"**K**id, I know what we gotta do," said Eddie B., chewing on cheese-flavored popcorn. "We gotta get her mailbox. We'll wreck that shit."

Marc shook his head, his lips curled in a disdainful grin. "What a bunch of losers. You don't have anything better to do? Don't you know any women?"

"Eddie, it's not happening," said Luca. He grabbed the popcorn and flicked his bangs to one side. "She's on the other side of 34. It'll take us all night to walk it." His left hand was wrapped around the rubber penis he'd stolen from the head shop beside his father's salon. Occasionally, he swung this object over his head, as if it were a lasso.

"We can take your mom's shitter," said Eddie, his orange eyebrows arching. "It'll fit right in with all that white trash."

"No way." Luca whipped Eddie's leg with the phallus. "Not tonight."

Siddharth was only half paying attention to their banter, but the sound of his friends' voices was soothing. The lights were dim, and he was lying on the shaggy multicolored carpet in Luca's family room. The door that separated this room from the kitchen was made of plastic and slid open like an accordion, and the wall behind the television was lined with wooden panels. He returned his gaze to the television, on which a dark-haired man was groping a large-breasted blonde. They were on a bed with silk sheets that overlooked the sea. Eddie had rigged Luca's cable box so that *Playboy* came in for free.

After Arjun had left, Mohan Lal poured himself a stiff drink and locked himself in his office. Ms. Farber cancelled their hotel reservations, then went to the kitchen and removed all of the silverware from the drawers, polishing each and every piece before putting it back. Siddharth couldn't believe it. What kind of freak would clean at a time like this? And why did she think she could go into their cabinets as if she owned them? He had ambled to his bedroom and sat on the floor, tapping his head against the closet door. Something bad was going to happen. Arjun was going to skid off the highway into the Delaware Water Gap.

By the time the phone rang, Siddharth had been sure it was the police calling to say that his brother was dead. But it was Arjun himself. He was spending the night in Pennsylvania and would push on to Michigan in the morning. Ms. Farber had taken the call. She told Arjun that they'd been counting on him. She told him they were disappointed. She put down the phone without passing it to Siddharth, who imagined punching her in the face. Mohan Lal was the one who decided to leave for Atlantic City in the morning. Marc's father was in upstate New York and Andy was in London, so Mohan Lal said the boys could stay with Barry Uncle. Siddharth said, "Dad, I'm sick of Barry Uncle. There's no way I'm staying with him." When Mohan Lal replied, "Fine, we'll cancel the trip," Siddharth thought he had triumphed. But Ms. Farber said, "Hey, I've got an idea. Why don't I put in a call to Mrs. Peroti?"

Marc was now on the Perotis' brown La-Z-Boy, his arms imperiously splayed on its ample armrests. With his legs propped in the air, he looked like a reposing king. "Look," Marc said to Luca, "you got dumped, and that sucks. And this Jeanette sounds like a real bitch. But trust me, only a few things are gonna make this better. You can get laid, or you can sleep for a couple of days. But the best thing would be to get really fucking wasted."

Marc pulled a lever to retract his leg rest, then sprang up and headed to the opposite corner of the room. "Yo, check this out." He grabbed his overnight bag and pulled out Siddharth's ornate Indian slingshot, the one Barry Uncle had given him.

Siddharth tensed up. "What the hell's that doing here?"

"It's for Luca's rectum," said Marc.

Eddie laughed.

"Come on, put it away," said Siddharth.

Marc dropped it to the floor, then extracted a rectangular bottle of liquor. It was green and had a deer on the label. He cracked it open. "I don't know about you, but I'm fucking thirsty." He took a swig and handed it to Siddharth.

He sipped the liquor, which singed the inside of his mouth.

"Pussy," said Eddie. "Take a real sip."

"Fuck off, Eddie," said Marc.

Siddharth handed the bottle to Eddie, who drank some and passed it on to Luca.

"I know a chick," said Luca. "I know a place where we can get a little pussy."

"Where?" asked Eddie.

Luca pointed his rubber penis at Siddharth. "Ask him. I hear his little friend can suck a mean cock."

"Who?" said Eddie.

Siddharth rubbed his neck and glanced down at the multicolored carpet. For the first time ever, he noticed that the rug's different colors formed a design. It might have been a tree.

"Niggerski," said Luca.

"Sharon?" said Eddie. "I thought she was a lezzie."

"Nah. Siddharth here says she likes it up the ass." Luca put the rubber penis near his rump and pantomimed the act of copulation. *"Oh, Siddharth, give it to me."* His voice was high and screechy. *"Fuck my hairy asshole."*

Eddie laughed. So did Marc.

Siddharth grabbed the bottle and downed a few glugs. The liquid passed straight into his throat and burned his belly. He gasped for air; his eyes were watering. "Yeah, I guess you would know how she likes it," he said.

Eddie cackled, then slapped him on the back.

The door suddenly slid open, and Luca's father barged in. Marc was quick to slip the bottle behind his back. Siddharth lunged for the remote, but Mr. Peroti got to it first. Siddharth sobered up quickly. He thought it was all over, that Mr. Peroti would get right on the phone with his father. But Mr. Peroti was smiling.

"I know what you're up to," he said. "You're all a bunch of little goats." His accent was thick, even worse than Mohan Lal's. "Relax, everyone. Oh, look at her. Isn't she beautiful?" Mr. Peroti seated himself on the sofa, dangling an arm around Eddie. "You boys can relax. I'm not gonna tell your parents. But you gotta promise me something."

Siddharth nodded. He would promise Mr. Peroti anything he wanted.

"Just stay away from the drugs—otherwise I beat the crap outta yous. Oh, and no homo business, please."

By twelve thirty, they had cracked open a second green bottle, and the words were flowing freely off Siddharth's tongue. He yakked about Nirvana being better than Pearl Jam, about Michigan's Fab Five being the best team that had ever existed.

"Yo, you don't know shit about shit," said Eddie. "Those guys are a bunch of ghetto-ass punks."

"Yo, that's racist," said Marc.

Siddharth brought up his recurring worry about memories—that there was no point in having them because they just made you sad.

"Yo, what you been smoking?" said Luca.

"He's right," said Marc. "My grandfather—he has to wear a diaper. He's not, like, *Oh, I'm so glad I can remember a time when I could wipe my own fucking ass.*"

Siddharth soon realized he had never been this drunk in his life. He couldn't stop smiling and wondered why people weren't drunk all the time. "Guys, I need to tell you something."

Everybody looked at him expectantly.

"Fuck Jeanette," he said. "Fuck her, and fuck our fucking parents."

"Yeah, kid," said Luca, putting an arm around him. "Tonight's your night. Tonight we're gonna get you a mailbox."

"Hell yeah," said Siddharth.

Eddie and Luca started their talk of shitting houses, bragging about a dead squirrel they had left on the front seat of a neighbor's Corolla, a fire they had once started during leaf season; it had gotten so big that a truck had to come from another town.

"Whatever," said Marc, annoyed. "You guys are a bunch of shit talkers."

"Don't believe me," said Eddie. "My dad's only a volunteer fireman."

"What about you, Marc?" asked Siddharth.

Marc looked stunned for a second, but then smiled. "What was that, Sidney?"

"I said, what about you? What have you ever shitted?"

"It's *shat*."

"Huh?" said Siddharth.

"It's not shitted, it's shat. Learn how to speak fucking English. And I got better things to do. But trust me, back in the day, these hands got pretty dirty."

"Shit talker," said Luca, waving his rubber penis.

Marc took a swig of booze. "Ask any Woodford cop. They still keep a picture of me on the dashboard."

"Stories are stories," said Eddie. "I'd like to see it with my own two eyes."

Marc told everyone how a couple of summers ago, when his parents had first separated, he used to sneak out with Corey Thompson, and they would break into rich people's houses. They played these people's video games. They ate their food and ordered pornos on pay-per-view. "Right before we left," Marc told them, "one of us always took a shit—right there in the middle of the floor."

"I hate Corey," said Luca. "White-trash motherfucker."

"Freaking hilarious." Eddie clapped his hands and keeled forward with laugher.

Siddharth turned to the television, where a naked woman was jogging down a beach at sunset. The boys passed the bottle around, and someone said it was time to get to work.

"Fuck that," said Marc. "I got no enemies in South Haven."

"Well, I do," said Luca.

Eddie smirked. "Niggerski?"

"Hell yeah," said Luca. "Fucking dyke."

Marc said, "Sidney, isn't she your friend?"

He shrugged, then reached for the bottle. As far as he was concerned, the only friends he had were sitting in this room with him right now. As far as he was concerned, loyalty was a myth. It was a bunch of bullshit that changed depending on the moment.

"Yo Luca," said Eddie, "tell 'em what she said."

"Screw you, Eddie," said Luca.

"Yo, we were on the bus, and Luca was ranking on someone up front, calling them a fag."

"Would you shut the fuck up?" said Luca.

"Let him speak," said Siddharth.

"So Niggerski stands up, her lips all quivering like a total spaz. She says, *Luca, takes one to know one. We all know you're gay.* The whole bus starts cracking up."

Luca batted Eddie over the head with his penis.

Eddie grabbed hold of the rubber dick. "Watch it, or I'm gonna ram this up your butthole. Oh wait, you'd probably like that."

All four of them were in stitches.

They strolled down Luca's street, Red Fox Lane, sucking on cigars with plastic filters. The others were telling jokes, talking shit. Siddharth was wobbly and warm, so he took off his gloves. He wished he had listened to Marc, who had said it was too hot to wear a jacket, but he didn't want to part with the red-and-green Columbia parka that Mohan Lal had bought him after one of their recent squabbles.

The moon was strong but it was foggy out, so the few streetlights were surrounded by little halos of moisture. The lawns they passed resembled cowhide, splotches of icy white mixed with puddles of mud. He could hear water dripping from every branch, from every tailpipe of every car. Snowmelts roared like rivers in the sewers, and Siddharth thought back to the river at the state park in Hamden. When he was seven, he had gone there with his parents, and his mother had suggested they try out a hiking trail.

Mohan Lal was resistant but eventually relented. They ended up getting in over their heads, walking two challenging miles over cliff and rock. Siddharth had been miserable and scared, but it was all worth it when they got to the top. The sky was so crisp that they could glimpse the Knights of Columbus building in New Haven. They could see all the way to the sound, a faint sliver of Long Island on the horizon.

Siddharth hoped his father had made it to Atlantic City okay. He was angry that Mohan Lal hadn't bothered to call but assumed it was Ms. Farber's fault. She was a freak. She probably wouldn't let the poor man take a break from banging. All the people who were supposed to take care of him were freaks, but in that moment, it seemed like the biggest one was Arjun. Siddharth was fed up with all his fucking Gandhi talk and his fucking Pakistani girlfriend—the way he complained about America and cars. Everything would be much better if it weren't for his brother.

They stepped off the road and cut into somebody's backyard. The grass was breathing steam, and it suddenly seemed as if they were in a movie. Siddharth thought about *Platoon*, picturing Charlie Sheen with a machine gun. But no, this was more *Stand By Me*. He wasn't sure if he was Vern, the chubby one who whined, or Wil Wheaton's character, who was smart and knew how to tell a good story. Eddie picked up a large rock and chucked it at a birdhouse mounted on top of a wooden pole. He slapped Luca five, and they both cheered.

Marc hung back, dangling an arm around Siddharth's shoulder. "Fucking morons."

Siddharth laughed, then grabbed the green bottle from him and took a swig.

Marc finished it off before throwing the empty onto a covered swimming pool. "You okay?"

"Yeah," said Siddharth. "But I gotta ask you something."

"Shoot."

"Do you think my brother's a druggie?"

"Arjun? I wouldn't worry about him. I'd say he's an upstanding young man."

Siddharth wasn't sure if Marc was being sarcastic or not. He grabbed the slingshot from him, the one that Barry Uncle had given him. He shot a stone at a stop sign, and the lights of a nearby house flicked on. The four boys broke into a run.

By the time they reached Sharon's, Siddharth was wondering if he would ever again regain control of his mind. He needed a bed. He needed sleep. A ragged old sofa sat on Sharon's lawn, about ten feet away from a stripped-down postal jeep. He took a seat on it, watching Luca and Eddie smoke their cigars on the driveway. When he closed his eyes, the darkness spun. He thought about Sharon. He wondered if she was still with her father or back at home. Regardless, she deserved what was happening. She was a downer, and she was nosy. She rubbed her boyfriend in Siddharth's face just to make him crazy, even though this so-called boyfriend was probably nonexistent. Siddharth thought about the things she had said to Luca on the bus. She was a hypocrite. They were all a bunch of hypocrites—not just her, but Ms. Farber and Mr. Latella, and especially Arjun.

Suddenly, he could see himself kissing Sharon's breasts, sucking on them like the muscled man had just done to the blonde on *Playboy*. He saw himself lying over her body on a beach. He tried pulling down her dress, and when she didn't let him, he had to yank it off. A crow cawed. He opened his eyes and observed the house across the street. It was a huge, modern home, completely the opposite of Sharon's. The place even had a three-car garage, which meant that whoever lived there was rich—whoever lived there was happy. A *For Sale* sign sprouted from the house's front lawn. In that moment, he glimpsed a pleasing vision of the future.

Despite what Arjun had said, Mohan Lal's book would make them millions. Mohan Lal would no longer need Ms. Farber; he could get someone prettier and younger, maybe a blonde—or maybe no one at all. Father and son would buy that house and live in it by themselves. That way, Siddharth would have a friend right across the street. A girlfriend. Somebody who had known him when he was happier. Or they could move into an even bigger house somewhere else. In a different town, where nobody knew him at all.

He remembered something Ms. Farber had said yesterday, when they still hadn't heard from Arjun: "Mo, you can't let other people control you—not your friends, not your family, and definitely not your children." Hadn't Sharon said something similar once? These two females were both insane. They both wanted to separate him from the people who truly loved him.

The sound of glass shattering, then voices.

"What the fuck?" Eddie's voice.

Siddharth turned to Marc, who was now holding the Indian slingshot. He had just cracked the glass on the lamppost on Sharon's front lawn. Siddharth burped, tasted the pesto Mrs. Peroti had served them for dinner. Sweat drenched his arms and legs. He burped again and thought he might vomit. No, he had to take a dump. He rose from the sofa and walked toward Marc. A set of headlights approached, and Marc told everyone to shut up. Siddharth felt a hand on his back. The next thing he knew he was eating wet earth. "What the hell?"

"Shhhhh," said Marc. "Stay down."

The car slowed but didn't stop.

Marc puffed on his cigar. "Luca, whatever you're gonna do, do it quick."

Eddie and Luca stomped on their stogies and walked over to Sharon's mailbox. They gripped its wooden stem and started grunting and heaving. The box yielded, and they placed it in the middle of the road. Siddharth couldn't stand it anymore. If he didn't go now, he might do it in his pants. Marc told him to be a man and wait.

"What if I can't?" Siddharth threw his cigar on the ground and crushed it with his shoe.

"Just drop trou and go for it," said Eddie. "Watch."

Eddie sprinted over to Sharon's front steps, undoing his belt on the way. Siddharth wanted to look away, but instead he watched as Eddie squatted down and defecated. He recalled an aunt's house in a dirty town near Delhi. Meerut or something. She had one of those hole-in-the-ground toilets, and whenever he had to stay there, he got constipated.

Luca and Marc were cracking up. Siddharth started laughing too, and he was laughing so hard that his bathroom attack vanished. Eddie ran across the street and pulled out the *For Sale* sign, placing it on top of Sharon's mailbox. Luca tugged at the Nagorskis' smaller newspaper mailbox, easily uprooting it. He pulled out a water bottle from his backpack, which was filled with gasoline meant for his father's tractor. The bottle gurgled as he poured it over the pile, the noxious stench of gasoline infiltrating Siddharth's nostrils.

The boys formed a semicircle around their makeshift hearth. Luca pulled out a Zippo from his windbreaker, flipped it open, and spun the top. Sparks flew, but it wouldn't catch.

"Pass it here," said Marc.

Luca handed it over. Marc sucked on the lighter, but it refused to yield a flame.

"Are you kidding me?" said Eddie. "Yo, Kaufman, I know you got matches."

"Just used my last one," said Marc.

Siddharth wondered if this was a sign. Maybe this wasn't supposed to happen.

"This is like blue balls," said Eddie. "Sidney, can't you just rub two sticks together?"

Siddharth noticed that Marc was the only one still smoking. "Hey, guys," he said.

Luca said, "Sidney, don't pussy out on us now."

"Listen," said Siddharth, "we can use Marc's cigar." His head was pounding, and everyone was staring at him.

"What the hell you talking about?" said Luca.

"Marc's got his cigar still," replied Siddharth. He wished he hadn't said anything. But now he had to finish what he'd started.

Eddie said, "So what's your point?"

"All he has to do is get it going and throw it down."

"Will that work?" asked Luca.

"It works in the movies," said Siddharth. "Here, give it to me. Marc, gimme your stogie."

Marc handed it over.

He pinched it between his thumb and forefinger. He took a strong drag, and the cigar's tip glowed cherry red. When he threw it onto the pile, nothing happened at first. But then there was a subtle boom. A blue flame spread across every inch of wood, every centimeter of plastic and metal. There were crackles. Some clicks and hisses. Soon, tall orange flames shot toward the sky. They were mesmerizing.

Siddharth closed his eyes, allowing the heat to soothe his cheeks and forehead. It felt so good, better than lying in front of the television with a blanket—better than lying in his father's bed and listening to him snore, better than watching his mother's hands sketch a landscape. When he opened his eyes, Marc's face was a warm shade of red, as if he had just returned from the beach. Siddharth looked over his friend's shoulder and saw two headlights approaching, then flashing red and blue lights atop the car. He didn't want to ruin this moment, so he didn't say anything about the cops.

"Holy shit!" Marc yelped. "Holy fuck." He grabbed Siddharth's sleeve and yanked him toward the woods.

EPILOGUE

WHY AND WHAT'S THE REASON FOR

I t is late May. The curtains sway, a breeze tickles his neck. Opening his eyes, he feels a pang of panic. He doesn't have the energy for school but then remembers it is Saturday. He stretches his arms and relaxes, nuzzles his head into his pillow. Pleasant thoughts fill his mind. Tonight he will see her again, the girl he has recently kissed. With tongue. Eighth grade will soon be over, sooner for him than for Eddie and Luca. He will take his exams early so that he can travel to India, where his father will talk about his book at a conference. Where Mohan Lal will speak beside a man who they say will be prime minister one day.

The thought of traveling to that dirty, godforsaken shithole puts dread in his stomach. But he will drink beer with his cousins. Will enjoy the smiling servants at his uncle's marble-laden home, the turbaned men who salute him at the Delhi Golf Club. Will enjoy a couple of weeks with his brother, who he hasn't seen in seven months. Arjun will arrive in India with his new girlfriend. She's from Ecuador, which is better than India. Better than Pakistan. She's from Ecuador, but looks European. Together they will all travel to the Himalayas. Then comes August. Then ninth grade. Then high school. A driver's license. Siddharth wants time to fly so that he can drive. Mohan Lal has recently inherited a small chunk of money from an aunt. Maybe he will use it to buy Siddharth a car. Maybe he will get rid of the minivan and buy himself a real vehicle. An Acura or a Lexus, or a souped-up Accord.

Siddharth gets up and makes himself toast without brushing his teeth. Makes himself a mug of instant coffee. Seats himself in front of the television and watches an episode of M*A*S*H. An episode of *The Jetsons*, though he would never admit it to Luca. A pair of blue jays is making a racket on the new squirrel-proof birdfeeder. He presses his head against the sliding glass doors. Bangs on the glass, so that the jays fly away. Stares out across the porch, which is spotless, with brand-new wicker furniture. A badger is foraging in a flower bed. A flock of turkeys struts toward the woods. He bangs on the window again. The badger looks up, then recommences its search.

The phone rings. He answers.

Luca's voice. Kid, have you heard?

Heard what?

About Sharon.

Who?

Nagorksi.

Luca sounds strange. Has uttered her name for the first time in months. Siddharth says, What about her?

Kid, she's freaking dead.

Fuck off, says Siddharth. That's not even funny.

I'm not kidding. They say it was an accident. But it's a cover-up.

What?

She freaking killed herself, dude. With her father's gun.

Her father? Sharon's father lives in North Carolina.

Luca says, I don't know her life story. But Eddie's dad was with the cops when they found her. It's kind of sad, really. I don't know why, but it makes me feel kinda weird.

Siddharth's stomach tingles. It is difficult to breathe. He returns his gaze to the yard. The blue jays are back. A squirrel has mounted the feeder and is knocking seeds to the ground, where another squirrel is gorging.

Luca says, You there, kid?

Siddharth says, I gotta go.

He puts down the phone. Can taste metal on the tip of his tongue. Tells himself this isn't happening to him, isn't happening to his family. The people he loves are still breathing. Usually this works. But today he cannot find calm. He can see Sharon. Her dimple, her eyeliner. He hasn't spoken to her in more than a year. He hasn't had anything to do with her. So this has nothing to do with him.

Footsteps.

They get louder.

He turns his head.

She is wearing her green kimono, the one Mohan Lal gave her last year on her birthday.

Oh honey, she says, walking toward him with open arms.

He stands there frozen, struck by how stupid she looks in that robe. This year Mohan Lal has given her a better gift, emerald earrings that had previously belonged to Siddharth's mother. He hated it when Mohan Lal gave Ms. Farber those emerald earrings. But Arjun told him it was for the best. That their mother wouldn't have minded.

She wraps her arms around him. But he is rigid.

She steps back. Looks him in the eye, grasps his shoulders. Says, I wanted to tell you last night, but I was asleep when you got home.

He stares at her messy head of curls, her small honeyed eyes that seem too far apart in this moment. She pulls him toward her, nestles his forehead against her neck. Her soft, small breasts press into his chest. A tear falls from his eye, moistens the silk on her shoulder. She places a hand on his back, starts rubbing it. Whispers, I need you to know this has nothing to do with you.

More tears fall. He knows this isn't true. This has everything to do with him.

She says, You're such a sensitive young man. Trust me, it was a complicated situation. You don't know the half of it.

If he were to step away from her, he would fall to the ground. He would fall, because he knows he could have done something. Knows he could have been her friend.

Ms. Farber repeats her reassurances: Son, this has nothing to do with you. Poor, sweet Siddharth, this just isn't your fault.

He gives her a squeeze, and she tightens her embrace. He likes the way she feels. Could remain in her arms for a very long time. Thinks, Maybe Ms. Farber is right. Maybe Ms. Farber's not that bad. Maybe it's time to start listening to her.

She keeps telling him he has done no wrong, and each time she does so, it is easier for him to believe her.

END

Acknowledgments

The account of the burning body in Professor Sengupta's newspaper article is partially inspired by Suketu Mehta's *Maximum City: Bombay Lost and Found*, and also by Omair Ahmad's short story "Yesterday Man," which originally appeared in *Delhi Noir*. Mohan Lal's brand of Hindu extremism is entirely his own, but texts by Pankaj Mishra, Amartya Sen, and Perry Anderson helped me to clarify his sense of politics and history.

I am grateful to Johnny Temple, publisher of Akashic Books, for having so generously nurtured my writing career for the past decade. Ibrahim Ahmad is a gifted, fastidious, and enthusiastic editor, and he has helped me make this novel a better book. The folks at Akashic work tirelessly to create opportunities for a truly diverse set of authors, and to infuse an essential dose of iconoclasm into literary culture. They have enabled me to publish work that remains true to my ideals, and all of my experiences with them have been defined by a spirit of rigor, professionalism, and camaraderie. Thank you Johanna Ingalls, Aaron Petrovich, Susannah Lawrence, and Katie Martinez.

Thanks to Rutgers-Newark University, for two years of generous funding, and to my instructors there, H. Bruce Franklin, Alice Elliott Dark, and Tayari Jones. Jayne Anne Phillips has always been willing to lend her support and share opportunities.

Caryl Phillips has been a steadfast friend, mentor, and reader, and his fiction has been truly inspirational. So many individuals have offered me indispensable guidance, including Hartosh Singh Bal, Patrick Phillips, Kavita Bhanot, Michael Reynolds, Anjali Singh, Nicholas Pearson, and V.K. Karthika. Toby Lichtig and Jouni Kantola have been true friends and benevolent readers. Jared Cozza, Mario Buletić, and Vicente García Pérez have helped me in ways that I will not put into words. The Cozza family once loaned me their home in Vermont, in which I hammered out certain chapters of this book. A special thanks to Margarita Sawhney; Susan Shah; Jyoti, Rajeev, and Sanjeev Wason; Jonathan Geal; the entire Kapur Khandaan, especially Gullu and Prikshat Puri.

My mother, Rama Sawhney, and my late father, Shiv Sawhney, have been supportive and generous in uncountable ways, and they raised us in an environment filled with love, ideas, debate, and books. My brother Vik has been a second father, and he has taught me invaluable lessons about discipline and focus—two necessary elements in writing. My sister Aarti has been an unwavering friend and guide, and she has opened my heart to so many of the good things in life, including fiction.

This novel would not have been possible without my wife, Anjali Wason. She has carefully read each one of my drafts, despite what's going on in her own life, and enhanced my prose with her acute sense of story and character. She has urged me to keep writing at the center of my life, regardless of its paltry material rewards, and even when my prose takes me away from her. I could not have asked for a more loving, sensitive, and wise partner.